R4/12

About the

Mark Robson was born   1966, and was raised, fc   .....a.
Carmarthen in West Wales. ... 1982, he gained a
scholarship to join the Royal Air Force as a pilot and
he is currently flying the HS125 on 32 (The Royal)
Squadron. His first book *'The Forging of the Sword'*
was largely written during tours of duty in the
Falkland Islands. The long quiet hours maintaining
the constant vigil of the Quick Reaction Alert Force
proved to be an ideal breeding ground for flights of
fantasy, mainly because the famous Falkland
Island's wet and windy weather prevented flights of
anything else! *'First Sword'* is the third in a series
of 'easy reading' stories that are suitable for fantasy
lovers of all ages.

Also by the same author:

The Darkweaver Legacy

    Book 1: The Forging of the Sword
    Book 2: Trail of the Huntress
    Book 4: The Chosen One*

* Not yet published

For up to date information on future releases see:

www.swordpublishing.co.uk

FIRST SWORD

Mark Robson

SWORD PUBLISHING

FIRST SWORD
ISBN: 0-9538190-2-7

First published in the United Kingdom by Sword Publishing

First edition published 2002

Copyright © Mark Robson 2002

Published by Sword Publishing,
12 Trenchard Avenue, Ruislip, London, HA4 6NP.
www.swordpublishing.co.uk

Printed and bound in Great Britain by Technographic, Kiln Farm, East End Green, Brightlingsea, Colchester, Essex, CO7 0SX

For my English teacher, Barry Childs,

And for all the unsung heroes of our schools who have the unenviable task of teaching the youngsters of today – with thanks.

Acknowledgements:

To Diane (Eagle-eyes) for help and encouragement that has been a godsend this year.

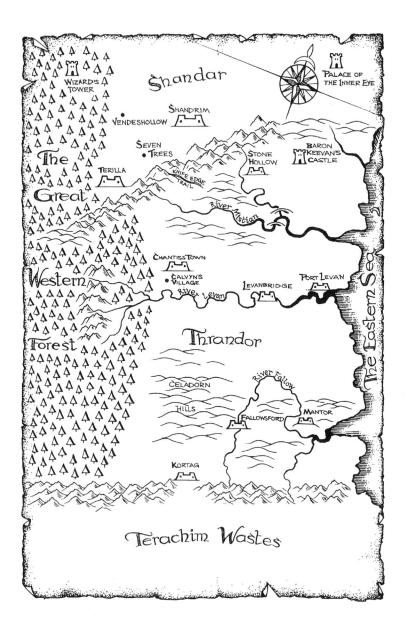

PROLOGUE

The Emperor lounged indolently in his deeply padded throne-like seat which, as one would expect, offered the best of views over the sandy-floored arena. With a languid indifference he picked at his teeth with a fingernail in a casual attempt to remove a piece of meat that had become lodged there a little earlier. The Arena Master had sent up tit-bits and snacks in an almost endless steam, doubtless in an attempt to make up for the depressingly predictable fights scheduled for the afternoon.

All of the glittering excitement that the Emperor craved so much seemed to have deserted the games over the last few seasons. Ever since Serrius had fought his way up to become the top ranked arena fighter in Shandrim three years ago, there had been a marked reluctance amongst the other fighters to issue challenges and thus rise through the ranks.

No one wanted to face Serrius.

The simple fact was that the man had created a legend in the arena in the space of three short years. Unlike most fighters in the games, Serrius fought to kill. Victory satisfied the majority of combatants, but no one who had entered the arena to face Serrius had ever left alive.

It was a fearsome reputation to have, and there was no doubt in the Emperor's mind that the man deserved it.

To the Emperor's surprise, as if just thinking about Serrius was enough to call him forth, the gateway to the fighters' pit opened again and the top ranked fighter strode out into the sunlight. The Emperor sat up straight, his finger withdrawn from his mouth and his attention immediately focused on the arena.

A buzz of excitement sounded around the tiered seats as the crowd became aware of Serrius. This was not on the programme. Had one of the other top fighters challenged him for supremacy? Nadreck maybe? Or Voldor? The iron gate clanged shut behind the broad-shouldered swordsman as he prowled out with the unconscious grace of a mountain cat towards the centre of the arena. The dark, hardened leather protective gear that Serrius favoured over the more traditional metal, glistened as the sunlight danced on the well-oiled sheen of the straps and plates.

'But who, and where, is the challenger?' everyone was asking.

Normally the challenger would walk into the arena at the same time as his opponent. This was completely unorthodox.

'If the Arena Master is doing this for effect, then he is more talented than I gave him credit for,' the Emperor growled to no one in particular.

Serrius stopped in the centre of the arena, drew the longer of the two swords hanging at his waist and saluted the Emperor's balcony.

The gateway to the fighters' pit opened again and the crowd hushed to an expectant silence. Who would it be? Whoever the crowd had been anticipating, it was not the young tyro fighter who emerged from the pit.

'An even bigger farce!' someone to the Emperor's right spat derisively. 'That poor kid won't last five seconds.'

Nevertheless, the Emperor held his peace, for despite the angry mutterings from the crowd, the young fighter walked forward with confidence and the Emperor's keen eye had noted that the gateway to the pit was not yet shut. Sure enough, after a few more seconds another fighter emerged. Two against one would be a bit spicier, but still the gate did not close. Another fighter walked out into the arena, and another and yet another before the gate finally clanged shut.

'Five against one!' the Emperor breathed.

It was hard to believe that the Arena Master was going to risk his best fighter in such a way, unless he was *trying* to get rid of Serrius. Maybe he had realised that the dominance of the arena by one man was slowly destroying the games. If so, then the Emperor had once again underestimated him, particularly as the Arena Master would have had to convince Serrius to agree to this fight. One of the perquisites of being ranked in the top five was that unless they were challenged, the fighters got to choose when and whom they fought.

Serrius had not fought for six weeks now, and yet here he was calmly awaiting not one, but *five* opponents to complete their salutes to the Emperor. It was hard to understand the mentality of the man. The Emperor had recognised four out of five of the men now lined up to salute Serrius as fighters who had won bouts in the arena over the last few weeks. One in particular had looked to have a lot of potential to the Emperor's experienced eye, so Serrius would do well to survive this encounter.

The five young fighters spread out and began to encircle Serrius. To everyone's surprise, including the fighters themselves, the deadly swordsman remained motionless, his sword held balanced, point upward in front of him and his feet planted firmly at shoulder width apart.

'Is he suicidal or something?' muttered someone, voicing a suspicion that niggled at the Emperor's mind.

'It's almost as if he's praying,' the Emperor thought to himself, his heart now beating harder with anticipation and excitement. 'Has something happened to make Serrius want to give up his life?'

The answer came swiftly.

Having completely encircled Serrius, the five challengers attacked simultaneously on a pre-arranged signal and the deadliest fighter in Shandrim blurred into action. Serrius leaped gracefully to his left, and the short sword that had an instant before been sheathed at his belt seemed somehow to have sprung into his left hand. With a speed and style that was all his own, Serrius twisted to block the nearest attacker with the short sword and had run the man through with the longer sword before his opponent had time to react. Using his momentum and the weight of the man impaled on his sword to turn himself around, Serrius whipped his shorter sword across to meet his second attacker's cutting stroke whilst wrenching the longer blade free. The second attacker managed one further stroke before he was virtually decapitated by a slashing cut that Serrius delivered with blinding speed. Within the span of two normal breaths, Serrius had reduced his opponents from five to three. One of the remaining three had found his attack balked by the falling body of the first man to die, whilst the remaining two each found their blades blocked by the lighting-fast reflexes of their single opponent.

The crowd exploded with cheers as the three remaining tyros backed off to regroup.

Serrius let them go.

Calmly the Master Swordsman turned his back on the three remaining opponents and walked clear of the two dead challengers to give himself space to move freely. Then he turned and waited for his opponents to come to him.

The three tyros consulted briefly before advancing in a line.

'They will die,' the Emperor decided silently. 'Their swords are too long to fight in formation. They will merely obstruct each other and give Serrius opportunities to pick them off at his leisure.'

Moments later, the three young fighters surprised both the Emperor and Serrius by breaking formation at the last instant. The two outside fighters leapt diagonally forward to flank Serrius on both sides and revert to their original tactic of multi-directional attacks. The best of the three fighters held the centre, and for several seconds Serrius struggled to fend off all three blades. Twice blades penetrated Serrius' defence, opening cuts on his upper arm and scoring the leather of his chest plate. For a moment it looked as if the Master Swordsman would simply be overwhelmed, but that moment was brief indeed.

With a breathtaking turn of speed, Serrius disarmed the man to his left, almost severing the man's sword hand in the process. At the same time, he evaded a sweeping stroke from the man to his right and blocked two quick strokes from the fighter in front of him. Then with the vicious speed and deadly precision for which he had become renowned, he pressed home his counter-attack ruthlessly. The blur that followed was so fast that neither the Emperor nor the two unfortunate fighters saw the death strokes fall. Indeed, their bodies were still in the process of falling to the ground as Serrius paused, perfectly balanced in a widespread crouch before the only one of his opponents still alive. The unarmed man was clearly in shock, having had no time to do anything but clutch at his badly sliced wrist. For a split second, the Emperor thought that Serrius would let the man live. Then, with a cold deliberation that chilled the Emperor's heart to the core, Serrius ran the man through with both of his blades at once.

The crowd was going wild with applause and the Emperor suddenly realised that he was also on his feet, his hands clapping enthusiastically along with everyone else. The Emperor's chest ached from having instinctively held his breath for much of the action. Despite the shockingly cold execution of the unarmed man at the end of the fight, he found himself smiling and nodding his appreciation to Serrius as the Master Swordsman gave his parting salute to the Imperial party.

'By Shand!' someone exhaled. 'The man is bloody invincible. Nobody in their right mind will fight him after that.'

The Emperor was inclined to agree. If only Serrius did not make such a point of killing everyone that he faced, other fighters might then be more inclined to challenge him. There was no doubt that Serrius' fearsome reputation had just climbed from deadly to totally legendary in the space of the last few minutes. Sadly, the Emperor reflected that it might be some time before he would see Serrius fight again.

CHAPTER 1

'It's changed!'

'I'm sorry, Lord Calvyn? What has changed?' enquired the immaculately attired Head of the Royal House Staff.

'I am not a Lord, Krider, I am merely a Corporal,' Calvyn said absently, as he stepped off the central carpeted walkway.

The great entrance hall of the Royal Palace of Thrandor was spectacular in size and steeped in history and royal tradition. Calvyn knew very little of either of these things, but something unusual had caught his eye and it drew him like a moth to a lighted window. A huge tapestry, one of many hanging in the enormous hallway of the King's residence, was the focus of his attention.

The tapestry depicted the scene of a magical battle from a famous Thrandorian legend. One Magician was standing with his back to the viewer and defiantly battling against five other Magicians, all depicted in various dramatic poses of spell casting. Four other characters were standing to one side of the battle, apparently just observing the struggle for magical supremacy.

'This tapestry, Krider, it's different!' Calvyn exclaimed again, as he moved closer to better examine the beautifully woven masterpiece.

'You must be mistaken, *Corporal*. That tapestry has been there for all of my forty-two years of service here in the palace. Indeed, all of these tapestries have. They are legacies of previous monarchs. King Malo has

13

commissioned several tapestries during his reign, but he feels that none of the new tapestries match the quality and content of these older ones. Apparently some of the Master Weavers took secrets to the grave, which is a great shame if you ask me.'

Calvyn ran his fingers over the figure dressed in black who, he had decided, must represent the evil Magician, Derrigan Darkweaver, and he shuddered.

'That is not what I mean, Krider. This tapestry was here the last time that I visited, but the picture has changed.'

'Impossible! No weaver would ever be allowed near these tapestries. You must be mistaken,' Krider said, clearly outraged at the mere thought that someone could possibly have tampered with a national treasure.

Calvyn shook his head slowly and moved back and forth along the tapestry, carefully examining the detailed figures.

'It's strange, very strange,' he muttered to himself thoughtfully. 'There were nine, I know there were nine.'

'There *are* nine,' Krider said adamantly, hearing Calvyn's words and leaping to a conclusion. 'Look, five are casting spells, and those four over there are watching.'

'No, I wasn't referring to the total number of characters,' Calvyn said, glancing across at Krider, who was now studying the tapestry with almost as much intensity as Calvyn. 'When I last looked at this, there were nine Magicians surrounding the central character, who I assume, is Derrigan Darkweaver. I wasn't counting those four over there. Now that I come to think of it, the background was more desert-like as well. I mean, I know the background is rocky here, but it's... well, it's just different,' he finished lamely.

The silver-haired old man in his immaculate dark blue doublet with its double row of gilt buttons down the front, looked more closely yet at the weave of the tapestry. For a full minute he walked up and down, carefully inspecting the weave before he turned to Calvyn with a mildly annoyed expression on his normally schooled face.

'Is this some sort of a joke, young man?'

'No, Krider. I swear I don't understand it, but the scene on that tapestry has definitely changed.'

'I can see no evidence of any tampering with the weave,' Krider asserted sceptically. 'I may not be an expert on the art of tapestry making, but that looks like the original work to me. Just look at the colours. There is no evidence to suggest that any of this hanging is newer than the rest, and the weave is perfect. There are no flaws of any kind. I simply cannot see how it could have been altered without some trace of that alteration remaining.'

Calvyn raised his eyebrows questioningly as he looked Krider in the eyes. Krider's eyes widened slightly in response and he spluttered in immediate denial at his interpretation of that look.

'No! Not here in the palace!' Krider exclaimed in disbelief. 'You cannot be suggesting that magic has been used *here*? Besides, I have walked past that tapestry every day for over forty years and I am sure that I would have noticed a change on the scale that you are talking of.'

'That's one of the things that I don't understand,' Calvyn admitted, chewing absently at his right thumbnail as his mind raced over the possibilities. 'I mean, why should *I* notice the change when no one here has noticed anything odd? Stranger, though, is why anyone would want to change the tapestry in the first place. It's not as if they can change history by changing a picture. Besides, the changes haven't really altered the story in the picture significantly. Darkweaver is still outnumbered and outmatched, so changing the number of Magicians responsible for his downfall achieves nothing. Also, I can't see how changing the setting is relevant either. It's mystifying!'

Standing quietly for a moment, Calvyn recalled his last visit to this hall. He and his friend, Jenna, had studied the tapestry closely. Calvyn vividly remembered being struck by the uncanny resemblance between the figure of Derrigan Darkweaver in the picture and the enigmatic Shandese Magician, Selkor. It was eerie that Selkor should now be in possession of Darkweaver's magical amulet, a silver talisman charged with dark powers. There was no way that Selkor could actually *be* Darkweaver: firstly, because if Selkor was the ancient scourge of Thrandor, he would be over two hundred years old and, secondly, because the things that Selkor had said when he had first obtained the amulet did not fit with him being Darkweaver. Yet there was no denying the likeness. Everything about the figure's posture, his hair, even the cut of his black cloak, reminded Calvyn of Selkor.

Then, of course, there was the other strange coincidence.

One of the other characters in the tapestry, one of the four apparently observing the battle, bore an uncanny similarity to Calvyn's mentor, Perdimonn. True, the details of the character were not particularly clear, for he was in the background standing alongside two other men and a woman. However, Calvyn could not shake the feeling that somehow, no matter how impossible it might seem, the character woven into the tapestry *was* Perdimonn.

A light touch on Calvyn's arm made him start slightly.

'Come, Corporal Calvyn, the King awaits, and it does not do to make royalty wait on your pleasure,' said Krider, beckoning him to follow.

Taking a final glance at the great hanging tapestry, Calvyn reluctantly followed Krider, but was unable to shake the feeling that the tapestry held an important secret that he needed to unravel.

'Calvyn, son of Joran, a Corporal in the army of Baron Keevan, your Majesty,' Krider announced at the doorway to the King's private audience chamber. The Head of the Royal House Staff moved aside and allowed Calvyn to enter the room before silently closing the door behind him.

The chamber was plush rather than opulent. A deep-piled carpet of a warm rusty red colour stretched from wall to wall, and between the many flickering torches hung numerous paintings and hangings depicting various parts of Mantor at different seasons. Situated as it was, right in the heart of the palace, the chamber possessed no windows. Despite the lack of natural light, however, the room seemed to have a welcoming feel to it that was hard to quantify.

'Come in, Calvyn, and join us at the table,' the King said, seemingly echoing the warm, friendly atmosphere of the chamber itself.

'Us' comprised a very select party indeed.

The King was flanked on his right by his staunch supporter and close friend, Baron Anton from western Thrandor and on his left by Lord Valdeer, a powerful Earl from northern Thrandor. To Calvyn's knowledge, no one ever referred to him as *Earl* Valdeer, but nobody whom Calvyn had ever asked had been able to explain why. Finally, to Valdeer's left sat Baron Keevan, who currently wore an unfathomable expression on his face. Calvyn was very tempted to reach out with his mind to try to discover what the Baron was thinking, but he resisted the urge and concentrated instead on bowing smoothly to the august quartet.

'Please, please, do come and sit down, Calvyn,' the King insisted, smiling warmly.

Anton and Valdeer also looked welcoming. Indeed, only Baron Keevan did not project any sort of warmth, as his expression remained distant and aloof.

Calvyn walked over, took his place at the oval shaped table, and immediately felt as if he was about to face an interrogation. The King and his noblemen sat at one of the longer curved sides of the table, whilst Calvyn sat at the other with all eyes upon him.

'Now then, Calvyn, I know that you have met Anton before, but have you made Lord Valdeer's acquaintance?' the King asked casually by way of introduction.

Calvyn could not keep his face from twisting into a

quirky sort of smile as he replied.

'Acquaintance might be a touch overstating our familiarity, your Majesty. I have seen Lord Valdeer at a distance on several occasions, but have not had the pleasure of an introduction,' Calvyn replied, as formally as he could.

Valdeer's smile widened and he chuckled slightly as he responded.

'I too have seen you at a distance, Corporal. You spoke well in His Majesty's Court when you defended the traitor, Demarr. That was a brave act under the circumstances. I also saw your duel and witnessed your control of the Shandese Legions from a distance. It is a pleasure to meet you face to face.'

'Thank you, my Lord.'

'Good,' said the King enthusiastically. 'Now, young man, you owe me a story. I intend to hold you to the promise that you made at Kortag, for the events that transpired there will undoubtedly spawn legends. Come, spare no detail, for I long to know how you arranged for our enemies to unknowingly fight one another, and if you do not object I will have my Scribe, Rexal, record the details.

Calvyn had not noticed the thin, reed-like man who sat at a bureau-style desk in the corner of the room, quill poised to start writing. Suddenly it struck Calvyn that his words here today would define how history recorded the events of the last few months. For who would question the word of the King's Scribe?

Thinking carefully and trying his best to maintain a logical sequence, Calvyn told his story. The telling was not short, for the plot was complex and both the King and the noblemen could not help but interrupt with questions as the unusual tale unfolded. Calvyn did not elaborate overly on his training in the powers of sorcery, but did his best to convey the structure and hierarchy of the sect of Sorcerers within which he had found himself.

All four listeners sat horrified as Calvyn related the diabolical methods that the evil Lord Sorcerer Vallaine had employed to gain Calvyn's compliance to his plot for gaining power in Thrandor. Equally, they looked genuinely touched as Calvyn told of how he had been aware of Demarr, once his mortal enemy, laying down his life to rescue Calvyn's soul from an unspeakable fate. Then finally, when Calvyn explained how he had used Lord Vallaine's prophetic vision to twist events to an outcome that served Thrandor instead of the Lord Sorcerer, the four all glanced approvingly at one another.

When Calvyn had finished speaking, his audience remained silent for a moment. The only sound within earshot was the furious scratching of Rexal's quill driving the last part of the story onto parchment, as the King and his advisers tried to digest the amazing tale.

'Well, young man, a story I asked for and a story I got. As I anticipated, much of it is laced with the subject that my ancestors, and indeed I, have tried to deny for the last two hundred years. It is time that Thrandor faced up to the fact that magical forces are all too real. Denying them has brought our nation to the brink of disaster twice in the last few months and we cannot allow that to happen again.

The King paused and looked back and forth, making eye contact with each of the nobles in turn before returning his gaze to Calvyn. King Malo's face was grim now, underlining his obvious lack of comfort with what he was saying.

'Magic, sorcery, wizardry and more than likely several other forms of supernatural arts exist and there is no point in trying to deny these powers any longer. That the rulers of Thrandor have tried to outlaw the use of arcane powers has led to a complete lack of knowledge and understanding of what such powers can achieve. It is apparent to me that our ignorance is a danger to our very survival as a kingdom. I am therefore appointing you to be my personal adviser in these matters and I would appreciate your thoughts on what we can do to prevent these sorts of events recurring in the future.'

Calvyn was stunned.

The King's personal adviser on all matters magical! It was a position beyond any that he had ever imagined possible. The potential for influencing the reintroduction of the practice of magic within Thrandor was immense, and suddenly Calvyn was swamped by thoughts of his lack of years and knowledge of magic. Calvyn had only a limited knowledge of basic magic spells and though he had witnessed a Wizard at work, knew nothing of his art. True, in but a few short months Calvyn had mastered sorcery to a level that many who trained in the art all their lives never achieved. However, he knew nothing of alchemy, necromancy, witchcraft, or any of a handful of other magical arts about which he might be asked.

The King sensed his turmoil and smiled.

'That you are speechless does you further credit, for I deem you to be an honest young man. Keevan assures me that you have always proved trustworthy in his service and I hope that you will serve me with the same loyalty that you have shown to him.'

'But of course, your Majesty,' Calvyn spluttered. 'I would be more than honoured to serve as your adviser, but I hardly feel qualified for such a position. My knowledge is sorely limited...'

'And yet so much more complete than any member of my court,' the King interrupted. 'Please, Corporal Calvyn, to my knowledge there *is* no one else in Thrandor who is more suitable to fill this role.'

Calvyn's heart was hammering in his chest, for he knew that he could not really deny the King's request, and yet there was one matter that he had not yet addressed.

'Why do you hesitate, Calvyn?' asked Baron Anton, his keen eyes watching Calvyn closely. 'Do you not want to serve your King?'

'Oh yes, my Lord. Very much so, it's just that...'

'Go on, man! Spit it out,' said Lord Valdeer a little impatiently.

Calvyn gulped at the lump in his throat that was threatening to stop him from being able to speak at all and he gripped his hands together tightly under the table to stop them from shaking.

'It's my friends, your Majesty, the two who sought to rescue me from the Shandese army camp that I, as Lord Shanier, have sent to Shandrim to fight in the arena. If you remember, your Majesty, I told you at Kortag that I intended to go and free them before the Emperor of Shandar had them killed. I have not changed my mind on this, and if I am to become your adviser then I beg you, please let me do this first. I will never forgive myself if I do nothing for them after they risked everything for me.'

A touch of warmth coloured Baron Keevan's, until now, cold eyes and Anton and Valdeer smiled openly. The King, however, looked at him gravely and his voice was serious as he replied.

'What you ask is dangerous,' he said slowly. 'It is dangerous for you, as you will need to travel to the very heart of Shandar to achieve your goal, and dangerous for me, as I will have to risk the only person in my kingdom who is capable of providing me with information vital to the security of my country. You have already made it clear to me that I should prepare for the worst with Selkor, the Shandese Magician, still at large with Darkweaver's amulet. What should I do if he moves against Thrandor in your absence?'

'In all honesty, your Majesty, there is little that you could do whether I was here or not. I am no match for Selkor and I know it. However, I may be able to locate someone who might help in such circumstance whilst I search for my friends. My mentor, a Magician named Perdimonn, managed to intimidate Selkor once. If I could find news of him, then maybe we would gain information on how best to protect Thrandor from anything that Selkor might try.'

The King scratched thoughtfully at the bridge of his nose and looked around firstly at Anton, who shrugged in a non-committal fashion, and then at Valdeer and Keevan. Valdeer gave a small nod of agreement, but Baron Keevan did not look happy.

'What say you, Keevan? Should I let him go?' the King asked, noting the Baron's discomfort. 'After all, it is an honourable request.'

'That I do not deny, your Majesty, but the wisdom of allowing him to go off on the quest alone is, I believe, highly questionable. I would feel much better if he had at least a few others to aid him. The journey is a long one and fraught with dangers that might be better faced by a small party than one man alone.'

The King nodded in agreement.

'That makes sense to me. Do you agree, Calvyn?'

'I was actually wondering if I could even broach the subject, your Majesty,' Calvyn said, hardly believing his ears. 'I already have a few people in mind, but it will depend very much on whether Baron Keevan can spare them.'

'Try me,' the Baron offered, rolling his hand slightly in a gesture for Calvyn to proceed without delay.

'Well, my Lord, I'd like to take Privates Fesha and Eloise and, if you can spare her, I'd like Sergeant Derra as well. I think that between the four of us we should be able to handle most things. I don't really want to take along any more than that, as the party would lose any chance of stealth if it were much bigger. Also, as a small group we should be able to travel lightly and swiftly.'

The Baron gave a tight smile and then grimaced slightly.

'Privates I have in abundance, Corporal. You are welcome to take whomever you wish from amongst them. Sergeants, on the other hand, are at a premium right now. Particularly Sergeants with the talents of young Derra.' The Baron paused and turned to the King. 'That said, your Majesty, if I had to choose someone to give this venture the best chance of success, then Derra would be high on my list of candidates. Very well, I agree – on one condition.'

'What is that, Keevan?' the King asked.

'Well, it is obvious to me that Calvyn can hardly remain a Corporal in my army if he is to be your personal adviser, your Majesty. I have no vacancies for any more Captains right now. Still, I suppose that as he will be spending more time here at Mantor than in the north, I could give him the rank without the command, but maybe it would be better if he transferred to the Royal Guard.'

The King considered this for a moment and Calvyn's breath caught in his throat. To hold any sort of rank in the Royal Guard would be an honour in itself, but to become a Captain would mean more even than the post of Royal Adviser. He could hardly believe that the Baron had put him forward in such a way, let alone that the King was taking the suggestion seriously. Then the King shook his head slowly and Calvyn's heart sank. For a fleeting moment his imagination had run riot and adrenaline had raced through his veins like a raging torrent, but now his emotions crashed down to reality like a dropped rock.

'No,' the King said sombrely. 'No, I have a much better idea than that.'

The King got to his feet and walked over to the corner of the room where a pair of swords hung on the wall. Carefully, he removed one of the long-bladed weapons from the wall and he walked back towards Calvyn.

'Come here, Calvyn,' the King ordered, his tone formal. 'Come here and kneel before me.'

Suddenly, Calvyn's adrenal glands went back into full production and his stomach knotted in response. This could not be happening. His mind was spinning with the enormity of it and he hardly realised that he had risen at the King's command and moved to kneel in front of him. Time seemed to skip from slow to fast and back to slow in a way that made the whole situation strangely surreal. Nevertheless, this was no dream. In a clear stately voice the King started to state the formal phrases that Calvyn had heard many times in his imagination since he was a small boy.

'Do you, Calvyn, son of Joran, swear fealty to the Crown of Thrandor? Do you swear to uphold truth and justice, maintaining the honour and traditions of those who have gone before? Do you swear to champion good against evil, and to drive darkness from our land wheresoever you find it?'

'I do so swear,' Calvyn croaked, his voice tight with emotion.

'Then I dub thee, Sir Calvyn, son of Joran, Knight of the Realm of Thrandor, Guardian of the Peace and Protector of the Innocent. May the gods guide and protect you.'

The King briefly rested the flat of the blade firstly on Calvyn's right shoulder and then on his left. With each brief touch a thrill like an electric shock fired through his body and childhood images of heroic characters saving damsels and fighting dragons flashed once more through his mind.

'Arise, Sir Calvyn, and serve thy King,' Malo ordered with a smile.

It was real. He was a real Knight of the Realm.

That thought obliterated all else, as firstly Lord Valdeer and then Barons Anton and Keevan came forward and clasped his hand in congratulations. Calvyn accepted their warm handshakes in a daze and Anton laughed as he joked that Calvyn's expression was almost as vacant as the expressions of those who had been born into nobility. Calvyn smiled in response, but despite the jibe could not force himself to focus his mind into any sort of coherent thought.

'Your elevation will be announced in court in the morning, Calvyn,' the King advised him. 'The news of it will then be sent to every province in the kingdom with the official news of the victory at Kortag. I do not suppose that I have to tell you that as a Knight of the Realm you are no longer tied to the service of Baron Keevan. Also, you will receive a stipend from the treasury, which should keep you from needing to seek other employment.'

'I... I don't know how to thank you, your Majesty,' Calvyn stammered, still in a state of shock.

'Your thanks are not required, *Sir* Calvyn. Your

continued support and loyalty are what I really desire.'

'Sir Calvyn' echoed in Calvyn's ears, as the enormity of what had just happened began to sink in. As a Knight he had rank and privilege enough to do everything that he had ever dreamed of, assuming of course that the King did not require his services elsewhere.

'My loyalty you will have forever, your Majesty. I am yours to command,' Calvyn answered wholeheartedly. 'My support, such as it is worth, you will also have. However, for now, your Majesty, I must beg your permission to withdraw and make preparations for my journey.'

'Granted, and good luck,' the King said with a warm smile, and he picked up a small silver bell from the table and rang it.

Almost instantly, the door opened and an immaculately dressed old man entered and bowed.

'Yes, your Majesty?' he asked in a deep voice.

'Veldan, show Sir Calvyn out if you would, and ensure that the stables give him a mount befitting his new status. He is shortly to depart on a journey, so please give him any assistance he requires to speed him on his way.'

'Yes, your Majesty.'

Calvyn bowed deeply to the King and his noblemen, then he turned and strode swiftly from the room with a bounce in his step that spoke volumes of his pride and excitement. Veldan followed more sedately, forcing Calvyn to wait just outside the King's private audience chamber for the old man to catch up with him. Once together, they progressed through the palace at the butler's measured pace. It was all that Calvyn could do to prevent himself from dismissing the old servant and stretching out his legs at the pace that they itched to set. It was not until they set foot in the great entrance hall that Calvyn realised that he had not mentioned the tapestry to the King.

'Blast!' he cursed, punching his right fist into his left palm with a resounding smack of annoyance.

'Sir?' the butler queried politely.

'Oh, it's nothing, just something that I meant to mention to the King. It's probably not important. Out of interest though, have you noticed anything odd about that tapestry over there recently?'

'Odd, Sir? In what way?'

'If I tell you, then I will prove nothing,' Calvyn said carefully. 'Please, humour me. I assume that you are familiar with the hanging?'

'Well, yes, Sir. It's been there for many years. The subject matter is odd enough – Magicians fighting is not something that you see everyday, but aside from that, I cannot see anything unusual. Should I?'

Calvyn thought about that for a moment.

'Do you know what? I'm really not sure whether you should or not,' he said, frowning as he considered the question. 'It was just something that Krider and I were discussing earlier.'

'Ah, well, Sir, if it's information about the palace you want, then Krider is the man to ask. No question about that, Sir. Krider is the only person to have served here longer than I. If he could not answer your question, then there is probably no one who can.'

Calvyn thanked the old butler and they moved on through the hall and out of the palace to the royal stables. Veldan relayed the King's instructions to the Master of the Stables and before long Calvyn found himself leading a magnificent horse out into the courtyard, complete with a set of leather tack of the highest quality. The Master of the Stables had wanted to give him tack that bore the Royal Crest and the insignia of a Knight. The only problem was that despite his deep desire to ride with those emblems emblazoned for all to see, Calvyn had to consider where he was going. Under the present circumstances, he hardly wanted to advertise to every citizen of Shandar that he was a Knight of Thrandor, so he declined the precious saddle and reins and opted instead for plain ones. To Calvyn's delight, once he explained his reasons for not accepting the

Knight's tack, the Master of the Stables promised to put a set aside for him.

'I'll keep it separate and ensure that the lads look after it properly for you, Sir Calvyn,' he said in a reassuring tone.

From what Calvyn could see, every piece of leather in the stables was immaculate in every respect. If his tack were to get special treatment, then it would be well looked after indeed, he decided happily.

After thanking the Master of the Stables for his help, Calvyn mounted his new chestnut stallion and left the palace grounds at a steady walking pace. The horse was obviously not pleased with his rider's choice of gait and it pranced and skipped every few yards in an attempt to encourage more speed. Calvyn, however, was not about to start their new relationship by letting the horse, Hakkaari as the Master of the Stables had named him, get away with anything. Calvyn had a sneaky suspicion that the name Hakkaari was very suitable. Apparently the name had been taken from a strong valley wind that, when the conditions were right, blew out of the White Falls Pass in the Terachite mountain range at the southern border of Thrandor. If Hakkaari ran as fast as the wind that was his namesake, then Calvyn had gained a steed indeed.

Sergeant Derra and a party of soldiers from Calvyn's old squad had arranged to meet him at a training area in the lower part of the city. When he reined Hakkaari to a halt, it appeared that his compatriots were similarly impressed by his new acquisition.

'Hey, Corporal! I said that I expected you to come back bearing gifts from the King, not come with the gifts bearing you,' Fesha joked glibly.

Calvyn smiled and decided that the best way to tell them about his abrupt change of status would be to work it straight into the inevitable exchange of banter.

'Nice horse, Corporal, now all you need is someone who knows how to ride properly to keep it exercised for you,' said Eloise loudly over the other whistles and mutters of appreciation at the beautiful horse.

'That's Sir Corporal to you, Private,' Calvyn replied with a grin, swinging himself out of the saddle and landing neatly on his feet.

Hakkaari pranced a few steps on the spot in a display of suppressed energy, and then walked calmly forward as Calvyn led him to where the group of soldiers had been practising their swordplay.

'Oh ho! He's getting ideas of officer status now that he's hob-nobbing with royalty,' Fesha said with a laugh to those around him.

Derra, however, caught his meaning straight away.

'Squad ATTEN... SHUN!' she barked suddenly, her gravelly voice cutting through the other voices like a freshly honed scythe through ripened wheat.

The soldiers reacted instinctively and in an instant they were all standing straight and still. Derra, who had also snapped to attention, marched a few paces across to stand face to face with Calvyn and then saluted.

'May I be the first to offer my congratulations on your new appointment, Sir Calvyn?' she said with enough volume that even the furthest of the soldiers could hear her. 'You will have to get your gear changed to reflect your new status.'

'Thank you, Sergeant. The Royal House Staff offered to do that for me, but I decided that under the circumstances it might be a good idea to travel incognito for a while,' he replied, keeping his voice low and his face in a friendly smile.

'The King has allowed you to go then?' Derra asked, obviously surprised at this development.

'Actually, no. He has allowed *us* to go, along with a couple of others.'

Derra's eyes widened even further.

'And the Baron agreed to this?'

Calvyn nodded, amused to have been able to throw the normally unshakeable Sergeant Derra off balance.

'Yes. In fact he thought that taking you along was a very good idea. I can't for the life of me think why though,' he said teasingly, savouring the chance to banter the previously unassailable Sergeant.

Derra's eyes narrowed dangerously for an instant and then opened wide again, as she realised that she could no longer reprimand him for impertinence. To Calvyn's surprise, she let out a short bark of laughter and then saluted him again.

'Undoubtedly the Baron wanted to ensure that the kingdom's newest Knight of the Realm didn't get himself spitted unnecessarily by someone who didn't appreciate his humour,' Derra said with a tight grin. 'May I stand the troops at ease, *Sir*?' she asked.

'Be my guest, Sergeant,' Calvyn replied.

As soon as Derra gave the 'at ease' order, the soldiers swarmed around Calvyn to shake his hand and pat his shoulder in congratulations. Several of them were more reserved, as they were suddenly acutely aware that Calvyn now outranked even the Captains in Baron Keevan's army. For the most part, though, the men and women who had been his compatriots for more than a year appreciated that this was probably the last chance that they would have to treat Calvyn as one of their own and they made the most of it.

Calvyn enjoyed the moment, only suffering a momentary pang of regret that there were several people not here to share in it that he would dearly have loved to be present. Sadly, his parents would never know the heights to which their son had climbed in such a short space of time. He was sure that they would not have let him join an army had they been alive. Nevertheless, his parents would have been incredibly proud to have their son awarded a knighthood.

Strangely, there were others missing from the celebrations, who in Calvyn's eyes might have appreciated the moment as much as, if not more than, his parents. Some like Matim and Sergeant Brett had been killed at the battle for Mantor. Others, like Bek, Jez and Perdimonn, he felt sure were still alive, but their fates were uncertain... and then there was Jenna.

More than anyone else, Calvyn missed Jenna.

His only knowledge of her whereabouts was that she and Demarr had somehow killed the demon to which the Lords of the Inner Eye had fed his soul some months before. Where they had confronted the demon, Calvyn could not tell. All he knew with any degree of certainty was that Jenna had survived the encounter and Demarr had not. Strangely, he could not even describe how he knew this much. The fragments of information were tormenting in their incompleteness. Unfortunately, to Calvyn's knowledge there was no way of filling in the gaps without finding Jenna, and his chances of doing that whilst trying to free Bek and Jez were minimal at best.

When Calvyn finally managed to escape the crowd and put Hakkaari into stabling, he sought out Sergeant Derra and filled in the details of what had happened in the King's chamber. Derra in turn called for Fesha and Eloise and ordered them to pack for a long journey. They did not need telling twice and rushed away to prepare at once.

'Let's just hope that we're not too late,' Calvyn muttered quietly as they left.

Somehow Derra's sharp ears picked up the comment.

'With your recent run of luck I find that unlikely,' she said with a tight grin. 'But we'll not dawdle – just in case.'

CHAPTER 2

The pits stank.

A foul reek of stale sweat combined with a strange smell of herbal concoction emanating from the many pots of clear grease that some fighters smeared over parts of their bodies before a fight. Bek suspected that the poor sanitary arrangements added to the odour, but permeating all was a smell that was more instinctive than it was olfactory: the smell of fear.

Many of those gathered in the pits were not fighters by choice. Most were small-time criminals whose punishment was to provide entertainment for the public to whom they had supposedly done harm. Bek quickly deduced that for some here, their only crime had been to be in the wrong place at the wrong time. The sickening fact was that by sending them here, the Shandese authorities had effectively sentenced them to death.

The real fighters, those trained in the art of single combat specifically for the arena, had their own pits. Bek did not doubt for one moment that their facilities were vastly superior to these squalid, dungeon-like accommodations into which he and Jez had been brought.

Dozens of men were sprawled around the chamber where Bek and Jez were being held, and there were many more in other similar rooms nearby. The guards seemed to take great delight in provoking the prisoners into fighting amongst themselves and then took equal pleasure in punishing them for it. On the day that they had arrived, Bek had taken a stinging blow across the shoulders from a whip when a group of guards had charged into the room to break up a fight over food. Twice a day a meagre amount of bread and meat was shoved under the heavy iron-barred gate that secured the men in the pit. Inevitably, frequent fights broke out over its distribution and Bek, although not involved in the fracas, had not been quick enough to avoid the whip that the guard was flailing with a fierce indiscriminate pleasure.

A burning flame of anger was smouldering almost constantly in Bek's gut now, as he became steadily more bitter about the situation in which he found himself. Jez, with his light-hearted outlook and seemingly eternal optimism, was all that kept him from fighting back. 'Bide your time, Bek,' Jez kept telling him. 'The time to fight will come all too soon. Let's save ourselves for when we can face them with better odds. They'll have to give us weapons when they send us into the arena, so let's marshal our strength and await our opportunity.'

He was right of course. Aside from getting himself badly beaten by the guards, there was nothing that Bek could realistically hope to achieve under the present circumstances. Knowing, this did not stop the seed of anger from growing like a malignant tumour in Bek's stomach, as he stored up each witnessed injustice in a rapidly growing list of grievances.

The worst part about his being here was that Calvyn, the man whom Bek had considered his best friend, had orchestrated their deliverance into this hell-hole. Calvyn, who had been his closest friend through military training in Baron Keevan's army, had somehow switched sides and was now a powerful leader in the Shandese army. Calvyn's duplicity had been a shocking blow, particularly as Bek and Jez, together with Derra and Eloise, had been on a mission to rescue him from the heart of the enemy camp when he had betrayed them.

Time and time again during the long forced march to the Shandese capital city, Bek had asked himself the question whether Calvyn had always belonged to the enemy, or whether he had somehow been subverted. It was still almost inconceivable that Calvyn could ever betray Thrandor, yet he had declared himself Lord Shanier, a Lord of sorcery, at their last meeting and had displayed a streak of ruthlessness that Bek would never have believed possible of his friend. With a coldness that even now chilled Bek to think of, Calvyn had killed another Sorcerer Lord whilst holding his four would-be rescuers under his thrall with powerful sorcery. Then he had handed them over to the Shandese military in such a way that made Bek doubt that Calvyn had an ounce of compassion in his body.

Jez still seemed to believe that Calvyn had been somehow forced into sending them here and that he would in turn mount his own rescue mission to save them. Bek knew better. He had seen Calvyn's eyes. There would be nobody coming to save them. If they were going to get out of here, then they would have to engineer their escape on their own. Jez was too much the romantic and he was placing his trust in a friendship that Bek now doubted had ever existed.

From overhead came the muffled sound of cheering. The arena apparently was full again and the weekly games were about to begin. The last time that this had happened, the guards had hauled many men out, and the vast majority of them had not returned. The few who had been brought back down the corridor in front of the gate to Bek and Jez's chamber, had all borne horrific wounds. When they had seen the wounded being dragged back down the corridor, and the extent of their injuries, it had become blatantly clear to Bek and Jez that whatever the 'games' were in the arena, they were anything but friendly.

'That must have been a week ago,' mused Bek, as he listened hard, straining once again to try and gain some sort of a clue as to what was going on up there. Few of the other men were talkative and those who were would not talk to Bek or Jez. The guards, it seemed, had made sure that everyone had known that they were Thrandorian prisoners before they had arrived. As such they were shunned totally.

A clang sounded up the corridor as the metal bars of the nearest door slammed, steel on steel. The approaching thudding of multiple sets of boots announced the arrival of the guards. There were six of them, all armed and dressed in uniform, which was largely black in colour with heavy diagonal belts of leather thrown over each shoulder. The design of the belts was such that it accentuated the guards' already broad shoulders. Other than this, and offering a minimal amount of protection, Bek could see no real purpose for them. Whoever had designed them must have thought that they looked good. To Bek's mind they would actually prove a dangerous hindrance if the guards were ever to get into a serious fight, as the thick leather would undoubtedly restrict the wearer's freedom of movement. Still, it was useful to catalogue the enemy's weaknesses before it came to a conflict, and Bek was more than happy to add another to his list.

'Come on you. You there, with the red hair. Yes and you as well, the other Thrandorian. Time to bleed for His Imperial Majesty's pleasure,' said one of the burly guards with a viciously vindictive grin. 'Someone once told me that you Thrandorians bleed yellow. Is that true? Something to do with the yellow streak that runs down your bellies it's said.'

The rest of the guards guffawed with laughter at this. Jez placed a hand on Bek's shoulder.

'Not yet,' he whispered. 'Patience.'

Bek all but growled. However, he gritted his teeth and did not struggle as the guards roughly manhandled him out of the chamber. Behind him guards were rounding up more of the prisoners and herding them out into the corridor.

Before long a group of ten, including Bek and Jez, was being shoved and pushed along the passageway and up several short flights of stairs. As they climbed the steps the sound of the occasional cheering above grew louder, and it quickly became apparent that it was not a small crowd that was making the noise.

'Tarmin's teeth! There must be thousands out there,' muttered Jez, as they stumbled up yet another flight of steps.

The nearest guard, who was as heavy-set as all the others but distinguishable by having a little black goatee beard that looked ridiculous on his large round face, heard his comment.

'That's right,' the guard laughed. 'Thousands of 'em. An' you know what? Not one of 'em will be cheering for you unless you're being spitted by one of the arena fighters.'

'Nice,' Bek breathed. 'What a charming society this must be.'

At the top of the final flight of stairs was an open area with a line of cages side by side. Before Bek had a chance to realise what was going on, he and Jez had been separated into different cages. Bek cursed himself for his inattentiveness. Each cage held two prisoners, and because of a moment's distraction, Jez and he would now have to act independently. This seriously shortened the odds of either of them escaping today.

Three sides of the cages were made of iron bars, and the fourth side was solid metal. Bek quickly determined that the solid metal side was also a door and that it almost certainly opened out into the arena. The other man locked in Bek's cage with him suddenly decided that as their fate was to go through that door together, it could not hurt to talk.

'What's your name, Thrandorian?' the man asked.

'Bek.'

'And can you fight?' he added, hopefully.

Bek looked the man in his eyes and saw the fear that haunted them.

'If they give me a sword, then I'll hold my own,' he replied carefully.

The man's eyes brightened a little, but the fear

remained. As a potential ally in a fight, the man displayed little to inspire Bek with any confidence in his usefulness. He was of medium height and slightly built. His dark, lank hair seemed to dangle permanently in his eyes and he was almost constantly pushing it aside with one of his shaking hands, or flicking his head to one side in order to clear his vision.'

'Oh, they'll give you a sword all right, but it'll be a toy compared with the one our opponent will have.'

'A short sword? About this long?' Bek asked, measuring an estimated length with his hands.

The man nodded and Bek grinned at him.

'Then I think that whoever awaits us with a long sword is in for a bit of a shock,' Bek confided softly. 'What is your name, friend?'

The man hesitated and Bek prompted him to answer by extending a hand of greeting.

'Come, we're about to become sword brothers in a fight for our lives, can you at least tell me your name?'

'Selek,' he answered softly.

'Well, Selek, anything else that you can tell me about what is about to happen would be very useful. How many opponents will we face? Will they be armed with more than just a sword? What armour, if any, will they be wearing? Anything, anything at all will be useful.'

'Oh, there will only be one man to face. The fighters virtually always fight alone.'

'So why are we being grouped in twos?' Bek asked, puzzled.

'Well, Serrius... you've heard of Serrius I presume?'

Bek shook his head and Selek looked shocked.

'I thought that everyone in the world knew of Serrius! Anyway, it doesn't matter. Serrius is the top fighter in Shandrim, and therefore by definition the best in Shandar. For some reason known only to him, Serrius decided about four weeks ago to fight five of the other trained fighters,'

'What, one after the other?' Bek asked in surprise.

'No, all at once. What's more – he killed all of them.

Ever since that, the other fighters have been practising against multiple opponents.'

'And who better to practise against than us?' Bek finished for him. 'Well that makes sense, I suppose.'

Just then, the guards shoved a couple of short swords through the bars of the end cage and they dropped to the floor with a clatter. Almost simultaneously, the door that opened out into the arena from that cage swung open, allowing the sunlight to stream into the room. All of the prisoners, without exception, shielded their eyes and squinted against the blazing daylight.

The two men whose cage had been opened to the arena scrabbled for their blades and then made their way cautiously out into the open air. A loud roar went up from the crowd outside that was abruptly muffled to Bek, Jez and the others as the metal door to the now vacated cage swung shut with a clang. Seconds later there followed the ringing tones of swordplay, but to Bek's practised ear it was obvious that there was no contest in it. There was no rhythm to the exchanges, which would denote opponents of equal skill.

Sure enough, seconds later the clashing exchange stopped and the crowd roared again.

The guards, who were watching the fight through small slits in the wall to the side of the line of cages, cursed loudly.

'Pah!' one of them spat. 'They hardly made him move his feet.'

'Come on,' said another. 'We'd better go pick up the pieces. The next lot will be on in a minute or so.'

A small door opened and again the bright sunlight flooded through it into the dim holding area. Most flinched from it, but Bek stared straight at the light and urged Selek to do likewise.

'Look at the light, Selek. Use these chances to allow your eyes to adjust to the brightness before we go out there. Whoever is waiting for us will be using every advantage that he can to dispose of us quickly. Any element of surprise that we can carry will help.'

Two of the guards disappeared out through the door only to return moments later dragging the two bodies of the men who had been in the end cage only a few minutes before.

'OK, Red Hair, let's see if your blood is really as yellow as they say,' one of the guards said with an evil grin, as he dropped two short swords through the bars to Jez's cage.

Jez did not answer, but snatched up one of the swords as the door from his cage to the arena swung open. Bek forced himself again to look at the light. It did not hurt his eyes anywhere near as much this time as the brief wave of sound and sunlight washed through the holding area again.

The door clanged shut.

Bek listened intently.

This time there was hardly a pause before the muffled ring of blade on blade sounded above the cheering of the crowd. The song was different this time. Fast regular patterns of steel on steel such that Bek could almost see the fight in his mind.

'Hey, young Red Hair is pretty sharp!' exclaimed one of the guards.

'Which is more than his partner is... was I mean,' said the guard with the goatee beard, as the pace of the fight changed slightly.

'Ow! That had to hurt,' said a third.

'What do you know! He does bleed red after all,' laughed the guard who had dropped the swords into Jez's cage.

Bek clenched his hands into fists as he forced down his anger. It would be his turn soon and he had to stay calm. 'To fight angry is to fight carelessly.' Derra's words had stuck with him from one of her early lessons to his squad during training. Now, more than ever, it was important to keep that principle at the forefront of his mind.

'Come on, Jez,' he muttered under his breath. 'Stay alive. Keep at him.'

The clashing exchanges continued at a furious pace, so Bek guessed that whatever the wound was that Jez had taken, it could not be overly serious. Then there was a gasp from the guards almost as one and the metallic song of steel stopped abruptly.

'What's he doing?' exclaimed the guard who kept referring to Jez as Red Hair. 'He could have finished him.'

'It seems that the Thrandorian has a sense of honour about not striking an unarmed man,' said one of the others, with a muted note of respect in his voice.

'Well, he won't last long around here with attitudes like that,' spat the guard with the goatee. 'Come on. Let's fetch him in before the crowd warms to him too much.'

Bek smiled grimly to himself. He had no qualms about killing anyone that awaited him in that arena. He was under no illusion that these so-called arena fighters would not hesitate to kill him if given the chance, so he intended to give no quarter in return. Besides, if he killed his opponent it was one less to face in the future.

The guards led Jez back in through the door from the arena. There was a large diagonal tear in the front of his tunic, and the material was soaked with blood. He looked pale in the dim light of the holding area.

'Are you OK?' Bek asked as Jez walked past his cage.

'Yes, but be careful out there. My opponent was supposedly a tyro fighter, but he was good, Bek. Don't get overconfident.'

Bek nodded, looking at Jez's torn tunic. He hoped fervently that the guards would get Jez some treatment for his wound quickly, before he lost too much blood.

The door to the next cage opened and Bek got his first real glimpse of the arena as the two men in the cage next to his moved out into the open. The layer of dusty sand that covered the floor of the arena had quite obviously been raked smooth before the day's events had begun. Now though, the more central area looked scuffed and dimpled with the footprints of fighters who had already battled for their lives that morning. The far wall was also visible briefly. It was far too tall for any thoughts of an easy scramble to escape. From the short glance that Bek got of it, he estimated that the first tier of seating must be eighteen to twenty feet above the sandy floor. Other metal doors were visible in the far wall of the arena, which suggested that the whole stadium was ringed with a series of pits from which men could be allowed entry into the central open-aired fighting ground.

His only thoughts today should be of survival. Jez had managed it. So would he, Bek decided grimly. Focusing inward, he calmed his anger and his thoughts of escape, carefully burying them deep in his heart. A sense of peace settled over him as he controlled his breathing into a slow, regular pattern, and he blocked out the sound of the comments from the guards and the dull noise of cheering from the arena outside.

Suddenly, the gate to Bek's cage opened to the arena outside and he looked up to see a formidable looking man standing in the middle of the arena waving to the cheering crowds.

'Shand alive!' Selek breathed, his voice projecting fear and dread. 'It's Barrock, we're as good as dead already!'

'I take it that he's good then?' Bek said, calmly picking up one of the swords that the guards had dropped into the cage.

'He's a ranked fighter and he's vicious,' Selek said, his voice flat and without hope.

'Stay back and leave him to me,' Bek replied softly.

'Go on! Get out there!' ordered one of the guards roughly, and made as if to jab at them with his own sword through the bars.

Bek, however, needed no further prompting, and he stumbled forward out of the cage and into the blazing sunlight. In the few seconds that he had had to assess their opponent, Bek had decided on a strategy that fitted the situation perfectly.

Barrock was a muscle-bound giant of a man. Standing a full six and a half feet tall with a broad chest, bulging biceps and forearms that appeared as thick as some men's thighs, Bek could not fail to see why Selek feared him. However, from the moment that Bek had seen the man waving to the crowd, he had judged that Barrock's ego towered every bit as high as his body. Bek hoped that the man's ego would prove his downfall.

Moving forward, Bek deliberately stumbled, and he squinted his eyes virtually shut against the bright sunlight. Feigning incompetence, Bek held his sword awkwardly in front of him and felt a slight glow of satisfaction as Barrock's face settled into a derisive sneer. Without warning, the big man leapt forward with surprising speed and agility for one so heavily built and his sword sliced through the air with whistling force.

Seemingly by pure fluke, the bright sun chanced to reflect off Bek's sword straight into Barrock's eyes even as the giant swung his sword down. At the same instant that Barrock was momentarily blinded, Bek shifted his grip on the sword, deflected the descending blade and whirled in close to Barrock. To the crowd's dismay, Bek opened the fighter's throat with a single whip-like cutting stroke and spun out of his reach before Barrock had seen him coming.

The anticipatory roar of the crowd as Barrock had moved forward for the quick kill, dropped away to a stunned silence as the huge man dropped to his knees. For a moment he knelt, clutching at his throat in disbelief as he tried in vain to draw breath. Then with agonising slowness, he tumbled forward to the ground and died. Bek walked calmly back and picked up Barrock's sword from where it had fallen at his side. However, the blade was far too heavy and long for Bek to use effectively, so he dropped it back on Barrock's body.

Someone, somewhere in the crowd, started to clap slowly. One by one, others joined in until the whole arena adopted the slow applause. Bek did not look up at the tiered seating, or acknowledge the crowd's acceptance in any way. Instead, he just walked slowly back to where Selek was standing, dumbfounded and staring at the body of Barrock in an obvious state of shock.

'Come on, Selek. We've done our bit for society today. Let's leave,' Bek suggested, gently pressuring his arm to turn his Shandese cellmate around towards the gate through which Jez had been led after his fight.

The Arena Master, however, did not agree with Bek's sentiments, and the door back into the pits remained firmly closed.

A sudden roar of approval from the crowd signalled the emergence of another fighter into the arena. The new opponent was nowhere near as imposing a figure as Barrock had been. He was of similar size and build to Bek, but like Barrock, he wore various pieces of protective armour. A bright breastplate and helmet were the most notable pieces, though he also wore stiffened leather greaves over forearms and thighs.

'Who is he?' Bek asked Selek warily.

'I don't know,' Selek replied. 'I've never seen him fight before. He's certainly not ranked here in Shandrim.'

Bek made a mental note to quiz Selek about this ranking system if they made it back to the pits alive. As it was, ranked or not, this fighter moved easily and looked as if he was perfectly at home out in front of this roaring crowd.

Once more Bek waved Selek back and advanced to meet the approaching threat on his own. However, this time there was no point in attempting deceit. This fighter already knew that Bek could use a sword and he was unlikely to fall for any simple tricks. Undoubtedly the impending fight would hinge on skill and an instinct for survival, both of which burned fiercely in Bek. The only question that remained was whether they burned fiercely enough.

The armoured fighter circled Bek slowly and the crowd started to stamp their feet in a regular rhythm, seeking to urge the two protagonists into action by beating out the passage of time.

Neither was going to be rushed.

Bek's grey-blue eyes drilled unblinkingly at his prowling adversary and his stare was returned with equal intensity. The blade that the armoured man carried was a full six inches longer than the one in Bek's hand, and its extra length and weight made it a weapon that was better handled with both hands. This in itself made the approaching battle one of uncertainty for Bek, as he had never faced a two-handed blade before. His mind raced as he followed his opponent's movement minutely. In theory, the double-handed blade would be wielded with more power behind the strokes, but would hamper the fighter's manoeuvrability and speed. As Bek's most deadly assets were his speed and anticipation, this should work to his advantage. However, he was not about to get overconfident.

The muscles bunching on the unknown fighter's right leg were the clue that Bek had been watching for and even as the man leapt in for the attack, Bek was on the move to intercept him. As Bek expected, the first swinging blow came with a lot of weight behind it. The shock of meeting it on his short blade jarred his wrist more than he had anticipated though, and this made the subsequent rapid exchange far more difficult than he had imagined it would be. The only striking blow that he managed to land glanced harmlessly off the leather guard on his opponent's forearm. The fact that Bek had met every stroke, and indeed made contact with a stroke of his own, albeit ineffective, placed a hint of doubt in the armoured fighter's eyes. The two had sprung apart from the initial exchange and resumed their stalking, completely oblivious to the fact that the crowd was cheering wildly.

These early bouts seldom produced any real fights. The norm was a slaughter. Blood flowed in great quantities, but almost never from one of the regular fighters. Most people viewed these fights as a warm-up for what they really wanted to see: the trained fighters facing each other. There was heavy betting on every bout involving ranked fighters, and great sums of gold changed hands on a weekly basis. Even the fights between the tyros drew great interest, but nobody betted on the pre-games slaughter of what they saw as the undesirable criminal element of Shandar. There were few among the crowds at the games who realised that the majority of those forced into the arena to their deaths were little more than petty criminals. To see someone fight back with skill and poise was almost unheard of, so to first see a tyro beaten by a lanky red-haired man, and then see a ranked fighter killed by this nondescript young dark-haired man had got them fired up to a frenzy of emotion.

Bek took the initiative on the second exchange, driving home a barrage of strokes that forced the armoured fighter back and left him bleeding from cuts on both upper arms. A glimmer of fear started to dawn in the fighter's eyes as Bek's cold grey-blue gaze impassively surveyed his bleeding opponent with no hint of mercy or compassion.

The pause that followed was very brief as Bek decided not to allow his opponent to regroup. With a dazzling turn of speed, Bek darted in close to his opponent and landed several more stinging cuts whilst easily blocking his adversary's counterstrokes. The fighter retreated, as he simply could not counter Bek's speed effectively. Even as he stepped back, he stumbled slightly, and before he could begin to recover, Bek was inside his guard again and had driven his blade up under the base of the man's breastplate and through his body.

The man dropped his sword, and looked down in shock at the hilt which protruded from the front of his body. His eyes glazed as death took him and he tumbled to the sandy floor at Bek's feet.

The crowd was on its feet and thunderous applause and cheers were reverberating around the arena.

Bek ignored it all.

Instead, he bent and picked up his opponent's sword with interest. It was longer than he was used to and the handle, being long enough for two hands, felt unusual. Strangely, though, the blade was not much heavier than the short sword that he had used.

Experimentally, he whirled the blade in a series of

elaborate strokes. By using the blade one-handed, the longer handle meant that his wrist had to roll more with any change in direction and this, he decided, would reduce his speed and flexibility. It was a nice sword, but it really did not suit him. There was no way that he would have been allowed to keep the blade, but it had been useful to try it, if only to begin to understand the limitations of the weapons that the arena fighters favoured.

'Holy Shand, Thrandorian! You are fast, and far more skilled than you let on,' Selek exclaimed, appearing at Bek's side. 'I thought that your defeating Barrock was a fluke, but I suspect that even if he had been wary of you the outcome might still have gone in your favour. Come. The Arena Master has obviously decided that he has lost enough fighters to your arm today. Leave the weapon and let's get out of here before he changes his mind.'

Bek shrugged and planted the sword point first in the sand next to the dead fighter. Guards were already dragging Barrock's body from the arena and a group of four of them was closing warily on Bek and Selek, their blades all drawn.

Selek threw his blade to the ground and walked forward alongside Bek towards the open door back into the holding area. The guards, realising that there was going to be no trouble, moved to shadow them. One fell into line either side of them, with two behind them and the applause from the crowd did not cease until they had disappeared back into the pit.

'Did you see the Emperor applauding?' Selek asked Bek enthusiastically, as they were shepherded back down the steps and along the corridors to the holding cell.

'Emperor? No! Where was he?' Bek asked in surprise.

'In the Imperial Box of course. To our right as we entered the arena. I've been to the games on several occasions as a spectator and have only seen him applaud in very few fights. Normally he just sits there with his crowd of sycophants and advisers, impassively observing the fights and ignoring all else. Rumour has it that he's followed the form of the fighters for many years and seldom fails to predict the outcome of any fight. Certainly, to see him applaud a prisoner is unheard of.'

'But that's hardly surprising as it's obvious that very few prisoners ever win,' Bek stated coldly.

'True enough, but it's said that the Emperor appreciates skill when he sees it, and they also say that he's very discerning,' Selek continued undeterred by Bek's lack of enthusiasm.

'Then it's a shame that he doesn't apply that virtue to his justice system instead of spending so much time on this barbaric waste of human life that you all describe as games,' Bek said flatly. 'From what you've just said of him, I suspect that he's not really very in touch with the ordinary people of his Empire.'

Selek looked at Bek as if he were mad.

'Oh, he's not bad, as rulers go,' Selek said stoically. 'Of course he isn't in touch with the people. What ruler is? Overall, though, he hasn't made matters any worse than they were under the previous Emperor and that's really all that we have as a measure.'

Bek considered what Selek had said and was still thinking about it as they reached their cell. The gate was unlocked and they were allowed to walk in without being shoved or manhandled in any way. Indeed, the guards treated them with such respect that the prisoners inside all crowded around them to find out what had happened. Bek pushed his way through the crowd to look for Jez, as Selek launched into an expansive tale of Bek's double victory in the arena. There was no sign of Bek's Thrandorian friend anywhere in the small series of linked rooms and he could only hope that Jez was somewhere having his wound treated.

When he returned to the first room, where he had left Selek beginning his oratory, no one hindered him as he entered. Indeed, the other prisoners all drew aside to let him walk freely and a hushed silence fell over the room. Bek decided to use this obvious rise in status to best advantage.

With a confidence that he did not really feel, he walked into the centre of the room and he swept the circle of faces with his steely grey-blue eyes.

'Does anyone here know anything of the whereabouts of my companion?' Bek asked, his voice cool and unemotional.

There was a short silence.

'The red-haired lad?' someone asked from Bek's left.

'That's right. Do you know where he is?'

'Taken down to the Red Room. We saw him led past here about half an hour ago I'd say.'

The man who had spoken was broad-chested, with a large livid red scar still bearing a line of uneven stitches, which ran diagonally down from his forehead and right across his left cheek. Like most of the men in the room he was dark-haired with thick, black eyebrows and dark brown eyes. Without the scar, he might have been considered handsome. With it, his appearance was forbidding.

Others murmured in agreement at his statement.

'The Red Room? What's that?' Bek asked coldly.

'Where the butchers the Arena Master calls medics carry out their work, of course,' the man laughed, his voice harsh and bitter. 'The place where I was treated to this masterpiece of healing skill,' he added, pointing at the coarsely sewn and puckered scar line across his face.

For a moment Bek was stuck for a reply, the image of Jez in the hands of such unskilled medics robbing him of his power of speech.

Don't worry,' the man said, his misshapen face twisting into a parody of a grin. 'Your friend won't be gone long. The surgeons may not be skilled, but they do work quickly. He should be back any time now, unless he died of course.'

'Thanks a bundle,' Bek muttered. But before he could ask anything more, the sound of multiple approaching footsteps forestalled any further conversation.

CHAPTER 3

Everyone in the cell waited expectantly as the footfalls of several sets of booted feet approached. Bek fervently hoped that it was the guards bringing Jez back from the red room, but logic made that unlikely. The footsteps were approaching from the same direction as the arena and the scant information that Bek had gathered so far indicated that the medics' domain rested somewhere at the opposite end of the corridor.

A group of four men arrived at the gate to the cell and the hush of anticipation amongst the prisoners turned into a buzz of excited whispers. Two of the men wore the standard black uniforms of guards but the remaining pair, although burly enough to be guards, wore richly coloured clothing made from fine cloth. There was nothing uniform about these two aside from the heavily-muscled build that spoke of an intensive regime of physical training. Bek was immediately reminded of the strutting figure of Barrock in the arena, and he instinctively knew that these were more of the trained arena fighters.

The guards opened the gate and Bek was not overly surprised when they singled him out.

'You... Thrandorian – come with us.'

There was no point in arguing and the rest of the prisoners moved aside as Bek walked, as confidently as he could, forward to exit through the gate. This might just be the chance that he had been waiting for. If only Jez had been here. Together their chances for escape would have been far greater and Bek was reluctant to consider making a break for it without his friend.

'Come on. We haven't got all day,' one of the guards growled in a vain attempt to sound dangerous.

Bek ignored him, more than aware that his own reputation for being dangerous had today grown to far exceed that of a blustering guard. The rest of the prisoners remained silent, save for a couple of quietly derogatory noises directed at the guard as Bek did his best to walk casually and unhurriedly out of the cell. The guard decided better than to say anything about the disrespect of the prisoners. Instead, he just locked the door behind Bek and then fell into place behind the rest of the group, who were already moving back up the corridor.

'Where are we going?' Bek enquired of the finely dressed fighter to his right. 'Am I to fight again so soon?'

Bek had done his utmost to keep his words cold and flat from emotion, trying really hard to keep any nervousness from his voice.

'Patience. You'll see soon enough,' the man replied with a grin.

The fighter's smiling response left Bek wondering whether his gambit had been successful and had won the man's approval for his calmness, or whether he was being quietly laughed at. Whichever it was, Bek was not about to venture any more attempts at conversation until he knew a bit more about his situation.

All the way along the corridor and up the flights of steps, Bek studied his surroundings for likely avenues of escape. There did not appear to be any that were obvious, but he absorbed himself in the detail of the route along which he was being taken in the hope of discovering a weakness.

The corridor walls appeared thick and strong, made with great blocks of sandstone that had not been totally smoothed to a flat surface but had been roughly hewn and yet cleverly fitted together. The torches bracketed to the walls at regular intervals had stained the stones behind and above, their orange flickering tongues of flame leaving a cooked-on blackness of sooty scorch marks. There were doors and metal gates in the walls on both sides of the corridor at times. Some obviously opened into more cells, and groups of prisoners watched with interest as the small party passed. Others yielded no clues as to where they led, if anywhere. For all Bek knew, every door along that corridor might merely open into more cells. There was no way of knowing and there were no clues as to possible escape routes.

When Bek and the others had been led along the corridor earlier in the day, the group had not turned aside from the main wide passageway. They had climbed the various flights of twisting stairs to the holding cages at the arena level. This time though, Bek was not taken all the way to the cage area. Instead, the group stopped short of the final set of stairs and one of the two guards unhooked a large bunch of keys from his belt. A large metal door on the left hand side of the corridor was opened to reveal a straight staircase leading off in a different direction.

Bek could hear the crowds quite clearly again by now, and as he climbed this new staircase he realised that the noise was no longer just coming from above him, but also from his right side. They had to be climbing up into the very seating area of the arena, he mused, but why? Why was he being brought up into the public viewing area? Suddenly a chill swept down his spine. What if he was to be visibly punished for killing the two fighters earlier? Or maybe even executed? After all, one of the two men that he had killed was a ranked fighter and probably had a large number of supporters who followed his fights.

Another metal door, this time on the right side, was unlocked at the top of the stairs, and once again the amazing atmosphere and noise of the Shandrim arena washed over Bek. This time he got to appreciate the immensity of the arena crowd even more, as he was not instantly faced with a life or death situation, even if his circumstance was still far from certain. A short set of steps led up into the open air at the top level of the tiered seating and Bek had to fight an almost overpowering urge to shoulder his way past the others and make a run for it into the crowd.

One of the two well-dressed fighters sensed his desire and muttered a word of warning to Bek in a low voice.

'Don't even think about it. You wouldn't stand a chance if you tried to make a break now. Just follow us and be patient. All will become clear soon enough.'

Bek was surprised, firstly because he did not realise that he had been that obvious, and secondly because he got the distinct impression that wherever he was going, something good was going to come of it. What that thing was, he had no idea, but he took encouragement from the fighter's reassuring tone, and his elevated heart rate began to calm slowly down to a more normal level.

As they stepped up into the sunlight, Bek's eyes were instinctively drawn to the two figures battling in the centre of the arena. The two protagonists were glistening with sweat as they weaved their deadly dance of steel, their blades clashing together in a vicious series of stroke and counterstroke. Both were skilled and moved with grace and balance, but even as he watched, Bek could tell that the heavier-set of the two men would win the bout. Although heavier, the man moved slightly more surely and his strokes appeared to have more of a sting to them. The other man did not appear to have any great advantage of speed, skill or mobility and would surely tire faster trying to defend against such an opponent.

A nudge on the arm prompted Bek to keep moving and he was led down an aisle of steps between two stands of bench-style seating to the very lowest level above the sands of the arena. Even before they reached the bottom of the steps Bek's judgement of the fight was proved correct and the crowd roared their approval of the winning blow. Both fighters bowed to the Emperor's Box, the loser bleeding heavily from a nasty wound on his right upper arm. The Emperor acknowledged them with the faintest of nods.

For a brief moment, Bek wondered if his escorts were leading him to the Emperor, for they were now moving in the direction of the special area of seating that was allocated to His Imperial Majesty. Thoughts of an Emperor's pardon crossed his mind, but they were quickly dashed when the two men in front of him stopped before a strange looking character dressed in a rich purple robe, trimmed with gold.

'The prisoner you wanted to see, Master,' said one of the fighters, bowing low to the purple clothed man sitting in the front row.

'Ah yes! A Thrandorian I'm led to believe?' he replied questioningly, and squinting slightly as he tilted his face up to look at Bek.

Bek could not help but stare at the man, for his apparently blighted body warranted more than just a quick glance. He was deformed; there was no other word for it. Short in stature with a pot belly and a viciously curved spine that forced his head forward and downward on his shoulders, the man hardly looked human. Hair that grew in random patches on the man's scalp gave him a naturally untidy look despite the fact that he obviously did everything he could to make himself look presentable. The man's hands, folded carefully on his lap, boasted perfectly shaped and trimmed nails and an odour of fresh scent wafted from him.

'Well?' the man asked impatiently. 'Are you Thrandorian or aren't you?'

'Yes... Sir,' Bek replied, unsure of how to address the odd-looking little man.

A shrewd smile spread slowly across the man's face, as he seemed to weigh the fact in his mind.

'You fight well, Thrandorian. What is your name?'

'Bek, Sir.'

'Bek... hmmm. No, that won't do at all. Far too simple and not dramatic enough, we will have to change that for a start. Can't have fighters with names that aren't dramatic. They need rhythm – something that the crowd can chant. No, Bek won't do at all.'

The strange little man looked at Bek thoughtfully, muttering half-heard names to himself and then shaking his head slightly with each mutter. Then, apparently disregarding the problem of Bek's name, the man decided to introduce himself.

'I am Garvin, Master of the Arena, Bek, and I would like to make you a proposition.' He paused to allow his introduction to sink in. 'Do you want to stay a prisoner, Bek?' he asked casually, almost as if he were just letting the question slide between his lips.

'No, Sir, I don't,' Bek replied firmly.

'Ever thought of being a professional fighter? I don't mean a soldier, for I can see that you've had military training, and I'll lay heavy odds that today was not the first time that you'd killed with a sword. I mean a true professional fighter. Someone who demonstrates his skill for the pleasure of others on a regular basis and gets well paid for those displays. Think of it, Bek... thousands of people clamouring to see you fight in the arena and shouting your name over and over as you come out onto the sand. They will worship you in your shining protective outfit as you cross blades with other like-minded men. It's a glorious profession, Bek, and one for which I believe you are well suited.'

Bek was not enamoured with the idea at all, but he did not want to shut off a potential escape route so he pretended to be interested and asked a few follow-up questions.

'It sounds great,' he lied. 'What's the deal? Do I get paid per fight, or on a results basis?'

'That is all negotiable. Initially, though, you will not be paid much, for I will have training costs to cover and equipment costs for your fighter's outfit and weapons. I think it only fair that my fighters pay for their keep. When all is taken into account the keep of a fighter is not cheap. Despite this, if you do well and progress up the ranks as quickly as I suspect, you won't want for money. Trust me on this. You will have all the money that you need and your pick of the sort of luxuries that most men dream of. Fine wine, beautiful women, the best food – what do you say? Will you become a fighter?'

'Do I have a choice?'

'There is always a choice, Bek. Your best choice now is to become a fighter, getting good accommodation and training, being well fed and paid. Alternatively, you can go back to your cell and expect to go into the arena every week against my best fighters until I find one to kill you. It is a simple choice.'

Bek gave Garvin a wry smile.

'When you put it that way, then I guess my decision requires little thought. Before I agree though, may I ask one request?'

'Ask away.'

'If I'm to be trained as a fighter, then I would like my fellow Thrandorian to be trained as well.'

'Fellow Thrandorian? Who is he?' the Arena Master asked curiously.

'He fought and won earlier today. A tall, red haired young fellow – disarmed his opponent...'

'Ah yes. The lanky-looking young chap.' The Arena Master paused to consider for a moment. 'He fought reasonably enough. He's a bit skinnier than I would normally consider, but... well I suppose he might provide the crowd with a bit of novelty. He was injured in his fight this morning wasn't he?'

'Yes, Sir, but I have no idea how badly. I haven't been able to discover word of him since he left the arena.'

'Very well,' Garvin said decisively. 'Chanis, go and find out the status of the lanky Thrandorian... what was his name?'

'Jez, Sir,' Bek offered eagerly.

'Jez? Don't any of you Thrandorians have interesting names?' Garvin shook his head disapprovingly. 'It doesn't matter. Names can be changed easily enough. Very well. Chanis go and find out about this Thrandorian, Jez. Providing that he isn't crippled then transfer him to the secure tyros' quarters. Maasich, take Bek to the secure quarters now and have him fitted with training gear. He is to join the training programme this evening with the other tyros.'

The two well-dressed fighters both bowed to Garvin and wasted no time in moving to fulfil their respective duties. Bek was ushered away even as the crowd began to cheer the next combatants who were already entering the arena.

Maasich proved to be the fighter who had warned Bek not to attempt escape earlier. This time as they walked back up the aisle of steps to re-enter the bowels of the stadium he spoke freely with Bek.

'I heard about your fights earlier. I wasn't in the crowd at the time, but from what I heard you made short work of killing Barrock. I'm impressed – he was a good fighter,' he stated, giving Bek an open smile.

'Well, he may have been good, but he was also very overconfident,' Bek replied depreciatingly. 'It wasn't really a fight at all. He didn't expect to face a prisoner who knew how to handle a sword. I fooled him momentarily and that was enough to give me the opportunity to end it quickly.'

'Karoth was more wary though,' Maasich continued enthusiastically. 'He may not have been ranked, but he probably would have been by the end of this season. He was one of the better young tyro fighters here and he had already won several fights. Yet, not only did you beat him, you also killed him and with a short sword at that. Whatever you say, those that saw you fight were all impressed. Somehow you walked away unscratched from two bouts against good fighters, and you had no armour and only had a short blade to fight with! That sort of thing just doesn't happen around here... unless, of course, your name is Serrius.'

'I've heard about him. Everyone seems to hold him in very high regard. Is he really as good as they say he is?'

Maasich grimaced expressively and nodded.

'Probably better,' he admitted. 'There is no one to touch him. What's more, even those who might have a vague chance of beating him don't want to try.'

'Why on earth not?' Bek asked in surprise.

'Because he gives no second chances for those who face him. Serrius does not strike unless he can make a killing blow. He will deliberately pass up opportunities to end a fight in order to make the kill. No one has ever survived an encounter with him – he has killed every man that he has ever faced in the arena. Strangely enough that seems to put people off from wanting to fight him.'

'Understandable. I heard about the five that he killed a few weeks ago. I've seen men hold off multiple opponents in the midst of a battle, I've done it myself – but to do it in an open area! He must be very fast.'

Maasich's eyes were distant and he did not answer for a moment.

'You have no idea,' he breathed. 'The man is faster than a striking snake. Facing him just does not bear thinking about.'

Bek decided that he had heard enough about Serrius for now. As he had absolutely no intention of facing anyone in the arena that he did not have to, Bek decided to see whether Maasich was as free with other information as he was about Serrius. In particular, he was interested in anything that might prove useful in attempting to escape the arena. All background information on the layout of the stadium would be useful, so that was where he concentrated his efforts.

They were back into the dimly lit corridors under the seating stands again by now and Bek had already become confused by all the turns and stairwells. It was a virtual labyrinth of passageways within the bowels of the stands and Bek realised that he would need to try to memorise at least some of the interior if he was to have a chance of finding his way out when the opportunity arose.

'How on earth do you know where you're going down here?' Bek asked Maasich as they turned through yet another nondescript doorway and into another almost identical looking passageway.

Maasich grinned at him.

'It does seem like a maze at first, but you'll soon get

used to it. We're nearly around to the tyros' rooms now. You'll be living in the secure rooms, which means that you'll be locked in when you're not out training. That will restrict what you can do other than training and fighting, but you'll be too tired to do much more than go to bed anyway.'

'Tough training programme?'

'Tough? It's a scorcher! You'll find out soon enough though. Garvin said you were to join the training session this evening, so you'll get a taster before you have to start doing full days of it.'

'I can hardly wait,' Bek said sarcastically.

When they arrived at the quarters, Maasich showed Bek into a large room with four beds in it. The room was empty of any personal possessions and spartan in its furnishings. There was a tall single-door wardrobe to the right of each bed space, and a small bedside chest to the left. Other than this the room was bare. The floor was paved with flagstones worn to a shine from years of use. The walls and ceiling were plastered roughly and whitewashed giving a cold, clinical feel to the place. However, even if there had been three others using the room, Bek would still have had much more space of his own than he had enjoyed as a Recruit, or as a Private in Baron Keevan's army. Even as a Corporal, he had shared his room with one other of the same rank, but the space that he had enjoyed even then did not compare to this.

'This will be your room for as long as you remain a tyro,' Maasich said, noting Bek's expression of surprise at the size of the accommodation. 'Of course, if you climb the rankings into the top thirty, then you'll be given a single room with a lot more trimmings. Garvin likes to work on a reward based work ethic.'

'I can see how that might be effective,' Bek said, forcing his voice to sound enthusiastic. Privately he thought it unlikely that fighters would be motivated by the size of their living quarters. Ambition, glory and gold were more powerful motivators in his experience, but if that went hand in hand with better accommodation, then maybe it might have an effect.

'Your friend, the other Thrandorian, will probably be quartered here with you, and you can expect the other beds to be filled at some time over the next couple of weeks,' Maasich was saying. 'As you've got no personal stuff to leave here, we might as well go and get you kitted out with your training gear.'

Maasich closed the door to the room and led Bek down another corridor, this one having door after door along its length. Turning first right at the next junction and then immediately left, they followed this passageway to the very end.

A stony-faced Storeman handed over Bek's protective training gear, though he was issued with no weapons.

'You'll get your weapons from the armoury at the beginning of the training session like all the other tyros,' the cold-faced Storeman said, his voice betraying an inexplicable tone of distaste.

'Thanks,' Bek replied, trying his best not to react to the Storeman's manner. 'I'll try to look after this as best I can.'

'See that you do. You won't get more without good cause.'

A muffled roar that was definitely not of human origin distracted Bek from being drawn into making any comment on the Storeman's persistently hostile attitude.

'What in Tarmin's name was that?' Bek asked, his eyes wide, as he looked across at the wall from behind which the noise had originated.

Maasich gave a wicked little grin.

'Not all the opponents that we face in the arena fight with swords,' he said, his eyes twinkling with amusement.

The roar sounded again, a deep-throated expression of frustrated blood lust.

'Have a nice day,' the Storeman said, his face twisting into a smirk but his voice losing nothing of its icy coldness.

Bek gave a shudder.

At least as a proper tyro arena fighter he could expect to be properly armed and dressed for battle when he went into the arena. He suddenly felt a surge of pity for the prisoners back in the cells who would not necessarily enjoy even that much of a sporting chance.

By the time that they had got back to Bek's quarters with his new gear they found Jez already there. He was lying relaxing on the bed, his chest bound with bandages and partially covered by a loose shirt that was unfastened at the front. He looked pale, but was smiling at the sight of Bek.

'Jez! How are you? Did they look after you OK?' Bek asked, immediately dumping his new gear on the nearest bunk and moving to his friend's bedside.

'I'm all right. The medic who did the stitching could do with a few needlework lessons, but he did stop the bleeding. When the fighter, Chanis, came and got me from the medics, he then took me to another set of medics who seemed far more competent. They tutted and muttered at the way that my wound had been treated, but they seemed to think that I'd be fully fit in three to four weeks with plenty of rest and no fighting or strenuous exercise.'

'So did Chanis tell you why you were being brought here rather than being taken back to the cells?'

'Yes. He said that I was to be trained as an arena fighter, but he wasn't forthcoming with news of you. I'm really glad to see that you survived out there today. Do I need to ask how it went?'

Bek shook his head and started on a brief description of his fight when Maasich interrupted him.

'You two go ahead and settle in. I'll be back later to take you to the training session, Bek.'

'Thanks, Maasich. Just one thing before you go though – are we likely to get fed at all today? I haven't eaten properly in a week.'

Maasich nodded.

'I'll get food sent down as soon as I can. The kitchens will be very busy right now, but I'll do my best.'

With that, Maasich left. The click of the lock and the thud of the bolt being driven home emphasised the fact that whilst their circumstances had improved, Bek and Jez were still very much prisoners. The reminder led them to discussing escape plans and all that they had learned of their prison so far. Bek had the better overall mental picture of the arena and he drew out what he had learned by using a finger on the bedcovers.

'From what I can tell, the arena complex is a rectangular structure, although the inner arena and the tiered seating are arranged in a wide sausage shape,' he began, sketching the outlines by indenting the covers with his forefinger. 'The prison cells are located underneath the stands on the north side of the sausage and this room seems to be underneath the south side. From what I could see, the arena has a fairly symmetrical layout, with eight main blocks of seating separated by aisles of steps. The Emperor's Box is there, on the north stand, and that appears to be the only side of the arena without a main entrance and exit way. It would not surprise me, though, to find that the Emperor has his own entrance somewhere behind that box.'

Bek paused, looking at the bedcover and concentrating hard. Most of the lines were fading even as he drew them, but both had the image in their minds and as he added things into the picture, he would occasionally refresh the outer oblong to keep the places in context.

'The Red Room, which is what the other prisoners called the place that you were taken to for treatment by the medics, must be somewhere towards the north eastern corner of the arena...'

'Yes, that makes sense,' Jez confirmed. 'And the better medics would have been over there in the south eastern corner somewhere.'

'They probably treat the arena fighters and leave the butchers in the Red Room to look after the lowlife prisoners.'

Jez nodded, the overall layout beginning to make more sense. 'So what about the western end of the arena?

What's under the stands there?'

'I'm not sure that I really want to know,' Bek answered, his tone ominous.

Jez looked at him quizzically.

'The equipment store that I was taken to earlier would have been here, in the south western corner,' Bek went on, pointing at the appropriate corner. 'While I was there I heard the roar of a beast like nothing I've ever heard before. The noise came from what must be some sort of holding area at that western end of the arena. I didn't get a straight answer out of Maasich, but they certainly hold dangerous animals of some sort down there.'

'What for?'

'For us to fight apparently,' Bek said, noting that Jez's eyes had widened as much as his had done earlier. 'It seems that the games here are not just about fighting one another. The Arena Master obviously likes to add a bit of variety to his shows.'

Bek and Jez talked over the information that they had gleaned for some time, each trying to devise some sort of plan for escape. However, as neither had actually come close enough to an exit to see what sort of security they were up against, they soon concluded that they needed more information before they could hope to make a breakout attempt that was likely to succeed.

A man bringing food eventually interrupted their planning and scheming. Hunger diverted all of their attention towards consuming the hot stew, bread and meat that the man brought them. More food than they had eaten in days did not last more than a few minutes, as they wolfed down every last morsel as if someone might take it away from them at any second.

When everything was gone, Jez was more than a little sleepy and Bek encouraged him to get some rest. Within a few moments Jez had sunk into a deep sleep and the slow regular pattern of his breathing quickly reminded Bek of how little sleep he had had recently. Placing his training gear in the bedside press and wardrobe next to his chosen bunk, Bek settled down for a quick snooze.

Only seconds later, or so it seemed, Bek was startled awake by Maasich noisily opening the door and informing him that it was time to get ready for the evening training session.

'Come on,' Maasich said loudly. 'You've got two minutes to get into your gear. Hammar will not like it if you're late and you really wouldn't want to upset him.'

'Who's Hammar?' Bek mumbled sleepily, tipping his legs over the side of his bunk and rubbing fiercely at his reluctantly opening eyes. 'And anyway, I thought you weren't going to come and get me until just before the evening session?'

'It is evening already,' Maasich stated in an irritated tone. 'Come on, come on! Hammar is the Weapons' Master and believe me, if you value your hide, you'll get out of here in the next minute.'

Bek scrambled to comply with the practised efficiency that only a military training regime could teach. Moments later he was back out walking the corridors with Maasich, who showed no surprise at Bek's speed of preparation. A short walk brought them up and out into the arena through one of the fighter's gates.

Perhaps fifty or so men were gathered at the eastern end of the arena, where a grizzled-looking old man was directing them to collect a wooden pole each and line up in a double file. Bek and Maasich moved swiftly to do likewise and get themselves into line with the others.

Hard-faced stares met Bek wherever he looked. Some were simply that – hard-eyed, unemotional stares. Others, though, harboured an intense dislike, a well of anger that promised violence at the earliest opportunity.

'Well, they are fighters,' Bek reasoned silently, 'and having killed two of their compatriots today will hardly have endeared me to them. I'll just have to lie low for a while and try not to attract any more attention.'

'Fighters, hup!' the grizzled old man called out in a voice that rivalled any of Bek's old army instructors.

All of the men responded immediately by holding up the wooden poles horizontally above their heads in both hands.

'Forward,' the instructor called, and the double file of men set off at a jog around the perimeter.

The poles were only a couple of feet long and about as thick as a man's wrist, so they were not particularly heavy. However, Bek knew all too well from previous experience that the weight of them would gradually seem to grow and grow with every passing minute until it felt as if it were made of lead. What he was not prepared for was how fast it happened.

Weeks of captivity during the long, slow trip to Shandrim, and also in the cells below the arena stands, had sapped much of Bek's stamina. Within two circuits he was breathing hard and his arms were burning with the effort of holding the wooden pole above his head. He was only glad that his fights had not lasted long in the arena earlier in the day. With hindsight, he was sure that if he had been faced with a long fight against a skilled opponent, then he would not have lived to tell of it.

From the moment that his breathing began to labour, sheer determination kept Bek going. Through circuit after circuit of that steady pounding jog, he gritted his teeth and drove his unwilling muscles through the punishing series of exercises. Sometimes the pole would be held in front of him, sometimes behind his neck. Sometimes it would be pushed up and down from shoulder level to as high as he could reach, and other times it would be lowered to touch the ground and raised again. Regardless of the exercise, though, the rhythm of the slow running pace never changed.

Finally, just when Bek thought that he could take it no longer, the instructor ordered them to stop running. In agony, a wave of relief swept over him, but it was to be short-lived. Before he could even get his breath back the torture continued with a long series of stretching exercises that were even more painful than the running. Pain seemed to fill every part of his body. Every fibre of every muscle screamed out through his nervous system for relief from the relentless punishment that it was taking. Even his bones seemed to ache a deep throbbing pulsation of hurt that made Bek feel as if he would never fully heal from this depth of physical abuse.

'OK, gentlemen – relax,' the instructor said unexpectedly.

Bek did not need telling twice and he slumped to the floor, a low groan escaping his lips despite his desperate desire not to display just how bad he felt.

'Ah! The new boy. What did you think of our warm up, Thrandorian?'

'Warm up?' Bek gulped, his voice unable to totally mask his disbelief at that apparently ridiculous description. 'Er... it was very... effective.'

The instructor looked at him with a grin that would not have been out of place on a large predator.

'Good. I'm glad that you think so. If you haven't heard yet, my name is Hammar. I am the Weapons Master here. My job is to train you – all of you – to be the best arena fighters in the world. So, now that you are all sufficiently warmed up, let's begin some real training.'

CHAPTER 4

The ship heaved and wallowed, tossing and rolling like a pregnant woman unable to sleep. Perdimonn silently cursed his fortune that, when he had reached the Shandese Port of Sevra, the only vessel bound for Kaldea was this barrel-like scow of a merchant ship that moved through the water as if it were treacle. Grinding his teeth in frustration, he was sorely tempted to try shapeshifting into a sea bird or a dolphin to pick up more speed. The problem was that each time he considered the difficult spell, his mind recoiled with the memory of his previous near disastrous attempts. Shapeshifting really would be a last resort, and he was not at the point of committing foolhardy spells, when it was not definite that the gamble would make any difference.

After speaking to the High Council of Magicians in Terilla, Perdimonn had learned that Selkor had been to Terilla ahead of him. There was no doubt now that Selkor had managed to get Darkweaver's amulet repaired and that he was wielding the dark magic of the talisman to his own ends.

Selkor had always desired power. Ever since Perdimonn had first met the Shandese Magician, he had seen that desire grow, until now it burnt like a raging fire that would stop at nothing to sate its appetite. The evil influence of Darkweaver's amulet would feed that deep-seated drive, forcing it to grow until it became all consuming. Selkor was sliding down the slippery slope to a living hell, but he almost certainly had no conscious awareness of the precarious nature of his situation.

Perdimonn gripped the polished wooden rail towards the prow of the ship and gazed out over the churning grey-green waters of the Eastern Sea. Somewhere out there laid Kaldea, the volcanic island where Arred had made his home. If Perdimonn's hunch was correct, and he was almost one hundred percent certain that it would be, Selkor would seek Arred next. What Perdimonn was not sure of was whether Selkor knew where to start searching. If Selkor did know, then Perdimonn was probably already too late. However, he was not about to give up on his quest before he had even begun. Selkor must not be allowed to gain control of any of the Keys to the Elemental Powers and Perdimonn was going to do everything in his power to stop that nightmare scenario from happening. Everything, that was, with the exception of using his own Key as a weapon – that he would not, no, *could not* do.

All of the Warders had been chosen for their pacifistic natures. The powers entrusted to them were never intended for conflict – they were just too powerful. To raise one of the Elements in conflict would risk devastation on a scale beyond anything the world had ever seen. Even the 'war of the gods' would pale into insignificance by comparison. That eventuality was one that Perdimonn would avoid at all costs.

If they were not to break their vows, the only option available to the Warders was that of retreat and secrecy. However, in order to retreat, the Warders first needed to be warned of the danger. That task was what drove Perdimonn now.

'If only I had been Warder of Air or Water,' Perdimonn thought to himself dully. 'I could have summoned a favourable wind or stirred a rapid current to drive this barge of a ship at a more dynamic pace. Instead I ward the Earth Element and find myself so far from its centre of power that I am as helpless as a babe in arms.'

The ship wallowed again, slapping down into a trough between waves and kicking a plume of spray outward from the bow. Another wave rose in front and the ship did not so much slice through it as bludgeon its way ahead. Whoever had named the ship 'Wavedancer' had clearly either had a warped sense of humour, or had known nothing whatsoever of sea faring vessels.

To be fair to the crew of Wavedancer, they had worked tirelessly since setting sail to make best speed to Kaldea. To Captain Ferdand, time lost was money wasted, so he drove his crew of rough, sea-hardened men as hard as he dared in order to shave whatever time he could from the journey. In truth the ship was making good time considering its design. Perdimonn just hoped and prayed that Selkor had not found himself a vessel more suited to the race that they ran.

'Rocks ten degrees to port!' called a voice from above.

Perdimonn could not restrain himself from looking up at the crow's nest high above him to where the man on lookout duty sat his watch. It was not an enviable job, particularly in the rough seas that they were currently sailing. However, as the Lookout had just proven – it was a vital task.

Trying to roll with the ship, Perdimonn staggered his way across to the port side of the bow and clung hard to the gunwale, as he scanned the heaving water for signs of the rocks. Sailor he might not be, but Perdimonn understood the dangers of reefs and shoals all too well. He had not come all this way to get himself shipwrecked within days of his journey's goal, so he disciplined his mind to concentrate on searching for spells that might prove useful.

The ship was far too big for him to try to translocate it to safety. Besides, if he had thought that possible, Perdimonn would have used the spell to speed up their journey by hopping them forward each day. Briefly he considered his time distortion spell, but without a team of oarsmen it would be pointless. True, the spell would halt the waves around the ship, leaving it free to manoeuvre at will around the rocks, but unfortunately the wind would also effectively die to nothing, leaving the ship with nothing to drive it around the lethal obstacle.

'There has to be something that I can do,' he thought, his mind racing through the possibilities.

'Helm, hard to starboard. Prepare to jib on my mark,' yelled the Captain, his voice anxious but holding no edge of panic. 'Navigator, what rocks be these? I thought we were due to be in deep water all day today.'

The pale, skinny looking man standing next to the Helmsman peered desperately at the chart that he held spread before him. His eyes were wild with shock and disbelief.

'As did I, Captain. There are no rocks marked in these waters on my charts, and I've sailed this sea for more than twenty years. I swear that I've never heard tell of them before.'

'More rocks twenty degrees to starboard,' the Lookout called from above.

'Hell and damnation!' swore Ferdand viciously. 'Range, man. Call the range.'

'Two hundred yards, now fifteen to starboard. Previous call now ten degrees to port, one hundred and fifty yards.'

'Anything between them?' the Captain yelled back and then held his breath as he awaited the response.

There was a pause that seemed to last forever before the Lookout responded.

'Nothing visible, Captain.'

'Helm, straighten her up. The old girl will never make that turn. Take her through the middle.'

'Aye, Captain.'

Perdimonn's heart began to pound as he sighted the jagged teeth of the rocks spitting spray into the air with every swell. His knuckles tightened and his jaw clenched as he assessed the line of the ship's trajectory between the visible rocks. Hard as he tried, he could not stop himself thinking about the possibility of hull-rending points of granite hiding just below the surface. As best he could tell, Perdimonn judged that the Helmsman was holding the ideal line to give maximum clearance on either side of the ship. However, who was to know what lay hidden beneath the path down which the wind was driving them.

'Holy Shand alive!' the Lookout cried in dismay. 'More rocks, Captain – loads of them. We're running straight at a reef!'

Captain Ferdand wasted no time cursing. Instead, he hurled a blistering series of orders, firing every crewmember into action.

'Drop sail to minimum rig. Helm, steady as she goes. Lookout, call the rocks, nearest first but discount the two already called.'

Crewmen swarmed up the rigging and within seconds the main canvas sails were being furled, and the ship was noticeably decelerating. The whizzing sound of ropes whistling through pulleys, the flapping of canvas and the creaking of the masts as the driving force was spilled from the sails were but incidental background to the rapid dialogue between Captain, Lookout and Helmsman over the following minutes.

When all sails were furled, barring one small canvas sheet atop the forward mast, the men hung silently in the rigging. All were watching and praying that the Captain could find a safe way through.

'Rocks dead ahead two hundred, suggest port turn. Further rocks to starboard at ten and twenty degrees, range two hundred and three hundred.'

'Helm, come twenty to port... now,' the Captain ordered, watching the first set of rocks slide down the port side and timing his turn as precisely as he could.

'Further rocks range three hundred, estimate ten degrees to port of new heading.'

Perdimonn felt helpless, yet determinedly he reviewed his repertoire of spells again. Even as he felt the scraping graunch of rock juddering down the port underbelly of the ship, an idea sprang to mind. It was not so much one idea but two, an ambitious combination spell that he would ordinarily have devoted hours of thought and study to, ordering the runes to maximise its effectiveness.

There was no time for any of that now. Even as the

Captain ordered men to go below to caulk any leaks and assess damage, Perdimonn began the casting. Runes flowed through the old Magician's vision in a torrent, as he visualised the effects that he sought to produce. Desperation drove him and the scrambling figures of the crewmen sliding and swinging down ropes to race below deck did not even register in Perdimonn's vision.

'More rocks to port, Captain. A line of 'em beyond the last call. Suggest five to starboard.'

'Helm, five to starboard... steady. Hold her there now... what in Shand's name? Are we beached?'

Ferdand ran to the port rail and looked down into the churning water below. There was no sign of shallow water, yet the ship was suddenly riding about a fathom higher through the chop. A quick glance around confirmed that nobody was ditching his cargo and even if they had been, they could not have raised the ship in the water that fast. He looked down again and noticed something else strange. The hull seemed to be glowing green beneath the water. Something unnatural was going on and he had absolutely no idea what it was.

A shiver ran down the Captain's spine, but he could not afford to dwell on the strange phenomenon. He had to concentrate on avoiding the rocks and staying alive. He had no idea at all why the ship was suddenly riding so high, but he vowed to himself that he would offer thanks to Shand for it later. The shallowing of the ship's draft by such a substantial margin might just give him the edge that he needed to sail her to safety.

'Come on, old girl. Hold together for me,' Ferdand muttered. 'We've got some sailing left in us yet.'

'More rocks to starboard, Captain. Range one fifty. We've got nowhere to go but straight ahead,' the Lookout called, the pitch of his voice rising involuntarily as the stress of the situation took its toll.

'Steady as she goes.'

Looking forward, Captain Ferdand could not help but notice the strange old man who had boarded at Sevra. Normally passengers were an unwelcome cargo on

Wavedancer, but this old fellow had offered ten gold Sen for passage to Kaldea. There was hardly a Captain on the Eastern Sea that would not put up with a little inconvenience for such a price; some would even consider it worthwhile if it meant committing an occasional murder. Ferdand was not of that ilk; though he had been only too glad to take the man's gold for what was a comparatively short voyage.

What caught Ferdand's eye was not that Perdimonn was standing towards the prow looking out at the rocks. It was the air of concentration and the hunched stance that the Captain would normally have associated with someone shouldering a heavy burden. If Ferdand had been looking at the old man for the first time, he might have mistaken the stance for the stoop of one who felt his long years. However, the old fellow had been on board for several days now, and his back had always been straight as a rod before. The thought flashed through Ferdand's mind connecting Perdimonn to the strange glow and the sudden lifting of the ship in the water. Just as quickly, common sense drove the ludicrous connection to the depths of his mental rubbish bin.

A sudden scraping judder warned of more sub-surface rocks threatening to grind the hull to splinters.

'Lookout! Report!'

'Nothing visible, Captain. We seem to be almost clear. Another fifty yards should do it.'

The waves rolling along from behind the ship drove the vessel forward relentlessly, the small pull from the remaining square of canvas almost negligible as the waves funnelling between the rocks accelerated the ship forward.

A particularly large wave lifted Wavedancer like a cork and, shunting her forward a few yards, dropped her full weight on the rocks that only seconds before had started their warning scraping sounds. The hull hit with a resounding crash and the whole ship heeled alarmingly on its shallow keel.

'All hands prepare to abandon ship,' Ferdand yelled,

grabbing a rail to prevent himself sliding across the deck.

Another wave lifted her forward and again the ship dropped with a booming impact onto the rocks. A third wave and the ship cleared the channel with a spine tingling grind of wood on rock. Wavedancer gradually, but noticeably, began to sink within seconds of finding deep water.

Ferdand ran to the nearest hatch and, dropping to his knees, stuck his head down and yelled as loudly as he could.

'All hands on deck. Prepare to abandon ship.'

Men poured back up out from every orifice of the ship, each coming to a confused halt as he reached the deck. It took a few moments, but eventually one crewman voiced the question on all of the men's lips.

'Why are we preparing to abandon, Captain?'

'Because we're sinking of course,' Ferdand snapped back as the ship settled lower again with the next wave.

'But Captain, we're not taking on any water. The hull is sound.'

Captain Ferdand was dumbfounded, but the men were all adamant, so after checking with the Lookout that all signs of danger were past, he went below himself to check. As incredible as it seemed, there was no sign of any major damage at all, yet he would have sworn that there had never been a ship constructed that could have withstood those last two impacts on the rocks.

Climbing back up on deck, Ferdand was greeted by lots of wicked-looking grins and several calls of 'Shall we all jump overboard yet, Captain?'

'I don't know about jump, but I might just throw one or two of you,' he growled with an answering grin.

They had no right to be afloat and yet Wavedancer was now sitting back at her normal laden draft and was easing her way along the rolling swell.

'Well, don't just stand there like a bunch of sun-struck layabouts! Get some sail on, or we will never make our fortunes.'

'Aye, Captain,' the crew responded as one, and

scrambled to comply.

The Navigator was already carefully aligning his sextant and making careful notations on his chart as the Captain climbed back up alongside the Helmsman. Much as Ferdand wanted to speak to the Navigator, he knew that now was not a good time. Instead he looked up and watched as Wavedancer's sails boomed into life once more and she slowly, but surely, began to accelerate away from the reef. Just as the last edges of adrenaline were draining from Ferdand's system, a call from the Lookout pumped them up again.

'Something in the water dead ahead, Captain. No more than fifty yards!'

It was then that Captain Ferdand noticed that the old man travelling as a passenger, although still at the bow and holding fast to the port grab-rail, was on his knees, his head sagging on his shoulders, 'Probably with relief,' the Captain thought to himself as his eyes scanned for this new danger.

If he had not seen what happened next with his own eyes, Ferdand would never have believed it. The balding old man looked up and forward, and with fist clenched raised his right hand slowly as high as he could reach. As he raised his hand the ship rose in the water, just as it had done earlier. At the same time a bright green glow of energy seemed to enshroud the prow with a heatless burning shield.

'Twenty yards... ten...'

It was too late to do anything but grab hold of the nearest rail and brace for the inevitable impact. Hanging on with all his strength and gritting his teeth against the expected crash, Captain Ferdand was as startled as everyone else when it did not come.

'Lookout! Report,' he ordered firmly.

'I... I don't understand it, Captain. It was there and then it was...'

At that moment there was a great roaring rush of air and a plume of watery vapour erupted just off the starboard side of the ship. A huge whale surfaced, and rolling slightly onto its side, eyed them briefly before sinking slowly back beneath the surface.

A ripple of nervous laughter ran through the rigging and across the decks as the whale disappeared silently back into the deep. However, the mirth was short lived, because with an almost audible snap, the green shield of energy shrouding the prow vanished and Wavedancer dropped the six feet or so that she had risen in the water. It was as if a great hand had started to lift the ship from the sea, and then let it slip from its grasp. A great spray kicked out from all sides of the ship as she settled, and everyone clung to rails and ropes like limpets, as they fought to keep their balance.

Captain Ferdand's eyes sought out the old passenger, only to see him collapsed and unmoving on the deck. With a muttered oath, Ferdand vaulted the rail in front of him and dropped lightly onto the foredeck. Seconds later, he reached the old man's side and was shocked to see the deep lines of exhaustion that clearly marked his face. Whatever it was that the old traveller had done, it had clearly taken its toll.

'You three,' Ferdand ordered sharply, indicating his choices with a decisive stabbing of his forefinger. 'Help me get this man to my cabin.'

'Captain?' one of the men asked in shocked surprise. No landlubber normally got to so much as see through the door of this Captain's cabin unless he sported a very impressive title, or flashed an inordinate amount of money around. True, it was rumoured that this man had paid well over the odds for his passage, but nothing in the league that would normally qualify him for such an honour.

'Don't ask questions. Just do it,' Ferdand ordered brusquely.

If, as Ferdand suspected, this old man had just protected his ship from disaster on the rocks, then the Captain intended to ensure that the traveller was justly rewarded for his actions. Carefully and gently, the sailors carried the old man across the deck and down to the Captain's cabin. There he was laid on the bunk and allowed to sleep as the ship and her crew concentrated once more on the mundane tasks that usually filled the time on a routine voyage.

* * * * *

High on the north side of the huge volcano that dominated the centre of the island realm of Kaldea, a weary-looking figure in a dark cloak stumbled into an opening in the rocky mountainside. It was more of a fissure in the rock than a cave – at least it was initially. The great cleft spoke volumes of the huge stresses that had once pulled and twisted at the very fabric of the mountain, as the earth had spewed its fiery, dusty vomit high into the air. Long years had passed since that violent eruption but still the evidence of the mountain's deadly history was plain for any with the eyes to see it.

The cloaked man picked his way carefully into the dark opening in the mountainside. A wrong step here could quite easily result in an abrupt death. Pausing before progressing into the true darkness of the cave hidden within the split in the rock, he raised a staff of plain wood in front of him. Silently his lips moved, as scarcely muttered syllables wrought their magic. The tip of the staff began to glow brightly and the darkness fled from it. After a quick glance around, the man moved on again, carefully but surely making his way past the mountain's outer defences and penetrating deep beneath its skin.

The cave twisted and turned, changing from narrow to wide, from a high roof to a place where he was forced onto his hands and knees by the low ceiling. There were places where the cave opened out into great caverns with huge spiralling stalactites and stalagmites twisting in impossible shapes towards one another. However, there was only ever one path forward – a single way that dragged the mountain's intruder deeper and deeper in towards its very heart.

Then... a sound: a simple clicking of a loose stone

disturbed from its resting place and the traveller spoke.

'Arred? Arred, is that you?'

There was a pause.

'Perdimonn? What in Tarmin's name are *you* doing here?'

'Well that's a fine greeting if ever I heard one!' Perdimonn replied, flicking his hood back to expose his bald pate. The old man's eyes glinted silver in the light of his brightly glowing staff and humour filled every line of his face. 'If you must have motive before greeting, then I've come to warn you that Selkor is probably not far away. He has already got Darkweaver's amulet, as well as some of the treasures that the Brotherhood has been guarding so jealously all these long years. Arred, Selkor is trying to lay his hands on the Keys – not just yours – all of them. He tried to take the Earth Key from me last year, but I evaded him. With the power that he now commands I doubt than any one of us could withstand him alone. Even together we would struggle without calling upon that which we guard.'

'That, of course, is out of the question,' Arred grunted harshly, stepping out from behind a corner and striding forward to meet Perdimonn. 'Though it is awfully tempting sometimes, isn't it?' he added with a grin.

Arred was quite a strange character to look at. His flaming red hair was seemingly at odds with his soft, slightly protuberant green eyes, and despite the fact that his youth was long since behind him Arred still appeared somewhat gawky. He was an awkward, gangling man, who had held on to the skinny, undeveloped look of an adolescent. There would certainly be no mistaking him in a crowd.

Maintaining his almost mischievous grin, Arred briefly embraced Perdimonn in an awkward hug. Then he laughed.

'Well you've passed on your warning, old friend. Have you seen Rikath and Morrel as well, or did you single me out because of Selkor's interest in fire spells?'

'You are the first for just that reason,' Perdimonn

replied. 'Besides, I have not a clue where Rikath is these days. I have not seen her in years and she was always a flighty young woman at the best of times.'

'Yes, well I suppose that is true enough, but she has always had a fascination with the Straits of Ahn. If I were looking for her, then that would probably be my first choice to start my search. The rip tides and whirlpools there seem to hold an eternal interest for some reason. Personally I hate water, whether it's raging in torrents or still as a millpond. Water is water: wet and, more often than not, cold. Horrible stuff.'

'The Straits of Ahn... of course! Now why didn't I think of that? It's obvious enough when you think about it,' muttered Perdimonn excitedly, his eyes distant. 'Thank you, Arred. You have probably just saved me a lot of unnecessary travelling.'

'You are welcome, old friend. Now shall we go have a drink, or did you plan to just run straight off again?'

'Oh, I think I have got time for a drink or two,' Perdimonn answered with a sly wink.

'Excellent! I think that you will be impressed with the latest brew. Come on. This way. It isn't far.'

Arred led the way onward into the mountain and before long the temperature began to rise sharply. The mild tang of sulphur in the air became progressively stronger as they went, and gradually an orange glow filled the tunnel with a light of natural origin. Perdimonn muttered a quick spell and the light of his staff died. The natural glow was more than sufficient to light the way and Perdimonn caught his breath as they rounded the next corner.

A wave of heat washed over him and his eyes watered at its intensity. The tunnel had opened into a chamber bright with a central burning fire. The fire, and apparently the majority of the heat, was contained within a column of magical energy, for the central section of the chamber bubbled and heaved with liquid magma. The temperature within the magical shield did not bear thinking about and Perdimonn realised instantly that should that shield fail, the two Magicians would fry to a crisp before they could blink.

'Interesting choice of accommodation,' Perdimonn coughed, unable to speak without gagging at the heat and sulphuric smell. Just opening his mouth caused his mouth and throat to dry up and he failed to see how anyone could choose to live in such an environment.

'It's not much, but I like to call it home,' Arred said with a knowing grin. 'Here, have a drink of this and make yourself comfortable.'

Arred tossed a wineskin to Perdimonn, which he caught deftly. Propping his staff against a nearby rock, Perdimonn unstopped the wineskin and took a healthy swig. Arred, who had been watching carefully for the old Magician's response, gave a hearty chuckle as Perdimonn's eyes bulged in shock. The old man doubled up in a fit of involuntary coughing and tears filled his eyes.

'What in Tarmin's name?' he wheezed, his voice cracked and barely audible.

'Fire water, what else?' Arred laughed, slapping his thigh in amusement and taking back the wineskin. With a casual nonchalance, the strange-looking Warder put the neck of the skin to his mouth and took a long draft, swallowing it as if it were ordinary water. 'Good, isn't it?' he said with a mischievous grin.

A distant rumble sounded deep beneath their feet and the molten rock at the centre of the chamber heaved in response. The smile vanished instantly from Arred's face to be replaced with a look of intense concentration. After a moment he looked at Perdimonn, his face serious.

'I am sorry, old friend, but I must ask you to leave after all. The old girl is brewing for another eruption and I need to divert the flows to calm her down.'

'Can I not help in any way? Surely together we could accomplish the task far more easily than if you work alone,' Perdimonn suggested. 'Earth and Fire together would make a potent combination. How are you diverting the flows?'

'By burning new outlets through the bedrock and feeding the magma out onto the ocean floor,' Arred said uneasily. 'That reduces the pressure here and prevents the mountain from blowing her top.'

'Why burn the passages? You show me where you want them and I will simply part the rock for you.'

Arred looked almost stunned in disbelief at Perdimonn's suggestion, as if he were suggesting something deeply heretical.

'Our vows, Perdimonn! What about our vows? No Warder shall ever gain knowledge of more than one Key, remember? How could we not gain such knowledge if we locked minds in such a venture?'

'I won't peek if you won't,' Perdimonn said, his blue eyes twinkling with the same sort of mischief that had been in Arred's eyes only moments before. 'Come on, Arred, we both know why we were picked as Warders. What harm could come of it? I am Warder of the Earth Key, why would I desire knowledge of the Key of Fire? Let's do what needs to be done, then I'll take another swig or two of that evil brew that you've concocted and I'll be on my way.'

Arred hesitated a little longer before another rumble, stronger this time, prompted a decision.

'Very well. Let's link,' he said suddenly. 'Give me your hands. It will make the link easier if we have physical contact.'

Arred held out his hands and, forming the rune for the Elemental Key of Fire in his mind, prepared to launch their combined spirits on a swift journey into the turbulent depths of the volcano. As his mind was open and fixed on his goal, he was not at all prepared for the shock that hit him as their hands and minds touched.

The Warder of Fire recoiled from that touch in horror as the man he had thought to be Perdimonn exhaled a self-satisfied 'Ahhh' of revelation and contentment.

'You! Selkor! But how?'

For a moment, Perdimonn shimmered and then it was not he, but Selkor standing before Arred. A varicoloured cloak hung about his shoulders, and the amulet of Darkweaver gleamed balefully from his chest like a single silver eye. The Shandese Magician wore a grin that threatened to split his face in two.

'Didn't you listen to a word I told you, Arred? I told you that I wasn't far away and that I was carrying items of power. Don't you recognise the cloak of the great shapeshifter Merridom? It really is quite effective, isn't it?'

'But the amulet! I should have felt the presence of the amulet,' stammered Arred. 'I even hugged you for Tarmin's sake!'

Selkor held out his right hand, knuckles forward.

'Recognise this at all?'

A ring, gold, with a single oblong-cut red stone mounted on it, glinted on Selkor's middle finger. Arred stared at it as if mesmerised and then slowly, comprehension dawned on his face.

'The Ring of Nadus! You shielded the amulet with the Ring of Nadus! What in Tarmin's name are you doing, Selkor? You are walking around with more power at your fingertips than any Magician for centuries. Why do you want to mess with the Keys?'

'What I do is my own affair, Arred. Now I am afraid that you have outlived your usefulness. I certainly do not want you, in a moment of weakness, to pass on the Key to anyone else. What's more, I don't want you wandering around with the power to use it either, so I am afraid that you must die.'

Selkor's eyes flashed silver, the smile gone, and an expression of self-righteous anger settled in its place. With a flick of his hand a bolt of blinding white energy flashed at Arred with a crack like lightning splitting the air but, incredibly, the Warder of Fire was faster. Even before Selkor began to twitch his hand, Arred had hurled himself into a flat dive straight at the magical barrier in the centre of the chamber. The lethal bolt of magical energy that Selkor had unleashed missed him by a hair's breadth and blasted rock from the wall of the far side of the chamber. Arred's body struck the barrier and to Selkor's eyes simply vaporised in a flash of flame and with it went the barrier itself.

The Ring of Nadus was all that saved Selkor in that instant, for it threw up its own self-protective barrier to shield its bearer from harm. Had it not done so, even the amulet would not have availed him. Liquid rock sprayed around the chamber as if a shaken bottle of champagne had just blown its cork, and the floor of the chamber shook as a rumbling tremor from deep within the mountain growled its eagerness to spew forth fiery death from the depths of the earth.

'How in Tarmin's name do the Warders do that?' Selkor swore in frustration, for he sensed that somehow Arred had not perished. Then, backing carefully out of the cave, he shouted into the boiling turmoil. 'You can't hide forever, Arred. We *will* meet again, you and I.'

Despite the frustration of Arred's escape, however, Selkor could not help but feel satisfaction. Arred was a pacifist, like all the other Warders, and therefore was not a serious threat to his plans. When all else was put aside, his ultimate goal of this encounter had been achieved. He now had the knowledge that he had so desperately desired. He knew the form of the master rune that was the Key of Fire. What was more, he knew where to search for Rikath, Warder of the Key of Water. All in all, it had been a most successful day.

CHAPTER 5

The sound of hoof beats brought Calvyn, Derra and Eloise to their feet. Each of them had automatically drawn their sword and they were all now standing, poised and alert, awaiting the approaching rider silently. A burning stick popped noisily in the little campfire that they had been sitting nursing. The noise seemed shockingly loud in the stillness of the evening, but nobody flinched.

'It's all right everyone. It's me, Fesha.'

The familiar voice floated into the campsite from the blackness of the night. Derra cursed herself mentally for allowing herself to fall into the hypnotic trap so subtly set by the dancing antics of the campfire flames. Her night vision had been totally ruined and she could not see Fesha at all, despite knowing his direction and that he was mounted. If he had been an adversary with a bow, all three of them would be as good as dead now. It was a sobering thought, particularly because they were poised to cross the border into Shandar.

The company of four had ridden hard from Mantor. The mile-eating gait of their horses had made quick work of the journey that had taken weeks of marching on foot only a short time before. Jokingly, they had bandied the idea between them of suggesting the formation of cavalry units to Baron Keevan upon their return to Thrandor. The supporting arguments that they developed as they rode were many and varied. The more outrageously obscure benefits of cavalry, more often than not suggested by Fesha, often had all four in gales of laughter as they rode.

Before crossing the border, Calvyn had insisted that they discard their Thrandorian clothes and don garments that would be less conspicuous. Fesha had proved to be a veritable mine of information on the fashions of Shandar and so Calvyn had sent him off to a Thrandorian market town to buy suitable clothes for the rest of their journey.

Derra and Eloise were under no illusions that they would be able to carry swords in Shandar, for they had made that mistake once before. It was decided that they were to pose as relatives of the men. Eloise had insisted that no one with even a modicum of common sense would believe that Fesha and she had shared even one parent, so Derra was to be Calvyn's older half-sister, and Eloise was to be the cousin of Fesha. Calvyn's hair and eye colour were different from Derra's, she being dark haired and brown-eyed, but Eloise insisted that people would be able to imagine enough similarities between them for the relationship to stand. Equally, as cousins, Eloise and Fesha were distant enough relatives that no likeness need be present to prove the relationship.

'Have you got what we need?' Calvyn asked the shadowy figure, as he rode forward and dismounted at the fireside.

Fesha grinned and patted full saddlebags.

'Everything and more,' he chuckled.

'Why do I get the feeling that I am not going to like this?' Eloise asked Derra in a pained voice.

'If he's wasted our money, I'll gut him here and now,' Derra warned in the dangerous tone that she used so well.

'Now, ladies, don't fret. I've purchased exactly what I was sent to get. The additions, albeit my own idea, I have no doubts will win your approval,' Fesha said confidently, and he immediately began unbuckling the bulging saddlebags. 'Here Eloise, these are for you,' he said, tossing some clothes to her. 'These are yours, Sergeant.

The other bag has gear for Calvyn and myself.'

'If this is another of your jokes, Fesha...' Derra growled, holding up a wickedly low cut bodice in front of her.

'Sergeant, you can blame me for many things, but I cannot be held responsible for current fashions in Shandar – even if I do heartily endorse their styles,' Fesha said, winking slyly at Calvyn and then ducking as the hard-flung boot whistled past his ear. 'Now, now! There's no need for that. Besides, you'll have to remember your place once we've crossed the border. Shandese ladies are demure and well spoken. They leave matters of a violent nature to their men folk.'

'Then it's time they had a cultural revolution,' Eloise said, waving the partner to the previously thrown boot as if it were a weapon.

'Enough!' Calvyn interrupted with a chuckle. 'Fesha, you've needled enough. Sergeant, Eloise, leave him alone. He's done what he was asked to do, now let's see what these extra purchases are that he's so proud of. Come on Fesha, out with it, what have you spent our money on?'

Fesha grinned enthusiastically at him and reached into the open saddlebag again. Then he paused.

'As you know, I consider myself to be something of an expert on throwing knives. I thought that as the ladies couldn't carry swords, they might like these instead.'

From the saddlebag he drew two straps of leather, each sheathing half a dozen small knives. He handed one to Derra and the other to Eloise, and was obviously pleased at the looks of approval that they gave him as they took them. Both of the women drew blades, trying them for weight and balance, and each seemed equally pleased with what they found.

'There is just one thing, Fesha...' Eloise said suddenly, pinning him with a hard gaze once more.

'Yes?'

'Where in Tarmin's name are we supposed to conceal these within this ridiculous garb?'

'I can show you if you like...' Fesha offered quickly, his

cheeky grin getting wider. Derra's eyes narrowed again and she looked as if she were about to test one of the knives when Fesha continued swiftly. 'If you just take a look inside the clothes I've given you, you'll see why I was late back this evening. I had each set altered to include hidden sheaths with appropriate padding to prevent any of them showing. Most of the sheaths allow quick and easy access, though there are a couple that might prove difficult to lay your hands on in a hurry.'

'Clever,' muttered Eloise, as she found some of the hiding places that had been carefully stitched into the fabric.

The clothes that Fesha had purchased for Calvyn and himself were not overly different from some of the styles of dress that Calvyn had observed in Mantor. Where they did differ was the piping around pockets, cuffs and collar, which was not something often seen in Thrandor. It made the clothes seem somehow more elaborate, although in truth the cut was as simple as that worn by any normal city dweller that Calvyn had seen.

Overall, the group were pleased with their disguises. Certainly none would take them at first glance to be Thrandorian whilst they were wearing these outfits. To be fair, Calvyn reflected later that evening, whilst looking across the campfire at Eloise and Derra who were now sporting their new clothes, it was unlikely that anyone would be looking at Fesha and he with these two around. Eloise, as always, looked devastatingly attractive. The big surprise, though, was Sergeant Derra.

Calvyn had never really considered Derra's appearance as a woman before. The Sergeant had such a fearsome presence, and was so much the soldier, that to see her in attire that accentuated her feminine curves was a complete revelation. Graceful and fit in combat was one thing, but her slim athletic build and unusual angular facial features made her a striking figure of a woman, particularly dressed as she was in a low cut bodice, short riding skirt and long, tight fitting leather boots. Calvyn would not be surprised if Derra drew nearly as much attention as Eloise.

Derra's hair was still very short, a style generally at odds with the Shandese fashion. However, Fesha had suggested that she could pretend to be in mourning for a recently deceased loved one. It was not unusual for a woman to shave her head as a sign of her anguish at such a time, so the stubble length hair that Derra preferred would not pose any great problem. With some reluctance, the Sergeant had agreed not to cut it again whilst they were in Shandar, just in case their mission took such a length of time that someone noticed that her hair was not growing back. To make her imaginary persona complete, Fesha had supplied her with a filmy black scarf, which he had advised her to wear visibly at all times, preferably tied tightly around her neck like a choker. This and the short hair should stave off any awkward questions.

Names were an issue as well. Generally, the Shandese people had slightly more convoluted names than Thrandorians. Eloise sounded acceptable enough, but Derra, Calvyn and Fesha were not typical. They had debated the pros and cons of adopting popular Shandese names, but in the end decided that the chance of a slip of the tongue was just too great. Fesha again had provided the solution.

'It's easy,' he had told them one afternoon as they were riding along a deserted stretch of country road. 'Just convolute the names we have a little. That way if one of us does slip and use our real names, it will just appear to be a natural contraction. Listen... I'll be Feshanoire, Sergeant Derra can be Derrania, and Calvyn can be Calveryne. These names are a little unusual, but not untypical of southern Shandar.'

Calvyn suspected more and more that this was not the first time that Fesha had posed as something other than his normal self. However, he did not quiz the wiry young Private, as he was not sure that he really wanted to know where the knowledge of such deception had come from. For now, Calvyn was just glad of his choice of Fesha as a member of his party.

The next day, the party gathered their belongings, packed the saddlebags and rode on over the unseen border into Shandar. It was about mid-morning when Calvyn heard the familiar voice calling, but to his surprise it was not calling him.

'Jenna? Jenna? Can you hear me, Jenna?'

The voice was faint but unmistakable.

'Perdimonn?' Calvyn exclaimed, bringing his horse to an abrupt halt.

'What is it, Calvyn? Is something wrong?' Derra asked, her eyes scanning the empty countryside for signs of whatever had caused Calvyn to stop so suddenly.

Calvyn held up a hand in the sign for silence. There was a short pause and then Calvyn heard Perdimonn's voice again, more clearly this time.

'Calvyn? Thank the Creator, the girl succeeded! Calvyn, listen to me – where are you?'

'I've just crossed the border into south eastern Shandar,' Calvyn said out loud. 'Where are you? I can't sense your presence nearby with sorcery, so how are you speaking to me? You are still alive aren't you? Selkor didn't...'

'No, he didn't kill me... although he came close. I formed a magical bond with you while we were together. It's an unusual spell and probably not in your grimoire yet, but to be honest I didn't foresee a need for you to know of it. Then, when the gorvath... well let's just say that I never thought that the link would survive.'

'So where are you, Perdimonn? And why were you calling Jenna?' Calvyn asked curiously. 'You sent her after the gorvath didn't you? Why her?'

There was another short pause and Calvyn seemed to hear a sigh, as if of resignation.

'I'm in Kaldea, Calvyn, and yes I did send Jenna after the gorvath. I had no choice. There was no one else. Listen to me for a moment, Calvyn. This sort of communication requires a great deal of magical energy, so I can't explain everything now. You must go to Terilla.

Find the Magicians' Academy and ask to speak to Akhdar. He's a member of the High Council. Tell him that Selkor has the Key of Fire.'

'But, Perdimonn! I'm on a mission to rescue friends in dire peril. I can't turn aside now.'

'You must, Calvyn. The High Council must know this news. They will need time to prepare, if indeed they have the resources to do so. Just tell them that Selkor has the Key of Fire and that Arred survived.'

Perdimonn's voice was fading now, and it was heavy as if laden with weariness.

'Arred? Who is Arred?'

'Just tell Akhdar, Calvyn. He will understand.'

Perdimonn's voice faded to nothing and Calvyn knew instinctively that the old Magician's presence in his mind had gone. His three companions were sitting watching him expectantly. Calvyn looked around at them and then swore explosively in frustration.

'What is it, Calvyn? Trouble?' Derra asked, as it became apparent that he had finished his strange communication. All three of his companions had seen him work magic before, although this one-sided conversation, as they perceived it, was most bizarre to watch. Calvyn swore again, which surprised them all, because his language was seldom fouled by such phrases as he was using now.

'I can't go with you,' he said finally, his shoulders slumping in defeat. 'Perdimonn has left me with no choice. I can't ignore his errand, because it involves Selkor. Apparently he has acquired something called the Key of Fire and I have been charged with getting this information to the High Council of Magicians in Terilla.'

'What is the Key of Fire?' asked Eloise, cocking her head slightly to one side inquisitively.

'I have absolutely no idea,' Calvyn replied with a sigh, 'but whatever it is, Perdimonn deems it important enough to make me drop everything and run to Terilla as fast as I can.'

'Why can't this Perdimonn person go himself?' asked

Fesha irritably. 'If he's so uptight about getting the information there, why doesn't he go? Or, for that matter, why doesn't he just put in a mental call to the High Council the same way as he just did to you?'

'He can't go because he's in Kaldea which, if I remember correctly, is an island several hundred miles out into the Great Eastern Sea. As for contacting the High Council directly, I don't know, Fesha, but I do trust Perdimonn implicitly and I'm not about to let him down. If this High Council has the power to stop Selkor from doing whatever it is that he's cooking up, then going will probably benefit everyone in the long run.

'But what about Bek and Jez?' asked Eloise anxiously. 'Surely you're not just going to abandon them?'

'No,' said Derra firmly, 'he is not going to abandon them.'

'Derra, I...' Calvyn began.

'He is not going to abandon them,' Derra repeated forcibly, interrupting Calvyn before he could say any more. 'Because he is going to send us to rescue them, while he goes and delivers his message. That's right, isn't it Calvyn?'

Calvyn held her gaze for a moment and then smiled thankfully.

'Absolutely, Derra, and as soon as I have delivered it I will race back to Shandrim, track you down and make sure that you haven't run into any difficulties.

Fesha laughed.

'By the time you've been to Terilla and returned all the way to Shandrim, we will have rescued Bek and Jez, gone back to Thrandor, and all been promoted!' he jibed light-heartedly.

'Don't count on the last part, *Private*,' Derra growled.

They all laughed.

'It's settled then. We will part ways, but we will not need to do so for some time yet. Our paths lie together for some days yet and we will have plenty of time to plan rescue strategies,' Calvyn said thoughtfully. 'Come, we need to pick up our pace, for this mission is becoming more important by the minute.'

With a gentle nudge of his spurs, Calvyn prompted Hakkaari into a steady canter and wheeled him slightly around to the west, a course that would cut the finest line to the eastern end of the Vortaff Mountains.

* * * * *

A rushing scurry of thudding little feet would normally have attracted an immediate response from Jenna.

'Did you get it, Jenna? What's the matter? Is something wrong?'

Alix came running through the brush of the forest, breathlessly excited at having disturbed more prey for Jenna to shoot. Skidding to a stop, her excitement turned to concern as she realised that Jenna had never even drawn her bow to shoot.

Alix had been so proud when Gedd had overruled Kerys' arguments against Alix going out hunting with Jenna.

'Alix is growing up, Kerys,' her father had said. His hazel-brown eyes had been solemn as he had interrupted Alix's mother. 'Let her go. It will do her good to stretch her independence a little. Jenna will look after her.'

Kerys had obviously wanted to argue, but Gedd's obvious trust in Jenna's ability to protect their daughter had won her around. It was not that she did not trust Jenna, but their guest had been the harbinger of dire trouble in the form of a very powerful demon. The demon was dead now, but not before injuring Gedd and killing a stranger that Jenna had named as an old friend of hers.

Gedd had recovered enough to be back up and about again. The bruising to his head, sustained during the fight with the gorvath had long since healed, but the dizzy spells that he complained of still came and went at random. Kerys was at a loss to explain these, and feared some internal head injury that her healing arts could not touch. Gedd's condition was a constant worry to her.

For her part, Jenna had been torn between two desires

after killing the demon. The desire in her heart to leave in search of Calvyn was very strong, but after burying Demarr near the old Wizard's tower, Jenna had been forced to all but carry Gedd home and her desire to help him and his family, and thereby repay their earlier kindness to her, had kept her from going. The blow that Gedd had been dealt by the demon had left him with lots of swelling on the right side of his face. His right eye had been completely closed and he had suffered severe concussion. He would never have made it home alone. Even with Jenna's help it had taken four days to cover the distance they had travelled in two on the way there.

Kerys and Alix had been worried sick by the time that they had returned. Men from the nearby settlement were gathering at the cottage when Jenna and Gedd had arrived. Apparently, after four days had gone by, Kerys had contacted two of the younger village hunters called Sam and Dreythus and told them where Gedd and Jenna had gone. Dreythus had tried to tell Kerys that Gedd would be fine, as he was the best hunter around and had hunted demons before. Kerys was no fool though and she had noticed the worried glance that Dreythus had shared with Sam when she had named the gorvath.

Eventually, after another two days had passed, Kerys had convinced Dreythus that a search party should go out armed to face the demon. It was this group that were gathered at the cottage when Jenna and Gedd arrived back, and the two were afforded a hero's welcome. With Gedd unable to hunt for the family, Jenna had felt obliged to take on this role until he was well again. It had seemed the least that she could do to repay Kerys for her tender healing of the vicious wounds that she had sustained from the same demon in an earlier encounter. Now, weeks later, Jenna was beginning to feel trapped by the commitment.

'Alix, be still,' Jenna ordered, raising her hand in a sign for silence.

It was most strange. A moment or two ago, Jenna could have sworn that she had heard a man's voice calling her name. It had sounded like Perdimonn's voice calling to her from a great distance. A chill ran down Jenna's spine as she suddenly realised that she could not be far from where the gorvath had fooled her by imitating a familiar voice. The demon had used Calvyn's voice and appearance to lure her out into the open before attacking. Slowly, she lifted the little silver arrow talisman from her chest and held it in front of her. If there had been a demon nearby, the arrow would have pointed at it. The arrow gently spun in a circle. The call had not been from a demon.

Alix looked around slowly and nervously. Jenna was normally chatty and fun to be with. This was not at all like the woman that Alix had come to know.

Jenna listened intently for several minutes and Alix listened with her. The woodland noises of birds, insects and small animals seemed unnaturally loud, as they strained their ears for anything unusual.

There was nothing.

Eventually, Jenna beckoned Alix to her and put a friendly arm around her shoulders. 'I'm sorry if I frightened you there at all,' she said gently. 'Maybe I'm just a little jumpy after recent events. Still, I think that it's time for us to head for home now anyway. We've got plenty of food for dinner and we'll need to give your mother at least some time to think about what she's going to do with our catch this evening. Come on, let's head back.'

Alix smiled up at Jenna.

'I wasn't frightened at all with you around,' she offered, trying to sound casual. 'You could hit the eye of a gnat at a hundred paces with that bow of yours, so what is there to be frightened of?'

Jenna laughed.

'Absolutely,' she chuckled. 'Though the shot might be moderately difficult if it was squinting!'

Alix skipped and laughed her way home and Jenna did her best to encourage that happy mood, but inside she knew that something was not right. The last time that

Perdimonn had called her, he had been in desperate circumstances. There had been a tinge of that desperation in his tone again today. It would be interesting to see what sleep brought her tonight, she decided, for sleep had brought his message most clearly before. Maybe an early night was in order.

Jenna told Kerys nothing about hearing Perdimonn's voice when they reached the cottage. Instead, she listened and smiled as Alix bubbled away enthusiastically to her mother and father about the hunting trip. The young girl's greatly exaggerated tales of Jenna's apparently miraculous shooting prowess brought a quirky smile to Gedd's lips. Jenna gave him a sly wink as he pretended to be astounded at Alix's descriptions of Jenna's abilities, and when the young girl had gone to bed he thanked Jenna for her patience with his daughter.

'Alix is a wonderful young woman, Gedd,' Jenna replied with genuine feeling. 'She is enjoying her last days of being a girl before the responsibilities of adulthood overtake her. I would not steal this time from her for anything.'

'You are a kind and patient woman, Jenna, but I sense that not everything went well out there today. Is there something that Kerys and I should know about? Did Alix misbehave in some way or get herself into trouble?'

'No! No, nothing like that. You're too perceptive for your own good sometimes, Gedd. Seriously, if it had been something about Alix, then I would have told you immediately. At the moment, though, I'm still not sure exactly what did happen in the woods today, so I would like to at least sleep on it before I tell you more. I don't mean to cause offence by keeping secrets from either of you. I promise that I'll tell you about it tomorrow.'

Kerys gave her a warm smile.

'Everyone is entitled to their secrets, Jenna. Tell us if you feel you should, but we will not press you if you don't want to share it.'

Jenna nodded her thanks for that and excused herself to her bed.

As is often the case when sleep is one's primary desire, it suddenly becomes impossible to achieve. Minutes marched slowly into hours and, despite trying to relax and allow her mind to rest, it was well past midnight before Jenna finally slipped into a fitful sleep.

The next morning Jenna felt awful. Her tired eyes burned as she cracked them open to filter the bright shaft of sunlight that had dived through the slight gap in the curtains. The small of her back felt stiff and her body ached with the sort of fatigue that Jenna would normally feel after having spent a full day's hunting. The worst thing though was that she had no memory of any dreams, and she had been so sure that Perdimonn would repeat his elusive call.

Maybe he could not call. Maybe he thought that she had got his message the first time. There again, she reflected doubtfully, maybe he had never called to her in the first place. It could have just been her imagination playing tricks on her... but no, the voice had definitely been calling. Jenna was certain enough to swear an oath on that. So why had the old Magician not followed up the call this time? The only conclusion that sprang into Jenna's mind was that he was in so much trouble that for some reason he could not call.

Jenna dressed slowly, mulling over her conclusion. Even when trapped inside a stone monolith at the top of a mountain, leagues from anywhere, Perdimonn had still been able to call Jenna repeatedly. He was a Magician of some talent, and with sufficient standing to think that he could gain an audience with the High Council of Magicians, whoever they were. These facts begged the question of what it was that could prevent him from contacting her if he so wished. Jenna shuddered at the thought of another quest as dangerous as the one that had led her here. However, just as she had not been able to ignore Perdimonn's repeated plea for her to come to his aid in the mountains, Jenna found that she could not ignore his call now.

With her mind made up, Jenna made her way through

to the small common room cum kitchen area of the cottage.

'Good morning, Jenna. Come and sit down. You'll be needing a good breakfast this morning to see you on your way,' Kerys said warmly, pointing to what had become Jenna's place at the table.

'I'm sorry, Kerys, what do you mean?' Jenna replied in surprise at the greeting.

'Well, you will be leaving us today, won't you? Both Gedd and I read it in your face last night. You need to move on. We understand. You have been very kind to stay as long as you have, but you will be wanting to go and find your friend – Calvyn, isn't it?'

'No... no that isn't... well, yes I suppose that I will have to leave, but...' Jenna spluttered uncertainly. 'It's not Calvyn that I have to find, though that would be nice. It's Perdimonn.'

'The old Magician?' Kerys asked, plainly surprised by this.

'Yes. I am sorry to have to leave you before Gedd is fully healed, but I think that Perdimonn needs my help in some way. It's strange, I know, for a Magician to need *me*... but, well, I'm sure that I heard his voice calling for me while Alix and I were out hunting yesterday and his tone sounded needy somehow.'

Kerys nodded thoughtfully as she spooned hot oatmeal cereal into a bowl and placed it on the table in front of Jenna.

'He called you before like this, didn't he?' Kerys asked.

Jenna nodded, carefully blowing her first spoonful of cereal before tentatively mouthing a little from the spoon. It was piping hot and laden with sweetening, just the way that she liked it.

'Then you must not ignore the call. Gedd is outside packing your carisak for you. We will all miss you, Alix in particular, but the Creator has his hand on you, Jenna. You have things to do. Important things. I have no idea what they might be, but I do know that we have no right to hold you back from the tasks that lie ahead.'

'But who will do the hunting for you?' Jenna asked. 'Gedd isn't really up to going out on his own yet.'

'Alix can go with him. As you have both pointed out, she's growing up fast and is no longer the little girl that we've been clinging to so hard. I'll give her directions on what to do if Gedd has a dizzy spell. Alix will cope just fine.'

Kerys was trying to sound supremely confident, but it was Jenna's turn to be perceptive as she detected a vague undertone of doubt in the kind woman's voice. Jenna placed her spoon down in her bowl and caught Kerys' arm as she bustled past.

'Alix *will* be just fine, Kerys,' Jenna stated firmly, catching the woman's gaze with her own and feeding encouragement and comfort through that look. 'Aside from which, Gedd is a superb hunter and won't need to travel far to find prey enough to keep you well fed. After a few days you'll be back into your old routine from before I inflicted myself upon you.'

'You never inflicted...'

'I was only joking, Kerys.'

Jenna got up and pulled Kerys into a hug.

'I owe you so much and I feel awful about leaving you now, but you are right – I cannot ignore Perdimonn's call. I have to go. Unfortunately, I have no idea of where I'm going.'

At that moment Gedd came through the door, Jenna's carisak slung over his shoulder. It looked very full.

'A huntress always knows where she's going,' he stated, his gaunt face twisted into the smile that always looked so out of place. 'It's instinctive. The prey is out there somewhere, and the true huntress uses her knowledge of the land and the prey to plan out her hunt.'

'I wasn't talking about hunting, Gedd.'

'Of course you were, Jenna. Life is one long hunt. So where is it that you don't know how to find?'

'Not where, but who,' Jenna said, feeling foolish even as she said it.

'You see? A hunt! What did I tell you? So what do you

know about this person who you hunt? Where was he last time you saw him? Where would you normally find him? Who does he associate with?' he asked, his eyes dancing with merriment.

'I last saw him at the foothills of the Vortaff Mountains and he was on his way to Terilla,' Jenna answered, realising immediately that Terilla would have to be her initial destination.

'Terilla is a fair distance from here,' Gedd said thoughtfully. 'Did he say how long he would be there?'

Jenna shook her head.

'No, he said that he was going to deliver a message, but he gave no indication of where he would go next,' she said, carefully sifting her memory for any other clues that Perdimonn might have let slip.

'Do you know who he was delivering the message to?' Gedd asked.

'Yes.'

'Then you know the first step of your hunt. You are a resourceful young woman, Jenna. You'll find the one that you seek. I'm sure of it. Come – finish your breakfast. It's getting cold at the table and you should always start a hunt with a good meal if you can.'

Jenna could not help but smile ruefully as she sat back down at the table. What Gedd had said all made perfect logical sense, but he did not know the full story. True, if she had just been going to Terilla armed with nothing but a name, Jenna would have been confident of finding that person. However, when faced with the prospect of tracking down a Council of Magicians, it was likely that if they did not want to be found, then Jenna could walk the streets of Terilla in vain for the rest of her life and never find anything.

'Still, it never pays to give up before you try,' she reasoned silently, as she finished her breakfast. 'Maybe it won't be so hard. After all, Perdimonn was a pretty distinctive sort of character. Someone must have seen him come or go.'

Alix came in just as Jenna finished her oatmeal. It took

the young girl only an instant to spot the very full carisak by the door and her eyes went wide with shock.

'You're not leaving, are you?' she asked anxiously. 'Please tell me that you're not leaving.'

Jenna looked at Alix, tears already welling in the girl's eyes, as she instinctively knew the answer before Jenna could give it.

'You can't go!' she wailed desperately. 'You haven't finished teaching me how to use a bow. You promised...'

'A promise that I fully intended to keep, Alix, but your father will finish what I have begun. He is the better hunter anyway. You will learn many skills from him that I could never teach you.'

'No! Please take me with you. I could help you as you travel. I'd be really useful and no trouble, I promise,' Alix begged pitifully.

'Alix, think for a moment and you will see that I cannot take you with me, if for no other reason than you are going to be needed here more than ever when I've gone. I know that you want to taste adventure and travel to strange, exciting places, but this is not your time. I am sure that when the time is right, your parents will let you go with their blessing. That time just isn't here yet. You are very young and very brave. You have time enough and spirit enough to find your own adventures one day. Trust me, Alix – this adventure is not for you.'

Alix ran across the room and threw her arms around Jenna, weeping loudly as she buried her head into Jenna's shoulder. Looking over the girl's head and meeting the thankful looks that Gedd and Kerys were giving her, Jenna acknowledged them with the slightest of nods. The last thing that she wanted now was a protracted farewell and so, gently disentangling herself from Alix's arms, Jenna swiftly gathered her few things from the guest room.

Digging through her various pouches she gathered half of the gold that she had left and clasped it tightly in her hand, then returned to the living area to say her last goodbye. Kerys and Gedd were standing either side of

Alix, each with an arm about her shoulders. Alix's face was tear stained, but she was doing her best to hold a watery smile.

Jenna smiled warmly at all three of them.

'I am afraid that I have nothing personal that I can afford to give you as a gift in appreciation of your kindness to me,' she said sadly. 'This seems so impersonal, but I want you to save it against hard times, so that when you most need a friend, you can remember me with some fondness.'

Kerys was stunned at the gold coins that Jenna thrust into her hand. Jenna had already given Kerys a larger stack of gold coins before going off with Gedd to hunt the demon. Protesting, Kerys began to say that it was too much and tried to hand it back, but Gedd gently stopped her.

'Peace, Kerys. The gift is a generous one, and well given. Do not dishonour the giver by turning it down,' he said, and then turned back with a grateful expression to Jenna. 'We also have a gift for you. I pray to the Creator that you never have need of it again, but in that respect the gift is similar to your own. Here, take this. I will hunt no more demons, so better to pass it on to someone who may yet have need of it.'

Gedd's gift was the knife that had killed the gorvath, its blade a single piece of Demon's Bane, sharp and deadly. It was Jenna's turn to be flabbergasted by the gift. However, after Gedd's little speech to Kerys, Jenna could hardly now protest this gift from them.

'Thank you, Gedd, thank you, Kerys and thank *you* Alix – you have all taught me many things that I will never forget. If I ever get the chance to come back this way, I'll be sure to come and visit.'

'May the Creator guide your path, Jenna. Hunt well.'

CHAPTER 6

'Ahem, your Imperial Majesty, there's a Commander Chorain from the Fourth Southern Legion outside insisting that he must speak to you about a matter of great urgency.'

'What? Oh, very well, send him in. He'll more than likely only make a nuisance of himself if I delay him. We might as well see what he wants,' the Emperor said irritably.

The Emperor had been studying his new piece of silverware. The large oval silver serving dish, engraved with a series of dragons and firedrakes, had arrived earlier in the day and he had only just found time to admire the workmanship when this latest interruption had spoiled the moment. Despite his position and the wealth available in his imperial coffers, the Emperor did not buy things lightly. He made it his business to see that he spent his money wisely on things of beauty and craftsmanship that would endure long beyond his reign. From what he had been able to tell from his first quick examination, this piece of silverware would become just such an heirloom.

The door to the Emperor's drawing room opened again, Commander Chorain was introduced, and the servant withdrew. Chorain dropped to one knee, his head bowed as he waited on the Emperor's pleasure.

'You may rise, Commander. Please tell me, what is such important news that you all but force your way in here during my rest time?'

'It's bad news, your Imperial Majesty, very bad news

from the south. The invasion force that you authorised to take Thrandor failed in their mission and was wiped out.'

'Wiped out!' the Emperor exclaimed in surprise. 'Surely you mean defeated? I find it hard to believe that there were enough men in the whole of Thrandor to so much as delay five complete Legions.'

Chorain shifted awkwardly. He was obviously uncomfortable with his task as the bearer of ill tidings and wishing that the responsibility had fallen to someone else.

'You are probably correct, if you are referring to Thrandorian men, your Majesty. Unfortunately, we were deceived and betrayed from within. The Sorcerer Lord that led the Legions was a traitor. He used his powers to fool us all into thinking that we were attacking Mantor when we were actually at Kortag. Thus we lost a large part of our force assaulting that city, which was held by the Terachite Nomads. Then, when all was in disarray after the successful taking of the walls, the Thrandorians hammered into our men from behind. We never stood a chance. It was slaughter.'

'Five complete *Legions*?' the Emperor stated more than asked, his voice low and full of shock. 'Surely some survived?'

'Oh, undoubtedly, your Majesty. A few will have recognised, as I did, the futility of the situation in the latter moments and managed somehow to escape. I was fortunate enough to capture a stray horse and so made my way back to Shandar relatively quickly. However, I doubt that many others will have been so fortunate.'

The Emperor fell silent, his fists clenched in impotent anger, as his mind tried to come to grips with the huge numbers of troops that he had lost. The ramifications of this defeat would be enormous. Politically, his potential successors would have enough ammunition to gain support for any plots they were hatching to remove him from power, to say nothing of the Emperor's standing and popularity amongst the people of Shandar. There would be few families in the whole of the south of the country that would not have lost family or friends in this debacle. How could he have been so foolish as to trust the assurances of a Sorcerer? Lord Vallaine would have a lot of explaining to do. He may be a Sorcerer, but Sorcerers and Magicians had crossed the Emperor before to their cost.

'How did it happen?' the Emperor asked finally. 'I want the full story, Commander. Spare no detail. This has to be dealt with properly, or there will be chaos amongst the populace.'

The Emperor sat back in his seat and composed himself to listen, as Chorain launched into a blow by blow account of the campaign in Thrandor. He told of the seemingly pointless raids into northern Thrandor that had continued for months, then the inexplicable ceasing of hostilities for a time, and finally moved on to the arrival of the two Sorcerer Lords, Shanier and Cillverne, and the march into Thrandor. Chorain had few details of why Shanier had killed Cillverne, or why he had sent two captured Thrandorians to fight in the arena here in Shandrim. However, he did speak at length about Shanier's apparent bloodless taking of Keevan Castle and the assault on what Chorain and his fellow commanders had every reason to believe was Mantor.

The description of the battle that Chorain gave the Emperor was graphic, and when he told of the revelation of Lord Shanier's duplicity, the Commander could feel the Emperor's anger building.

'I have seen the two Thrandorians he sent here to fight in the arena. One of them is good. He has the potential to be *very* good,' the Emperor muttered thoughtfully. 'I wonder why this Shanier fellow sent them here. It just doesn't seem to fit with the rest of his actions... unless he sent them here on some, as yet unfulfilled, mission. That doesn't fit either, though, for what could they hope to achieve? They are restrained within the arena. There is very little that they can do there other than get themselves killed. Maybe they knew of his allegiance and were seeking to use that knowledge against him somehow, but for what purpose? If they truly were working against him, why didn't he just have them killed? It is most puzzling.'

'Are the two that he sent still alive then, your Majesty?' Chorain asked, clearly surprised.

'Yes, they both live. One was injured during his first fight, but the other is being trained as a regular fighter. He will probably gain a ranking before the end of the season unless I am much mistaken.'

'Interesting,' Chorain said absently, his mind already racing away with the possibilities that these two Thrandorians might open up to him.

The Emperor stirred from his own musing at the Commander's tone. Chorain was hatching something and the Emperor was not about to let the Commander meddle without his knowledge or permission. He certainly did not want Chorain to harm the two Thrandorians in any way, as they might well prove to be an invaluable source of information. In particular, they might be able to shed some light on this character, Shanier, who appeared to be a Lord of the Inner Eye, and yet the Emperor had never heard of him before.

'Whoever Shanier is and whatever his allegiance, he is just too powerful a Sorcerer for his own good,' the Emperor decided silently. Somehow he would have to be disposed of. Vallaine had created this mess and if the Emperor had his way, Vallaine would not only take the full blame for it, but he would also sort it out satisfactorily, or pay the price with his life. However, in the event that Vallaine proved incapable of disposing of Shanier, then a backup plan would certainly not be a bad idea. Chorain could well provide a suitable medium with which to formulate that plan. It would take thought, but it would not prove impossible – nothing was impossible.

'What are you thinking, Commander? I trust that you are not considering any rash, unilateral revenge plans?' the Emperor suggested matter of factly.

'No! No, nothing like that your Majesty. I was merely

considering whether these two Thrandorian fighters might have reason to help Shandar rid the world of this traitorous Lord of the Inner Eye, if that is truly what he is.'

'Really? And how exactly did you plan to find out this information?'

'Well, your Majesty, I thought that I might just take the direct approach to begin with. With your permission I would like to go and question them. If that proves fruitless, then I propose to use more devious methods,' Chorain said, a sly smile crossing his lips.

The Emperor considered for a moment or two, and then agreed.

'With one proviso,' the Emperor said sternly. 'Neither of them is to be harmed without my permission. That restriction does not extend to the games of course. I want no fixing of the fights. If they are killed in the arena, then so be it.'

'You have my word, Your Majesty,' Chorain assured the Emperor solemnly. Then, with a deep bow, the Commander took his leave and withdrew quietly out through the door to the chamber, only to be immediately replaced by the Butler again.

'Is there anything that I can get you, Imperial Majesty?' the butler asked respectfully.

'Yes. Fetch Femke, would you?'

'Certainly, Imperial Majesty.'

The Butler withdrew and the Emperor scratched his chin thoughtfully. He did not trust Chorain as far as he could pick the Commander up and throw him. The Emperor had therefore decided to have Chorain followed, and if anyone could do the job discreetly, Femke could.

Chorain strode away from the Emperor's chamber oblivious to the Emperor's distrust and completely set on getting to the arena to see the two Thrandorian fighters. It would not be long now, maybe a week or two, before rumours of the defeat in Thrandor would start. If Chorain had any work to do in order to turn the two fighters firmly against Shanier, then he had better do it

quickly before the men heard news of the effectiveness of
Lord Shanier's clever manipulation of the Shandese
Legions.

Pleased to have such an immediate and positive course
of action available, the Commander marched straight into
the guard house at the front of the Imperial Palace and
used his rank to acquire a fresh horse. Without so much
as a backward glance he rode through the streets as
directly as he could to the huge arena in the south
quarter of the city.

The streets of Shandrim were wide, with paved roads in
the most central areas. Broad walkways for those on foot
were kept swept clean of litter, and the tall town houses
and mercantile stores were solidly constructed, with
sandstone frontages and slate roofs. Good quality roads
and walkways were also maintained around the great
arena, which was the largest of its kind in Shandar. As
such, Chorain's route avoided the poorer areas of the city
entirely, making the short ride a pleasant one.

As with all cities, Shandrim had its darker side, and
only the very brave or the very foolish rode into those
areas alone. The city militia patrolled the poorer sectors
of the city regularly, but even they took care to move
around in reasonably large sized groups. It was said that
there was an organisation that controlled crime in the
city, though no one in authority had ever succeeded in
proving its existence. Whenever such questions had been
asked, the individuals being questioned had either
vehemently denied any knowledge of a criminal
organisation, or they had clammed up and refused to say
anything – even under torture.

Chorain carefully avoided catching the eye of any of the
scantily clad women who roamed the streets around the
arena looking for custom. Several of them called out to
him, trying to attract his attention, but the Commander
was not going to be distracted from his goal. He kept his
eyes firmly on the road ahead and refused to allow
anything to divert him. The alluring calls often turned
abusive once it had become clear that he was not going to

stop. Chorain allowed himself a little smile at some of the names that he was called, but otherwise did not react to anything.

It did not take long to reach the towering arena. The building was easily the largest in Shandrim and would have dwarfed the Palace had it been situated nearby. Again, Chorain used his rank and status as a Legion Commander to gain immediate access, and he moved up the steps to the stands where he could sit and watch the fighters training in the oval arena below.

Down at floor level, Bek had noticed the Commander arrive and commented on the observer to Maasich. The Fighter, who was counting the chin-ups that Bek was performing on the high metal bar, glanced up at the stand.

'Probably trying to work out who to bet on at the next fight day,' Maasich commented dully, and continued counting, '...thirty-eight, thirty-nine, forty.'

Bek dropped to the ground and started counting for Maasich. He was rapidly becoming accustomed to the circuit training sessions that Hammar ran on a daily basis. The exercises concentrated largely on upper body strength and stamina. Aerobic fitness was covered in the 'warm up', and the pure fighting skills were taught once all of the other fitness elements had been covered. It was a gruelling routine, but there was no doubt that it produced results. Bek had already noticed that his arms were 'muscling up', and he could feel the extra power that this was allowing him to generate in his swordplay.

Hammar was an excellent instructor, and despite his advancing years he was still a formidable swordsman in his own right. Bek had discovered through talking to some of the other fighters that in his day, Hammar had been the top ranked fighter in Shandrim. He had retired from the arena whilst at the very peak of his popularity as a fighter and, despite numerous challenges from subsequent champions, had never returned for so much as an exhibition fight.

Bek had felt confident that he was a match for just

about anyone with a sword... until he had first sparred against Hammar. Within seconds he had found himself hard pressed and in under a minute he had suffered several light touches of Hammar's blade, without so much as getting close to gaining a touch of his own on the old Blademaster.

To Bek's surprise, however, there had been respect in Hammar's eyes as he had called a halt to the brief sparring bout, and modest praise on his lips.

'Not bad, my boy – not bad at all,' he had said with a strange hint of uncertainty in his voice. 'You're fast, but I sense something more. You were holding back on me there. You can do better than that, can't you? Why were you holding back?'

'I wasn't holding back as such,' Bek had replied honestly, 'but we were only sparring and if I'd taken openings that I did see, I would have risked maiming or even killing you if you hadn't reacted quickly enough.'

Hammar had smiled broadly at that.

'Indeed. Well, you will certainly prove a new flavour around here. Most of this motley bunch would love to land such a blow on me – even whilst sparring. You're quick, young Bek, but you are not invincible. Never forget that. There's always someone faster and stronger, with a more powerful will to survive than you have. Even Serrius acknowledges that. Indeed, for him it's become an obsession. He is convinced that his nemesis is closing in on him and so he presses himself ever harder to become the very best that he can be. He's the best swordsman that the arena has seen in many years, maybe ever, yet he's convinced of his vulnerability.'

From then onward, whenever Bek had seen Serrius working on his swordplay and exercising in the arena, Bek had been constantly on the lookout for signs of Serrius' paranoia. However, there had been little sign of it on the surface. Serrius was clinical in his fight preparation. He had faultless footwork and balance, combined with a grace and speed that was unmatched by any that Bek had ever seen before.

What had fascinated Bek the most about Serrius, though, was that he fought with a sword in both hands. Normally the top swordsman would fight with the longer blade in his right hand, but occasionally Bek had noticed him practise with the blades in opposite hands. The vast majority of fighters that Bek had ever met before fought either with a sword and shield, or with just a sword. The idea of fighting with a sword in both hands brought all sorts of possibilities to a fight that Bek had never considered before. He had often trained at fighting left-handed in case his right was ever injured, but to fight with both hands simultaneously was not something that he had ever considered before.

One thing was certain – Bek was in no hurry to meet Serrius in the arena.

The hairs on the back of Bek's neck prickled and he glanced up at where the high ranking soldier was looking down into the arena. The soldier was looking at him, Bek was sure of it. No matter what Maasich thought, Bek felt it unlikely that the man was here to seek out a profitable wager. It was most unnerving. The Arena Master appeared in the stands and spoke briefly with the soldier. Whatever it was that they spoke about, it appeared that they reached an agreement. The Arena Master nodded to the soldier and then left only a minute or so after greeting him. Bek could not shake the feeling that whatever they had been talking about somehow concerned him.

At the end of the training period Bek was proved correct, for the Arena Master appeared and asked for Bek to be taken to his office. The soldier disappeared from the stands and Bek did not need to guess where he had gone. A few minutes later, flanked by Maasich and Hammar, Bek was led into the Arena Master's office. The two escorts remained outside, whilst Bek went into the room where the Shandese officer was sitting at the desk waiting.

Chorain got straight to the point as soon as the door had closed behind Bek.

'I want Shanier. Dead or alive – it makes no difference.

Are you interested in helping?'

Bek could hardly believe his ears. This might be just the opportunity he needed to escape, but he was not about to leave without Jez.

'That depends,' Bek answered cagily. 'Firstly, what's in it for me? Secondly, what about my fellow Thrandorian? Where I go, he goes.'

'I am not here to negotiate deals, Thrandorian. I am here to recruit people who have a reason to see that Lord Shanier is removed from his present position of power. Are you interested or not?'

Bek thought fast. He needed more information, but he felt sure that this officer could be his ticket out of the arena.

'I am interested. My colleague and I have no love for Shanier. He sent us here to die. It would be fitting justice if we were to sentence him similarly.'

'I am not interested in your colleague. He is injured, is he not?' Chorain said icily.

Bek nodded.

'Then he would jeopardise the whole mission. It is *you* that I need. Are you interested?'

A flare of anger flashed through Bek as he took in Chorain's cold expression.

'If Jez cannot be a part of it, then no, my desire for revenge is not so strong that I would leave him behind. You will have to work your plan without me.'

Chorain did not even pause.

'Very well, I will not keep you from your cell, Thrandorian. If you decide to change your mind during the next week, then tell the Arena Master and I will arrange for us to talk again. If not, then you can be sure that you will never set foot out of this arena alive.'

With that, the Commander got up and strode around the desk to leave.

'Wait... Sir,' Bek said hurriedly.

'Yes? Changed your mind already?'

'No, Sir. It's just... whom should I ask to see?'

'Just ask to see the Commander,' Chorain answered

cryptically. 'The Arena Master will know who you mean.'

Commander Chorain opened the door and moved out into the corridor with a driving purpose punctuating every stride. Maasich and Hammar were caught off guard by the officer's rapid departure. Clearly, they had been expecting the interview to last a while longer. Both watched Chorain striding away for a moment and then moved to the door to meet Bek, who was emerging with a thoughtful expression on his face.

'That didn't take long,' Hammar said, his curiosity at what a Legion Commander could want with Bek getting the better of his tongue. 'What did he want?'

'He wanted me to kill someone for him,' Bek replied bluntly.

'And did you agree?' asked Maasich.

'No,' Bek replied flatly. 'I kill when I have to, but I am not an assassin.'

'Good,' said Hammar brusquely. 'I don't have a lot of time for the military at the best of times, but when they come to us to do their killing for them, it just reinforces my view that they are a waste of the taxpayer's money.'

Bek looked up at Hammar in surprise at the vehemence in his voice and noticed Maasich grinning from ear to ear.

'It's good to see that your views are mellowing in your old age, Hammar,' Maasich teased. 'There was a time when you would have said something really radical.'

Hammar made a sort of a grunting 'humpf' of irritation and then waved Bek on down the corridor, back towards the living quarters.

Maasich laughed.

Outside, Chorain mounted his borrowed horse and allowed a tight smile of satisfaction to creep across his lips. He had cast his lure; now all he had to do was make it the most attractive bait possible. The deal that he had struck with Garvin, the Arena Master, should make it irresistible, he decided. All he had to do now was to sit back and wait. The next games would zip the lure up to the perfect speed and force Bek to bite. Then it would be a simple case of reeling him in.

Even as Chorain rode sedately away from the arena, a shadow seemed to detach itself from the wall and follow him down the broad street. Chorain was far too preoccupied to notice.

* * * * *

Jenna had found it hard to believe that the militiamen and jurismen were still actively looking for her after all these weeks, yet her description was still being circulated in many of the villages. Apparently the local authorities still believed her to be responsible for the horrific killings committed by the demon that she had been tracking.

The first time that Jenna had entered a village, she had been forced to leave at a run. A little boy had been playing with a round cloth sack, stuffed hard with old material filling to form a ball, kicking and throwing it against a wall. As soon as the boy had seen her, he started shouting at the top of his voice and running away from her, clearly petrified.

'It's her! It's her! It's the bow lady!'

Jenna had not waited around to be caught. At full tilt, she had fled back out of the village the way she had come in. Then, circling in a wide arc, she had run around the village, being careful to use whatever available cover she could find to avoid being spotted again. From then on, Jenna had avoided contact with anyone for a week, and she had followed the edge of the Great Western Forest southward towards the mountains, using the trees to keep her out of plain sight.

Food had not been a problem during this time. Jenna's hunting skills had improved markedly whilst living with the Arissalt family. Gedd had taught her many tricks for recognising where to look for game, and her natural ability with the longbow that she carried had made the rest easy. So Jenna had lived comfortably as she travelled, never going hungry and never short of water to drink from the many small streams and rivers that crossed her path.

Eventually, as the mountains had started to loom like great towering thunderstorms against the skyline, Jenna had decided that she was far enough from all previous contact with the Shandese people for it to be safe to travel by road again. Tentatively she had entered a village that she had spotted a mile or so out from the edge of the forest. Sure enough, no one had batted so much as an eyelid at her presence, so she had stocked up with bread from the village baker and had purchased some local cheese. A woman had been selling apples in front of her cottage door and Jenna had bought a small bag from her for two copper sennuts. On chatting to the woman Jenna had discovered that Terilla was not much more than a day's travel away. Jenna had known that she must be getting close, because Perdimonn had described the city to her as sitting in the crook of the elbow formed between the Vortaff Mountains and the Great Western Forest. There were not many miles left to the foothills of the mountains, so finding the city was fast becoming inevitable.

Doubts sprang up in droves within Jenna's mind, like weeds in a fertile flowerbed. Would Perdimonn still be in Terilla? Would the Brotherhood of Magicians be easy to find, or would their location be a closely guarded secret? How big was Terilla? It was a city, Jenna knew that much, but how big did a town have to grow in Shandar to be called a city? Even if Perdimonn was still in the city it might turn out to be like looking for a pin in a hay barn. Had Perdimonn really called her, or had it been a figment of her imagination? Had she really just been looking for an excuse to move on? Maybe she should be trying to make her way home to Thrandor.

All was turmoil within her mind. Even if she did abandon Perdimonn and head back to Keevan's Castle, would she be welcome there? Would the Baron punish her for deserting his army, or reward her for her heroic efforts to restore Calvyn's soul? Had Calvyn ever even made it back to the Baron's army? They might know nothing of her journey, in which case it was unlikely that her story of magic and demons would be believed.

There were so many questions and seemingly no answers available without an element of risk in one place or another. Gritting her teeth with determination, Jenna decided that having come this far she might as well make some effort to find Perdimonn. No matter how Jenna tried to convince herself that the call she had heard in the forest that day had been a figment of her imagination, the conviction that the call had been real just would not go away. The very least that Jenna could do was to look around Terilla for him. If she could find no trace of him, then she would head back to Thrandor and try to find Calvyn.

Having finally made up her mind on this simple plan of action, Jenna felt much better. Unconsciously setting a renewed bounce in her step she marched on towards Terilla and some of the tension dropped from her shoulders.

The roads gradually became busier and busier with increasing proximity to Terilla. Great wagons carted iron and copper ore away from the city in long lines, whilst a wide variety of merchants carried their goods towards the city in the hope of favourable prices and hefty profit margins.

Despite there not having been a snowfall at all during Jenna's journey, there were patches of icy snow lingering on the roadsides and along the edges of fields now, bearing witness that the winter had been making some impact here, if only in fits and starts.

Looking up at the snowline on the mountains, it was considerably lower than when Perdimonn and she had crossed them some weeks before. Jenna would not even consider trying to cross the Vortaffs alone at this time of the year, so she decided that she might as well look long and hard for Perdimonn, or else face a very long and lonely road around the mountain range.

A merchant whose wagon proved to be full of woollen winter cloaks invited Jenna to catch a lift, which Jenna gratefully accepted. As with most travelling merchants, the man did not appear at all disturbed when he identified Jenna as Thrandorian by her accent. Cities, even provincial ones like Terilla, attracted all sorts of people. Tolerance to outsiders was always higher amongst such a large pool of people.

'Been on the road long?' the Merchant asked her, as she climbed up onto the driver's bench next to him.

'Long enough to be looking forward to a hot meal and a comfortable bed,' Jenna replied with a smile. 'Thanks for this. Walking is pleasant enough, but it palls a bit when you have to watch everyone else ride by in relative comfort.'

'Aye! I know what you mean,' agreed the Merchant. Judging by the paunch overhanging the belt on his trousers, Jenna doubted that he truly understood at all. 'So what brings you out to Terilla? It's not often that one meets a Thrandorian in these parts, and even less frequently a Thrandorian woman.'

Jenna decided that there was little to be gained from lies, so she told him the truth – at least, as much of it as she felt it necessary to give.

'I'm here looking for an old acquaintance,' she told him, as the team of horses started forward at a walk. 'He told me that he was heading for Terilla some weeks ago and I need to track him down.'

'Any idea where in Terilla he might be? Is he a merchant? Miner? Tradesman?'

'No, no, none of those,' Jenna said carefully, wondering just how merchants viewed the practice of magic in Shandar. There was only one way to find out. 'Magician. Perdimonn is a Magician. He was coming to Terilla to meet with some sort of a Magicians' Council. Would you by any chance know where I would find something like that?'

'A Magicians' Council, eh? You joking with me, girl? A Magicians' Council! Ha, ha, ha! That's a good one! Ah well, your affairs are your own I suppose and I was prying needlessly. I just wondered how far our paths would coincide, that was all. Never mind, though. Your company is welcome however long you decide to ride.'

Jenna was confused. Of all the responses that she had been expecting, complete disbelief had not been one of them. Her experience of the Shandese people thus far had led her to believe that here, magic was an accepted practice and that Magicians were respected for their abilities. This Merchant, however, seemed ready to either dismiss Magicians as myths, or ridicule them for their abilities – which it was, Jenna could not quite decide. Rather than risk her lift to the city, she just smiled as if she had deliberately made the joke that the Merchant had perceived and instead turned the conversation towards him and his errand to Terilla.

The Merchant, it seemed, was more than willing to talk about himself. Indeed it quickly became apparent to Jenna that this was his favourite subject. The man prattled away incessantly all the way to the city gates about his career as a merchant and how he had built his business from nothing over the past fifteen years. By the time they reached Terilla, Jenna reckoned that she could probably have calculated his total net worth from the detail of all the triumphantly recalled positive trades the man had boasted of. He had hinted at a few less rosy times and deals that had gone sour, but even allowing for exaggeration, the Merchant would be wealthy by most scales.

Thoroughly bored by the Merchant, Jenna was ready to jump down from the wagon and bid him farewell at the main gates to Terilla. When he offered to buy her lunch at a tavern, which he assured her served good food, Jenna was forced to change her mind. His company was dire, but his money would be useful, as she had precious little left of the gold that Perdimonn had given her. The majority of her money Jenna had given to Gedd and Kerys, and she did not regret that decision for one moment, though it might make survival here in a Shandese city a lot more difficult.

Reluctantly, Jenna remained with the Merchant, who then resumed his seemingly endless stories of his business acumen with even more gusto. As they passed into the city one of the first things that Jenna noticed was the huge number of street entertainers vying to win the approval of the passers-by.

Men and women everywhere seemed to be doing endless bizarre things to attract attention and money for their abilities. One woman, who was extinguishing flaming torch after flaming torch with her mouth, suddenly turned to one side and blew a great roaring flame of her own. A man just along from her was doing mind baffling tricks with a series of bits of coloured rope. Several young lads were literally running in and out of the crowds whilst juggling an incredible number of objects in the air. Balls, batons and pieces of fruit flew from hand to hand passing over, under and in between the passers-by as if nothing could make the pattern overly complex.

Jenna was transfixed and the Merchant noticed that her attention had finally wandered from his stories.

'Do you see your friend?' he asked her with a grin.

Suddenly, the Merchant's attitude towards Magicians became clear. He thought that Perdimonn was a street entertainer. No wonder he had thought she was joking when she had mentioned a Magicians' Council. If this was the 'acceptable' face of magic in the city, then the Council of Magicians and Perdimonn would probably prove difficult to find.

CHAPTER 7

Lava had still been pouring down the sides of the great central volcanic peak on the island of Kaldea when Captain Ferdand had reluctantly steered Wavedancer in towards the shore. If Perdimonn had not promised to protect the ship with his magic, Ferdand would never have agreed to go anywhere near the island. However, Perdimonn was persuasive and adamant that he wanted to go ashore despite the obvious dangers.

The port, and only major settlement on the island, had been virtually sliced in two by a river of molten rock that even now crept down into the sea like a huge, hissing orange and black serpent. Fires burned unchecked in its wake and where the lava slid into the water of the harbour, a small plume of steam was constantly rising. Every so often, the water where the lava flow hissed gently into the harbour erupted in an explosion of steam, though what triggered it, none could say.

Clouds of thick grey ash hung in the air above the island choking the sunlight into a perpetual half-light that was neither day nor night and, in the background, the mountain growled deep within its fiery throat. The constant rolling rumble that sounded like distant thunder was unnerving and held the attention of the superstitious sailors aboard Wavedancer much of the time.

The earth was angry, they muttered to each other. The gods of the underworld were fighting and spilling their wrath out through this mountain. They were to a man intent on putting as much distance between themselves and Kaldea as they could, and it had taken all of Ferdand's force of character to drive them into the coast in order to drop Perdimonn off.

Once the skiff had dropped Perdimonn at the northern edge of the harbour, as far from the lava flow as possible, the old Magician had not been surprised to see the crew hoisting every piece of canvas possible, the instant that the skiff had returned to the ship. He had not waited around to watch the ship leave, but had started straight away to work his way inland and up the mountainside towards the cave where he had last seen Arred many years before.

The cave entrance had not been penetrable. Perdimonn had been blocked from entering by a flow of molten lava that crept and rolled its way out from where his fellow Warder had once made his home. Perdimonn had been worried, but not distraught, for if anyone could survive in such a hostile environment, it would be the Warder of Fire. So, with little to lose by trying, Perdimonn had performed a spell of summoning. His intention had not been to drag Arred to him, so much as inform him by a sort of 'magical tug at his coat tails' that someone was waiting for him.

Whatever result Perdimonn had expected, it was not the one that he had achieved. For even as he had watched, a figure seemed to form in the lava flow at the entrance to Arred's old cave. The lava had seemingly coalesced into human form, beginning with a fiery blob, coarse in shape, with barely distinguishable arms and legs, then, with almost frightening speed, had rushed into the gangling form of Arred, who had stepped smartly from the flow of molten rock, anger flaring in his eyes.

'Perdimonn?' he had said, his voice unsure and his hands raised as if to strike.

'Who else?'

'Selkor. Who do you think?'

Perdimonn and Arred had spoken briefly and when Perdimonn discovered that Selkor had gained knowledge of the Key of Fire, he had then put out the mental call to Jenna that had resulted in his brief contact with Calvyn. Now, the two Warders sat on the side of the volcano surveying the destruction and contemplating what aid they could give to the people below.

'It is only the beginning, Perdimonn,' Arred said glumly, his elbows on his knees and his chin in his hands.

'We can stop the eruptions, Arred. It will take some effort, but between us we can prevent the mountain from blowing her top again for eons if we put our minds to it.'

'That's not what I meant. Selkor is after the rest of you as well. He means to become "The Chosen One." He means to wield all four Keys.'

'I know,' sighed Perdimonn. 'I must admit that when I saw the mountain erupting, I feared that Selkor had gained the Key of Fire... though I feared more that he had killed you on attaining it. That he didn't gives us some hope of defeating him.'

'Hope? What hope?' Arred asked in surprise. 'Perdimonn, he already has one Key that will give him a vast source of power and he is not bound by any vows. If he learns to channel that power through the Ring of Nadus, or Tarmin forbid, that monstrosity of an amulet, then there is no force in existence that could stop him from getting whatever he wants.'

Perdimonn nodded.

'I know,' he said calmly. 'Selkor certainly holds a strong hand right now, but I still think that he can be thwarted. I refuse to believe that there is nothing that can stop him. At least he doesn't know where Morrel and Rikath are yet. That should buy us a bit of time. If we can get to them first, maybe we will prevent him from gaining any more Keys.'

'Oh no!' Arred exclaimed, burying his face completely in his hands.

'What is it?'

'Perdimonn, I told Selkor where to look for Rikath. He is probably on his way there already.'

Perdimonn gritted his teeth and swore quietly under his

breath. Somehow, Selkor had managed to be consistently one step ahead of him and it was immensely irritating to Perdimonn that he remained powerless to redress the balance. He had to do something, but what? What could he possibly do to prevent Selkor from trapping Rikath and Morrel in the same way that he had trapped Arred? Somehow he had to get to them first, or at least contact and warn them to be on their guard.

'Arred?' Perdimonn asked slowly. 'Have you ever "linked" with Rikath or Morrel?'

'Linked? In what way?' Arred replied, his voice curious.

'A mental link. Mind to mind contact. Thought projection over distance,' Perdimonn explained, fumbling for the best description. 'I used the process only a few moments ago to talk to a young Magician in Shandar.'

'I didn't realise that it was possible over any distance. I have used a link when standing next to someone, normally with some form of physical contact to ensure the bond. I mean, I trust you that it can be done, because you wouldn't be asking if it couldn't. In fact, isn't that what Sorcerers do?'

'No, Arred, it isn't quite the same sort of thing, although the results are in some ways similar. A shame. I had hoped that maybe we might be able to contact them that way. Still...'

Perdimonn's voice trailed off as the glimmer of an idea began to form. Arred looked across at him, intrigued. The Warder of the Key of Fire knew Perdimonn well enough to perceive the beginnings of a plan formulating in the old man's head. The wheels were definitely turning in his mind, and if he had come to know Perdimonn at all in his time as one of the Warders, then the plan that he was devising was more than likely both clever and unorthodox. That was one of the things that Arred liked about Perdimonn most: the old man never held with convention.

'Maybe it could be done, Arred, but I will need your help in this,' Perdimonn said thoughtfully. 'I cannot guarantee anything, but it has a chance of success.'

'What do you have in mind, Perdimonn? I'll help if I can.'

'Well, normally, in order to link minds you need to have a close relationship to the person that you are trying to link with. However, I recently crossed a boundary that I'd never thought possible. I used my apprentice's close relationship to a companion as a bridge between our minds. By using his knowledge and intimacy with the girl, Jenna, I was able to contact her mentally despite having never met her physically in my life.'

'So?' Arred asked, puzzled. 'How does that help us?'

Perdimonn looked across at him slyly.

'You were intimate with Rikath at one time, weren't you?'

'That was a very long time ago Perdimonn! What's more, we weren't exactly compatible... fire and water don't mix too well at the best of times. It was a brief "acquaintance", nothing more.'

'But that acquaintance might just be enough – particularly if we attempt it together. I can teach you the spell and then we'll link our minds. Once we have achieved a link with each other, then we'll reach out to Rikath. Together, we might even have sufficient power and knowledge of Morrel to reach him as well, but let's not get ahead of ourselves. One step at a time. Come, let's go back down to the city and get something to eat and drink. We will start work on this a bit later. Selkor is not likely to reach The Straights cf Ahn for another week even by fast ship, so we have some time in hand.

Arred was obviously not convinced by Perdimonn's confidence in his past relationship with Rikath supplying what they needed to perform this mind-linking spell. However, he had no real frame of reference to judge by, and now that Perdimonn had mentioned food he suddenly felt a wave of hunger grip his stomach. There was certainly little to be gained by remaining here on the mountainside.

'A shame,' he muttered to himself, with a last backward glance at where lava still flowed from the entrance to his old cave dwelling.

'There are other caves, Arred.'

'That wasn't what I was referring to,' Arred said mournfully. 'My last brew of fire water was really quite good... and to think that I gave some to that slimy, good for nothing, Selkor!'

'You did?' Perdimonn laughed. 'I don't remember Selkor being very keen on strong liquor. If it was up to your usual gut-rot standards, I should think that his reaction would have been priceless!'

'Come to think of it, he was pretty bug-eyed after the mouthful he took,' chuckled Arred. 'I guess he just doesn't have our appreciation for the finer things in life.'

'Finer things?! If I didn't know better I might have suspected that spontaneous combustion of your stock of fire water was responsible for blowing the guts out of this mountain!'

The two Warders laughed together as they made their way down the mountainside and back towards the port city of Kaldea. Descending into the outskirts of the city had a rapidly sobering effect on their mood, for many people wandered the streets almost aimlessly – homeless and still in shock at the violent eruption of the volcano.

Fires were even more widespread than before, and although many people were working together to fight fires in the lower quarters of the city, the upper quarters had largely been abandoned to the flames. The logistics of getting water to the upper city were simply unworkable, but that did not make the anguish of watching one's house and belongings burn any easier to bear. Everywhere that Perdimonn and Arred went, they saw the pain and suffering caused by the fallout from the explosive eruption and the fiery destruction of the molten river of lava that continued to flow relentlessly down through the houses to the harbour below.

Children huddled in their mothers' arms, their tear stained faces smudged with ash and taut with fear, as knots of people gathered together to offer mutual support and comfort as best they could. A few were more organised. These moved through the streets offering first aid where it was needed, and gradually working to encourage those sitting around, rooted by shock, to get up and get on with life. For shocking and calamitous though the events of the last day or so had been, life did go on.

One group of women had set up an outdoor soup kitchen, with great cauldrons of hot steaming broth bubbling away to be offered to any who were hungry and in need. Arred led Perdimonn over to where the women were ladling the brew into mugs, bowls and anything else they could find to serve it in.

'We must help here before we do anything else,' Arred told Perdimonn determinedly. 'If we can calm the mountain and prevent her from causing any more damage, then we must do so – and quickly.'

'Agreed,' Perdimonn answered, sipping gratefully at the piping hot soup. 'How do you want to do it?'

Arred considered for a moment and then made his decision.

'There is a narrow tunnel from the central bowl of the mountain that runs westward out under the sea bed. I have used it for several years now to run off excess pressure from deep in the mountain's root. If you can widen the tunnel sufficiently, I'll shunt the flows in the right direction. We can sort the problems within the city afterwards, but the mountain could blow again any time, so let's tackle that first.'

'Very well. That should work well enough,' Perdimonn agreed. 'But we'll have to bend a few rules here, because to do as you suggest I must use my Key.'

'Me too,' Arred admitted.

'I won't look at yours if you don't look at mine,' Perdimonn said with a grin.

'Fair enough.'

The women standing nearby were looking at the two men as if they had lost their minds. Were they really talking about calming the anger of the volcano between the two of them? A bald headed old man and a strange looking gangly fellow with bright orange hair – an unlikely duo at any time. 'Maybe the eruption has driven them into a fantasy world, stripping them of their sense of reality,' the women muttered to each other. If so, it was yet another sad thread to the tale of woe that had been woven on Kaldea this day.

Perdimonn and Arred were oblivious to the undertones of muttered conversation between the women. Instead, they prepared themselves. Perdimonn finished off his soup and passed his mug back to one of the women at the cauldrons. Arred held on to his cup, as he had not yet finished its contents, and the two men walked out into the centre of the street, already muttering in the strange runic language of magic. The Warder of the Key of Fire placed his cup down on the road next to him and nodded his readiness to Perdimonn. As if anticipating the imminent intervention the earth shook, and the mountain gave a particularly loud and ominous rumble of defiance.

Somewhere close by a woman screamed in terror, but the two Magicians ignored her and remained focused on the task in hand. Raising his old wooden staff in front of him, his hands gripping it firmly like a sword, Perdimonn formed the master rune that was the Elemental Key of Earth Power in his mind.

Magical energy flooded into him, filling him until he felt fit to burst like an overfull wineskin. Feet spread at shoulder width, Perdimonn reached down into the earth with his mind, searching through the strata of the rock for the opening that Arred had spoken of. Sinking through layer upon layer of rock, Perdimonn's consciousness spread with the surfeit of magic released by the Elemental Rune of Power, widening like a great net sifting for its catch. Deeper and deeper, down into the earth's roots his mind sank until there, exactly as Arred had described, Perdimonn felt the channel that he was searching for.

Narrowing his focus, Perdimonn raced along the channel, following it from the very throat of the volcano out along its length to where it eventually opened onto the sea bed. The channel was already lava filled, but it was narrow and constricted in many places and at these points the flow reduced to no more than a trickle at best. Already the lava was cooling in the channel such that chunks of re-solidified rock were beginning to block the passage and restrict the flow even further. The task was clear and with the Earth's power still streaming into him, Perdimonn felt as though nothing was beyond his ability.

Forming new runes in his mind the old Magician created the spell that he required to widen the tunnel. At the same time he constrained the vast energy source that he had unlocked to produce only the effects that he desired. With an inarticulate cry Perdimonn drove the foot of his staff at the ground in front of him, stabbing down at the earth as if with a spear. The earth heaved beneath his feet as power blasted from him in a tightly controlled bolt of magical energy. Simultaneously, around the city people cried out in renewed fear as it seemed that the volcano was surely going to commence another major eruption.

A cracking sound of rock splitting was audible even to folks in the streets, but for Perdimonn it was deafening. He was there, riding the wave of power as it tore the earth asunder deep below the city. The channel widened and Arred, filled with the burning power of his own element, forced the boiling magma from the belly of the mountain to flood the new passageway with its burning pressure.

For a moment, Perdimonn thought that they had overdone it, and that the crack he had opened would just continue and literally split the earth open like an overripe melon. However, after an intense moment or two, the earth's quaking subsided and he felt the flow settle into the widened passageway, pumping like blood through a major artery.

Spinning another web of runes Perdimonn sealed off the flow of lava that was currently running down through the city, blocking it with a magical plug that would withstand more pressure than the mountain was ever likely to apply. Then, slowly, he withdrew.

The return of consciousness to his body was a painful one. He had unwittingly thrown much of his own energy into the coursing flow of power drawn from the earth and his body felt totally drained of strength. Releasing his hold on the huge power source that had surged and filled his senses to overflowing left a bittersweet desire to be filled again.

He sagged against his staff, feeling totally spent.

Arred, however, looked fresh and his eyes sparkled. Beaming at their success he put an arm around Perdimonn and assisted him over to a low wall where the old man sat down, shoulders slumped with exhaustion.

'Ah! What a feeling!' Arred breathed happily. 'That's what makes our task worthwhile, Perdimonn. That rush of god-like power makes all the long years of nothingness disappear into an inconsequential speck of inconvenience.'

Perdimonn said nothing, concentrating instead on getting his breath back. However, he strongly suspected that Arred had been making use of his Key more frequently than was strictly necessary, or, for that matter, advisable. Perdimonn took his vows as a Warder very seriously and he had carefully avoided the danger of addiction to the adrenaline rush of power that use of the Key brought. Arred, on the other hand, had always been the rebellious one of the four, stretching the boundaries of his vows whenever and wherever it suited him. Strictly speaking, each Warder was not supposed to allow the others any possibility of discovering knowledge of their Key. Knowledge of more than one Key was inherently dangerous, as the ability to draw on power from more than one elemental force had been decreed too dangerous for any one individual to control. By using their Keys whilst standing side by side, Perdimonn and Arred had both opened themselves to the possibility of the other discovering their Key. Whilst he had not attempted to gain the Earth Key in that moment of vulnerability and opportunity, Arred was nevertheless exhilarated by the

experience of using two Keys of Power in concert to avert
further disaster on Kaldea.

'Now, if we just put out a few of these fires around the
city the people here can concentrate on rebuilding their
lives,' Arred said eagerly.

Perdimonn said nothing initially. He felt bone tired and
the thought of using more magic was about as appealing
as a bar room brawl right now. However, the city was
still burning in many places and the tail end of the lava
flow was still creeping its way down the mountainside
and triggering more fires as it went.

'Very well,' he agreed eventually. 'How do you want to
do it?'

'Well I can control the flames, if you can dissipate the
heat sources to prevent the fires from restarting.'

Perdimonn nodded. The principle was sound. He could
not cut off the oxygen to the fire, as control of the Key of
Air was Morrel's domain. Besides which, removing the
oxygen might kill many of the people in the vicinity of the
fires. Also, he could not remove the fuel that the fire was
consuming without destroying the city in the process.
However, he could force the earth to redistribute the heat
of the fires over a wide area, thus removing the hot spots
and preventing the chance of re-combustion. If Arred
reduced the flames to nothing whilst he dissipated the
heat, the fires should die instantly and stay extinguished.
It was a good plan.

Gritting his teeth against the overwhelming fatigue that
he felt, Perdimonn forced himself to his feet and leaned
heavily on his staff. He had no choice. He would have to
use his Key again.

Arred started his spell, constantly muttering the runes
as he once again pictured the Key of Fire in his mind and
stretched his power, this time across the city. Like a
circular wave rippling outwards from a pebble thrown in
a still pond, so the fires died in an ever increasing circle
centred on Arred.

Perdimonn saw this and began formulating runes to
complete the effect. Eyes closed and runes flashing in a

rapid sequence through his mind, he pictured the whole city as a heat sink, a pit where all heat was sucked down into the depths of the earth like a giant plughole sucking water down a drain. Finally, he formulated the Earth Key and once again felt the unending well of power flooding him as he released his spell.

Initially, with Arred having killed all the flames in the city, Perdimonn's spell appeared to have no effect. However, the lava flow gradually slowed and within a minute had lost its orange glow, turning instead to a dark grey street of rock. A sudden chill seemed to sweep through the city, and where men and women had stripped off clothes and were sweating from their efforts to fight the fires, now they shivered and scrabbled around for extra clothing.

Lost in the flow of power, Perdimonn poured more and more magical energy into the spell.

The ground grew cold to the touch and within another minute frost iced everything with its glistening white mantle. Any water gathered in buckets to be hurled in vain at what had been raging infernos only moments before, froze and split the buckets as it rapidly expanded.

Arred ceased his spell casting and turned in amazement to where Perdimonn was locked in the thrall of his magic, still pouring more and more power into the spell.

'Stop!' he cried. 'Perdimonn, enough!'

But Perdimonn was beyond hearing and the ecstasy of the flow of the Earth Power pouring through him refused to let him free.

The soup that had only moments before been bubbling in the cauldrons across the street was now filmed with a layer of ice and still the temperature dropped. All across the city men and women cast away anything made of metal as it reached temperatures which threatened cold burns.

In desperation, Arred slapped Perdimonn hard across the face. Despite shielding himself, Arred was thrown back by the power flow that back-lashed through him in the instant of that blow. However, the contact was enough to snap Perdimonn out of his magical trance, and he opened his eyes slowly to a silent audience, all viewing him with awe and fear.

Arred got up and brushed himself down.

'Well, old friend,' he said casually, 'I think that should about do it.'

Perdimonn looked around him in surprise at the unseasonable ice and frost that seemed to meet his eyes wherever he looked. He had been so lost in his spell that he had no awareness of just how effective it had been.

Arred wandered across to where the soup cauldrons were frozen over. With what appeared to be a casual flick of his fingers, the fires under the cauldrons sprang back into life. The women leapt away from them, exclaiming aloud in surprise and fear. With a look of concentration Arred pointed at one of the large pots, which within a few seconds melted back to a liquid and began bubbling with heat once more.

'Could you possibly spare some more of your delicious broth?' he asked one of the ladies, smiling gently at her with encouragement. 'My friend has finished his and I'm afraid that I let mine go cold.'

* * * * *

Calvyn was tired as he entered Terilla, but also excited. Ever since Perdimonn had first mentioned the Magicians' Academy here, Calvyn had imagined what the Academy would be like. Perdimonn had never divulged any details, which had left his dreamtime to build it into a place of great majesty and magic. Consequently, Calvyn entered the city with a mixture of anticipation and trepidation, as he was not sure that he wanted to have his dreams dashed by a possibly less than salubrious reality.

Street artists thronged the area just inside the city gates, but Calvyn sensed no true magic. All of the entertainers were just that – entertainers. The fancy tricks and illusions used clever props and sleight of hand and some required great agility or strength, but ranging through the crowds with his Sorcerer-trained mind, Calvyn found no real Magicians. For a moment Calvyn wondered how he would have approached finding the secret Academy without his abilities as a Sorcerer. The question was pretty irrelevant though, because his powers gave him the perfect tool for searching the city.

Keeping Hakkaari moving forward at a steady walk, Calvyn allowed his mind to range through the city, sweeping through area after area in an attempt to sift through the babble of thoughts for anyone using the runic language of magic. For several minutes he kept up his mental search with no results until he discovered a strange anomaly, an area of the city where he could sense no thought at all. Initially, Calvyn swept past it on the assumption that the area was uninhabited, but then realised that it was the only area like it in that entire quarter of the city. It was almost as if his mind just slipped over the area like a puck sliding over an icy surface. There was nothing for his mind to gain a purchase on, so he just slipped on by. Intrigued, Calvyn tried it again, specifically feeling that area with his mind, only to skate straight over it and find himself surfing through the thoughts of an adjacent neighbourhood.

Someone or something was blocking his mind out from that area of the city, and that could mean only one thing... some form of magical power. It was certainly a good place to start looking, so he mentally traced a route through the city and steered Hakkaari on as direct a course as he could towards his chosen area.

Looking around as he rode, Calvyn found Terilla fascinating. The only other cities that he had been in before were Mantor and Kortag, both of which had been very different indeed. This city seemed almost like a large village in the sense that everyone appeared neighbourly to one another. The whole atmosphere of Terilla was friendlier than the impersonal feel of Mantor. Kortag had been all but in ruins when Calvyn had been there, so no comparison was possible there, but from his mental sweep of the city, Calvyn had learned enough to like what he had 'heard'.

People took time to laugh and joke together in the streets and there was much community spirit within the different quarters of the city. Whether this was because it was a provincial city, or whether the Shandese people took life a little less seriously than the Thrandorians, Calvyn could not say. However, his discovery dispelled any last prejudicial thinking that the Shandese people were 'the enemy'. Most of the people here were ignorant of there having been any conflict between the Shandese Empire and its neighbouring kingdom. Aside from the general wariness of strangers from foreign lands, Calvyn realised that he had little to fear from the general populace here.

Looking up the street at the front of a tavern not far ahead, with his mind only half on his immediate surroundings, it took a few seconds to register that the figure disappearing in through the door was hauntingly familiar. All in a rush it dawned on him who it was that he had just been looking at.

'Jenna? Jenna!' he yelled, spurring his horse forward into a fast run.

A scant few seconds later, Calvyn leapt from Hakkaari's back. Looping the reins loosely over the stile outside the tavern, he burst through the door. The public taproom was busy, but not overly so. Calvyn's abrupt entrance caused all conversation to stop, and everyone turned to see who had all but thrown himself through the door.

'Jenna?' he called loudly, his eyes searching the room, darting from face to face with an almost bird-like intensity and speed. At the same time, his mind scanned the room for his friend with a similar rapid bouncing from one to the next. Both searches drew blanks. Then, as one of the women at the bar turned away from him to continue ordering, Calvyn saw his mistake. From behind, the woman looked so like Jenna it was painful. Calvyn muttered an apology and rapidly backed out of the door to the sound of a smattering of laughter from within. Embarrassment flared his cheeks. With a single bound he remounted Hakkaari, and cursing himself for allowing his imagination to get the better of him, Calvyn gently encouraged his great horse onwards up the road and away from the tavern.

What on earth had possessed him to believe that the girl was Jenna? The chances of Jenna being here in Terilla were so ridiculously slim as to be almost non-existent. Even if Jenna had been in Shandar, then she would probably be well on her way back to Thrandor by now, not stuck here in a city about as far from the nearest logical border crossing-point as possible. There were some people who considered braving the depths of the Great Western Forest an option, but most sane people dismissed that option out of hand. The Forest was not a place to be approached lightly, any more than the Vortaff Mountains were a sensible picnic spot in wintertime.

Berating himself soundly for his stupidity, Calvyn resolved to focus on the job at hand and find the Magicians' Academy just as fast as he could. Derra was resourceful, and with the talents of Eloise and Fesha to draw on, he felt sure that if anyone could rescue Bek and Jez, it would be the battle-hardened Sergeant. Despite his trust in Derra, though, Calvyn was desperately aware that without his powers of sorcery and magic to aid the little rescue party, their chances of success had been drastically reduced. The quicker that he could complete his task here in Terilla and race back to Shandrim, the more chance he had of aiding Derra and the others to rescue his friends.

Hakkaari had truly been well named, Calvyn reflected, patting the horse affectionately on the neck. The horse really did run like the wind when called upon to provide speed. Calvyn would never have believed it possible to cover so vast a distance in such a short time, but Hakkaari had raced along tirelessly day after day. Now Calvyn felt that if he could just find the Academy quickly and deliver his message, Hakkaari might just speed him back to Shandrim in time to be of help.

If there could be such a place as a backwater section of a backwater city, then that was where Calvyn found himself a short while later. The area within which his powers of sorcery could not penetrate appeared to centre on a large building, square fronted with a single wooden door. The frontage of the building did not seem out of place amongst the buildings around it, but there were hints for those who had the eyes to see that it outdated its surroundings by a considerable period.

Calvyn halted Hakkaari in front of the steps that led up to the single door. Dismounting, he patted the horse affectionately on the neck again and ordered it kindly, but firmly, to stay still while he went up to knock on the door.

The traditions of Magicians, and in particular the Academy at Terilla, had been something that Calvyn had questioned Perdimonn about on several occasions. For the most part, Perdimonn had not revealed much, maintaining that as he had never trained at the Academy, he could hardly convey anything of their customs and traditions. However, the one thing that Perdimonn had taught him was the ritual greeting, so if nothing else, Calvyn at least felt as if he knew how to say hello properly. When the door opened at his knock, though, for a moment it seemed as if even that small gem of knowledge might escape him. If there was such a thing as a giant, then surely the man who opened the door to Calvyn's knock qualified for the title. For a moment Calvyn was speechless, simply staring up in awe at the size of the doorkeeper.

'Yes?' the man's deep bass rumbling voice enquired, as he looked down at Calvyn with scarcely disguised amusement.

'I... I... I come in p...peace to see and s...serve my brothers,' Calvyn stammered.

'As a servant, so we all begin,' the man responded formally. 'Should I know you? I do not recall your face.'

'I am here to deliver a message to someone called Akhdar.'

'Really? And what might that message be?'

'Are you Akhdar, Sir?' Calvyn asked tentatively.

'No, but I am sure that he would not mind my carrying a message to him for you.'

'I'm sorry, Sir, but Perdimonn said that I was to give the message to Akhdar.'

'Perdimonn, I see.   Then you must be Calvyn, I presume?'

'That's right, but how...?'

'I think that you had better come in, young man. That way I can take you to see *Grand Magician* Akhdar right away.'

CHAPTER 8

If ever a man was born to look the part of a Grand
Magician it was Akhdar. His long hair, beard and long
moustache were all snowy white with age. Bright,
piercing blue eyes looked out from under his bushy white
eyebrows and his long, slim fingers looked to have
retained their dexterity despite the Magician's obvious
advancing years. An artist, given a free hand to draw his
impression of how a Magician should appear, might well
unwittingly draw such a face without ever having met
Akhdar.

Calvyn was certainly more than a little overawed by his
first meeting with a Magician who quite obviously held a
position of authority here at the Academy. The giant of a
doorman, who had introduced himself to Calvyn as
Lomand, had been awe inspiring in one manner. Akhdar,
on the other hand, oozed power and magic as if he were
made of it, thus inspiring a level of respect beyond even
that which Calvyn had instinctively given to the King of
Thrandor. It was respect for the authority Akhdar held in
a world that Calvyn had desperately wanted to become
involved in for several years.

'Brother Akhdar, this is Brother Calvyn. He bears a
message from Brother Perdimonn,' Lomand announced,
having been granted entrance to Akhdar's study.

'*Brother* Calvyn, is it?' Akhdar asked, one bushy
eyebrow rising quizzically and his bright eyes seeming to
see straight into Calvyn's soul.

'Well... Sir... um, well I don't really know whether I am a

"Brother" as such,' Calvyn spluttered, his cheeks turning bright red at Lomand's introduction.

'Brother Perdimonn asked me during his last visit with us whether he could sponsor a bright young apprentice of his into the Academy,' Lomand interrupted, his deep voice rich with rolled 'r's and booming vowel sounds. The apprentice he mentioned was this young man. I believe that Brother Perdimonn's recommendation should accord young Calvyn here enough status to be named a "Brother".'

Akhdar smiled and his bright blue eyes twinkled with mirth at Calvyn's obvious discomfort.

'Truly,' the Grand Magician said benevolently. 'Though if he is to become a "Brother" in the total sense of the word, then he will have to work long and hard to earn that accolade. Now, what brings you to my study? Even new Acolytes sponsored by such worthies as Brother Perdimonn are not introduced to the Masters without reason.'

'I bring a message, Sir,' Calvyn said quickly, 'though I fear that it is not good news.'

'Indeed? Then out with it, young Brother. What news from Perdimonn?'

'Well, Sir, Perdimonn said to tell you that Selkor has the Key of Fire...'

'What! Are you sure?' Akhdar gasped.

'Positive, Sir. He said it twice, but he also said to tell you that Arred survived.'

'Well that's something, I suppose,' Akhdar muttered, pacing up and down, twining hair from his beard around the forefinger of his right hand and unravelling it again as he walked.

'Did he say anything else? Did he mention Rikath or Morrell?'

'No, Sir.'

'You are sure?'

'Yes, Sir, absolutely sure. Perdimonn impressed on me the urgency of this message, such that I had to abandon an important quest of my own to deliver it. He said something about giving the High Council time to prepare.'

'"Said something about?" That's not very specific. What were his exact words, lad? Think now. It's very important.'

Calvyn closed his eyes tightly and ran through what he could remember of his mental conversation with Perdimonn.

'Yes, Sir, I have it,' he said. '"The High Council must know this news. They will need time to prepare, if indeed they have the resources to do so. Tell them that Selkor has the Key of Fire and that Arred survived." That's it, Sir, as exactly as I can recall the words.'

Akhdar had paused briefly to listen to Calvyn's specific phrasing, but now he paced up and down once more. The Grand Magician's face was grave and he was obviously lost deep in thought. Calvyn watched him for a moment or two, but now that the Grand Magician was no longer focusing his interest in Calvyn's direction, the young man found that many fascinating things drew his attention away from Akhdar and his pacing.

The chamber was cluttered with no end of books, scrolls, maps and odd-looking pieces of apparatus that had no discernable function. Every nook and cranny of the room was filled with oddments and Calvyn found himself wondering if everything in the room was magical in one way or another. It would certainly be most appropriate, Calvyn decided, for such a magical looking Magician to have a study crammed with items of power for all conceivable circumstances.

Yet now it appeared that a circumstance had arisen for which Grand Magician Akhdar had no plan or magical remedy. His face was grave as he paced and he showed no sign of awareness that Lomand and Calvyn were still in the room. After a few minutes Lomand gave a loud cough in his throat that caught Akhdar's attention.

'What? Oh, yes! Lomand, take Calvyn and settle him into the Acolytes' quarters, would you? Also, you had better summon the rest of the Council. They need to hear these tidings. There can be no hiding from this any longer. We will have to do something about Selkor now.'

'Very well, Brother Akhdar, I will see to it at once,' Lomand said, giving a bow. With one shovel-sized hand placed on Calvyn's shoulder, the doorkeeper steered him out of Akhdar's study and back into the corridor. Once the door to Akhdar's chamber was shut, Lomand turned as if to lead Calvyn deeper into the building rather than back to the entrance.

Calvyn hesitated, unsure what to do.

'What is it, young Calvyn? Is something wrong? You heard Grand Magician Akhdar. You have been accepted as an Acolyte. From what Perdimonn told me of you there is every chance that you could gain your robes as a Magician within a very few years.

'Years!' Calvyn exclaimed. 'I can't... I mean... that's a very long time and I have duties that I have to attend to.'

'Don't you want to become a Magician, Calvyn? I thought that I could feel your desire from the moment I met you.'

'Well, yes, I do want to become a Magician. It's been an ambition ever since I learned that magic was real, but I have friends trapped in the arena in Shandrim because of me. I must attempt to rescue them.'

'Must? Why?'

'Well, I was responsible for getting them sent there in the first place; it is my responsibility to free them. Besides, that was the basis on which the King of Thrandor gave me leave to abandon his court at a time when he craved my counsel.'

'The King of Thrandor craved *your* counsel? Are you not a little young to be offering advice to kings, Calvyn? Normally kings take care in choosing elders who have years of experience and a history of sound leadership and wisdom to bring them counsel. Meaning no disrespect, but you are barely out of childhood. Why would this King bring his problems to you?'

'The King made me his Counsel in all matters magical because none of his elders had any knowledge or experience of such things. Whilst I protested that I knew little of magic and the arcane arts, the King decided that what I did know was more than anyone else at his disposal. Therefore, despite my protestations I was given a Knighthood and made one of his personal counsellors.'

Lomand laughed, his great barrel chest convulsing as his deep booming voice reverberated his mirth along the corridor.

'Well indeed,' Lomand said at last. 'So you will be a celebrity Acolyte! A king's counsellor and a Knight, that is certainly a first.'

'But my friends...'

'Was no one else seeking to free them?' Lomand asked, his eyes searching deeply as he turned to study Calvyn's face.

'Well... yes, but...'

'Then let them do the rescuing,' the big man advised. 'Let them go. Don't miss the opportunity that you have here, for it's highly unlikely to be presented to you a second time. The Masters take a dim view of anyone not putting the Academy first. Magic must be foremost in your priorities if you are to become a Magician. Come. Study magic with the greatest teachers in the world today and you'll be able to go back to your King with the knowledge that you require to fill his post properly.'

Calvyn was terribly torn. It was a tremendous opportunity and if anyone could engineer to rescue Bek and Jez, it was Derra. He just felt immensely guilty that firstly he had sent his two friends to the arena, then he had been sidetracked here from his original plan to rescue them, and now he was seriously considering abandoning the rescue team entirely.

'Come,' Lomand said again, and started to move down the corridor into the depths of the Academy building.

Reluctantly, Calvyn followed Lomand, his mind playing over his options. If he stayed, he would most likely gain the knowledge of a true Magician, but he would not be able to help his friends. If he left, he might never get the chance to study here again. It was a terrible decision to have to make and he was not at all sure that he would be comfortable with his choice whatever he decided.

Lomand looked back and noted Calvyn's tortured expression.

'Don't worry,' he said kindly, 'I won't lock you in. You might as well stay the night before you make your choice. Sleep may well bring you resolution one way or the other.'

Lomand led Calvyn down a series of corridors. It was strange, because the building seemed somehow larger inside than it had appeared from the street. Calvyn could have sworn that the corridor he was in now was longer than the whole building had appeared from the outside. The décor along the passageways was spartan, with a thin central walkway of carpet down each corridor, most of which had seen better days. Pictures dotted the walls at irregular intervals with no consistency of size, layout, or for that matter, composition. Some were portraits of Magicians, most of who looked venerable rather than powerful. Others were pictures of objects that Calvyn could only assume had some relevance to the Academy, though how a pair of battered old shoes, or a quill and an old chipped ink bottle were of significance, Calvyn could not begin to guess. All in all, the entire place was nothing like he had imagined it to be.

The giant doorkeeper stopped outside a plain door. There had been many doors in each of the corridors, all of them seemingly identical. Navigating around this place must be a nightmare, Calvyn decided silently, as Lomand opened the door and waved for Calvyn to precede him into the room.

Inside, the décor did not improve significantly. The room held a threadbare rug, an old narrow bed with bedding that looked as if it had been around since Darkweaver's time, a battered desk and chair and an old four-drawer press for storing clothes. There were also a couple of pictures on the wall. One was a portrait of a particularly dour-looking Magician holding a huge grimoire of spells on his lap, the other a picture of a cloak hung on a tall cloak and hat stand. What really caught Calvyn's attention, though, were the two long shelves packed end to end with books. Aside from Akhdar's study, which had contained a veritable library, this room held more books than Calvyn had ever seen before.

'Please, make yourself comfortable and get some rest,' Lomand said, smiling knowingly at Calvyn's wide-eyed reaction to the long lines of books. 'I'll have one of the Acolytes bring your saddlebags up from the stables.'

'Thank you, Sir, I would appreciate that. Please, before you go, could you tell me if all Acolyte rooms have this many books in them?'

Lomand's eyes twinkled as he answered.

'Indeed they do. In fact, each has the same books, for those volumes make up the required reading to be able to attempt to gain a Magician's robes. Sleep well, young Calvyn.'

Hardly had the door closed behind Lomand before the first book was in Calvyn's hand. It proved to be a history of the Shandese Empire. Interesting, but not what Calvyn was looking for. Working progressively down the shelf, he opened each in turn until he found what he was looking for. It was surprising to Calvyn's mind just how many of the books were not related to magic at all. Odd for an academy of Magicians, he mused. The reading material was more attuned to producing a scholar than a Master of magic, but the book that he had found was exactly the sort that he had hoped to find – *Basic Magical Theory* by Grand Magician Therone Jexis. The year that it had been written meant nothing to Calvyn, as it was related to a dynasty of the Shandese Emperors about which he knew nothing. It could have been last year, or a hundred years ago as far as he could tell.

Settling himself down on the bed to read, Calvyn quickly became absorbed in the text. True, Calvyn already understood and had utilised the vast majority of what he was reading but he found that the different perspective offered on many of the basic principles opened his eyes to a whole new way of viewing the practice of magic. The writer had a very regimented mindset on how one should progress on the road to learning the skills of a Magician, almost as if there was only one path to success and every flagstone on that path had to be trodden in turn if the Magician was to become complete in his abilities. This Calvyn knew to be a stifling method of progression, which allowed no room for creativity, individuality and flair. Surely becoming a true Magician did not really need such a restrictive regime, he thought grimly.

When he finally placed the book down, having read it right through, it was very late. Calvyn's eyes burned, feeling dry and gritty, as he extinguished the lamp on his desk. In moments he was asleep, and seemingly seconds later there was a knock at his door.

'Come in,' he mumbled, and prised his eyes open into a squint as Lomand appeared in the doorway.

'Sleep well?' the doorkeeper rumbled and then smiled as he noticed the book on the desk. 'Ah! Good old Therone. So what did you think of the old Master's philosophy on magic? Did you read much?'

'All of it,' answered Calvyn sleepily, rubbing at his eyes. 'He's a bit... rigid in his thinking, isn't he?'

'All of it! Ho, ho! The Masters will just *love* you! Between you and me, I think he must have been one of the most tiresome old windbags ever, but unfortunately some of our more distinguished Magicians might disagree with me. His teaching practices are highly revered by one or two of the Masters here at present. Not all of them mark you. Some are still flexible enough to allow original thought, but many are stuck in the traditions and learning practices handed down over centuries from Master to Master. Anyway, be that as it may, are you ready for a bite of breakfast?'

Calvyn's stomach rumbled at the mention of food and he instinctively placed a hand across his middle.

'I guess that spoke for itself,' Calvyn chuckled. 'Please, just give me a moment to straighten myself up.'

Rifling through his saddlebags, which had been placed by the door sometime the previous evening, Calvyn found a clean tunic and performed a rapid change. Ruffling his hair with his hands, he then used spread fingers to comb it flat, and rubbing at his teeth with the side of his finger to remove that almost furry feel, he signalled his readiness to Lomand.

The doorkeeper led Calvyn once more into the maze of corridors and brought him eventually to a door that looked no different from the others. From behind the door came the noise of many voices, and Calvyn was quite shocked visually to find that the door opened into a large, high-ceilinged hall. Three rows of long tables extended the length of the hall and a shorter line of tables ran across the width, joining the far end of the three lines together. The Masters apparently sat at the head tables and the Acolytes and lower ranked Magicians filled the rest.

'Why don't you take a seat over there with that group of Acolytes?' Lomand suggested. 'I'll come and collect you when the meal is finished and you can go, or stay, as you will.'

Calvyn thanked Lomand and went, as the Magician had suggested, to join a group at the end of the right hand set of tables. The entire group wore the mid-grey robes that Calvyn presumed designated them as Acolytes. What struck him instantly about the group though was not their dress, but their vast age range.

Boys as young as about twelve sat alongside men in their twenties, thirties and even forties, yet all of those in the group chatted like equals. 'Where else would you find such an unusual circumstance,' wondered Calvyn as he made his way to join them.

The group fell silent as Calvyn took his seat and all eyes turned to look at him. Not intimidated in the slightest, Calvyn met their gaze with a slow, sweeping look of his own.

'Good morning, gentlemen. Well met. I am Calvyn,' he said loudly enough to be heard by everyone nearby.

'Are you going to become an Acolyte?' asked a boy in his mid teens who was sat to Calvyn's right.

'Maybe,' Calvyn said slowly. 'I haven't decided yet.'

'Haven't decided!' scoffed an older man across the table. 'What sort of commitment does that show?'

'I haven't decided yet whether I should go and attempt a dangerous rescue mission, which would almost certainly need the magic that I already know if it is to succeed, or whether I should stay here and learn magic formally. It's a difficult choice,' Calvyn said pointedly, locking eyes with the scoffer and staring him down. 'Which would you choose?'

'Well, I...'

'He would stay here until he rotted given half a chance,' injected one of the others mockingly. 'Saernall is far too cowardly to attempt anything that didn't conform to the Masters' will.'

Several of the others laughed and the older man huffed and looked away, like a spoiled young boy a third of his age.

'So you can perform some magic already?' the first boy asked again. 'Which spells have you learned?'

'Oh, not many,' Calvyn said modestly. 'A few healing spells, a light spell, a defensive barrier, a spell to bring things to hand from a distance...'

'Translocation! You can translocate!' exclaimed the man immediately to Calvyn's left. 'I've heard that half of the Magicians don't know how to do that. Where did you get the spell from?'

'I made it up,' Calvyn said to a shocked and disbelieving audience. 'It wasn't that difficult really, I just took elements of two other simpler spells and combined them to make the effect that I wanted.'

A shocked silence fell around the table, followed by a series of muttered whisperings back and forth that excluded Calvyn completely until the man to his left spoke to him again.

'Have you any idea how dangerous making up spells is?' he asked in a quiet voice. 'If you had got it even slightly wrong, the effects could have been disastrous.'

Calvyn had no idea what the man was talking about. Perdimonn had not mentioned anything about any potential dangers and it was difficult to imagine what could go wrong other than nothing happening at all when the spell failed.

'So how are new spells created then, if no one is supposed to make them up?' Calvyn asked, a little exasperated by their attitude.

'The Magicians and Grand Magicians spend years in research, looking at combinations of runes that have been used before to make sure that there have been no catastrophic effects recorded of such attempts in the past. Classic examples of this would be the invisibility spell that left the Magician like a hollow glass, or the growth spell that caused whatever it was used on to explode.'

Calvyn found both examples pretty ludicrous, and began to wonder if the Masters were duping the Acolytes into blind obedience. After all, why would something explode if it were subjected to a growth spell? The effect of the runes was controlled by the mental image, or at least that was the understanding that he had gained from Perdimonn. So if the runes were of the right sort, almost regardless of the order, providing the mental image conforming the runes to the desired effect was strong enough, the magic would work. Undoubtedly, the Academy would teach set patterns for runes in order to give conformity to classes, but from what Calvyn understood of magic, exact sequences were not necessary. The Acolytes would probably have a blue fit if he told them about the magic sword he had created, he thought to himself with a mental chuckle. He would save that little gem for another time.

'Well, I can't say that I've ever had a problem with any of my spells to date,' Calvyn said carefully, 'but then I've not really been overly ambitious *that* often.'

'Not overly ambitious, he says,' laughed the teenage boy to Calvyn's right. 'He makes up a spell for translocation, but he's not overly ambitious. Is that why you have come here then? To learn enough to become ambitious? Or to discipline your magic into a safer, more controlled skill?'

'Actually, I came to deliver a message to Grand Magician Akhdar. I never intended to stay, but now that a place here has been offered, I must confess that the idea is becoming increasingly intriguing,' Calvyn replied with a mischievous grin. 'Let's face it – if I can make you lot wince, imagine what I'll be able to do to the Masters.'

Most of the group laughed, but the older man across the table from him continued to look sour.

Breakfast proved to be a hearty meal of bread, thick slices of bacon served with eggs and a strangely spicy variant of piping hot dahl. When the meal was finished, everyone stood up and remained still whilst one of the Masters read out a class rota that meant nothing to Calvyn. Judging by the grimaces of some, and the grins on the faces of others, the rapid-fire list obviously made perfect sense to those around him. After the class rota had been read, those sitting at the top table dispersed first and only when they had all left the hall did anyone else move.

Lomand appeared at Calvyn's side and the Acolytes quickly dispersed, none of them staying a moment longer than was absolutely necessary in the giant man's presence.

'I intimidate them for some reason,' Lomand said with a grin, once the last one had left. 'So, young Calvyn, what's it to be? Will you stay? Or shall I have one of the Acolytes saddle up that fine horse of yours?'

Calvyn thought for a moment longer. The King of Thrandor really needed someone with a good grounding in magic to be his adviser. Also, as a Knight of the Realm, Calvyn had a duty to serve his country to the best of his ability in whatever he did. Learning magic here would enable him to better serve Thrandor in the role into which he had been cast. Calvyn desperately wanted to help Bek and Jez, but would have to cast aside his duty to king and country to go to their aid. In his new role as a Knight of the Realm, he would then have to justify why he had put his companions above his duty to serve the King. Reluctantly, he pushed the last of his doubts to the back of his mind and made his decision. He would trust Bek and Jez into Derra's hands. Derra was a seasoned soldier, an excellent leader, and the perfect person to lead the rescue mission to free Bek and Jez.

It was clear that Perdimonn had intended for him to study here, or he would not have made provision for his entry into the Academy. The King had awarded Calvyn a Knighthood giving him a position of responsibility and some freedom to make difficult choices for the good of Thrandor. This was the first of those choices and Calvyn desperately hoped that he had chosen correctly. There was no doubt that being trained as a Magician would better qualify him to advise King Malo on matters of magic, though Calvyn knew in his heart that in some ways this was an excuse for him to do what he had always wanted – to become a real Magician. The opportunity was unique, beneficial to his country and altogether too good to turn down.

'I would like to stay, Sir, if that is all right?' he said, trying to sound convinced that he had made the right choice.

'Excellent. I am sure that you will fit in here just fine. Come. Let us get you settled into a class. I am afraid that I am pretty much obliged to put you in with the juniors to begin with, but as soon as the Masters have placed your abilities and knowledge, I am sure that they will move you up to a more suitable group.'

Lomand strode off and Calvyn had to all but run to keep up with him. They did not leave by the same door that they had entered the dining hall, though Calvyn would not have known it had he not marked in his mind the way they had come in. He had still not discovered a method of distinguishing one corridor from another, so similar did the passageways appear.

They did not have to go far before Lomand stopped and knocked on one of the doors on the left hand side of the corridor. The doorkeeper did not wait for an answer, but merely opened the door and marched straight in.

'Ah, Brother Jabal, I have a newly arrived Acolyte to join the juniors. I know that you have been working with this group for some months now, but I suspect that you'll find young Calvyn here will be able to catch up in a reasonably short order.'

'Really, Lomand! Can he not wait for the next set of juniors to start? Protocol is that *every* student should attend *all* of the classes at the basic level. Why should this young man be any different?'

'Well, Brother Jabal, Calvyn has been sponsored here by Brother Perdimonn. I suspect that he would find the initial classes something of a waste of time,' Lomand replied with a smile.

Jabal's eyebrows rose slightly at the name of Perdimonn, but he remained unrepentant of his attitude.

'No class is a waste of time unless the student's mind is closed to learning the nuances of our craft. Very well, he may join us. However, if he cannot keep up with the rest, then he shall be excluded in future until a new group of Acolytes is ready to begin.'

Lomand gave Calvyn an encouraging smile, and with one of his massive hands, he steered him forward with a gentle pressure on his shoulder.

'Go ahead. You'll be fine,' Lomand said to him in a low voice, then withdrew from the room, closing the door gently behind him.

Calvyn moved over to an empty seat. There were only a dozen or so other students in the class and Calvyn recognised one of them as the teenage boy who had spoken to him at breakfast.

'Now then, class, let us hope that there are no further interruptions. Back to the exercise please. Close your eyes and picture in your mind a blanket of white...'

Calvyn smiled. He was on familiar ground. The exercise was the first of the mental exercises that Perdimonn had set him over a year before. With a practised ease he cleared his mind and focused on nothing but a white background. The Master was droning on and on, trying almost to hypnotise his students to success and Calvyn found his patience quickly tested.

Out of interest, whilst still maintaining the pure field of white within the open area of his mind, Calvyn reached out to look into some of the other students' minds to see how they fared. Using the powers of sorcery learned during his time with the Lords of the Inner Eye, this proved a simple exercise. None of the minds that he touched had achieved the goal. Some were close, but allowed minor distractions to prevent them from the complete, stable mental image of white nothingness that Calvyn knew the Master was looking for.

Carefully and subtly, Calvyn touched the Master's mind, and instantly regretted doing so. Jabal's eyes flicked to look at him the moment Calvyn touched on his consciousness and the look that the Master gave him was stern and penetrating.

'It seems that Lomand was correct,' Jabal said slowly. 'You are not only capable of joining this class – you are well beyond it. However, you are most certainly lacking when it comes to magical decorum, young man. Attempt to look into a Master's mind again without his express permission, and believe me, you will wish that you had never learned the degree of mental control to do so.'

Jabal was not nasty, nor even threatening with his words. He stated them as he would a line from a textbook. Calvyn gulped and went back to concentrating wholly on his field of whiteness. He had thought that his powers of sorcery would have been such that he could enter and leave any mind without trace, except perhaps that of another Master Sorcerer. It appeared that he would have to redefine his thinking.

The class continued for another three quarters of an hour or so, during which time Calvyn maintained the required image without break. In his inner mind, he mulled over his reading from the previous evening and entered a debate with himself. Trying to remain as objective as possible, he weighed the benefits and disadvantages of the rigid progression to gaining a

Magician's robes that Therone Jexis advocated. He found that on reflection, he could appreciate some of the advantages, but overall still felt that more flexibility to cater for individual strengths and weaknesses would produce better results.

At the end of the class, Grand Magician Jabal asked Calvyn to remain behind for a moment. He also ordered one of the Acolytes to wait outside in order to guide Calvyn to the next class. Calvyn remained seated, nervously wondering whether Jabal had waited until the others were gone in order to punish him privately for his impudence at trying to see into the Master's mind.

The Grand Magician sat silently, waiting until the door had closed behind the last student before he spoke. When he did so it was in a quiet voice that held no malice or anger.

'I look forward to having the time to find out exactly what Brother Perdimonn has taught you of our craft, Calvyn. Your mental control is quite good for one so young, though your technique is strange. I would almost question that a Magician had trained you at all. I appreciate that Perdimonn never studied here, but there are some things that I have always taken for granted as being standard by necessity. In future, you shall join the senior Acolytes for your training in mental clarity. You shall, however, attend classes in Magician etiquette with the juniors. You should prove an interesting student. Work hard and you will do well here.'

'Thank you, Master.'

'Go now. You have another class to attend. History if I am not mistaken.'

Calvyn left swiftly at the Master's directive, relieved that he had not got into too much trouble over his ill advised attempt to read the Magician's thoughts. How had the Master detected his touch so swiftly though? Calvyn could not understand that at all. He had tried to be so subtle, and yet Jabal had felt Calvyn's touch before he had even settled in the Master's surface thoughts. Yet Calvyn had not felt Jabal touch his mind at all. It was very strange, though Jabal had inadvertently given Calvyn the clue to solving the puzzle, for the majority of his mental training had *not* been given by a Magician. The Sorcerer Lords of the Inner Eye had progressed the majority of Calvyn's mental ability, so it was perhaps unsurprising that the skills were not identical.

The Acolyte waiting outside in the corridor led Calvyn quickly around the corridors to another classroom where the next class was about to begin. This lesson was uneventful enough, though Calvyn left it with the realisation that he had a lot of reading to catch up on if he was to take part fully in the debate element of the class.

The final class of the morning was a science class that today happened to be about minerals. It seemed an appropriate subject somehow, with the Academy based in a city whose existence was based around mining ore from the mountains. The class was far more comprehensive than just the basics of the local geology, however, and Calvyn found himself wondering just how the subject material related to magic.

At lunch, Calvyn asked some of the other students when the practical magic sessions were scheduled for and was surprised to be rewarded with a roar of laughter for his immediate answer.

'Practical magic?' chuckled one boy. 'Well I suppose if we do well in our assessments, our class should be ready for basic spell casting in a year or two.'

'A year or two?' gasped Calvyn in horror. 'But that's ridiculous! I didn't agree to stay here to be pumped with years of theory and no practical. I've already progressed my spell casting to include a fair number of spells and I was really looking forward to building on what I have learned on my own.'

'Then you will have to take the assessments in all the basic theoretical subjects sooner rather than later,' the Acolyte suggested. 'It's the only way that you'll be allowed to move beyond the beginners' classes.'

'Good old Therone Jexis, I suppose?'

The boy nodded.

'Very well.   Give me the reading list for the tests,' Calvyn asserted.   'If it's assessments they want, then it's assessments they'll get.'

CHAPTER 9

'The arena will be open tomorrow,' Fesha said, keeping his voice low and seemingly concentrating on watching the bubbles rise in his mug of ale. 'The gates open at the tenth hour and the entrance fee is three copper sennuts each.'

Derra and Eloise sat sipping wine, feeling distinctly uncomfortable in their low cut garments and short skirts. It was certainly not in their imaginations that many of the male eyes in the tavern lingered on their table as often and as long as courtesy allowed – often longer. Eloise was more uncomfortable with the clothes than the attention. The strikingly attractive Private was used to being stared at, but Derra was finding the whole experience did not sit well with her military training.

'If that man over there winks at me one more time, I'll poke his eyes out and spread his fat red bulbous nose right across the rest of his face,' Derra growled in a low voice.

Eloise started to choke on her wine and grabbed a napkin from the table, trying desperately to delicately hide her mirth at Derra's annoyance. Unnecessarily drawing the attention of the locals would do the Thrandorians no favours. Derra flashed Eloise one of the looks that she was famous for back at Keevan's Castle.

'What's the matter, Eloise? Did your wine go down the wrong way? Would you like some assistance?' Derra asked sweetly, making her voice as ladylike as possible.

Eloise looked at Derra's hand just poised to thump her

153

on the back and decided that whilst unwanted attention would be bad, getting backslapped by Derra might just be worse.

'No thanks,' she croaked and coughed into her napkin, her eyes watering.

'Ladies, ladies! Please, let's try to keep our minds on the matter at hand,' Fesha smirked, his voice low and teasing. 'Perhaps we should go to the games tomorrow and try to find out a bit more about the security of the prison sections. I've already discovered that the cells are under the northern stands. Apparently the southern side of the arena is fitted out with quarters for the trained fighters, and the western end houses the wild animals.'

'Wild animals?' Derra asked quizzically.

'Why yes, Derrania, there are great bears and mountain cats and the like. Apparently they are released into the arena for the fighters to contend with as part of the show. Isn't that exciting?' Fesha said, raising the volume of his voice just slightly, and using his eyes to warn Derra that someone on a nearby table was taking an interest in their conversation.

'Exciting indeed, Feshanoire. Tell me, where do you think that we should attempt to sit in order to get the best view?'

'Well I'm really not sure...' Fesha said uncertainly.

'Pardon me, but I could not help overhearing your dilemma,' interrupted a man from the adjacent table. The eavesdropper was obviously the reason why Fesha had been being so circumspect with his information. 'Please, if I can be of assistance in aiding your decision, then I will be most happy to do so. I am a great fan of the games and have attended them almost religiously for years now. Can I take it that you have never been to the games here in Shandrim before?'

'That is correct, Sir. We're visiting Shandrim for the first time and have heard so much about the arena and the spectacle of the games. There's nothing like it where we come from, so we felt that we really had to attend at least once during our stay.'

'I'm glad that you think so. The games are one of the most attractive things about city life in my view. They are really not to be missed. If I were you, I would sit in the north stand tomorrow. You'll need to get to the gates early if you want good seats though, for the best ones fill quickly. You need not worry about prisoners escaping, or wild animals for that matter, for they are very safely secured and guarded.'

Derra's eyes narrowed at the man's assurances, for it showed that he had probably heard everything that Fesha had said. They were being far too careless. Fortunately, the man had interpreted their interest in the prisoners as worry for their own safety, but they could not afford to ride their luck overly much, or they might well discover the location of the cells all too quickly – from the wrong side of the bars.

'Why thank you, sir. It is always good to get advice from an expert,' Fesha replied gratefully. 'Is there any particular reason for advising the northern stand?'

'Three reasons really,' the man answered, obviously pleased to be able to demonstrate his knowledge. 'Firstly, being south facing, the stands will be warmer than the others, which is always pleasant as winter approaches. Secondly, the Emperor himself sits on the northern stand in his Imperial Box. As a visitor to the capital, you will no doubt wish to at least get a glance at His Imperial Majesty.'

'Indeed,' agreed Fesha, as the man paused. 'And the third reason?'

'Well, as I myself shall be sitting in the northern stand, I might gain another chance to be introduced to these two charming young ladies,' he said, a smarmy smile spreading across his face as he was given his chance to attempt flattery.

Eloise flashed him one of her devastating smiles and Derra tried to follow suit, although hers looked more akin to a snarl.

'My apologies, sir, may I introduce my cousin, Eloise, and her travelling companion, Derrania? Eloise and I have been visiting relatives in one of the villages nearby. Derrania offered to come along and provide Eloise with female company. Apparently my small talk is not up to much and Eloise was delighted to have a soul mate to talk to on our long journey.'

'Delighted, Eloise, Derrania. It is always a pleasure to have the chance to meet such lovely ladies,' he fawned, almost drooling as he kissed their hands in turn. 'I am Jarom Trebaryn and I am at your service.'

Fesha happened to catch the look on Derra's face as Jarom kissed her hand and decided to get them out of the tavern quickly. The danger signals were all there, and whilst the Sergeant was maintaining her self-control, Fesha judged that it would not take much for Derra to lose her cool and do something that they might all regret.

Pleading a prior arrangement with private dressmakers, Fesha excused them from Jarom's company and led Derra and Eloise outside. No sooner had they walked fifty paces from the tavern door, than Derra all but exploded.

'Obsequious, snivelling, scum sucking little... urghh!' Derra growled with a shudder.

'Oh come on! He wasn't *that* bad,' chuckled Eloise, with a wicked grin. 'I've met a lot worse!'

'Well let's hope that Derrania here doesn't,' said Fesha fervently. 'The way she curled her hand into a fist as Jarom kissed it, I thought she was going to knock his teeth down his throat at any second!'

'The thought did cross my mind,' Derra growled.

'Well next time, don't let it,' Fesha whispered forcibly. 'You may be a Sergeant and I would certainly follow you into battle in an instant, but that doesn't mean I'm going to sit back and let you get me locked up because you can't control your emotions. I suggest that you bottle it, or we might as well go home now.'

Derra stopped dead in her tracks and fixed her very hardest gaze on Fesha. Most men would have withered under that fearsome stare, but Fesha met her eyes coolly and waited her out. After a few moments, Derra looked away and muttered angrily to herself for a few moments.

'You're right, Fesha. I'll keep a firm grip on my temper from now on,' Derra stated with a dangerous edge of fire still in her voice. 'Just remember that whilst you know more than I do about this place, you still follow *my* lead, is that clear? If I decide that it's necessary to start a fight, I'll do so and I'll expect you to back me up – whether I'm right or wrong. I appreciate your experience, and I'll bow to it at times out of necessity, but don't let it to go to your head. Let's go find somewhere to stay tonight – and Fesha?'

'Yes Derrania?'

'Tomorrow we get seats as far from where that Jarom fellow recommended as we possibly can. Understood?'

'Absolutely,' he replied, his voice more subdued than it had been since they had entered Shandar.

* * * * *

'Ah, Femke! Come in, come in,' the Emperor beckoned. 'Tell me, what have you discovered?'

A young woman in plain clothing, neither rich nor exactly poor, walked confidently into the Emperor's personal quarters. There was little that could be said of Femke other than that she was unremarkable. Indeed, she had made 'unremarkable' an art form of the highest order. It was the quality that had made her the Emperor's most successful spy.

'Your Imperial Majesty, Commander Chorain has negotiated with Garvin concerning the Thrandorians, though so far I have been unable to discover the exact details of the agreement that he has struck. All I know in truth is that Chorain is more than a little satisfied with whatever it is that he has arranged. He spoke with the dark-haired Thrandorian as well, and I have it on good authority that Chorain asked him if he would assassinate someone for a price. Who and for how much I do not know yet, but I'm working on it.'

The Emperor nodded and pursed his lips as he

considered again whether he was doing the right thing by having Chorain involved in anything to do with sorting out the disaster that had occurred in Thrandor. The Commander was a wild card, liable to play his own games, and as such, Chorain was dangerous. Yet Chorain's connivances might prove useful, providing the Emperor was aware of what he was up to and could prevent the Commander from doing anything too disruptive to the Emperor's own plans.

'Very well, Femke, continue to monitor Chorain for now. Anything that you can discover about his agreement with Garvin would be useful and I'm very intrigued to know more about his offer to the Thrandorian. Do keep me informed, but don't compromise yourself to do so, unless you deem it absolutely necessary.

'Yes, your Imperial Majesty. As you wish.'

The young woman withdrew, leaving the Emperor to his thoughts and little realising just how important her role was in the current play of political events. Word was already beginning to spread of a defeat in Thrandor, and it would not be long before the Emperor would start being asked difficult questions. He had little time for manoeuvring people and events to his advantage, and much hung on the reports brought by Femke and the other spies as to how the Emperor would word his replies.

High Lord Vallaine had already been summoned to Shandrim, though privately the Emperor doubted very much whether the self-styled High Lord of the Inner Eye would present himself at the Emperor's request. If Vallaine did not arrive as requested and soon, then the Emperor fully intended to send every assassin he could spare to ensure that Vallaine never messed with Shandese politics again. After the demise of five legions in Thrandor, the Emperor decided that he could more than afford to lose the Sorcerer Lord who had promised a glorious victory by sending them there. Vallaine would have to decide quickly – present himself to the Emperor to offer an explanation, or dodge assassins for the rest of his life.

'Somehow,' thought the Emperor grimly, 'I think he'll choose the latter course and I almost look forward to the report that announces him dead.'

* * * * *

Bek awaited his contest with trepidation. It was his first fight since beginning his training as an arena fighter. He was clothed totally differently from his first encounter in the arena. Then he had worn the tattered remnants of his old uniform and had sported only a short sword. Now he had a longer blade, though not as long, or as heavy as many of the fighters favoured. Also, he wore a protective leather jerkin, leather greaves over his thighs, a hardened leather cap and a small round shield. He still had no idea who he was due to fight, but after the last few weeks of training under the Weapons Master, Hammar, he felt ready to face just about anyone.

The crowd had been a bit more vocal today than they had over previous weeks, or at least it seemed so. Bek was realist enough to recognise that it could well just be his nervousness amplifying the cheers as he waited for his turn to contend for his life in the arena.

'It's not always to the death,' he reminded himself, and as he ran through the list of fighters' names that he now knew, he realised that there was not one that he would deliberately kill. They were generally likeable men who had chosen to fight in the arena for a variety of reasons. There were few amongst them who would deliberately try to kill him now that he had been included in their ranks as an arena fighter in his own right.

Suddenly, the crowd roared louder than anything that Bek had heard that day, and the noise level remained high for the next couple of minutes. Whoever was in the arena was obviously a crowd favourite and there were many gasps, cheers and eventually a large roar of approval as the fight concluded.

Bek was closer to the gates now, as his turn to fight

came ever closer. The gates opened ahead of him and the victorious fighter descended back into the pits.

It was Serrius, and not only was he sporting a cut across his right cheek that was bleeding profusely, but he was also wearing a look that personified the sky-splitting crashes of the most powerful thunderstorm. The crowds were still going wild out in the arena and Bek realised that whomever he had just fought had obviously put on an impressive show.

Serrius passed and Bek nudged the fighter ahead of him in the line to enter the arena.

'Who gave Serrius the cut?' Bek asked in a low voice, half looking over his shoulder to ensure that Serrius was out of earshot.

'You mean you haven't heard?' the man replied, his surprise obvious that anyone did not know whom Serrius had fought. 'I would have thought that you, of all people, would have known.'

'Why should I know? I don't even know who I'm going to be fighting, so why should I know the opponent that Serrius was up against? I seem to be the last to find out anything.'

'Well I just assumed that your friend would have told you about it, that's all. He fought well it appears. Serrius is rarely marked during his fights, and I have never even heard of anyone touching his face.'

'Jez? Where is he? Is he all right? He shouldn't have been fighting anyone. He wasn't fully recovered from the wound he took during his last fight,' Bek fired back, his voice fast and heavy with concern.

The fighter looked back at him with sadness in his eyes. 'Come on, Thrandorian. You know better than that. Nobody who enters the arena with Serrius is ever all right. He is dead. The guards will probably be taking his body down to the pit of the dead, where they strip the bodies prior to disposal.'

'Dead? Are you sure? He might just be injured, or have left the arena by another gate,' Bek asked, unable to accept Jez's death without evidence. 'You didn't see the fight any more than I did. For all we know, Jez might have defeated Serrius. That might be why he looked so angry.'

The fighter looked at him pityingly and shook his head slowly.

'Don't get your hopes up, Thrandorian. There are few amongst the fighters here who would have so much as an outside chance of defeating Serrius on their very best form. There is no way that anyone not fully healed from an injury would beat him and that can only mean one thing. Serrius does not leave anyone alive in the arena.'

'But why? Why Jez? It doesn't make any sense. Serrius is the top arena fighter in Shandrim. Why would he want to fight a man that was not fully fit, let alone not in current practice, nor for that matter even trained in the techniques of arena fighting. If he wanted an easy victory, surely there were others who would have been more respectable opponents, yet offered no great challenge. Jez could not and would not have challenged him, so Serrius must have dictated Jez as his opponent. There is something very strange going on here, and I mean to get to the bottom of it.'

Bek gradually began to feel more and more angry as he considered how, and why, Jez must have been sent out to fight such a mismatched battle. By the time his own turn to enter the arena came up, he was absolutely steaming mad. Eyes blazing, he strode out onto the sand with his jaw clenched hard against the desire to just charge his opponent and hack at him, abandoning all of the discipline that his experience told him was essential to victory. Fortunately, his common sense won him over.

The fighter awaiting him in the arena was fairly experienced, but was not a ranked swordsman. Bek had seen him at training but did not know his name. On seeing the madness in Bek's eyes as they met in the centre of the arena to salute the Emperor, the fighter's lips twisted slightly into a look of satisfaction.

Moments later, he was bleeding from several minor cuts, held no weapon and had the point of Bek's blade at his throat. Angry or not, Bek's instincts guided him faithfully when faced with a dangerous opponent. His blade work was faster than ever, and his temper, although roused, was firmly under control.

Barrock and Karoth he had killed out of necessity, but he was an arena fighter himself now and there was no need to kill this opponent. Instead, Bek concluded the fight in short order, leaving no doubt in anyone's mind as to who the victor was.

With the slightest of bows to the Imperial Box, Bek marched straight out of the arena again and started calling for Hammar the second that he was through the gate to the pits. So fierce was his anger as he demanded to see the Weapons Master, that people raced to comply with his demands. Sure enough, within a few minutes the old Master Swordsman arrived.

'What's the matter, Bek? I saw no foul play during your fight. Indeed, your victory was most impressive. You won far faster than I would have cared to wager.'

'Why did Jez fight today?' Bek snarled angrily. 'He was in no fit state to fight anyone and certainly not Serrius. His wounds were still not properly healed and he hadn't even begun to train for the arena as Garvin promised that he would, so why did he fight?'

Hammar looked sympathetically at Bek and shook his head slightly.

'I am not the one to ask,' he said slowly. 'Serrius arranges his own fights unless he is challenged by one who has the right to do so and that has not happened in some time. If you want to know why, then you must ask Serrius.'

'Then Jez *is* dead.'

Hammar nodded.

'I want to see him,' Bek insisted firmly, his anger making the words a statement rather than a request.

'Very well. I will take you there myself.'

Hammar took Bek's weapons from him, much to the relief of the guards, and led him out of the fighters' pits. A roar went up from the crowd as another fight got underway. As they twisted and turned through corridors and down stairs, Bek realised that the noise of the crowd had washed over him unnoticed today. Strange, really, how he could block out something so loud, and yet he had genuinely not noticed the noise whilst he was out in the arena. His anger and his focus on the fight had been so complete that all else had become irrelevant.

Hammar led him into a bleak chamber, where bodies lay in a line on the floor at one end. There were no furnishings here. No pictures hung on the wall and no carpet covered the cold stone floor. There were no chairs or tables. The chamber was completely bare.

The room gave the impression of clinical cleanliness. The floor had obviously been scrubbed time without number to remove any trace of blood from the weekly pile of bodies that were laid here. Now it would have to be done again, as some new smears of darkness traced across the floor to where the latest casualties of the arena lay.

There, at the end of the row, was the familiar lanky shape of Jez, his red hair standing out starkly against the line of otherwise dark-haired bodies. Bek ran across to his side and knelt beside his body. Gently, Bek grasped Jez's hand. It was as cold as the stone he lay on. A tear ran down first one cheek and then the other, as Bek involuntarily began to weep over his friend.

'Serrius will pay for this, Jez,' Bek whispered, his vow amplified by the bare chamber. 'I promise that you will not go unavenged, Jez. Serrius will regret the day that he decided to fight you before you had fully recovered from your wound. What is more, I will make Calvyn pay as well. Sending us here was an evil deed. I had counted him my friend – our friend. His betrayal of that friendship will be his undoing. When I have finished here with Serrius I will go after Calvyn. By Tarmin and all the gods, I swear that I shall not rest until I see justice done to both of them.'

Bek gently laid Jez's hand back at his side. His face looked strangely peaceful for one who had suffered a violent death. There was no trace of pain on his face and, save for the hint of blue about his skin in general, and his lips in particular, one could almost have been forgiven for thinking that he was just sleeping.

Bek rose to his feet and muttering a last farewell, returned to where Hammar was waiting quietly by the door. The Weapons Master met Bek's sad gaze with a sympathetic expression and he turned and led Bek silently back up the stairs and into the corridor system that honeycombed the stadium. Bek followed grimly, saying nothing, but mentally reinforcing the vows that he had made over and over again in his mind.

When they reached Bek's room, Hammar opened the door, let Bek in, then made as if to close the door and paused.

'He will kill you, Bek. You are not good enough to face Serrius. I understand your anger. I have been where you are myself on occasion, but I am warning you that if you face Serrius you will die.'

'Thank you, Hammar. I appreciate your advice, but I have sworn an oath and I intend to keep it. I will challenge Serrius at the next games.'

'And what if he will not face you? He doesn't have to, you know,' Hammar asked.

'Then I'll fight until I'm ranked high enough that I can force him to face me,' Bek replied, his voice flat and his face unmoving.

Hammar pursed his lips, and with a simple nod of acknowledgement he closed the door and locked it. The bolt driving home with its loud metal clank no longer rang with the tone of a prison. To Bek, this had become a home – a home until vengeance was sated.

* * * * *

Derra, Fesha and Eloise sat midway up the southern stand, watching with a mixture of horror and fascination as the pattern of the games unfolded before them. The early fights between trained fighters and prisoners produced no upsets and lots of bodies. After the first few minutes, Fesha had muttered to Derra that they might already be too late.

'That may be so, but we're not leaving until we know for sure. Both Bek and Jez are good fighters. They would certainly fare better than those poor souls,' Derra had whispered back, being careful not to say anything aloud that might draw unwanted attention from the crowds around them. 'Keep your eyes and ears open. Anything that you can find out about this place will be useful.'

When Jez had walked out into the arena with Serrius, Fesha's nudge on Derra's arm had been unnecessary, for the crowd had gone wild at the sight of Serrius, drawing all eyes to the arena.

Eloise had turned to the man sitting behind her, and explaining that they were not from Shandrim had asked what all the fuss was about. It had been hard to conceal her horror at learning of Serrius' reputation, but the man was not really looking at her anyway. His eyes, and those of everyone else in the stadium, had been on the two protagonists down on the dusty floor below.

'If this Serrius is the top ranked fighter in Shandrim, what is he doing fighting someone who is obviously injured?' Derra had muttered through gritted teeth.

The Sergeant's keen eye had noted Jez's restricted movement, and had known the outcome of the fight almost the instant that it had begun. Anyone with half an eye could have seen that Jez was in no fit state to fight anyone, let alone an accomplished swordsman. Nevertheless, Jez had fought bravely and well, considering his injury. It was just galling that Serrius had killed Jez in front of them, when there had obviously been no need for him to do so. He could have finished the fight as the victor within the first few seconds, if he had been of a mind to do so. However, Serrius had deliberately forced the opening for a killing blow. Derra knew that they had been powerless to prevent it, but she silently made a promise that if she ever met Serrius with a weapon within reach, she would not hesitate to kill the man where he stood.

When Bek had entered the arena, also dressed in the garb of one of the trained fighters, all three had found themselves holding their breath for much of the fight. Again, it had not lasted long, but this time they found themselves cheering with the rest of the crowd when Bek expertly disarmed his opponent and stopped short of killing him. Bek had fought superbly. Again, the keen eye of Derra noticed details that slipped by the others. His style had altered slightly to cope with the longer weapons, but his speed and balance were as superb as ever. He had well deserved his victory.

The question facing them now was how to get Bek free. They had seen all that they had needed to of the games. Now they concentrated on extracting as much information as possible from those around them whenever there was a break in the action in the arena.

Before long they had gleaned as much as they were likely to between them, and Derra called the other two to follow her as she made her way to the nearest of the aisles a little later in the morning. The games were scheduled to go on well into the afternoon, and Derra had decided to pool their knowledge quickly to see if they could do anything before the games finished.

The three made their way to the public toilet facilities down at the lowest levels, where the crowd noise was just a muffled roar.

'Right,' Derra started, having first checked that no one else was within easy earshot. 'What have you found out?' she asked in a low voice.

'Well,' Eloise answered, 'prisoners like the ones we saw being slaughtered at the start are held in cells under the northern side of the arena. Neither Bek nor Jez were dressed like them though. · They were dressed as trained fighters, and they are quartered here, under the southern stands.'

'That checks with what I learned,' Fesha confirmed. 'The quarters under here are not heavily guarded, because the majority of fighters are here by choice, so we should not be overly outnumbered if we were to try and fight our way in to where Bek is being held. The only thing that we cannot guarantee is how the fighters would react. If they get involved on the side of the guards against us, we will be in serious trouble.'

'I agree,' affirmed Derra. 'A straightforward assault is out of the question. We will need some subtlety, but not much. I doubt that the Arena Master – Garvin I believe he is called – really expects a rescue attempt to free Bek, so the security should be fairly lax. Here is what I propose that we do...'

Derra outlined a simple plan, which the others agreed was worth a try. They had learned of only one entrance leading to the fighters' quarters, and when they approached it, they noted that there was just a single armed guard holding the door.

Fesha led the two ladies forward, one on each arm, until the guard told them to halt.

'What do you want?' the guard asked suspiciously. 'If you are looking for the toilets, you are in the wrong place. They are over there and down the steps.'

'No, no, my good fellow, nothing like that,' Fesha said boldly. 'Between you and me,' he said, dropping the arms of his two companions and lowering his voice in a conspiratorial fashion as he moved forward on his own, 'the two ladies here would like to show their appreciation to a couple of the fighters.'

'Show their appreciation? In what way?' the guard asked dully, and then flushed at the coy look that Eloise threw him.

'Oh, they were *very* impressed, and I'm sure that the fighters would just *love* to see them, if you take my meaning?' Fesha said, moving closer still to where the guard was holding his post at the locked door.

'No, I'm afraid that it's out of the question,' the guard answered. 'Garvin would have me flogged if he found out. He is very strict about such things.'

'I was afraid that you might say something like that,' Fesha said disappointedly.

Moving so fast that not even Derra saw where it came from, Fesha suddenly held a knife at the guard's throat. The guard's hand went belatedly to the hilt of his sword, but immediately dropped away from it again, as Fesha's blade increased its pressure slightly against the guard's skin.

'Now I am afraid that I am going to have to insist,' Fesha said, his voice sounding disappointed but his eyes flashing with amusement. 'My female friends here are really *very* keen to meet the fighters, aren't you ladies?'

'Just get on with it, Fesha,' Derra growled dangerously.

'Yes, of course, my lady,' he said with a grin. 'Now, my good man, would you be so kind as to take us to the Thrandorian's quarters?'

Fesha increased the pressure of the blade slightly more again, which got the desired effect. The guard fumbled the keys from his belt and turned awkwardly to unlock the door. Fesha maintained his knife at the man's throat throughout.

Once the door was open, Derra asked the guard if they were likely to meet other guards on their way.

'No,' he answered. 'Most of those on duty will be working in the cells area on the north side. The few off duty will most likely be up in the crowd watching the games. The only people that we might meet are the fighters returning to their quarters.'

'Very well. Eloise, unbuckle his sword belt and give it to me, then check him for any further weapons.'

Eloise took the belt off the guard whilst Derra had a quick look to see whether the guard had been telling the truth about the lack of any further guards inside. When Derra saw the size of the belt that Eloise had removed from the guard, she changed her mind about strapping it about her own waist.

'Here, give me the sword and ditch the belt. It would take too long to adjust to my size. Have you checked him for weapons? Then let's get on with it, we don't have all day,' Derra ordered brusquely.

Eloise nodded, showing Derra knife that she had

removed from his right hand boot. Content that the guard was now unarmed, they moved quietly down the steps into the levels below the stands. With Eloise ahead ensuring the way was clear, and Derra watching behind, Fesha got directions from the guard whilst keeping the blade constantly at his throat.

They had to stop once in a stairwell, all crowded behind a door, whilst two arena fighters passed by. To the three intruders and their hostage the sound of their own breathing seemed to echo loudly in their ears, but the two fighters passed by oblivious to the potential explosion of violence lurking just a few feet away. Once the two fighters had gone, Eloise checked to ensure that the way was clear and they pressed on towards their goal.

The final corridor that the guard led them into was long and dreadfully exposed. No one appeared to be around, but they would have to be quick about getting Bek out, or they would be discovered for sure.

'OK, which room is he in?' whispered Fesha softly to the guard.

'Down that way. Fourth door on the right I think,' the guard answered, his brow beaded with sweat.

'Think? Think is no good. I don't want to open the door to a hornet's nest,' Fesha whispered, his voice dangerous and his pressure of the blade on the guard's throat increasing again.

'I'm sure! I'm sure it is! Fourth door on the right,' the guard replied, his voice full of panic as the blade threatened to cut.

'Which key is it?' Fesha asked, holding up the bunch that he had taken from the guard after he had opened the door at the entrance earlier.

The guard's eyes widened in terror.

'None of them. I don't hold the key to his room. There are only two or three that do. Please, don't hurt me. I'm telling the truth,' he gasped.

'Where are we likely to find the nearest key?' Derra asked, her eyes glittering under her dark brows, as she fixed the guard with a stare that would have drilled through granite.

'No need, Sergeant. I have a way with locks,' grinned Fesha, removing two lock picks from his pocket.

'I should have known,' Derra growled. 'How long will it take you?'

'Depends how well oiled the lock is, but no more than a minute at the outside,' Fesha said with a shrug.

'Very well. Eloise, stay here and keep the guard quiet. Keep an ear open for anyone coming down the stairs. I'll go with Fesha and keep an eye out down the corridor whilst he unlocks the door. If anyone comes down the corridor, we'll leg it back up the steps. If you hear someone coming down the stairs, Eloise, come and join us and we'll hope that Fesha gets the door to Bek's room open in time for us all to hide in there. Any questions?'

There were none, and moments later Fesha and Derra moved swiftly and silently down the corridor to the fourth door on the right. Derra, sword in hand, put aside her curiosity at what Fesha was doing and waited with her back to the door. Her head slewed left and right, constantly scanning both ways for signs of trouble. Behind her, the scratching, clicking sounds of Fesha's lock picks sounded unnaturally loud.

True to his word, well within the minute he promised, there was a louder click and the sound of the door creaking open drew Derra's attention.

'Bek? Bek, are you in there?' Fesha whispered loudly and carefully opened the door fully into the room, which at first appeared empty.

He entered cautiously.

'Fesha? Is that really you?' Bek answered softly, and appeared from behind the door where he had obviously been poised ready to attack.

'It was the last time I looked,' Fesha replied with a grin. 'Come on, we're getting you out of here.'

Bek hesitated, obviously torn with indecision.

'Come on! What are you waiting for?' Fesha urged, sensing that Bek needed a push. 'We need to get out of here now.'

Bek teetered for a moment and then his resolve hardened.

'Go. I appreciate what you've done, but I'm not coming.'

CHAPTER 10

'Not coming? Don't mess around, Bek. This isn't a game,' Fesha urged impatiently. 'Let's get out of here – now.'

'I can't. If only you had come yesterday... but you didn't. Now Jez is dead and I've sworn a vow to avenge him. Go, Fesha. Tarmin go with you, but I'll not leave here until I've faced Serrius.'

Fesha looked at the determined set of Bek's jaw and the steely, immoveable look in his eyes, and realised that nothing that he could say or do would make any difference.

'What's taking so long?' rasped Derra in a low voice from the corridor. 'This isn't visiting time at the medics' quarters – let's go.'

'He says he's not coming, Sergeant.'

'I didn't come all this way and risk myself for nothing, Bek. Get out of there now. That's an order.'

Derra raised her voice sufficiently to project her anger, but before Bek could make any sort of response, a shout came echoing down the corridor.

'Hey! You! What do you think you are doing?'

'Out. Both of you. Now,' Derra barked in a tone that would normally have soldiers running as fast as they could.

Fesha raced out into the corridor, but Bek did not follow. There were two guards running down the corridor towards them, weapons already drawn. Fesha did not hesitate. The way back to the stairwell, where Eloise was

172

waiting, was still clear. Not pausing to see who followed, Fesha sprinted off towards their escape route.

Derra paused for a second and looked at the stubborn set of Bek's face.

'Tarmin damn you for a fool, Bek,' she snarled, then turned and ran after Fesha.

When Derra reached the stairs, she instantly saw that the guard they had been holding at knifepoint was slowing Eloise and Fesha down hugely. The three had only climbed one short flight of stairs, and keeping their hostage was only likely to get them surrounded and trapped. Quickly catching up with the others, Derra hit the guard hard on the back of the head with the pommel of the sword that she had liberated from him earlier. The man went down like a pole-axed cow and, as he fell, Derra caught him and twisted his body such that it rolled back down the steps towards the two pursuing guards.

All three guards tangled and fell back to the bottom of the flight of stairs whilst Eloise, Fesha and Derra sped away upwards. At the top of the stairs, Derra paused briefly to listen for signs of pursuit. The sound of feet pounding up the stairs was plain to hear. The guards were still coming.

Eloise and Fesha had built up a bit of a lead over Derra now, and were well along the passageway towards the next flight of stairs. Derra gritted her teeth and sprinted after them. A sudden shout from behind announced that the guards had caught sight of them again and Derra glanced over her shoulder to see how many were following. Unfortunately, as she looked back, a side door in the passageway just ahead of her opened and she ran full pelt into it.

For a split second, Derra saw stars and the world spun as she crashed to the floor. There was no time for any thought or worry as she fell, for the inky blackness of unconsciousness wrapped her in its dark void before she had even finished falling.

* * * * *

Calvyn ground his teeth in frustration. He was in trouble with a Master for the third time in but a few days and yet he had excelled at the tasks he had been set and worked harder by far than even the most dedicated of the other students. It just did not seem fair.

This time was even stranger than the previous occasions. Having proved himself capable of progressing to the practical spell casting classes by passing some of the assessment tests in little more than a week, Calvyn thought that he might find favour with the Masters. Inexplicably, this did not appear to be the case. He had read texts so late into the night that he felt as if his eyes must surely be bleeding, and his head was swimming with so much history, geography and science that it felt bloated with knowledge. Yet for all of his obvious drive, enthusiasm and ability to learn, Calvyn found himself constantly in trouble with the Masters for one reason or another.

Grand Magician Jabal interceding on his behalf and pronouncing him fit to progress to the practical spell casting classes, despite his not having completed all of the assessments, was undoubtedly part of the problem. The majority of the other Masters appeared to be of the opinion that Calvyn should start on the road to his robes by attending every class that a raw Acolyte would take. Credit for knowledge already attained was not a factor in their thinking. Certainly the idea of an Acolyte who had not yet passed all of the assessments, taking classes in spell casting, caused much frowning and shaking of heads.

Some of the other Acolytes also shunned Calvyn because of what they saw as preferential treatment. In particular, those who had spent years studying to complete all of the assessments before being allowed to progress to casting spells, resented that he was joining their classes. This was a predictable response, so Calvyn did not allow himself to be overly bothered by the cool reception from his peers.

Master Jabal had argued that progressing Calvyn early

was a necessity. Calvyn already knew how to cast spells at a basic level and restricting him to only learning theory was merely going to force him into practising his magical abilities in secret. This line of argument was a particularly powerful one and had gained him access to Master Chevery's class. Unfortunately, whilst his first spell-casting lesson had been successful enough, the second had been an unmitigated disaster.

Annoyingly, the trouble had all been over something that in Calvyn's opinion was completely ludicrous. The class had been set a homework assignment to learn the basic pattern of an illusion spell, and to prepare a suitable illusion for the next lesson. This, Calvyn had done, but he did not understand why a Magician would bother using such a complicated method of producing an illusion. Even a novice Sorcerer could make something equally as effective with a single wave of thought. True, the Magician's illusion could be made permanent, whereas the Sorcerer's lasted only as long as he maintained a tendril of thought on it. Nevertheless, it seemed a lot of effort for something so simple.

Calvyn had prepared his spell meticulously, but with his insight into sorcery, he had explored a second method of achieving the same result with a fraction of the complexity. His chosen illusion had been that of his sword. It was familiar and easy to picture in detail, thus making the rune-casting simpler. Having prepared his pure magic spell, Calvyn also prepared another spell using sorcery to produce the illusion and magic to solidify it. The results were identical, and Calvyn had looked forward to showing off his work. The initial amazement of the Master had been gratifying, but when Calvyn explained how he had achieved the illusion, the look that flickered between outrage and horror that tortured Chevery's face almost caused Calvyn's heart to stop in his chest.

'You did *what*?' Chevery asked incredulously.

'I blended an illusion formed by sorcery with a simple holding sequence of runes to duplicate the effect of the purely magical spell. As you can see, the results are the same, but the effort involved is much less,' Calvyn said, expanding his explanation of the second illusory sword.

'Blasphemy!' the Magician spluttered. 'You come to the finest Magicians' Academy in the world and you have the gall to use *sorcery*! *Here*?'

For a moment, Calvyn thought that Master Chevery's bulging eyes might actually pop out of his head. There was no question that Calvyn was in trouble, deeper than any that the jealousy of other students, or the inflexibility of the Masters had brought him. It appeared that this time he had broken a rule that bordered on being sacrosanct.

'Well, it was not really sorcery, Master Chevery. I agree that it was not true magic either. I suppose that the true description would have to be somewhere in between,' Calvyn said, wishing for all the world that he had never conceived the idea at all.

Master Chevery was virtually apoplectic with rage and outrage by now, and looked as though he was about to explode. His normally serene face was puffed up and red, and he literally quivered with an indescribable fury.

'Out!' the Master yelled suddenly. 'Get out! Now! Go and see Master Jabal and tell *him* of your experiment. We shall see what he thinks of you attending my classes then.'

Calvyn left the room just as fast as his feet would carry him without running. He refused to run, even though his body was itching to do so. Surely, Magicians were not so narrow minded that they would not use a tool because of rivalry, or simply because of a label that placed one arcane art as totally divorced from the others? Calvyn had already discovered many areas in which the teachings of Sorcerers and Magicians overlapped, and who was to say that Wizards, Necromancers and practitioners of other arcane arts did not learn some common skills? In truth, probably the biggest difference between magic and sorcery was that whilst magic was generally used to actually alter and affect things, sorcery was all about appearances. Sorcery could well be described as the art of illusion, so using magic to achieve something for which it was not really suited seemed ludicrous.

Once outside of Chevery's classroom, Calvyn closed the door behind him and took a deep breath. Maybe he should have gone to rescue his friends after all, he reflected mournfully. Facing a whole city of potential enemies seemed by far preferable at this moment to going and facing Master Jabal. Would Jabal really stop him from progressing his practical skills in magic because he had transgressed a rule through pure ignorance? Surely there would be little justice in such a decision.

Dragging his feet dolefully along the corridors, Calvyn made his way slowly to see Master Jabal. When he reached the Grand Magician's classroom, Calvyn could not decide whether he was pleased or horrified that the Master was not teaching. In one way, Calvyn was glad that there were no other students watching, because he did not want any more of the other Acolytes to witness his humiliation. However, having seen Chevery's anger at Calvyn's apparently heinous crime of using sorcery, he could almost wish for witnesses in case Master Jabal did something hasty and unjust.

'Ah! Young Calvyn,' Jabal said, not sounding in the slightest surprised to see him. 'Pray tell me, why are you not in Chevery's class now? Have you so disappointed him that he has sent you back to me already?'

'Well, not disappointed exactly, Master Jabal,' Calvyn said apprehensively. 'I think horrified might be closer to the mark.'

'Really?' Jabal asked, his eyes alight with curiosity. 'And he has sent you to me for judgement I suppose?'

'Yes, Master. At least I think so. He said that I was to tell you what I had done and to see whether you still think that I should be attending his classes.'

'Come then. Tell me what it is that you have done to upset Master Chevery so. It intrigues me that you have managed to get yourself thrown back to me so quickly when you showed so much promise.'

Calvyn explained what had happened and waited for the storm to break, his shoulders tense in anticipation of the inevitable onslaught of emotion. He was surprised though, for there was no barrage from Jabal, only a thoughtful, considered curiosity.

'Sorcery, you say? Yes, it all makes sense now. No wonder your mental imagery is so clear and your mind power so well developed for your years. Being taught by Sorcerers would more than account for that. So how did you come to be sponsored here by Perdimonn if you were trained by Sorcerers?'

Calvyn's mind raced, trying to assess just how much to tell Jabal. Should he admit to his betrayal of the Lords of the Inner Eye? The sect of Sorcerers was, after all, Shandese. The Magicians' Academy claimed to owe allegiance to no empire or nation, but it had been situated in Shandar for hundreds of years. Surely the fact that the Academy had dwelt here so long would give some bias to the thinking of the Masters?

With a start, Calvyn realised that he had paused overly long. Grand Magician Jabal would almost certainly detect a lie now. There was nothing for it but to tell the truth.

'I'm not sure that Perdimonn knew anything of my training by the Lords of the Inner Eye when he sponsored me,' Calvyn admitted slowly. 'My training with the Sorcerers came after I had been parted from Perdimonn for some time. The story is a long one and very involved, but I will share it if you have time.'

Master Jabal considered for a moment and looked about to answer when a discordant bell started ringing loudly from somewhere within the depths of the building. Jabal's face dropped into a deep frown and he thumped his hand down in frustration on his desk top.

'Will they *never* learn?' he exclaimed in exasperation.

'What is it, Master Jabal?'

'Some blasted fool Acolyte has tried to conceal a magical object in his quarters again. They never learn!

Wait here. I'll be back shortly.'

The Grand Magician got up and swept out of the classroom with the purposeful stride of one on an urgent errand, his firm footsteps echoing several other sets that were hurrying along the corridor outside. Whoever had sounded that alarm had certainly stirred up a hornets' nest of activity, Calvyn mused as he tried to decide where to begin his story for Master Jabal on his return. The disturbance had worked in his favour if he wished to conceal things, for he now had a chance to bury anything that he did not want to come to light deep in the innermost areas of his mind before Jabal returned.

The more that Calvyn thought through his recent history, though, the more he perceived the futility of attempting to cover up what he had done. It would quickly become obvious to anyone with their wits about them that Calvyn was not telling the whole truth. There was no doubt that his tale was a strange one, which included many things that an ordinary man would dismiss as fiction. Master Jabal, however, was not an ordinary man. He was a Grand Magician who probably knew more of the arcane arts than Calvyn would ever know and, as such, he would listen with a far more open mind than most.

The door to the classroom swung open again, startling Calvyn such that he jumped to his feet. It was Master Jabal, back much more quickly than Calvyn had anticipated – and he was not alone. Four more Grand Magicians followed him into the room, including Akhdar and Chevery. Also the hulking figure of Lomand lurked in the doorway behind them.

Calvyn's eyes fell on the item in Grand Magician Akhdar's hands and his heart sank. It was his sword.

'Is this yours?' Akhdar asked, his eyes flashing dangerously under his bushy white eyebrows.

Calvyn nodded slowly. There was no point in denying it. In fact Calvyn realised that he should have known the instant Master Jabal named the reason for the alarm that the cause would be his sword. Until that moment,

Calvyn had not been aware of the restriction on Acolytes to not keep magical items in their quarters. The reason for the restriction was not entirely clear to Calvyn, but whatever it was, the presence of the five Grand Magicians right now certainly gave weight to its importance.

'Yes, Master Akhdar, the blade is mine. My apologies for causing such a disturbance, I was not aware of the restriction until a few moments ago. Why, even when told by Master Jabal what the alarm was for I did not think of the sword. I suppose that I have just got used to having it around,' Calvyn explained as confidently as he could.

All of the Masters looked at him disbelievingly, and inside, Calvyn was certain that he was in deep, deep trouble.

'How could you not know of such a basic rule?' Master Chevery asked, quite obviously pleased to see Calvyn in such a difficult position.

'Ignorance is no excuse,' one of the other Grand Magicians added grimly.

'Normally, I would agree with you,' Akhdar said carefully, interrupting before Calvyn had a chance to try to defend himself further. 'This circumstance is a little different from most though. Calvyn only arrived a little over a week ago and has not had much of the early groundwork teaching that is drummed into most new Acolytes. Therefore, it is quite conceivable that he would not know some of the rules here. It is up to us, as teachers and overseers, to ensure that we impart all of the pertinent knowledge to Calvyn, and every other new Acolyte that misses the indoctrination lectures.'

Akhdar paused for a moment or two to allow his words to sink in, and then to everyone's astonishment he handed the sword over to Calvyn.

'Here – you had better take this back, for it is obviously of no use to anyone else here.'

'But will the sword not cause the same fuss on the next time that the Acolytes' rooms are checked?' Calvyn asked dubiously.

Akhdar blinked as if dumbstruck for a few seconds. All of the other Magicians were still watching him, not quite sure what the old Master was thinking of.

'Oh... er, yes. I suppose that it would at that,' Akhdar answered uncertainly.

'Are you all right, Akhdar? You are not making any sense at the moment,' Jabal asked, concern running deep in his voice. 'What properties does that sword have, Calvyn? What spells have been laid on the blade that might cause Akhdar to act out of character?' he asked, his attention switching suddenly, as the new train of thought struck him.

Calvyn considered for a moment and then gave a small gasp as he put two and two together.

'There is one possibility, Master Jabal,' Calvyn replied quickly. 'I laid a compulsion on the blade such that it would encourage any who handled it to return it to me. There are other spells, but it could be that the sword is fogging Master Akhdar's mind in an attempt to get back into my possession. I had not thought that the compulsion would be strong enough to work on a powerful Magician. I wonder...'

Calvyn's eyes were the ones to glaze this time, as a strange and wondrous thought occurred to him.

'Yes, Calvyn? What is it that you wonder?' Jabal asked curiously.

'I wonder if that is why Selkor gave me the sword back at Mantor?' Calvyn said in a rush. 'You see, he took it from me and I had heard that he collected objects of power, so I just assumed that when he handed it back and described it as a toy that it was not really of any great value. Now I am beginning to wonder whether the compulsion was such that it fooled even Selkor into returning the sword to me.'

The five Grand Magicians glanced around at one another as if looking for any support to Calvyn's theory. There was a brief exchange between some of them on a telepathic level, but Calvyn caught none of it. To him it was like the murmuring whispers that echoed unintelligibly around one of the great city temples at prayer hour. Occasionally, a word would seem to pop up that was tantalising in its familiarity, but still it made no sense.

The Magicians obviously reached a decision because as one they turned to face Calvyn again. Five sets of penetrating eyes drilled at Calvyn, not hostile, but searching, each attempting to discover truth from deep within him. It was most unnerving; Calvyn felt stripped of all ability to hide anything from those intense, powerful minds, but he stood his ground. Using every ounce of determination that he possessed he forced the truth of the forging of his sword to the front of his mind.

'Calvyn,' Akhdar started, sounding much more sure of himself again, 'we have all agreed that there is little point in any of us taking the sword for safekeeping, as without weaving spells to counter the compulsion, it is likely that we would just give it back to you one way or another. It would be better all round if you were to place it somewhere for safekeeping – somewhere like my study for instance, where you can come and recover it should you feel the need. I am assuming that if you stored it there, then the compulsion would not be triggered, is that right?'

'Well, I'm not really sure, Master. It does make sense though.'

'Very well, come and bring your sword to my study. I would like to learn what spells you have placed upon it aside from the compulsion before we are done today. Just so that I am not caught off guard if I am to look after it.'

Akhdar led Calvyn out of the room and down the corridor to the right towards his already cluttered study. Behind them the four Grand Magicians broke into open discussion the moment that they left the room.

'He should be expelled from the college right now,' Chevery exploded angrily. 'First he used an abomination spell in my class and now this. I do not care who has sponsored him, it could be the Creator Himself for all it matters, that young man is a danger to us all.'

'Yes, but a danger in what sense, Chevery? You saw what just happened. An object, spellbound by that young man, who could barely be described as a junior Acolyte as yet, just fooled Akhdar into doing something against his will. When was the last time you saw an object so bound in magic, other than the Staff of Dantillus, the Cloak of Merridom, or the Ring of Nadus? Never, I'll guess!' Jabal answered calmly.

'And what does that have to do with anything?'

'Oh, come on, Chevery! The boy has all the hallmarks of greatness virtually stamped on his forehead. Here we are, a withered bunch of old fools, too frightened to go out and face what we know that we must and along comes this prodigy. What are we to do? Throw him out of the Academy because he does not fit into the comfortable mould that we usually hammer the Acolytes into? Do not be hasty, Chevery. Before long, we are going to need all of the strength that we can muster if we are to face Selkor. I fear that even with such raw talent and power that young Calvyn displays, our chances are worse than slim. We cannot afford to be narrow-minded, not with Selkor having already gained access to one Elemental Key of Power.'

'Pah! What good will one more undisciplined Acolyte do against the power, knowledge and experience of a Magician like Selkor?' Chevery mocked. 'Are you going as senile as old Akhdar then? He should have given the sword to me. I would have put it out of Calvyn's reach.'

Jabal looked at Chevery sadly and shook his head. He turned briefly to the other two Grand Magicians with a mute appeal in his eyes, but their response was non-committal, as if they were not sure on which side of the argument to fall.

'I doubt that you would have fared any better than Akhdar, Chevery,' Jabal said, his voice measured and resigned to Chevery's prejudice. 'That blade had a truly complex weave of spells around it. Also, there is power in the blade of a depth that I would never have thought possible in something made by one with so little knowledge. The binding is clever, complex and true. Who amongst even us here could claim to have made such a thing? None! What is more – you know it. The truth is that we as an Academy, and we as a Council, have become hidebound in tradition and overly comfortable in our customs. The boy is unorthodox – that is granted, but he does have talent. Talent that is raw and untamed. Let us harness that talent and use some of his radical ideas to our advantage before we all rot in our musty old robes!'

Chevery grunted sourly and frowned as he sensed the other two Grand Magicians becoming swayed by Jabal's arguments.

'Talent or no talent, I will *not* have him using sorcery in my class again,' Chevery growled, and then shouldered his way between his colleagues and out through the door.

Jabal shrugged at his fellow Masters, while the angry, pounding footfalls of Chevery retreated at pace away down the corridor.

Akhdar led Calvyn through the maze of passages to his study. The cluttered room was as fascinating to Calvyn as it had been on his first visit, if not more so. Now that Calvyn had soaked himself in the books allocated as reading material for Acolytes, he appreciated even more the value of what was collected here in this room. The grimoires of many Magicians lined whole shelves with lifetimes of accumulated spells. Gathered alongside the tomes of magic was volume after volume of knowledge on just about any subject that one could think of. From plant classification to bridge building, from geology to the study of the movement of the stars in the heavens, there seemed to be books that covered every subject. Calvyn could not help but marvel and wonder if Akhdar had read even half of what was stored here. If so, then he must be knowledgeable indeed, Calvyn thought, lost in wonder at the thought of having the opportunity to study such treasures.

'Here, young Calvyn, come and place your sword over

here,' Akhdar suggested politely, gesturing to a place in a corner of the study next to an old wooden staff.

Calvyn followed promptly and carefully balanced the sword, in its scabbard, point down and hilt into the corner. It was only as he was turning to leave the sword that Calvyn really took note of the top of the staff. The carved fist clenching a red gemstone that had been crafted as the top knob of the Magician's staff was unmistakeable.

'That's the Staff of Dantillus!' Calvyn exclaimed, unable to restrain his tongue.

Akhdar smiled at Calvyn's incredulity.

'Indeed it is, young man. So you have heard of it? That is interesting... very interesting,' Akhdar said thoughtfully.

'Well, Master, not heard of as such. I read about it a couple of evenings ago. I think that it was in one of the volumes about the history of the Academy. If I remember correctly, this staff is older even than Darkweaver's amulet.'

'Indeed it is. A hundred and fifty years older. Dantillus was an extraordinary Magician by all accounts. Do you know any more of him?'

'No, Master... that is, I know that he made the Staff to aid the channelling of spells. It is said that it focuses spells in the same way that a convex glass lens focuses light. Of the man, Dantillus, the book said little.'

Akhdar nodded wisely and ran his fingers thoughtfully through his beard, as if assessing quite how much information he should reveal.

'Dantillus was a radical,' he said eventually. 'He was all but exiled from the Brotherhood of Magicians. Does that surprise you?'

Calvyn nodded, remaining quiet in the hope that Akhdar would tell him more. He was not to be disappointed.

'Dantillus did not hold with the views of the majority of the Magicians of his day. He felt very strongly that magic should be used as a tool for the good of the masses.

Apparently he was not the most powerful deliverer of spells, but he was innovative. To make up for his lack of power, Dantillus fashioned this staff to enhance the effectiveness of his spells. The effect of the staff was not quite what he had envisioned, but unknowingly he paved the way for another Magician to succeed in creating a true magical amplifier some ten years or so after his death. Do you know what it is that I am describing?'

'I'm not sure, Master Akhdar, but if I was to guess, then I would have to say the Ring of Nadus,' Calvyn answered.

'Very good. You are quite right. Shortly after that, a Grand Magician called Merridom fashioned a cloak that aided transformation spells, or shape-shifting spells as they are sometimes called. After all three had passed away, the Staff, the Ring and the Cloak were all used by the Council of Magicians and held in the Academy for study and use only in times of dire need. Now two of those icons have been stolen.'

'Selkor!' Calvyn breathed.

'Correct again. Do you also know of the Keys of Power?' Akhdar asked, his blue eyes sparkling particularly brightly.

'No, Master. Perdimonn mentioned something about Keys, but he was not specific and I've not come across anything in my reading so far. All that I know for certain is Perdimonn's message to you, which told me two important things. Firstly, Selkor is apparently trying to gain the Keys, and secondly, he has already gained at least one of them. What the ramifications of Selkor's latest acquisition are, I honestly have no idea. The tone of Perdimonn's message suggested that this turn of events was of the direst consequence, so I am guessing that the Keys are very important.'

'Your guess is most astute, Calvyn, but I do not think that now is quite the right time to enlighten you. Please, keep what you know, and what you suspect, to yourself. Do not discuss these things with anyone other than the Masters, and only then if you have something new to tell. Something tells me that one way or another, you will know as much of these things as the Masters do before all is complete. Somehow, you are tied up in the current crisis in a way that I do not pretend to understand. Events seem to twist you into the centre of things in a way that suggests higher powers at work. My only advice to you is one of common sense: study like you have never studied before, Calvyn. What you learn over the next few days, weeks or months, before events sweep you away again, may dictate the fates of us all.'

Akhdar's words sounded very melodramatic to Calvyn's mind, but the old Magician was obviously deadly serious, so Calvyn nodded and schooled his features into a sombre front. It was true, Calvyn thought grimly, that circumstances had dragged him into pivotal positions during the recent conflicts in Thrandor. Now that he was here at the Academy, though, it appeared highly unlikely that he was going to be called upon to do anything unless it was to be punishment duties for breaking yet more rules.

Calvyn glanced back at his sword. If it could speak, then it would certainly be boasting of the company that it kept, standing as it was, next to the Staff of Dantillus. Calvyn smiled to himself at the thought of his sword talking. Praise Tarmin that he had not tried to include anything so foolish into the spells that he had placed on the blade.

'What is the matter, Calvyn? Does the blade exert an influence over you as well?' Akhdar asked, intrigued by the look that Calvyn had given the sword.

'No, Master, not at all. I was merely thinking nonsense. By your leave, I should be returning to my lessons now.'

Calvyn hoped fervently that Akhdar knew nothing of his being cast out of Master Chevery's lesson earlier. Although Akhdar was bound to find out eventually, Calvyn did not really want another roasting just now. To his intense relief, the Grand Magician mentioned nothing of the incident, but merely dismissed Calvyn to return to his class. Making the most of this turn of fortune, Calvyn made for the door as swiftly as courtesy allowed, but just before he made his exit, Akhdar stopped him in his tracks.

'Wait just one moment, Calvyn,' he ordered peremptorily. 'I meant to ask you to describe just what other spells that you have woven into this blade. Indeed, I am intrigued that you could weave any at all, for steel is all but impervious to magic. Tales of magic blades in the legends and histories are, for the most part, a fabrication of the minstrels to add colour to the stories of the heroes of ages past.'

Calvyn smiled at the memory of the great hulking figure of Gerran, the Master Smith who resided in the smithy at Keevan's Castle, being adamant that forging the sword was a waste of good metal. Gerran had been convinced that Calvyn was mad to attempt to blend silver with steel, for even a novice blacksmith knew that the two would not mix.

'Well, Master Akhdar, to tell the truth I did not bind the spells into the steel, for I was aware that to do so was all but impossible. So I sort of improvised,' Calvyn confessed. His face reddened slightly, as he thought of what the Acolytes had told him about the designing of new spells and how much research and deliberation was carried out before trying something new. If the Master realised how little thought had gone into this in comparison, then Calvyn could be sure that he would be up to his neck in seriously hot water.

'Improvised? And just how did you do that?' Akhdar asked, his voice more curious than anything else. Calvyn explained what he had done: the fooling of the Smith into thinking the silver was special, the effects that he had tried to set into the blade and the mysterious way that the runes had appeared on the tang of the sword.

'Fascinating!' Akhdar exclaimed softly when Calvyn had completed his story. 'You blended the silver and steel with a form of diffusion spell, which, if you were not aware, draws its power from the water element. The flame spell drew from the fire element, the lightness spell from the air element and the binding spell from the earth element. All four elements were utilised in one form or another. Your ingenuity has served you very well, young Calvyn. I suspect that you have wrought an effect far more powerful than you ever imagined, and you did it by instinct. Interesting – very interesting indeed.'

The old Magician scratched at his beard for a moment whilst contemplating the sword that was standing up against the wall.

'Calvyn, listen – this is important. Firstly, do any of the Acolytes know anything of the sword?'

Calvyn shook his head.

'Good. I would like you to keep it that way please. By all means talk with the other Masters about it, but only in private, and only when there is no chance of you being overheard. The less people that know of the sword, the better.'

Akhdar scanned his bookshelves, obviously searching for something in particular. Then, with a grunt of satisfaction, he picked up a small set of steps and placed it carefully against the packed shelving.

'Here, add this to your reading list. You might wish to read it sooner rather than later. When you have done so, return it to me here.'

Akhdar pulled a dusty old book down from a high shelf, blew the excess dust from it, and handed it to Calvyn. Hovering at the doorway and poised for a quick exit, Calvyn took the old book almost reverently for it was obviously ancient. There was no doubt in Calvyn's mind that this was one book that would definitely not be on the Acolytes' general reading list.

'Thank you, Master, I will read it as soon as I may,' he murmured thankfully. Then he left the room and closed the door quietly behind him.

Quietly excited, he looked down and read the cover of the book that Akhdar had lent him. *The Oracles of Drehboor – Seer of Shantillia*, he read, struggling even with the lettering on the cover. A strange book to lend, Calvyn mused. It was not the normal sort of literature that the Masters recommended to Acolytes, that much was certain. Still, Akhdar would not have lent him such a book without purpose, Calvyn reasoned, so he resolved to take it back to his quarters quickly before returning to see Master Jabal. For some reason, Calvyn had a feeling that the other Masters might not wholly approve of Akhdar's decision to lend him this book, so he resolved not to let any of them find out about it from him.

A few minutes later he had hidden the book in his room underneath some of his clothes in the little press. It was hardly a secure hiding place, but the Acolyte's quarter did not lend itself to concealing anything. Still, with the room having just been searched once after the incident with his sword, Calvyn doubted that anyone would search it again for a few days. The book would be safe enough, he decided.

As he had not completed his talk with Master Jabal earlier, Calvyn elected to return to find him before attempting to gain re-entry to Master Chevery's class. Wincing in anticipation of his welcome, Calvyn wondered how friendly his reception would be this time. Getting thrown out of Master Chevery's class was one thing, but being responsible for all of the Masters being called from whatever they had been doing was quite another. Things were not working out at all the way Calvyn had expected, yet he had been trying just as hard as he could with every moment the day brought.

On reaching Jabal's classroom, Calvyn gave a tentative knock on the door. The 'Come in,' that ordered him past its archway sounded very irritated. Calvyn took a deep breath and swallowed hard against the lump that seemed to have formed in his throat. Becoming a Magician, it seemed, was not going to be an easy road.

CHAPTER 11

Derra awoke with a start as the door to her prison opened. The guard was in through the door and had dumped a pile of equipment on the floor before Derra had managed to move.

'Wait!' she called after the guard as he began to leave without saying anything. 'What is all that lot for?'

'What does it look like?' the guard spat angrily. 'For some reason Garvin is under the impression that you might just stand a chance in the arena against one of the *real* fighters. He always likes a novelty, does Garvin. If you survive, I get the impression that you will be billed as something of a showpiece – "The first woman arena fighter in Shandrim in a hundred years". You had better get dressed. Garvin had that stuff made especially to make you at least *look* the part. I'll be back to take you up to the arena shortly.'

The guard left and Derra took a closer look at the pile of things that he had left behind. There was a thick leather skirt, studded with steel that was marginally longer than the embarrassingly short skirt that Fesha had supplied. A jerkin of the same material was shaped to accentuate her feminine curves, whilst calf length leather boots and leather wrist guards were purely practical. There was a hardened leather helmet as well, but Derra discarded it the instant that she tried it on. The eyeholes were well placed, but she found even the marginal reduction in peripheral vision unbearable. Derra had never fought in such a constricting helmet before and saw no reason to start now.

The rest of the gear fitted remarkably well. How Garvin had gauged Derra's size so accurately she could not begin to guess. Indeed, the thought was irrelevant. What mattered was that she had been provided with a fine set of protective gear. There were no weapons, but that was hardly surprising. Only a fool would furnish a prisoner with weapons and then leave her unsupervised, and Derra had already deduced that the Arena Master was no fool.

Garvin had been there when Derra had regained consciousness. The strangely deformed little man had already worked out much about Derra before she had awoken. Just about the only thing that he did not seem to know was her name, and Derra had seen little value in trying to deceive him about something so meaningless. For some reason, Garvin had been almost amused by the attempt to rescue Bek, which Derra found strange, as they would probably have succeeded if only Bek had come with them straight away.

The Arena Master had quizzed Derra about the other two would-be rescuers, but she had told him nothing. Indeed, Derra had learned more from the interrogation than Garvin, for the fact that he had asked about her two companions confirmed to Derra the one piece of information that she had really been interested in – that Fesha and Eloise had escaped. That meant they were out in Shandrim somewhere, probably hidden, and almost certainly planning a way of rescuing her.

Derra had expected to be taken and put in the cells with the other prisoners, but instead had found herself locked in a room of her own. The room was hardly luxurious, but it was not uncomfortable and Derra had spent the last six days nursing her swollen left eye back to normality. There was enough floor space for her to exercise as well, so Derra had passed several hours a day pushing her body through a gruelling routine. Escape from here was unlikely to be achieved without a fight, she reasoned, so it was only sensible to be as prepared as possible for that eventuality.

Now it appeared that Derra's preparation was not to be in vain. Though the Sergeant had been preparing herself to have to fight her way along the corridors and out of the building, her determination to stay fit and able to fight would pay equal dividends in a hand-to-hand arena fight.

The arena fighters were good swordsmen – Derra had seen that much during the games last week. Also, they all appeared to be very fit and strong. In that respect, Derra knew that she would be at something of a disadvantage, for although she was fit, skilled and fast, the Sergeant could never hope to put on enough muscle to truly contend with the majority of these men for pure brute force. 'Still,' she thought, a quiet smile pulling her lips up at the corners, 'if there hasn't been a woman fighter in the arena for a hundred years, then it's unlikely that the man I face will have fought a woman before.' That fact brought its own advantages.

The sound of booted feet approached down the corridor outside and stopped outside Derra's door. A key rattled in the lock and the door swung open once more. Two guards had come this time. The one who had brought the fighting gear stepped inside and eyed her approvingly.

'You'll do,' he said gruffly, and waved her out into the corridor. 'Come on! Hurry up! You don't want to keep Garvin waiting. He is very strict on punctuality. The punishment for being late for anything here is very severe – in many cases fatal.'

Derra was ushered out and forced along the corridors at a brisk walk. The noise of the crowds above cheering and jeering, ebbed and flowed as they went, wafting down stairwells and diffusing along the passages. Then, when they reached the set of steps up which the guards directed her, the noise began to get louder and louder. The images of last week's games flooded back and Derra drew comfort from the fact that despite being high in the stands, she had still made observations on weaknesses of the swordsmen that she had seen fight. Even Serrius had not been faultless, for Jez had managed to open a cut on the man's face. However, Serrius had been formidable in his response to that cut and Derra harboured no desire to fight such a swordsman. To do so would be to court death in such a way that compared evenly with being in the midst of a raging battle, completely outnumbered and with little chance of victory. Somehow Derra felt she would have more hope of leaving such a battlefield without taking the dark spectre's hand, than facing Serrius would offer.

They reached the fighters' pit with the wooden gate that opened out into the arena. Three other fighters were waiting to enter the arena and were each covering their nervousness in different ways. One sat apparently calm on a bench, though the way that his eyes kept darting to the gate with every loud cheer gave voice to his apprehension. Another was working through a series of limbering-up exercises, whilst the third was quite openly praying. Bek was not among them.

Derra turned to the guard who had brought her the protective leather gear and asked him which of the three she would be fighting.

'None of them,' the guard replied sourly, as if her lack of knowledge was somehow offensive. 'You go out of that door, your opponent will enter the arena from somewhere else.'

Thinking back, Derra realised that this was indeed what had happened the previous week. Maybe that was what was making the three men so nervous. Not knowing whether you faced a novice or a Master Swordsman before entering the arena was enough to set even the most accomplished of fighters on edge. It was affecting Derra as well, but instead of trying to bury the nervousness, Derra embraced it. A healthy nervousness would sharpen her senses and, providing she did not allow the feeling to overwhelm her, the energy that the nervousness generated should prove beneficial.

A great cheer went up outside and a guard standing at an observation port, next to the door into the arena, beckoned to the fighter who was still stretching and exercising his muscles.

'You're up, Charis. Good luck.'

Charis nodded and drew his sword. The guard took one further quick look through the observation port and then opened the gate to let Charis out.

The noise of the crowd invaded the pit like a flood and Derra felt a sudden surge of adrenaline rush into her stomach. In a few minutes time she would have to walk through that gate and fight. The noise in the stadium was unlike anything that she had experienced in battle before. Battles were noisy, confusing, and chaotic. The noise here though was almost coordinated. Everyone was reacting with noise at the same moments, the result of which was great crescendos of ear splitting volume and a mind-numbing intensity of emotion.

Unexpectedly, the guard called Derra forward next and her stomach turned over again.

'OK, lady, it's your turn next. Good luck – you're going to need it.'

Gritting her teeth in a semi-snarl, Derra snatched the short sword and the dagger that the guard was holding out to her. For a split second she was tempted to kill him where he stood, but common sense took over and instead, when the gate opened, she strode out into the arena as confidently as she could.

It was bright in the arena, far brighter than it had been in the pits. Derra squinted against the light and stopped for a moment to look around. Her opponent was to her left and was moving onward towards the centre of the dusty floored arena. He was young, Derra noted, and he looked every inch the part of an arena fighter.

The man moved easily on the balls of his feet, his gait exuding an energy and enthusiasm that marked him as either very good at what he did, or very inexperienced. To just look at him, Derra guessed at the latter, but she was determined not to underestimate her opponent before they crossed blades.

Drawing his sword, the fighter saluted the Emperor's balcony. Derra had no intention of saluting anyone here, though she could not resist glancing up at where the Emperor sat watching. The Emperor was leaning forward slightly in his chair and looking straight at Derra as if intrigued by the prospect of seeing a woman fight.

'If it's a fight you want, then you won't be disappointed,' Derra snarled quietly to herself as she looked back at her opponent.

With a slight grunt of annoyance, she noted that he was left-handed. Derra could fight equally effectively with both hands, but she slightly favoured the right. Fighting right-handed against a left-handed opponent always seemed awkward somehow. Still, to switch hands with her weapons now would only give away the element of surprise at that ability, so she advanced with her sword gripped firmly in her right hand and her dagger in her left.

The man saluted her formally with his sword, clashing it noisily against the small round shield that he carried instead of a dagger. Derra simply nodded an acknowledgement of that gesture and then leapt nimbly forward to strike quickly and test his defence. The man's blade danced up to meet hers and for a few seconds the sound of steel resounding on steel rang out its tones amid the yelling, screaming encouragement of the crowds.

Even in those first few seconds, Derra learned enough to realise that both of her earlier surmises had been true. The man possessed a lot of raw talent, but he was also as green as a fresh spring shoot shunting its way out of the earth. Derra would have to be careful, but she was sure now that she was not facing a Master Swordsman.

With a flashing series of strokes, Derra pushed forward again, testing the man's defences at every corner. The fighter blocked and countered well throughout the rapid exchange, and some of his counterstrokes were fast and very well thought out, Derra noted grimly. This was not going to be a fight that she would wish to drag out in any way.

Suddenly, the man launched his own attack and Derra

found herself backing away under a seeming rain of heavy blows. The barrage of strokes was fast and hard, but repetitive. Derra countered them comfortably enough despite being physically driven back, and within a few moments had developed an effective counter-attack sequence that left the man with a scored jerkin and a shallow slice on his upper arm.

The fighter backed off for a moment, a new respect showing in his eyes, and that was when Derra played her trump card. In a lightning fast exchange, Derra swapped the sword into her left hand and the dagger to her right, then sprang straight into the attack before the man had a chance to mentally adjust to the difference.

The following few seconds were not pretty. Derra opened several more gashes on the man's sword arm and managed to stab through the leather jerkin and into the man's side with her dagger. The wound was not fatal, but it was certainly incapacitating. The fighter could no longer stand truly upright, as the pain in his side was too great to be ignored. He backed away and saluted, then laid his sword aside in a signal of surrender and clutched at his wound. Blood dribbled through his fingers in a steady flow.

'You had better get that looked at by your medics,' Derra growled, her gravelly voice rasping and harsh.

The man nodded, but Derra had already turned her back and started walking back to the wooden door through which she had entered. When she got inside, the guards greeted her with a wary respect. There was no point in attempting to fight her way out of here. There were several guards and Derra already felt emotionally and physically drained by her fight in the arena. Recognising the futility of resistance, Derra handed back her weapons without a fuss.

Before being led out of the pit and back into the maze of passages to her room, Derra spotted Bek sitting on a bench by the wall. He was grim-faced and silent, his eyes cold and deadly in their intensity. This was not like the Bek that Derra knew of old. He did not show so much as a flicker of recognition, or even awareness, of her presence. It was as if he was lost in a world of his own, unfeeling and uncaring of anything outside the prison of his mind.

Derra's assessment of Bek was not far removed from the truth. He had been aware of her return and deep within him, his soul rejoiced that she had survived the encounter in the arena. For now, though, his thoughts and focus were totally fixed on the opponent that he knew awaited him when he walked out through the gate. Unfortunately, the opponent was not the one that Bek most wanted to face. Serrius had, as Hammar had predicted, declined Bek's challenge. Instead, Tabernar, ranked twenty-fifth in the table of ranked fighters and the highest ranking fighter that Bek was allowed to formally challenge under the arena rules, awaited him beyond the gate. If Bek won the bout, then he would assume the ranking position of his opponent.

Bek had no grudge against Tabernar. Indeed, he had sparred against him in one of the recent training sessions and had enjoyed some light-hearted banter with the fighter while they had practiced. Bek had also learned plenty of respect for Tabernar's speed and strength, though he was fairly certain that he had identified a weakness in the ranked fighter's style. Today would prove whether or not his suspicion was correct.

The only way that Bek could guarantee to face Serrius in the arena was to rise through the ranks into the top five. Only then would Bek be allowed to challenge Jez's killer and attempt to exact his revenge. Of course, if Serrius were to challenge Bek, then Bek would get his wish early, but Serrius had no real reason to challenge anyone, except maybe to keep in practice. He could afford to sit back and wait for any challengers to come to him, as he all but owned the top ranking spot now and there was no one else who wished to face him.

Bek felt guilty that his desire for revenge had caused Derra to get captured and forced into the arena, but he also knew that Derra could look after herself. There were few among even the ranked fighters here who could match her weapon skills. It would take Garvin a while to work that out of course, so barring mishaps, Bek was fairly convinced that Derra would stay alive for some time yet. That period of uncertainty would give Fesha and Eloise a chance to rescue her and get her well away from here. Bek just hoped that they would waste no further time on him. His mind was firmly set. His first priority was to take his revenge on Serrius. Once that had been achieved, he would look towards finding and confronting Calvyn, or Shanier, or whoever he really was.

'Come on, Thrandorian! You're up next. Look sharp.'

The guard was standing right in front of him and Bek suddenly realised that he had been so lost in his thoughts that the guard might well have already spoken to him several times. Bek got to his feet and brushed past the guard as if he was not there. The gate was already opening, so Bek just continued walking straight out into the brightness of the arena.

In his mind, Bek had decided to follow all protocols of the arena to the letter. The last thing that he needed was to have a fight disallowed on a technicality, so he marched out to the centre of the dusty bowl and saluted the Emperor's balcony. Tabernar was about half a pace behind him and that was precisely where Bek intended to keep his opponent throughout this fight.

With the formalities complete, Bek and Tabernar began to circle one another. Both fighters had opted to carry a single blade and no shield, so neither man was hampered by any cumbersome extra equipment. To look at the two, there was little to separate them for grace of movement. Tabernar was very slightly taller with a fractionally heavier muscular build, but otherwise they could almost have been cast from the same mould.

The Emperor sat transfixed. This was going to be a fascinating contest. He remembered only too well how quickly the Thrandorian had killed Barrock, a well-respected fighter of several seasons. However, Barrock had been complacent. Tabernar, on the other hand, was wise to Bek's skill and ready to test him to the full. For the first time since Serrius had taken on five tyros in one bout, the Emperor did not really have an inkling of which way the fight would go. The uncertainty set his blood racing.

One of the courtiers nearby called out a wager of a hundred gold sen on Tabernar to win at two to one odds.

'I'll take that wager,' the Emperor stated loudly, his eyes never leaving the circling fighters.

Everyone else in the Imperial Box looked around at one another in shock. The Emperor had not gambled on a fight in two seasons. This was a strange bout to choose to break from that long abstinence... and to bet on the Thrandorian! The interest level in the fight suddenly increased immensely amongst the Emperor's toadies. Did the Emperor know something of this Thrandorian that they did not? Was the Thrandorian a part of some scheme or plot that the Emperor was hatching? Or could it be that the Emperor had arranged for the Thrandorian to be brought to the arena and had rigged his fights? The Emperor was certainly devious enough for any of these things to be true.

The Emperor, in fact, was almost oblivious to the stir that he had caused amongst those around him – almost. He did allow himself a sly smile, for his sycophantic advisers and courtiers would all probably spend the next few weeks trying to find out all that they could about any possible links that the Emperor had with the Thrandorian. That should keep them off balance sufficiently for him to slide some other more important things past them without notice.

Tabernar made the first attack, springing at Bek and driving blow after blow in a rapid sequence of shifting strokes. Bek gave ground, but parried each attacking blow with comfortable ease.

With eyes hard as agate, Bek concentrated fiercely on Tabernar's upper body, watching the body-set, balance and shift of muscles. Instinct and experience did the rest, and he danced the deadly tango of blades with a precision and speed greater than anything he had ever known in the past. What had always been a skill to be drawn on now became a natural extension of what he was. The shifting patterns of the two blades made perfect sense and fitted together in a strange symmetry that would have been impossible to articulate in words. Strengths and weaknesses to the pattern also became obvious but, to begin with, Bek did not exploit the weaknesses for he did not want to lose the wonder of his newfound discovery.

Tabernar disengaged from his attack and a glance at the fighter's eyes told Bek that his opponent now knew he was outmatched. Bek was now positive that providing he maintained his concentration, the victory was his to take. There was no point in dragging the fight out. Kaan had taught him that during his training at Keevan's Castle. If you dragged out a fight unnecessarily, you merely allowed fate more time to intervene and take away the victory that was rightly yours.

Moving forward smoothly, Bek turned the tide of the fight and began his own offensive. The ring of steel on steel sang loud in his ears and the patterns once again filled his mind with their intricacies. A poor shift of balance was instantly identified and exploited, Bek's blade connecting hard with Tabernar's left side. The hardened leather jerkin protected Tabernar from being sliced open, but Bek could see that the clout to the side of his opponent's rib cage had made his breathing less regular.

A moment later and Bek had opened a deep slice in Tabernar's sword arm that pumped blood from a severed artery. Bek stepped back. The fight was over. He had no intention of killing the now defenceless fighter unnecessarily. The only life he was interested in taking was that of Serrius and it was satisfaction enough to have just moved one large step up the ladder towards the chance to make that goal a reality. At the moment, Bek suspected that Serrius was a better swordsman than he, but that did not matter one iota. Bek wanted revenge so desperately that he would rather walk into the arena knowing he was going to die fighting Serrius, than to walk away and let Jez's untimely death go unavenged.

Bek turned and saluted the Emperor. Strangely, it was then that Bek noticed the cheering of the crowds for the first time since entering the arena. His mind had been so fixed on the fight with Tabernar that it had shut out all else.

The Emperor was applauding.

Bek suddenly remembered the comment of Selek, the prisoner, about how infrequently the Emperor showed any emotion, or approval of fights.

'So the Emperor was impressed by the fight,' Bek muttered under his breath. 'I wonder if gaining the Emperor's notice and approval might be useful?'

His mind raced as he ran through the possibilities. Would the Emperor allow him to challenge Serrius out of turn? It was a possibility that might bear some thought. Bek would just have to make sure that he established himself firmly at the forefront of the Emperor's thoughts, he decided. With a grim smile to himself, he realised that he knew just the way to achieve exactly that result.

Striding back into the pits, Bek was greeted by an enthusiastic welcome from both the guards and the two tyro fighters who were waiting for their turns to fight. Nadreck was there as well, but the highly ranked fighter ignored Bek with an arrogant disdain.

'Good fight, Thrandorian. I guess that we're going to have to put a lock on the door of Tabernar's old room now!' one of the guards noted with a chuckle.

'Don't bother,' Bek replied coolly. 'I'll not be sleeping there tonight.'

'Why not?' asked Karoth, one of the tyro fighters who had first taken Bek to see Garvin. 'You're a ranked fighter now. That entitles you to some privileges, even if you are not a free man.'

'I will not be sleeping there, because one way or another I will no longer be ranked twenty-five,' Bek stated matter of factly. 'Guard, would you go and advise Bitranis that he is challenged. I will meet him in the afternoon bouts.'

There was a sharp intake of breath at this. Even Nadreck looked at Bek sharply. However, later that evening, sitting in his comparatively luxurious suite of two rooms, Bek reflected with satisfaction that he had done exactly the right thing. The Emperor, along with everyone else who had been present in the stadium that day, would be thinking and talking of nothing else but the explosive emergence of a newly ranked fighter into the games – a Thrandorian fighter whom, as a lowly prisoner, had already gained some fame for having killed the ranked fighter, Barrock, with nothing but a short sword. Now, in a single day, the same Thrandorian had made not one, but two successful challenges, climbing a full third of the way up the ranking table in one fell swoop.

Ranked at twenty, Bek was entitled to challenge any of the five fighters ranked immediately ahead of him on the table. The simple fact was that, to Bek, four of those five were irrelevant to his purpose. It was the fighter ranked at number fifteen that he would face next. Who that was, Bek did not have a clue. What was more, he did not care. All that mattered was to face Serrius and the fewer fights he had to take part in to meet that objective, the better.

To Bek's surprise, despite having beaten Bitranis in the afternoon session of fights, it was Tabernar's rooms that he had moved into that evening. Bek had never really understood the way that the system of rooms worked for the ranked fighters, as he had not really had much interest in it until now. It transpired that anyone ranked twenty-five to thirty, beaten by an unranked fighter, lost his ranking altogether and moved out of the suites. The suites for the fighters ranking from thirty up to sixteen were all pretty much identical, therefore any moves in ranking within those numbers did not mean that the fighters had to swap accommodation. From a ranking of fifteen up to six, there were a set of more sumptuous suites, and from rank five to one, each accommodation was different, getting more luxurious at every increase in rank.

The ranking system worked on a ladder system. A fighter could challenge another up to five ranking places higher than his own for that fighter's place on the ladder. If the challenger won, the displaced fighter moved down by one rank, as did any intermediately ranked fighters, unless the defeated fighter was killed, in which case all of the fighters in the ladder below would move up one place. The accommodation system was such that only the very highest ranking fighters and those middle ranked fighters at the changeover rank of fifteen/sixteen would be likely to move on a fairly frequent basis.

A polite knock at the door seemed ludicrous, followed, as it was, by the jangling rattle of keys in the newly fitted lock outside. The door opened and Hammar, the Weapons Master, entered, his eyes filled with questions and his rapid steps conveying a sense of agitation that Bek, in turn, found curious.

'What can I say, Bek? Well done does not seem to begin to cover it. That trick you used to disarm Bitranis, would you mind teaching it to me? I did not quite see what it was that you did, but it was very effective.'

Hammar looked hard at Bek, trying to assess how he would react to the request.

'Thank you, Hammar,' Bek acknowledged with a wintry smile. 'I will gladly teach you the trick, for you have taught me much – but not just yet. I may need it again shortly, and the less that the others can glean of my little tricks for the moment, the better. Give me just a few more weeks and I will teach you every little trick that I know.'

Hammar nodded.

'So you are aiming high then?'

'Is there anywhere else to aim?' Bek asked, scorn for the question leaking into his tone.

'No, but with you it is more than that. This is personal. I can see it in your eyes and I witnessed your vow. Revenge for your friend is a poor reason to get yourself killed in this fashion. You are after Serrius, that much is plain – so plain that every fighter in the arena is talking of nothing else. He watched you fight today, you know?'

'Who? Serrius?' Bek asked, surprised.

'Who else? He is far from stupid, Bek. I saw him watching your second fight, and I would not be surprised if he has already figured out that trick you pulled on Bitranis and come up with a countermove. Unless you are *dem taqat* then you will not survive an encounter with Serrius. I am beginning to seriously believe what many others have been voicing for the last three years – Serrius is *dem taqat*. If that is true, then neither you nor anyone else in this world will kill him in single combat.'

Bek had no idea what Hammar was talking about. The term *dem taqat* was not one that he had ever heard of before, but he did not care what it meant. Words were not about to dissuade him from his course. His mind was made up. He would get his showdown with Serrius, or die attempting to get it. What was more, when he fought Serrius, Bek would have no thoughts of dying. There was no room for negative thoughts. Negative thinking was what did get fighters killed. Serrius had cleverly and ruthlessly filled every fighter in Shandrim with so many negative thoughts that they could no longer so much as look at him without seeing their own death staring back from his cold eyes.

'You may be correct in everything that you say,' Bek said, his voice defiant and his eyes hard and determined, 'but you will not dissuade me. My intention remains. I will fight Serrius.'

Hammar sighed heavily and nodded.

'I expected no less,' he replied, his voice heavy. 'I didn't think that I would be able to change your mind. Therefore, I shall just have to help you.'

'Help me? Why?'

'Well, aside from the fact that you're probably the most promising young fighter that I've seen enter the arena in a long while, you don't kill your opponents unnecessarily. I know that you killed Barrock and Karoth, but that was different. You were in the arena as a prisoner, not a fighter. They would have killed you without blinking, so you despatched them before they had a chance. That was pure survival on your part and perfectly understandable. Since becoming a fighter, though, you have already risen through the ranks to twenty and have neither killed anyone, nor taken so much as a scratch from an opponent. That is unusual.'

Bek thought about Hammar's reasoning, but it still did not ring totally true. He was not telling the whole truth. Just because he was talented and did not kill his opponents was not reason enough for the Weapons Master to help him.

'Not enough, Hammar. Come on – what's the *real* reason that you're offering to help me?'

Hammar looked Bek in the eye, but could not match Bek's stare for long. He looked away.

'Two reasons really,' Hammar admitted slowly. 'Serrius has been singling out the most promising tyros and killing them in the arena to prevent anyone new with talent from learning enough to be a real challenge. The fighters who are already ranked are frightened stupid by him, so he has no fear of them. I hate seeing young men die unnecessarily. It gripes me. If I can by some miracle give you enough of what it takes to beat Serrius, then the killing would stop.'

'That's one reason,' Bek prompted. 'And the other?'

'That Commander who came to see you has offered me a large pot of gold to do it.'

Bek's eyes widened in surprise and his mind raced. That Commander again! 'What game is the man playing?' he wondered.

'So he bought you to train me? How much did he offer?'

'A lot,' Hammar admitted with a grin. 'More gold than I would earn as Weapons Master here in the next ten years. Enough to make me comfortable in retirement when my strength and abilities as a teacher fail me.'

Bek nodded thoughtfully. No wonder Hammar was keen to offer his services. Well, this was an unexpected turn of events, but now that Bek was sure that he understood Hammar's motives, it would be foolishness to turn the man's help and experience aside.

'So, Hammar, what is it that you think I need to do in order to beat Serrius?'

'Well, to be honest, you need a miracle,' Hammar said, gritting his teeth at the thought. 'The first problem that you'll have to overcome is not Serrius at all – it is Mandarbe. I'm assuming of course that you intend to continue your pattern of challenging the highest rank that your current position allows?'

Bek nodded.

'Well, Mandarbe is ranked at fifteen and is a very sound fighter. I can certainly teach you his weaknesses and those of the other fighters that you will face before meeting Serrius. If you work hard, you should not have too many problems along the way, but to face Serrius... have you ever fought with two swords at once?'

'No,' Bek replied. 'I have seen Serrius training with two blades and tried to run a few sequences myself. He makes it look very easy, but for me, the balance is awkward and I find that coordinating the strokes is a nightmare. I can fight almost as well with my left hand as my right, but together – no.'

'Then I will teach you that as well, but I suspect that we won't have much time. If you slow down your advance to the top ranks now, then I think that Serrius will challenge you. He will not give you much time to consolidate your position, but he will want to see you fight a bit more to research your weaknesses before he forces a contest. Therefore, we must make sure that all of your fights are as short as possible. That way, he won't have a chance to learn much and he may delay bringing the fight to you.'

* * * * *

'Your Imperial Majesty?'

'Yes? What hour is it? It feels like the middle of the

night,' the Emperor muttered dozily.

'I am afraid that you are right, your Majesty, but there is a woman here to see you. It appears that she knows all of the appropriate passwords and she insists that it is urgent, your Majesty,' the servant said apologetically, his voice sounding very tired, but as precise as ever.

The Emperor shook his head slightly, blinking hard and rubbing his face with the palms of his hands in an effort to awaken fully. There was only one woman who knew that many passwords, and he wanted to be as sharp as he could to listen for every nuance in what she had to tell him.

'Light a couple of the torches, then send her in,' the Emperor ordered, while at the same time rearranging his pillows such that he could sit up in bed comfortably. 'Oh, and get me a drink as well. A light wine will do,' he added before the servant disappeared out of earshot.

A minute or two later, several torches around the walls were alight and the servant re-entered the Emperor's bedchamber leading a well-dressed and very attractive young lady on his arm. If he had not known whom it was that he was awaiting, the Emperor would never have recognised his most reliable spy.

The servant placed a small tray with a decanter of white wine and two glasses on the bedside table, then, bowing deeply, retreated from the room and carefully closed the door behind him.

'Femke, you said to my servant that you had urgent news. Is it about Chorain?'

'Yes, your Imperial Majesty... and no. I have news of Chorain and have discovered much of what you wanted to know, but there is other news as well. Perhaps more important news than the Commander's schemes, but that is not for me to decide,' Femke answered hesitantly.

'Ah! I suspect that I know already about this other news that you bring, so humour me. Tell me what Chorain has been up to first, then we shall see if your other news is the harbinger of doom that I am expecting.'

Femke looked curiously at the Emperor, unsure of his

mood. His anticipation of her news unsettled her, as there was always the possibility that the bad tidings she carried would bring a new problem to add to one that the Emperor already had foreknowledge of.

'Chorain made a deal with Garvin to get rid of the red-headed Thrandorian so that he could take the other Thrandorian off on some quest without the possibility of having the red-head getting in the way.'

'That sneaky son of a... I told him not to harm the Thrandorians.'

'Actually, your Majesty, you gave him a gaping gateway to a get out clause – the arena. You told him not to interfere with fights in the arena and if the Thrandorians were killed in combat in that environment then so be it.'

The Emperor looked at Femke in stunned amazement.

'How did you...?'

'Information is my business, your Majesty. I'm the best. That's why you pay me so well,' Femke answered with a sly smile. 'Anyway, Chorain decided that he would twist your words to suit his own purposes. He didn't interfere with the fights directly; he simply spoke to Garvin and arranged a fight that could only finish with one possible conclusion. The red-haired Thrandorian, whose name incidentally appeared to be simply Jez, would be killed and conveniently out of Chorain's way. Unfortunately for the Commander, however, his plan backfired in a way that he had not expected.'

'Really? In what way?' the Emperor asked, fascinated.

'Well, it appears that Chorain's intention was to cut the other Thrandorian's ties to anything in the arena by eliminating Jez. This was supposed to leave Bek, the second Thrandorian, free to join him on some mission to kill someone called Shanier. I have not yet managed to find out who Shanier is, but I do have a few leads.'

'Don't worry about it. I will tell you who he is in a minute. Please, continue.'

'Well, your Majesty, it appears that far from freeing Bek from his ties to the arena, Chorain has bonded him there in a trap stronger than tempered steel. Bek has sworn revenge on Serrius for killing his friend and is now hell-bent on meeting him in the arena. Now all Chorain has for his troubles is the prospect of seeing Bek get himself killed by the very instrument that was supposed to set him free.'

'Hmm... Bek and Serrius. It will be an interesting fight but you are right – Serrius will kill him. A shame, and possibly an opportunity lost, but I'll not interfere with the arena fight schedule.'

'Neither will Chorain any more, your Majesty. Despite the Commander offering Garvin a small fortune, the Arena Master will not hear of avoiding what is already being noised around amongst the lower ranked fighters as an inevitable confrontation. The higher ranks still regard him as a tyro, despite his rapid rise into the rankings today.'

'So Chorain has manipulated himself right out of the game,' the Emperor chortled. 'A fitting finish to his scheming.'

'Oh no, your Majesty. He is not finished. Chorain has now offered Hammar, the Weapons Master, an extortionate amount of money to individually train Bek to beat Serrius.'

'Really? Now that could make the confrontation *very* interesting. I remember when Hammar was ranked first among the arena fighters. He was awesome in his day and he retired at his peak. Not many do that. Most find defeat at least once before they leave the arena. If Hammar can inject even more pace and variety into the Thrandorian, the fight might get very close indeed.'

The Emperor fell silent, lost in thoughts of the possibility of a truly memorable clash looming in the near future. Femke remained standing quietly, respectfully waiting while the Emperor allowed himself to dream.

A yawn built inside Femke such that she could not totally contain it and the movement of her hand to cover her mouth brought the Emperor back to the present.

'I'm sorry, Femke. I was miles away. Chorain, it appears, is being more meddlesome than I had bargained on. I think that it is time that he was taken out of play. Would you mind dealing with it?'

'Not at all, your Majesty.'

'And while you're at it, could you speak with Shalidar and have him despatch more people to dispose of Lord Vallaine. The High Lord of the Inner Eye has not seen fit to answer my summons and has somehow eluded the assassins I sent after him recently. His death should prove an instructive example to the rest of the Sorcerers and Magicians who feel led to dabble in politics.'

'Certainly, your Majesty.'

'Now then, Femke, you had other news. Speak it, and then we can both find our rest again.'

'Well, your Majesty, it's not so much news, as a rumour. It's just that the nature of the rumour is so damaging that I felt it had to come to your ears – and quickly. It's being said that Legions sent into Thrandor have suffered a crushing defeat so bad that there were very few survivors. This is not yet circulating the streets openly, but it will not be long, your Majesty.'

The Emperor merely nodded.

'So,' he said with a heavy sigh, 'it has started.'

CHAPTER 12

There was a strange peace about the city as Jenna began her final day of trudging the streets in search of Perdimonn. The Council of Magicians had proved an elusive group to find and Jenna had decided that enough was enough. There had not been so much as the faintest of leads to the Council's whereabouts. Now her money had run out, and the only way that she would be able to continue her search would be to get a job to earn her keep.

'Maybe it was just a dream after all,' she muttered to herself for about the hundredth time. Shivering slightly against the chill, frost-filled early morning air, Jenna stamped her feet against the flagstone pavement in an effort to spur her sluggish circulation into motion. 'Why am I still here? I should have given up a week ago. At least then I could have spent a few nights in relative comfort on the way back to Thrandor. Damn you and your dream-calls, Perdimonn. If you wanted help so badly this time, why did you not make your message more clear?'

Jenna continued muttering in this fashion for some time, but throughout it all, her large brown eyes constantly scanned her surroundings, looking for something, anything that might just be the hint or clue that would lead her to the mysterious Council, and so to Perdimonn.

The city was not really that large as cities go and Jenna felt that she must surely have walked every street a dozen times. Perhaps it was that familiarity that almost made her miss the obvious. On a couple of her early morning starts, Jenna had met stable boys out exercising their horses, and this morning was no exception. Jenna had already said 'hello' to a couple of stable boys when chance finally allowed the dice of life to roll in her favour.

The young lad leading two horses on reins in the opposite direction down the street had smiled at Jenna's cheery greeting and had returned it warmly. It was only when the boy had almost passed her by totally that Jenna suddenly recognised one of the two horses that he was leading. It was Perdimonn's old horse, Steady.

Before Jenna could prevent herself, a surprised call of the horse's name escaped her lips and Steady nickered in response.

The boy stopped.

'What was that?' he asked in surprise, as Jenna ran over and started patting the old mare's neck. 'Did you call this horse "Steady"? Or did one of them kick out at you as we passed?'

'You heard correctly,' Jenna said excitedly. 'This horse belongs to an old friend of mine. I've been searching high and low for him. Could you tell me where he is?'

The young stable hand looked uncomfortable and fidgeted with the reins, wrapping them around and around his fingers and then allowing the coils to fall free.

'Can you tell me anything about the owner that will prove to me that you really know him? My Masters will have me beaten if I take you to them without clearing it with them first.'

'Very well. The owner's name is Perdimonn. He is an old man with a large bald patch on the top of his head. The hair that remains around the sides of his head is iron grey and he has bright, mischievous blue eyes. For an old man he is surprisingly fit, but that may be attributable to his being a Ma...'

'Enough!' the boy said sharply, looking all around to see if anyone was close enough to hear what Jenna had been saying. 'You obviously know the person of whom you speak, but you won't find him here in Terilla.'

'Really, then how do you explain his horse being here? Perdimonn wouldn't have sold Steady for any price, so surely he must be somewhere close by?'

'Er... well I'm afraid, Miss, that I can't possibly tell you about that without first speaking to my Masters,' the poor stable boy apologised. 'They'll know what to do with you. Just follow me along to the stables and then I'll do my utmost to get one of the Masters to come and speak with you. You should find answers to your questions in one form or another.'

'Do with me?' Jenna thought irritably. 'They had better not try to *do* anything with me other than tell me what I want to know, or let me go on my way.'

With a shrug of her shoulders, Jenna accepted the stable boy's offer and agreed to walk with him as he took the horses out for their morning exercise walk. Jenna had no desire to get the boy into any trouble, so she did not insist that he go straight back to find his Masters. Instead, she chatted to him about life in Terilla, about horses, about archery and all manner of other things. The stable boy was bright and easy to talk to, which made the walk with the horses pass quickly despite her desire to get back to the stables, where she was certain that she would find the home of the Council of Magicians.

When the boy finally led the horses around the side of a deceptively large building in a residential area, Jenna could have kicked herself. The tavern at which she had been staying was no more than two to three hundred paces away. The place that she had been searching for had been right under her nose the whole time.

At the stable boy's direction, Jenna waited in the large porch-way at the top of the broad steps whilst he stabled the horses and disappeared inside to find one of his Masters. After a few minutes the front door opened and a huge man stepped out to greet her. Jenna could scarcely believe her eyes at the sheer scale of the man. He was huge, but somehow completely unthreatening.

'Now then, Miss, how can I help you?' the man

rumbled, his voice deep and completely in keeping with the rest of his appearance.

'Do you know of an old man named Perdimonn?' Jenna asked in return.

'Maybe I do... and then again maybe I don't. Who are you and what do you want with him?'

Jenna took a deep breath and quickly assessed how to play this situation to best advantage. With a quick look around to see if anyone else was in earshot she made her opening gambit.

'Do you really think that we should talk about magic out here on the doorstep?' Jenna asked in a stage whisper.

The man smiled. 'No, probably not,' he agreed. 'Come inside. My name is Lomand, incidentally, and you are?'

'Jenna.'

'Welcome, Jenna.'

Lomand led Jenna into the hallway and closed the front door behind them.

'Now then, Jenna, what brings you to our door asking about Brother Perdimonn?'

'Well, Lomand, a couple of weeks ago I heard Perdimonn calling to me in my mind. He sounded as if he was in trouble and needed help. He has called me before in a similar fashion, but last time he kept repeating the mental call, whereas this time he called once, and then... nothing. I was aware that when we last parted company he was bound for Terilla to speak to the Council of Magicians about the threat of a Magician named Selkor, therefore, I made my way here in search of him. By chance I recognised Perdimonn's old horse being exercised by your stable boy and here I am.'

Lomand considered her words for a moment, scratching absently at a spot just behind his right ear.

'So you are not here to take up training in magic?' he asked slowly. 'Perdimonn did not send you to us to learn our skills?'

'Great Tarmin, no!' Jenna exclaimed with a laugh. 'What a preposterous idea! A woman Magician!'

'Not as preposterous as you might think,' Lomand said thoughtfully. 'However, that is irrelevant right now. What is more important to you is the fact that Perdimonn left here weeks ago. He was bound for Kaldea. I don't know any more than that, though I believe that the Council have recently received some word of him.'

'Kaldea?' Jenna asked questioningly. 'I've never heard of it. Where is Kaldea exactly?'

'About a hundred leagues or so off the coast of Thrandor,' Lomand answered candidly. 'It is not the most hospitable of places to visit as it is comprised mainly of volcanic rock and ash.'

'Then why would Perdimonn wish to go to such a place?'

Lomand looked at Jenna with a gaze that seemed to see much more than her surface features. For a moment, Jenna felt as though the gigantic man was staring into her mind and stripping away layer after layer of who she was, until all of her innermost secrets lay open before him. Hopes, fears and deep desires all felt exposed before Lomand's penetrating eyes. Jenna fought down the urge to shudder at the sensation and let out a slow, controlled breath of relief when he finally looked away.

'If Perdimonn did not share his purposes with you, then it is hardly my place to speak about his intentions,' Lomand stated coolly, his expression and tone suggesting that he would not be moved on this point. 'But, if you would like to take some refreshment here, I will ask one of the Masters of this house to consider your arrival and decide what advice or direction to give you.'

Jenna nodded thankfully, and wondered whether she had the gall to ask for provisions and money to aid her onward journey. Lomand seemed friendly enough, despite his intimidating size and penetrating gaze. Maybe he would see fit to aid her on Perdimonn's behalf. Jenna certainly had little to lose by trying, but she decided to wait until after she had enjoyed whatever refreshment Lomand was leading her towards.

Calvyn had finished his breakfast and was just leaving

the dining hall by one of the doors diagonally opposite to the one that Lomand entered through. Calvyn caught sight of Lomand out of the corner of his eye and gave him a jaunty wave as he left the dining room and strode away to his first lesson. Lomand grinned and nodded in response, then turned to gently direct Jenna, who had been just behind him, forward to one of the nearby tables.

'No wonder Lomand is so big,' Calvyn laughed to one of the other Acolytes from his class who was hurrying along the corridor beside him. 'I just saw him coming in for a second sitting of breakfast. I wonder whether he does that at lunch and dinner as well?'

* * * * *

'And I still say it's our best chance,' argued Fesha, his voice low but full of passion.

'You're far too small for anyone to believe that you're one of the arena guards and I'd be even less convincing for obvious reasons,' Eloise retorted hotly.

They had debated a whole host of options since escaping the arena. Both had agreed that they could not abandon Derra, so they had plotted and schemed to devise a feasible rescue plan. Until now, none of their plans had leapt out at either of them as having a great chance of success and while Fesha was enthusiastic about his latest idea, Eloise considered it little more than lunacy.

Fesha was convinced that by relieving one of the off duty arena guards of his uniform, Eloise would be able to make a few rapid alterations to the clothes so that Fesha could take the guard's place. Eloise had pointed out that needlework had never really been her calling in life, and the alterations likely to be needed would be major indeed to scale down clothes to Fesha's stature. Nevertheless, Fesha refused to be put off by her pessimism.

'Trust me, my size won't matter,' Fesha said confidently.

Eloise raised her eyebrows suggestively and gave him a wicked grin before bursting out laughing.

Fesha shook his head as he laughed along with Eloise, and tried to turn the conversation back on course.

'You're not taking this seriously, Eloise but I am. I came here with you and Derra to rescue Bek and Jez. Jez is dead already, and Bek might as well be, but I'll not abandon Sergeant Derra to that barbaric excuse for public entertainment.'

'You're wrong, Fesha. I'm taking this situation *very* seriously. It's you and your madcap idea that I'm ridiculing. Show me one arena guard who is not at least a head taller than you, and doesn't carry double your bodyweight and I'll admit that your plan has vague merit. But you can't, because there are no such guards. They appear to have been hand picked for their imposing stature and sheer bulk. They've certainly not been chosen for their wit and repartee.'

'Give me a better idea and I'll gladly attempt it,' Fesha offered, his tone challenging.

'You know I have none.'

'Then let us at least *try*,' Fesha pleaded.

'Oh, very well,' Eloise replied, her tone expressing resignation. 'When?'

'Tomorrow. Tonight we'll follow another shift of guards coming off day duty, and see if we can identify a likely target. The current shift pattern has two days to run, so we'll pick our target tonight, take him out tomorrow and then I'll attempt to take his place on what would've been his first night shift.'

'It sounds like a plan. A mad plan – but it is a plan. Tarmin help us, for we're going to need the gods to smile on us indeed if this is going to work.'

* * * * *

'Faster, Bek, faster!' urged Hammar. 'Come on, if you can't get through the defences of an old man like me, how do you expect to beat the best fighter in the arena?'

Bek grunted with effort and did his best to comply. Over the last couple of days, his respect for the Weapons Master had risen time and again. Hammar might be nearly twenty years older than most of the arena fighters, but Bek found it hard to believe that there were any out there who would easily defeat the old Master. In truth, Hammar was not really that old, but few arena fighters lived to see thirty, let alone forty, and Bek's estimate placed Hammar as approaching the latter figure.

As Bek had no possessions of his own to add to the furnishings of his new accommodation, it was not difficult to clear a sparring area in his spacious room. The ceilings were more than high enough to not interfere with stances or overhead strokes. Also, the limited area available meant that retreat during sparring was difficult to achieve effectively without being hampered by walls or furniture. This limitation made the sparring sessions much more intense.

'Stop, stop! Come on Bek, you can do better than this. You were faster with a steel blade against Bitranis. Why are you holding back? These blades are only wooden and are lighter than even the short steel blade that you favour. What *is* your problem?'

'The point is still sharp enough to cause a serious wound if lunged,' Bek grumbled, breathing hard after his exertions. 'The only openings of any worth that you left unguarded were all for lunge attacks.'

'Oh, so you *were* still awake! I was beginning to wonder whether I should go and get a sign saying lunge at me and wear it around my neck. Try it next time you see the opportunity. Trust me. If you injure me, I'll not hold it against you in any way.'

'Very well.'

They resumed, the clacking of their wooden weapons sounding not unlike the wooden shuttles of weavers' looms hitting the stops in a rapid-fire sequence. For a while, Bek saw no openings and concentrated instead on defending himself from a whistling series of attacks from Hammar. Sweat ran freely now in rivulets down from his forehead, threatening his eyes with their salty sting – still no chances. Then for a fleeting instant a tantalising opportunity for a lunge appeared, which Bek could no longer ignore, nor refuse. With a lightning-like change of speed and direction, Bek lunged, only to find his blade deflected and his opponent's blade cracking into the side of his ribcage.

'Ha! Another strike for the old man!' Hammar crowed annoyingly. 'Come on, Bek... faster! Surely you're not going to let an old has-been like me give you a hard time.'

Bek did not hesitate. He attacked again with a viciously fast sequence of strokes, but somehow Hammar always seemed to meet his attacks with a solid defence. Bek was just beginning to feel that the Weapons Master was infallible when he managed to get in a touch on Hammar's arm.

'Hold!' Hammar ordered, stepping back and giving Bek a quick salute. 'Good. That last attack was much better. You stuck at it more, and pressed on with more conviction than you have been showing up until now. We are making some progress it seems. Let's break from sparring for a bit and see how your double sword drills are coming along.'

Bek caught Hammar's wooden blade in his left hand as the Weapons Master tossed it to him. Without pausing, Bek smoothly spun into a rapid sequence of simultaneous blocking and cutting strokes. Whirling both blades at blinding speed through the pre-set sequences that Hammar had taught him only the day before, Bek demonstrated his progress in style. The Weapons Master looked on approvingly, and nodded with a pleased smile as Bek finished and held the final stance.

'Not bad – not bad at all. Very well, I have two more blades here. Let us try that same sequence with an opponent. Don't vary the drill yet. Stick to the patterns. We'll spar in good time, but sparring with two blades each is more than twice as dangerous as regular sparring. Now, begin slowly and we'll pick up the pace as we go.'

* * * * *

'Rikath... Rikath? Can you hear us, Rikath?'

Perdimonn and Arred stretched out their joint consciousness far across the sea to the Straights of Ahn, searching and calling for their fellow Warder. This was their fourth attempt and Perdimonn was rapidly losing hope that this attempt at long distance mind-to-mind contact would work.

The people of Kaldea were today counting the cost of the recent volcanic eruption. The two Magicians, after their spectacular intervention the day before, had been treated like royalty. Word had spread rapidly of the powerful magic that they had worked to stop the eruption, hold the lava flows and extinguish the raging fires throughout the city. The more superstitious amongst the people avoided Perdimonn and Arred, rapidly weaving fingers in a traditional warding hex against evil if they so much as saw the two Magicians. The vast majority of the people, however, were more than grateful for the cessation of the volcanic eruption, no matter how it had been achieved.

Perdimonn and Arred had spent the night in the plushest, most comfortable guesthouse left standing in the city. The pick of the food and drink available in Kaldea could have been theirs had they wished it, but Perdimonn had never really liked rich food and Arred had lived rough for so long that he preferred simple, hearty fare. The end result was that they had asked for a plain meal of local fare with a light white wine and then both had retired to their rooms to sleep.

After the euphoria of being washed in the deluge of power unlocked by his Key, Arred's excess of energy had rapidly dissolved until he found himself as tired as Perdimonn. Both had slept from early that afternoon right through the night until early the next morning and, even then, they arose feeling weary. All surplus energy seemed to have been sapped from their bodies such that even the simplest of tasks was far more taxing than normal.

This attempt to contact Rikath would have been difficult under normal circumstances but, tired as they were, the task had appeared all but impossible from the beginning. Brows furrowed with concentration and beads of perspiration growing, the two hurled their thoughts through the great void to where they hoped to find Rikath and warn her of Selkor's approach.

'Rikath! Hear us, Rikath. We need to speak with you.'

Bodies reclining in comfortable armchairs in Perdimonn's guest suite, they could have been enjoying a mid-morning nap. That was certainly the conclusion that the maid mistakenly reached. She had knocked on the door twice with no response, so had quietly opened the door and peeped inside. On seeing the two Magicians seemingly asleep in the armchairs, the maid had withdrawn again with an almost fond smile. 'Poor souls,' she had thought. 'Magic must really be tiring to cause them to sleep so long and then still need more.'

'Rikath? Rikath? Answer us, Rikath.'

Then it came... a faint response.

'Perdimonn? Arred? Is that really you?'

Clutching at that thought, the consciousness that was both Perdimonn and Arred rejoiced at its success.

'Yes, Rikath, it is. We have linked to warn you that a great peril approaches. Selkor is on his way to try to learn your Key. You must get away from the Straights of Ahn at once. Run like the wind, Rikath. He already has the Key of Fire and he carries objects of power to deceive and overwhelm. You must not let him find you.'

There was a short pause.

'You're too late with your warning. Selkor has already gained knowledge of my Key.'

The words dropped like cold leaden bombs into the stomachs of Perdimonn and Arred. Disbelief and incredulity filled their minds as they forced themselves to come to terms with Rikath's news.

'But how is that possible?' thought Arred, his mind filled with dismay and shock. *'Selkor could only have left here*

two days ago at most.'

'I don't have the answer to that, but the fact remains – he has been and gone. I only escaped him by luck. He came yesterday and deceived me by...'

'Save the details for now, Rikath,' Perdimonn interrupted gently. *'We have to contact Morrell before Selkor gets to him as well. Arred and I are already weary, so we can't afford the time now to hear your tale. Do you know Morrell well enough to guide us to him?'*

'I? No, I never really had anything to do with him,' Rikath replied, sounding surprised that they had even asked. *'The last I heard of him, he was planning to go to the Mountains of the Sun in the heart of the Terachim Wastes. Why anyone would wish to go somewhere so dry and barren, I could not begin to imagine.'*

'Then you know as much as I,' Perdimonn admitted. *'But that was a very long time ago, Rikath. I doubt that he would have stayed there all this time.'*

'Most of us are not wanderers, Perdimonn,' Arred disagreed. *'I have been here pretty much since our last meeting. Rikath has obviously not roved far either. It's only you who have felt the need for travel. The rest of us have felt at home nearest to our elements. Morrell will likely have stayed in the region that he sought, having parted ways with us all those years ago.'*

'Very well, if we have no way of linking to Morrell, then we'll just have to go and find him – though I fear that with the speed that Selkor is moving, we're unlikely to win this race. Somehow, our greatest enemy seems to have become time.'

Perdimonn paused for a moment or two as his thoughts seemed to echo around in his mind. 'Enemy... time... time...' With a flash of inspiration, light seemed to dawn in the old Magician's thoughts. It suddenly became clear what Selkor was doing.

'Damn me for a fool!' Perdimonn exclaimed through the link. *'I know how Selkor is staying ahead of me and I gave him the means to do it myself!'*

'What?' came the surprised simultaneous response

from Arred and Rikath. *'How?'*

'Never mind that now. Rikath, wait for us on the beach on the northern side of Finger Point. We'll be there tomorrow. I'll explain everything then.'

With that, Perdimonn broke off the link.

Arred and Perdimonn both opened their eyes at the same moment. Initially, Arred watched quizzically while Perdimonn immediately began to berate himself for his foolishness. The Warder of Fire knew better than to interrupt the old man whilst he was in mid flow, so he waited patiently for a break in the flood of angry words. He had to wait longer than he expected, but at last there came an opening in which he could speak.

'I assume that there's a point behind all this verbal self-abuse?' he asked innocently. 'Perhaps when you've calmed down a little, you might like to share it with me?'

'Yes, yes – of course I will,' Perdimonn snapped irritably. Then he took a deep, calming breath and apologised for his waspish behaviour. 'I'm sorry, Arred. I just feel a bit of an idiot for not realising that Selkor would figure it out eventually. You see, about a year ago we had a chance confrontation in a market place in northern Thrandor. I used a spell that altered the flow of time around certain objects, namely Selkor, my apprentice and I. I fooled him into thinking that I had frozen time altogether...'

'But that's impossible...'

'Of course it is, but Selkor was too rattled by the unexpected turn of events to think straight at the time. Unfortunately, it didn't take him long to realise that I'd duped him and now it appears that he's mastered the spell that I used, or one that has similar effects. He's literally making time for himself by changing the flow of time around his body such that he's probably moving ten, twenty, maybe even a hundred times as fast as we are.'

'So what are we going to do?' Arred asked, still grappling with the concept of manipulating time.

'We'll play him at his own game,' Perdimonn answered

fiercely. 'Come on. We need to find a boat and a crew of oarsmen if we're to get to the Straights of Ahn by tomorrow.'

* * * * *

'Yes? What is it?' the Emperor asked, as once again there was a knock at his study door. He had been poring over a stack of trade reports, military reports, domestic infrastructure reports and other documents that all supposedly needed his attention. Privately, he felt that there were far too many people writing far too many reports and not actually *doing* anything useful. However, with the trouble that he had brewing amongst the populace over the fiasco of an invasion attempt into Thrandor, now was probably not a good time to be alienating the bureaucrats as well.

'A visitor, your Imperial Majesty,' answered the servant, who was already opening the door.

'A visitor? Surely you know by now that I don't accept visitors during my study time?' the Emperor snapped angrily.

The servant did not so much as flinch at the Emperor's ire. His eyes were distant, and his voice distracted as he answered.

'This visitor must see you, your Majesty. It is extremely important.'

A man entered the room slowly. His face was not one that the Emperor recognised, but there was something vaguely familiar about the way that he walked. For a moment, the man's identity was tantalisingly elusive and then he spoke.

'Thank you, serving man. That will be all.'

The voice seemed to echo, not so much around the study, but in the Emperor's mind. With a thrill of recognition, the Emperor suddenly realised who it was that now faced him from the other side of his desk.

'Hello, Vallaine. I wondered when you would get around to dropping by.'

'Your Imperial Majesty,' the Sorcerer Lord replied, his appearance blurring subtly as his disguise dissolved. High Lord Vallaine, leader of the sect of Sorcerers known as the Lords of the Inner Eye, leaned on his staff as he stared into the eyes of the Emperor. 'I'd like to say that it's a pleasure, but to be perfectly honest it isn't. The assassins that you sent were really quite irksome, so I decided to come and stop you from sending any more.'

'And what makes you think for one moment that I will agree to that? Your Sorcerer's powers have no hold over me, Vallaine. After you have squandered five entire legions in an attempted invasion that you claimed to have foreseen with your powers would be successful, do you really expect to have any credibility left? Or have you come to stave the maddened hordes from my doorstep with your sorcery? For they *will* come. My spies tell me that the rumours of our defeat are already spreading.'

Vallaine stared even more intently at the Emperor but, despite his best efforts, once again the power of sorcery seemed to just slide off the Emperor's mind. It was sickeningly frustrating, but the Emperor spoke the truth when he said that Vallaine had no hold over him. Illusion worked well enough, but he could gain no control over the Emperor's mind by force of will.

'I have not come to gain any agreements, your Majesty. I have come to take your place.'

The Emperor's heart was racing. He had prepared well for Vallaine's inevitable appearance, taking all sorts of outlandish precautions against his powers, but he still had no idea whether his planning had yielded the results that he intended. The next few moments would be critical. He had to keep Vallaine talking.

'Really? And of course the people of Shandar will simply fall at your feet and hail you as the new Emperor.'

'They will not even realise that you have been replaced,' Vallaine answered, his face blurring again and becoming a mirror image of the Emperor's features.

'Hmm... yes, it might work – for a while,' the Emperor admitted thoughtfully, pretending to scrutinise Vallaine's illusory face intently. 'But thanks to your own bungling, this is not exactly the best time to be taking on the mantle of the Empire. You'll merely be substituting my assassins for a different bunch. My guards caught the first one today, but I'm sure that there'll be many, more skilled than he lining up to take his place over the next few weeks.'

Vallaine smiled and a chill ran down the Emperor's spine. The Emperor would hardly have described himself as pure of heart. Indeed, he had spent his entire life plotting and scheming. These attributes were those of survival in his seat, but the look that crossed High Lord Vallaine's features now made the Emperor feel positively naïve by comparison.

'Ah, but it will be so much easier to protect myself here. There are so many more people to draw on to ensure my safety. Assassins will have to be skilled indeed to survive my traps, particularly as no one attempting to assassinate the Emperor will even suspect that they are pitting themselves against a Sorcerer. I must congratulate you on your choices of killers by the way. They were all really quite skilled.'

'Fortunately, I saved the best until last,' the Emperor replied softly.

'Yes, I know,' Vallaine replied, his smile widening even further. 'Come in, Shalidar. You would not want to keep your Emperor waiting, would you? You see, I know all about your preparations for my arrival. I even prompted some of the more exotic arrangements myself in case any of my fellow Sorcerers showed the wit and foresight to attempt what I'm now going to do. Of course, none of them did. The only truly deceptive and astute mind among them was the one of my making, and he, unfortunately, chose to go his own way. He will pay, of course. Oh, how he will pay! But you do not need details of such things, for you will not have any use for them in the afterlife. Look at yourself. Go ahead. Look at yourself in a mirror. Take one last look at what the world will see of you after your death.'

The Emperor was terrified now. Why was Shalidar looking at him so strangely? How had Vallaine subverted his best assassin? Why did Vallaine want him to look in a mirror?

With a reluctance born of fear, the Emperor walked slowly across the study to where a small upright rectangular wall mirror hung next to a bookcase. As he traversed the room, he crossed his arms over his chest in what he hoped would be taken as an instinctively defensive posture. In reality, he was carefully retrieving a dagger from the inside of his left sleeve. Events were not running at all as planned and he now had to resort to desperate measures.

On reaching the mirror, the Emperor could not restrain the gasp of shock. The face that looked back at him was not that of his own. Instead, the evil, wizened old face of Lord Vallaine stared back at him, wide-eyed with shock.

The real Vallaine laughed, and even as he did so, the Sorcerer Lord's voice changed in timbre until it matched that of the Emperor's perfectly. The Emperor whirled, whipping his hand forward to hurl his dagger at Vallaine, but the dagger flew well wide of its mark as another knife seemed to erupt from the Emperor's chest.

'Fast, isn't he?' Vallaine chuckled. 'It's a great shame for you that I bought Shalidar over a year ago. He was *very* expensive. At the time I saw it as insurance and it appears that my policy has just matured.'

With a low groan, the Emperor fell first to his knees and then to the floor. He could not seem to breathe. Pain had exploded in his chest and now lanced its way into every part of his body. 'It cannot be,' he mouthed, his vision dimming with the overwhelming pain. 'This cannot be happening.'

Even as his vision dimmed and his life slipped away, the last thing that the Emperor saw was his own face looking down at him with a mocking smile, infused with evil.

CHAPTER 13

'Stop fidgeting! You'll give us away for sure if you do that in front of the real guards,' hissed Eloise angrily, as Fesha adjusted his diagonal shoulder belts for what seemed like the hundredth time.

'Nonsense,' he replied hotly, but quietly. 'Anyone new to this uniform would shift it around until he became comfortable with it. I'm hardly going to claim to have been a guard at the arena for long now, am I?'

Eloise tutted, unable to totally believe that they were going to go through with this crazy plan. There were so many gaping holes in it that it was barely a plan at all. Fesha argued that it left plenty of room for flexibility and improvisation, but in truth, Eloise knew that he was more than aware of the precarious nature of the tightrope they had chosen to walk.

'Anyway, I've noticed you twitching your skirt often enough. How is that any different?' Fesha asked, his voice accusing.

'For a start, this hardly qualifies to be called a skirt. It would be better described as a belt,' Eloise pointed out. 'If I didn't twitch it occasionally, I'd probably be arrested for indecent exposure!'

Fesha's annoyance melted with Eloise's obvious discomfort at her own costume.

'Yes, well I can't fault the fashion sense of the Shandese women,' he said with an impudent grin. 'Come on. Let's see whether the duty guard approves of Voldor's choice in women.'

The plan had matured very slightly since Fesha had first decided to try and replace one of the guards. Eloise had pointed out that replacing the gate guard really would not achieve much, as if he left his post, someone was bound to notice that he was missing and raise the alarm. Instead, they had targeted one of the day shift with the intention of relieving him of his uniform and bluffing their way past the gate guard. Their new ploy meant that Eloise could come as well, for they had discovered that another of the perquisites of the top five fighters was to be allowed women in their quarters twice a week. It did not take long to find out that Voldor, ranked third in the arena, was something of a ladies man. It was said that he always used this privilege to the full and almost invariably had a different woman brought to his quarters every time. Fesha was going to try to pass Eloise off as a 'visitor', and supposedly escort her to Voldor's quarters.

Eloise was hardly a prude when it came to clothing, but even she had baulked at the skimpy outfit that Fesha had supplied her with. Derra and Eloise had thought that the clothing that Fesha had supplied when they had first entered Shandar was scanty, but the outfit that she now wore was practically nonexistent. Unfortunately, Eloise could not fault it for accuracy. Just walking along the streets in the late evening, one could see the sort of women who would relish a visit to the fighters' quarters on certain street corners, similarly clad in next to nothing.

'I believe I'll be able to convince the guards that I'll meet with Voldor's approval,' Eloise stated haughtily. With that, she all but dragged him around the corner and out into the main street a mere hundred and fifty paces from the guarded entrance to the arena.

As Fesha had hoped, the guard on duty could hardly drag his eyes from the strutting beauty of Eloise as they approached. Fesha was vaguely aware out of the corner of his eye, of the exaggerated hip swinging walk that Eloise was performing, and it was all that he could do to keep his own gaze forward.

They reached the arena entrance and the guard seemed to notice Fesha for the first time.

'Who are you, short guy? I've not seen you around before,' the guard grunted, hardly taking his eyes off Eloise who was giving him one of her most devastating smiles. The guard grinned back at her stupidly.

'New guard,' Fesha answered. 'Only started on the day shift yesterday.'

'What? Is Garvin hiring midgets now?' The guard laughed coarsely, unable to tear his eyes from Eloise, who was now standing provocatively with her hands on her hips.

'The Arena Master didn't hire me for my stature,' Fesha said calmly. 'He hired me for my skill. Look. Could you do this?'

'Shand's teeth!' the guard exclaimed, leaping to his left.

Three knives had thudded home into the wooden doorframe only a span from the guard's head. The blades had impacted the wood so closely together that all three handles were touching. More important in the guard's eyes was the fact that they had been thrown so rapidly that he had hardly seen Fesha move. Some of that might have been to do with his preoccupation with staring at Eloise, but the third blade had still struck home before he had moved. The man was fast.

The guard's instinct after jumping to one side had been to look at the knives embedded in the door frame. An instant later, when he looked around at the little fellow who had thrown them, he found him juggling three more knives in a flickering circle of steel. From somewhere, a fourth knife appeared. The guard did not see where it had been drawn from, but it smoothly joined the circle without so much as a glitch in the rhythm of the little man's hands.

With a casual change of emphasis, Fesha flicked each knife in turn at the doorframe. They struck in a smooth, regular flow, each plucked effortlessly from the air and sent with remarkable speed and accuracy to form a perfect vertical line. The guard stepped across to the doorframe and looked in wonder at the precision of the strikes. Each of the blades was precisely one finger width below the last.

Looking back at Fesha with new respect in his eyes he let out a low whistle. 'Amazing!' he admitted. 'I can see how skills like that might be useful.'

'Fortunately for me, the Arena Master decided that a man with my abilities would be able to handle a guard's duties equally as well as someone of greater stature. I have other abilities, but I would rather not reveal all of my secrets.'

'So if you're on the day shift, what are you doing here in uniform at this time of night? And who is the woman?'

Fesha let out a wicked little chuckle.

'I made a rather unfortunate boast about my abilities when it came to locating attractive women. The boys on my shift decided to hold me to it and arranged for me to bring in Voldor's next six to see if I was telling the truth. This is my first effort. What do you think?'

'I think that Voldor is a very lucky man,' the guard said, giving Eloise a wink. 'If you want to dally with a real man sometime, lady, then be sure to look me up.'

Fesha laughed again.

'If you can afford her on a guard's wages, then Garvin held out on me when we talked money,' he said wistfully.

The guard laughed as well. 'Now *that* I can believe,' he chortled. 'Go on in. Do you know where Voldor's quarters are yet?'

Fesha nodded confidently, and wondered to himself whether the guard had meant that he believed it was not possible to afford Eloise on a guard's wages, or whether he had believed that Garvin would have short-changed Fesha. It did not really matter. They were being let into the arena, which was all that really counted at the moment. Fesha quickly retrieved his knives from the doorframe and stowed them with practised ease about his person, then with a florid sweeping gesture, he waved for Eloise to precede him in through the door.

They were in.

Now all they had to do was to locate Derra and somehow get her out. The initial bit of the plan had worked perfectly. Unfortunately, the next part was one of the gaping holes in his plan. The arena was vast and they only had the vaguest of ideas about where Derra was being held. The fact that she had appeared in the arena dressed like the other fighters had told them that she was being held in the rooms under the South Stand rather than the North. That, though, was the limit of their knowledge. Now they needed a bit of luck.

When they had talked it through over the previous couple of days, they had decided that their best course of action would be to begin looking in the area in which Bek and Jez had been held. Although the corridors and levels below the stands were maze-like in their complexity, Fesha was fairly certain that he could find his way back to the room in which they had found Bek on their last rescue mission.

Without an unseemly haste, Fesha and Eloise made their way up the stairs and into the arena stands. They had entered through the East Gate, the only one not barred and bolted at night, so on reaching the stands-area they turned left and traversed around the seating area to the south eastern corner of the arena. Climbing up to the back corner of the stands, they located the door to the stairwell that they had used last time.

The door was locked, but Fesha produced a set of lock-picks from his pocket and within a few seconds there was a click and the door swung open.

'Neatly done,' Eloise whispered. 'I won't ask where you learned to do that.'

'It's best not to,' Fesha agreed with a grin.

They had learned from their research of the layout of the arena since Derra was captured that there were actually three entrances to the fighters' quarters along the southern stands. These, of course, were aside from the entrances through the pit gates down on the arena floor. The central of the three entrances was almost certainly closest to where they hoped to find Derra, but as they had entered through the south eastern stairwell last time it made sense to go that way, as they were already familiar with it, rather than chance wandering around blindly.

Like two shadows, they slipped inside and crept quietly down the stairwell. Flitting from one level to the next and darting along corridors like weasels, they silently wove their way into the depths of the labyrinth of passages and levels. Twice they narrowly avoided detection. The first time was by a group of three fighters who emerged from a door a little way down the passageway that Fesha and Eloise were just entering. The two Thrandorians just managed to duck back into the nearby stairwell without being noticed. The second time was by Garvin himself, who entered a stairwell just above them. Fesha and Eloise had frozen to the spot, poised to attack or run as appropriate. Fortunately, Garvin, and a fighter who sounded older somehow than any that they had seen in the arena, turned up the stairwell instead of down.

'Phew! That was close,' breathed Eloise so quietly that Fesha barely heard her. He declined to respond, but waved for her to follow again as he moved on down the stairs.

Finally they reached the corridor in which Bek had been held. Once again, Eloise waited in the stairwell while Fesha dashed down the corridor to open the door. A few seconds later, he returned.

'Well?' Eloise whispered.

Fesha shook his head.

'The door wasn't locked, and the room was empty. It was a long shot at best. So where shall we go from here?'

Eloise thought for a moment, then smiled as an idea popped into her head.

'How many doors have you noticed with locks on?' she asked in an excited whisper.

Fesha caught her meaning immediately.

'Not many. They don't normally hold prisoners in this part of the arena, do they? Excellent! Well, let's just hope that Derra isn't far away. If I have to keep picking locks for long, we're bound to get caught sooner or later,' Fesha replied in a very low voice. 'Come on, Eloise. There's little point in us getting separated now. If we meet anyone, we'll just have to bluff our way out.'

With a quick glance to make sure that the corridor was still empty, the two strode boldly from door to door, checking each for locks. They opted initially to work their way down the passageway in the direction of the room where Bek had been held prisoner. The stairwell had opened into the middle of the corridor, so the choice was fifty-fifty, but they had to start somewhere.

Fesha found the first door with a lock and immediately fell to working at the keyhole with his lock-picks. Seconds later there was a click and Fesha opened the door carefully. It was a store cupboard for pieces of armour and other arena garb. Fesha scanned the interior briefly for anything that might be useful, particularly more weapons. There were none. With a sigh and a shrug, he closed the door silently and moved on.

Eloise located the next locked door. Unfortunately, this proved to be a store cupboard as well, stacked full of items similar to the last one. They moved on again, further and further along the corridor, but found no more locked doors. Several times they heard voices in conversation behind closed doors and they moved swiftly and silently onward until they reached the last door.

Nothing.

There was no choice but to go back and try the other end of the corridor. Instinct kept them moving quickly and their search finally proved fruitful. A little way down the corridor in the opposite direction to that of Bek's cell, they found a door with a newly fitted lock. Unfortunately, before Fesha had so much as a chance to try opening it, their fears of discovery were realised.

'You, there! Guard. What are you doing bringing a woman down here? Surely you know the rules?'

It was a fighter, judging by his build. He had emerged

from a room just a short distance behind them in the corridor. Eloise wasted no time, but immediately employed the full power of her most devastating smile.

'My, but you're a healthy looking fellow,' she said in a low seductive voice, and with a slinky, swinging walk, she closed the distance between them quickly. My friend here was just trying to find somewhere quiet so that we could have a little fun. You wouldn't want to get us into trouble over a little fun now, would you?'

The fighter spluttered a little, frozen to the spot as Eloise ran her hands over his chest.

Fesha gave a clicking sound with his tongue. Eloise leaned almost casually to her right, and then staggered as she caught the full weight of the fighter who was collapsing with a knife in this throat. Fesha sped quietly over to help her, and together they dragged the man quickly back into his room. Using the fighter's bedding and a basin of cold water that was on the floor by the man's bed, Fesha helped Eloise to clean up the blood that had run down her left arm and leg. Explaining that away to a guard patrol would certainly have proved all but impossible.

Having recovered Fesha's knife, and satisfied themselves that Eloise was presentable again, they checked the corridor for signs that anyone might have heard their exchange with the fighter. The passageway was empty. Fesha dashed across to the door with the new lock and got to work as quickly as he could. Eloise followed more sedately, having silently closed the door to the fighter's room behind her.

As always seems to be the way when you are desperately trying to do something swiftly, Fesha took over twice as long to spring this lock as he had to open the previous two. Time seemed to drag interminably, but in reality Fesha had taken no more than a minute to unlock the door. Sure enough, when he pushed the door open, Derra was waiting silently just inside.

Fesha and Eloise stepped inside quickly and closed the door behind them until it was just slightly ajar.

'What in Tarmin's name is that outfit you're barely wearing?' Derra asked Eloise, her hawkish eyes looking the younger woman up and down disapprovingly.

Eloise sighed. 'It was Fesha's idea, and though I hate to say it, he was right. Dressing like this has proved useful in getting us this far. Luck has run with us. All we need to do now is to get out of here without creating a major uproar.'

'That might be easier said than done,' Derra said urgently. 'The guards are due to arrive any time now on their rounds to ensure that all room torches are extinguished.'

'Damn,' Fesha muttered angrily. 'If we had only guessed the correct end of the corridor to begin with, we might have been out of here by now.'

'Someone's coming,' Eloise announced, listening intently at the door.

'It must be the guards,' Derra said quickly. 'Close the door. Quickly. And extinguish the wall torch. I'll pretend to have turned in early. You two hide behind the door. Only tackle the guard if you have to. There will be another just outside who will raise the alarm if he senses anything wrong.'

Eloise quietly closed the door fully. There was no time to get Fesha to re-lock it, and the noise involved would probably have drawn unwanted attention. Derra leapt into bed, drawing the covers up over her fully clothed body, while Fesha quickly doused the flaming torch in the pail of water placed beneath it for that purpose. Fesha and Eloise then moved to huddle tightly against each other with their backs against the wall behind where the door would open. Then they waited.

Suddenly a startled exclamation sounded out, not far down the corridor.

'Oh no!' groaned Fesha quietly. 'They've found the body. Why didn't we put the body behind the bed and extinguish the torch? They might not have noticed.'

'We weren't to know that the guards were about to come room to room,' Eloise answered consolingly.

'But it was such a schoolboy error,' Fesha moaned softly. 'Any self respecting footpad would have done a better job of concealing that body than we did.'

Sure enough, the conversation between the two guards out in the corridor was legible enough that they caught odd snatches which confirmed their fears. The words 'murder' and 'fetch Garvin immediately' were clearly distinguishable. It did not take the greatest of intellects to deduce that within the next couple of minutes the place would be swarming with guards.

'What shall we do?' Eloise asked softly. 'If we stay here we'll be caught for sure. Then we'll all end up in the arena.'

'Just sit tight for a minute,' Fesha replied, his brain whirling through various options. 'Let's just see how the situation evolves over the next minute or two. This might work out in our favour yet.

Eloise could not see how, and Derra was still oblivious to the whole interchange, as her bed was too far away for her to hear their quiet whispering.

'Back in your rooms please, gentlemen,' a gruff voice ordered from just outside the door. 'You'll all be told what has happened in good time, but for now it is of no concern to you. Get some sleep. It's lights out time now anyway.'

The guard repeated his order in the other direction down the corridor. He was quite obviously standing almost directly outside their door now and Fesha was half expecting it to burst open at any second, but it remained shut. Instead, Fesha was perfectly placed to hear the gruff voiced guard order his compatriot to go and fetch Garvin. The other guard must have agreed silently, for Fesha then heard a set of footsteps receding down the corridor into the distance.

With only one guard in the corridor, Fesha was about to suggest that this was probably their best chance to make a break for it, when the door handle rattled and the door lurched open slightly.

'What the...?' the guard started, more than a little

surprised that the door was unlocked.

'What's the matter?' Derra mumbled, feigning waking up in her bed.

The door opened wider and the gruff voice of the guard sounded wary as he looked in from the doorway to the darkened room.

'Why was your door unlocked, Thrandorian? And how long has it been that way?'

'Unlocked? Tarmin's teeth!' Derra swore, as she seemingly woke up more thoroughly at this point. 'Are you telling me that the guard who brought me my last meal didn't lock the door properly?'

Derra punched her pillow in apparent annoyance at the missed opportunity for escape and the guard laughed cruelly in response to her gesture.

'Well I'll deal with his lapse of security later, but other things have been afoot this night. You haven't heard anything unusual this evening have you?'

'How long ago are we talking?' Derra asked. 'I must have been asleep a little while.'

The guard took a step forward into the doorway, oblivious of Fesha, poised with knife in hand only a couple of feet away. 'Just a little further,' Fesha thought to himself.

'Oh, not long. The body was still warm and blood was still pooling,' the guard answered.

'Body? Whose body?' Derra asked.

'Some tyro fighter. I don't know his name,' said the guard and took another step forward.

That was it, the step that Fesha had been waiting for. Before the guard knew what had hit him, Fesha had grabbed him and slit his throat. The guard died a few seconds later. This time, Fesha took no chances.

'Quickly,' he urged.

Together, the three heaved the guard's body up and into Derra's bed. Then they raced quietly out into the corridor and shut the door behind them. Derra and Eloise headed straight for the stairwell, but Fesha knelt by the door and inserted his lock-picks into the lock.

Determinedly he jiggled at the lock until he got the satisfying click that he wanted. The door was locked again.

'Figure that one out,' he muttered gleefully to himself as he darted down the corridor after the others. The guard still had the key on his belt, but was dead and inside a room that could only have been locked from the outside. Someone would have a headache working through that little conundrum later.

As Fesha entered the stairwell to begin the climb back up through the levels, he found Derra and Eloise coming back down the stairs. Derra signalled silently at him to hide quickly. The sound of multiple footsteps rapidly descending the stairs towards them indicated that there was no time to look far for a really good hiding place. Pointing to the darkly shadowed area under the wooden stairs, Fesha ushered the two women ahead of him and then squeezed into the light space alongside them. They concealed themselves in the nick of time, for no sooner had they squeezed into the small dark space under the stairs than a series of pounding steps hammered down the staircase only inches above their heads.

Six sets of footsteps pounded down into the corridor. There was no choice now. The three Thrandorians knew that if they did not make a break for it, they would quickly be found. With two dead bodies in the vicinity, they did not want to wait around to face the consequences.

The moment that the last person had left the stairwell and gone out into the corridor, Fesha started dragging Eloise and Derra out of their hidey-hole. Within seconds they all leapt lightly up the stairs and away from the commotion below. Flitting up stairs and along corridors like three rodents trying to escape a predator, Fesha, Derra and Eloise fled at top speed for the exit.

Fate, it seemed, had finally decided to give them a clear path to follow, with no obstacles to slow them down. They paused briefly at the exit out into the empty stands to see if there were any guards outside in the arena.

None were in evidence, so they sprinted around the tiered seating to the East Gate. It was locked, but when they knocked on the wooden door leading out to the street, the guard opened it without a thought for trouble emerging from *inside* the arena. There was no need to kill this man. A quick punch to the midriff from Derra took his breath away sufficiently for them to knock him aside and run away unhindered down the street.

Fesha had worked out a twisting escape route designed to disguise their eventual destination. Aside from a couple of quick glances back to check for signs of obvious pursuit, none of them really worried overly about being followed. There were no shouts or sounds of booted guards clattering after them, so they relaxed and concentrated on getting to their pre-arranged accommodation as swiftly as possible, without drawing any unnecessary attention to themselves.

Unnoticed and unlooked for, a shadow seemed to detach itself from a wall not far from the arena gate and silently it followed them through the city. When they reached the place at which they were staying, the shadow-like figure stopped, waited a few moments to confirm that this was indeed their final destination, then it melted away unseen into the night.

* * * * *

'That is definitely the headland, Arred. Finger Point headland. My goodness, it's been a long time indeed since I last came here.'

Arred grunted, pulling on the oars of their little skiff and giving Perdimonn a sour look.

'Surely there must have been an easier way to get here than this, Perdimonn?' Arred asked, leaning back into his stroke with another grunt.

'Easier? Why yes, of course there was. We weren't looking for ease though. Speed was our goal and here we are at Finger Point in time for our meeting with Rikath. There was no other method of travel that would have got us here this quickly.'

Arred looked around at the eerily silent sea with its apparently stationary waves and he shuddered. He could not argue with Perdimonn's logic, but it had been a very strange and uncomfortable journey. Moreover, Arred was uncomfortably aware that Perdimonn would probably want to use this spell again to speed them on their way. As a Magician, Arred was used to disrupting the natural order of things. After all, that was probably as good a way of defining what magic did as any that Arred could conceive. This disruption of time, though, was probably the most unnatural-feeling result of magic that he had ever experienced.

The trip from Kaldea had taken many sessions, of what had seemed like hours at a time, pulling at the oars of their little boat. During that time, the sun had barely moved and the clouds had gone past only at the rate they were rowing. It had been strange seeing shoals of fish lying motionless in the water and sea birds hanging in mid-air, as if suspended on invisible wires. Once they had even passed through a rain shower where the rain drops did not move. All in all, Arred had found the experience most unnerving and he was looking forward to getting ashore so that Perdimonn would restore their place within time to normal.

Now, as Arred rowed the little skiff towards the northern shore of Finger Point, he reflected that he would just be glad that this part of their journey was complete. Perdimonn was looking forward, past Arred, towards the shore. He was obviously searching for something or someplace in particular.

'Ah! There she is!' he exclaimed suddenly.

Arred stopped rowing for a moment and glanced over his shoulder at the shoreline. It took a moment to pick out what Perdimonn was pointing at. It was Rikath. The Warder of the Elemental Key of Water was standing on the beach as still as the surf at which she was staring.

'Time to give Rikath a little surprise,' Perdimonn chuckled, sounding mischievous, like a little schoolboy who had just devised a particularly amusing prank. 'Keep rowing us in until we're right in the shallows just in front of her, then I'll restore us into normal time.'

Arred was not averse to the occasional practical joke and immediately saw what would happen. To Rikath it would seem as if they materialised out of thin air in front of her. Arred smiled as he looked at the amusement on Perdimonn's face. The old Magician had looked terribly weary and somehow depressed since their efforts at Kaldea and the discovery that Selkor now had knowledge of two Keys of Power. It was good to see him more like the jolly old fellow that Arred remembered of old.

Working their boat into the stationary surf just in front of Rikath was not difficult. Arred positioned them right in the shallows where they would merely need to hop over the side of the boat and they would be in no more than knee deep water. Then he pulled in the oars and watched Rikath's face with interest as Perdimonn completed his reverse time-disruption spell.

Unfortunately for Arred, he was so amused by watching Rikath's amazed expression as normal time resumed that he did not concentrate at all on what was happening to the boat. He was therefore unaware that Perdimonn had already stepped out into the water and that the boat had rapidly drifted around such that it was broadside to the shore. A wave crashed into the side of the boat behind him and Arred was pitched head first over the side. As he rolled along the sandy bottom of the shallows he felt the boat, lifted by the surf, slide over him. When he surfaced, spluttering and coughing at the inadvertently swallowed salty water, Arred found that *he* had suddenly become the butt of the joke. For an instant he was annoyed, but then he saw the funny side of the situation and joined in with the laughter of the other two.

A little while later, the three Warders sat around a small fire and discussed what to do next over a breakfast of roasted fish. There was little choice really. They had to chase after Selkor in a race to reach Morrell before the Shandese Magician added the Elemental Key of Air to his collection.

'Could he really be The Chosen One?' Rikath asked, her narrow lips pursed in thought.

'Anything is possible I suppose, but there is nothing in the prophecies that I've read to suggest that The Chosen One will gain the four Keys by deception and force. Come to that, there is nothing to say categorically that The Chosen One will wield all four Keys,' Perdimonn answered thoughtfully.

'What about "He shall wield the Keys of the World to determine its fate..."?' Arred asked doubtfully. 'That seems pretty clear to me.'

'Well it does only say "the Keys", not "all of the Keys",' Perdimonn replied. 'It's a fine distinction maybe, but then the text of *The Oracles of Drehboor*, to which I assume you refer, is so cryptic and open to interpretation that it's almost worse than useless. All I know is that if I had to choose someone in whom to entrust the fate of the world, then Selkor would *not* feature highly on my list.'

'Agreed,' echoed the other two.

Rikath ran her fingers through her long dark wavy hair, sweeping it back out of her eyes on both sides of her face.

'Of course, the whole thing might just be nonsense,' she said irritably. 'Drehboor was a pompous old bore at the best of times. Who knows – he might have made the whole thing up just to cause discussion and argument between Magicians everywhere for centuries to come?'

'No,' Perdimonn asserted quickly. 'Drehboor was genuine. He may have been a little closer to the edge of sanity than most, but I've seen too many of the other parts of his prophecies come true to begin doubting now. Whatever else he was, he was the most accurate Seer that I've come across. His prophecies of Darkweaver all came true, didn't they?'

Rikath and Arred both shrugged in unison.

'I suppose that you could interpret the words to fit the events,' Arred said, his tone dubious. 'It really doesn't matter that much, though I think that we're all agreed. We vowed to protect the secrecy of the Key Runes. Given a choice of a person to be The Chosen One, none here would choose Selkor. We must therefore try to prevent him from gaining any more Keys. Darkweaver caused enormous devastation without access to any of the Keys. Imagine what havoc Selkor might wreak with the ones he has, let alone more.'

'I certainly agree,' Rikath said forcefully, her green eyes flashing with fervour. 'Can we use your time distortion spell again Perdimonn? Given the speed that you got here, we could easily make it to the Mountains of the Sun before sunset.'

'It would be terribly dangerous,' Perdimonn answered, his face grave. 'We would have to be incredibly careful. I was happy enough to use the spell on the water because I could wrap the whole boat in the bubble and thereby remove the risk of injury. I couldn't do that if we were to travel overland. Any interaction with our bodies and their surroundings would actually be happening at hundreds of times faster than normal. A stubbed toe could mean a mashed foot. A fall from a horse would almost certainly be fatal. I could speed our way by two or three times that of normal quite easily, but we will have to be careful to avoid being seen. Explaining magic in Thrandor hasn't been easy for two hundred years or more now.'

'Will Selkor know about this effect?' Arred asked thoughtfully.

'I'm hoping that he's already found out the hard way,' Perdimonn said, smiling slightly at the thought. 'He never was one for anticipating the consequences of his actions.'

CHAPTER 14

'... and it will come to pass that in the time of
the ascension will the Chosen One arise.
Eternal damnation shall be at His left hand
and lasting peace at His right. He shall wield
the Keys of the World to determine its fate,
and though the faithful may clear the way,
only the Chosen One shall walk the final
road. The road to the abomination shall be
His alone to tread. If any but He and the Key
itself doth tread the path, then the World
shall end. All paths for the Chosen One lead
to the final road. The Key will choose the
time and the Chosen One shall know no
other choice. Eternity for all nations shall
reside in His hands.'

Calvyn had read this passage over and over again and it
chilled his soul with every reading. 'The Chosen One' –
why did seers have such fascination with a person known
as 'The Chosen One'?

The old Seeress in the market place who had tried to kill
him with a knife had rattled on about 'The Chosen One',
yet she had been talking about Demarr, named 'The
Chosen One' by the nomadic peoples of the Terachim
Wastes. At least, he assumed that this was the case,
because the events that had followed her pronouncements
had appeared to fit her words. The problem with prophecy
was that often it was so open to interpretation that

virtually anything could be twisted to fit the words. This book was no different. In reading the earlier sections of the oracles, Calvyn had thought that he had identified sections that spoke of Derrigan Darkweaver and the making of the silver amulet that Selkor now carried. Calvyn had read these sections over and over as well, but the more that he read them, the less certain he became that they related to Darkweaver at all.

Frustrated again by his lack of understanding and inability to interpret the twisted words and phrases of the book, Calvyn closed the cover and pushed himself back in his chair. Closing his eyes he allowed images conjured by the strange prophecies to run riot in his mind. Pictures of Demarr carrying a bunch of huge keys along the edge of a precipice dominated his thoughts, and his mind's eye added a fiery pit on one side and a peaceful Thrandorian style countryside on the other. But Demarr was dead, so he could not be 'The Chosen One' referred to in this text. He had ended, but the world had not. No, if these so-called Oracles were anything more than the rantings of a madman, then the answers did not lie with Demarr.

Why had Akhdar given him this book? He had seemed to think it important that Calvyn read it quickly for some reason. Yet having read it right through twice, and sections of it many times, Calvyn could not understand why Akhdar had lent it to him at all. Surely the Grand Magician had not made a mistake and given him the wrong book by accident? He had certainly seemed to be very deliberate in his choice. Maybe it might be better to return the book and ask Akhdar directly, though it irked Calvyn to think that he had somehow missed the point. At least if he asked Akhdar about the book, it might stop plaguing his mind with unanswerable questions.

Sighing in resignation, Calvyn decided that he would return the book the next day and, setting his questions aside for a while, he settled into practising spells for his next class with Master Chevery. The class had been set the task of mastering a basic levitation spell for moving objects by using magic. When he had studied the spell,

Calvyn had quickly realised that it was a variation of the one that Perdimonn had used when Calvyn had first met him. On that occasion, Perdimonn had used magic to lighten his wagon enough for them to free its wheel from a deep muddy pothole. This spell was actually simpler, though its effects were more spectacular. With it, the spell caster could cause an object to fly around at will, controlling its direction and velocity with simple rune sequences. Theoretically, with enough power to draw on, even large objects could be made to defy gravity with equal ease.

Calvyn began conservatively, using the spell to lift a silver coin that he had placed on the table. Initially the coin jerked and bounced as Calvyn struggled to control it, but it quickly settled into a steady swirling flight path as he directed it around the room with increasing skill and confidence. Once happy with moving the small silver coin, Calvyn tried moving a book and was delighted to find that it was just as easy.

'I wonder if I can handle more than one object,' he mused. 'If I change the runes in the second line of the spell, I should be able to handle a second.'

Calvyn studied the runes for a minute or two and quickly identified a short sequence that would enable him to introduce a second object. Grabbing an old parchment from a pile at the side of his desk, he scratched out his amended spell in a few seconds. The new series of runes was not really any more difficult than the original one and with a slight start of revelation, Calvyn realised that there was no reason to limit the number of objects to two. A simple recurring pattern of runes in the centre of the spell would allow him to handle as many objects as he wanted, with the proviso that they would all describe the same flight path.

Delighted at his discovery, Calvyn was anxious to try it out. He had long ago mastered the ability to carry out spells with his eyes open, but for a few seconds before he began the spell, Calvyn closed his eyes and ran through the amended sequence of runes in his mind. Once convinced that he could remember his new spell, he moved to the centre of the room and began.

Initially, he used the magic to lift his coin once more from the desk and send it flying around the room. Next, he introduced his new sequence and the book on his desk took off and began circling the room as well. A smile began to curl the corners of his lips and in an almost rapid-fire sequence, other books from his bookshelf leapt into the air. They joined the circle until there was an almost solid ring of flying objects racing around the tight circuit. Laughing with pleasure, he watched them for a moment before sending the books back to where they had come from on the bookshelf in a reversal of the pattern that had dragged them into the air to begin with. Finally the book and coin that he had begun with settled gently back on the desk.

'Ha! Spit the bones out of that, Master Chevery,' he chuckled.

Calvyn knew full well that none of the other Acolytes would even think to progress the spell that they had been set to learn. The Masters had apparently drilled them into thinking that it was terribly dangerous to design new spells. Why that was, Calvyn just could not understand. After all, the spell would either work, or it would fail. There was no middle ground that Calvyn could distinguish. Determined to prove his abilities to Master Chevery and thus win back his approval after his disastrous demonstration of sorcery, Calvyn continued to study the spell late into the night and discovered two other points in which the spell could be altered to advance its effects.

Strangely, his thought processes were interrupted twice during the evening by the sense of a familiar presence nearby. Both times he looked around from his desk, almost expecting someone to have crept unheard into his room. Each time he had started to reach out with his mind to locate the source of the feeling and had stopped. His ability to reach out with his mind using his powers of sorcery was severely limited here in the Academy building.

The shield that he had sensed on approaching the building when he had first arrived had obviously been designed to prevent sorcery from being used outside to look in. As Calvyn had quickly discovered, it also had the unusual effect of reflecting and refracting sorcery within its bounds. At very short range on a one to one basis, sorcery still worked well enough, but trying to range around the building with his mind had proved to be an extremely disorientating and uncomfortable experience. Having realised the cause, Calvyn was not in a hurry to repeat the sensations.

At first Calvyn wondered whether Perdimonn had somehow managed to return to Terilla, or whether he was trying to contact him. Based on the little information that he had on Perdimonn's whereabouts, this seemed unlikely. Eventually, Calvyn decided that it must be one of the Masters, maybe Akhdar or Chevery, 'looking in' on him. Although this seemed a huge invasion of privacy, it was consistent with the room searches for magical objects and Calvyn had already managed to draw a lot of unwanted attention over various things in the last week or two, so it would hardly be surprising if the Masters were keeping tabs on him.

The next day, Calvyn entered Master Chevery's class confident that he would be able to perform something with pure magic that would impress the crotchety old Grand Magician. On arrival, Master Chevery gave each of the Acolytes a small wooden ball about half a finger length in diameter and told them to go and sit at their desks. As Calvyn looked around at the class he was surprised to find most of them looking apprehensive. Some of the Acolytes looked so nervous that Calvyn wondered if something was happening today that he had somehow not found out about.

Master Chevery closed the door behind the last Acolyte and swept the room with his keen gaze.

'So!' the Master pronounced loudly, making several of the nearer Acolytes jump slightly. 'Who will be the chosen one today?'

It was Calvyn's turn to be startled at the mention of 'The Chosen One', but he settled quickly as he realised that it had been a chance remark.

'Sevendral,' Chevery nominated, stabbing a gnarled finger in the direction of a particularly nervous-looking young Acolyte, 'please show us how you progressed with your homework. Lift your ball by means of the spell that I gave you until it is stable at head height please.'

'Yes, Master,' the boy gulped.

'The rest of you take note of his efforts. Your turn will come,' the Master intoned ominously.

Sevendral began his spell and the ball he had been given began to wobble on the desktop. Frowning with concentration the Acolyte started subconsciously gesturing at the ball to rise while he repeated the spell. Reluctantly, the ball danced higher, bobbing back, forth, up and down like a prairie dog's head on the lookout for predators. Ever so gradually the jiggling ball rose until it was about head height.

A bead of sweat rolled gently down Sevendral's temple.

'Good enough,' Master Chevery said gruffly. 'Now make it fly around in a circle.'

That was too much.

The moment that Sevendral tried to make the ball move sideways it danced out of control and dropped to the floor with a clacking bounce. The Acolyte hung his head, clearly embarrassed at his failure. To Calvyn's surprise, though, Chevery did not chastise him for the failure – far from it.

'A good first effort Sevendral. The spell can be tricky to begin with. Practice will enable you to stabilise the spell and steady out all that bouncing around. Adding direction to the object's flight path can sometimes take a little while to master. Now then, go and collect your ball and we shall see if any of the others fare any better. Are there any volunteers?'

Calvyn looked around tentatively. He was in a quandary. To show off his progress after Sevendral's performance would seem like bragging to the other students, so he watched and waited. A couple of the other Acolytes volunteered and Chevery allowed them each to try in turn. One of them was little better than Sevendral, but the other, an older Acolyte whom Calvyn understood to have been here at the Academy for some years, completed the spell almost flawlessly. If his ball dipped and climbed a little as it flew in a circle around the classroom it was not overly noticeable. All of the other students were watching with fierce concentration, their faces mirroring their respect for their fellow Acolyte's control of the spell.

Calvyn was so lost in his indecision that at first he did not hear Master Chevery name him as next to go.

'Calvyn! Are you with us?' Chevery asked irritably.

'Sorry, Master Chevery. Yes I am,' Calvyn answered, ignoring the sniggers from the less discreet young Acolytes.

'Well? Are you going to show us how you have progressed? Or does the fact that sorcery cannot be used for levitation mean that you have failed in your homework?'

The direct slur was enough to make Calvyn's decision for him. He was not going to allow Chevery to use him as the class whipping boy. It was plain that the Grand Magician was out to embarrass him, so Calvyn decided to turn the tables. He knew in his heart that it was probably unwise, but his anger at Chevery's obvious prejudice drove him on.

'On the contrary, Master Chevery, I found the homework most stimulating and I decided to progress it along the lines that seemed most obvious. For instance I assume that the flying in a circle was merely a starting point.'

Even while he was speaking to Chevery, Calvyn began the spell silently in his mind. He did not need to look at the ball to know that it had risen smoothly from the table and had begun to fly a perfect circle around the classroom.

The Grand Magician's eyebrows rose slightly as he noted the perfect control and the lack of effort that Calvyn had required to carry out the spell.

'So I started playing with slightly more complex patterns,' Calvyn continued as he directed his ball into a figure of eight pattern. 'Then I realised that the obvious progression would be to control more than one object...'

'More than one? Don't tell me that you can weave multiple spells, young man! I once saw my old Master weave three levitation spells simultaneously, but the complexity...'

Chevery broke off his recollection and his jaw dropped as Calvyn added one after another of his fellow Acolytes' wooden balls into the figure of eight. Finally, all fifteen balls raced around the interlocking pattern, narrowly missing one another at the cross-over point in the middle. Calvyn's eyes did not leave that of the Grand Magician's.

'You don't have to weave simultaneous spells, Master Chevery. The one you provided was perfectly adequate. All that's needed is a repeat of the sequence in the second line and you can add as many items as your mind can imagine. Of course it's easy when the items are all the same shape and size, but it equally applies for other objects.'

Chevery was speechless and Calvyn did not doubt for one second that the rest of his class was equally as stunned. Calvyn had not finished yet though, he was just warming up.

'Of course the next obvious progression from that was to try to make multiple objects go in different directions. That seemed almost impossible at first, until I found that if you vary the fourth juncture and "nudge" the items in the direction that you want them to go with a sort of mental push, then it's really not that difficult.'

Five of the balls spinning around the figure of eight suddenly changed direction and began a vertical circle through the two loops of the figure of eight. If it was possible, Master Chevery's jaw dropped a little further.

'This can also be continued as with the multiple objects so long as your mind can sustain the picture.'

Five more balls left the figure of eight and started their own tight little horizontal circle inside the upper half of the vertical circle.

'Of course, the final trick would be to send the objects to somewhere other than where they had originally started from. It is easy enough to reverse the spell and send the items back to their original resting place, but to do otherwise...'

All fifteen balls raced down to Calvyn's desk to coalesce into a perfect equilateral triangle.

'...requires a change at the seventh juncture and another mental nudge. It's not particularly difficult, but it does require a bit of practice to get it perfect.'

Calvyn stopped talking and continued to look at Master Chevery expectantly as if awaiting his thoughts on the matter. The Grand Magician took a few moments before he managed to gather his thoughts sufficiently to react.

'Ah, well, yes Calvyn. Very good. Very good indeed. I see that your former tutor taught you the elements of levitation well.'

'Oh no, Master Chevery. It's true that I once observed my mentor use a variation of this spell to aid the release of a wagon wheel lodged in a pothole. Unfortunately, at the time I thought that he was a crazy old man who was spouting gibberish, for I'd been taught that magic was a myth. I didn't begin my training in magic in earnest for another two years after that incident. You're the first person to introduce me to levitation spells, but I do have a few questions. The rune sequence at the fifth juncture...'

'Later, Calvyn, later. Let us progress this lesson for now. Today we are going to look at basic transmutation – the altering of one substance such that it becomes another. This is the first step along the road to the shapeshifting spells that enable accomplished Magicians to alter the appearances of objects, and ultimately themselves, into other shapes and forms. Let us begin...'

The Grand Magician launched into his spiel on transmutation with his normal self-assured style, but Calvyn noticed once or twice during Chevery's lesson that the Grand Magician looked at him with a strange expression on his face. It was a mixture of wonder, uncertainty, anger, disbelief and wariness. Calvyn knew only too well that he had over-stepped the mark with his demonstration at the beginning of the lesson and in some ways he regretted it. However, the glow of satisfaction that he had felt at seeing Chevery's astonishment would carry Calvyn through any repercussions of his lack of diplomacy for a considerable time to come.

At the end of the lecture, the Grand Magician once again set homework. This time the task was to master a spell that would change milk into pure water. Calvyn was not surprised when Master Chevery asked him to stay behind and he waited patiently while the rest of the Acolytes gathered their things and left. Ignoring the furtive whispers and the uncertain stares of his classmates as best he could, Calvyn realised that after today's demonstration he would never be a true member of the group. The looks that the other Acolytes gave him as they left held the wary expressions that one might expect when looking at a strange and dangerous animal.

Having dismissed the class, Master Chevery ignored the departing Acolytes with a cold disdain. He waited until the last one had exited the room and closed the door behind him. Then, looking up from the papers on his desk, the Grand Magician fixed Calvyn with an icy stare.

'That was an impressive display that you put on today Calvyn. Tell me, where did you get that spell? I have never seen anything like it before, so don't give me that rubbish about it being the one I gave you. Is it in your grimoire?'

Chevery's tone was so cold and accusing that Calvyn was momentarily taken aback. He had expected Chevery to be annoyed at being made to look foolish in front of the class, but had not expected such a biased and vitriolic attack on his integrity.

'Yes, Sir, I wrote it into the grimoire last night. Here, look.'

Calvyn took out the grimoire from amongst the small pile of books that he had been carrying under his arm and passed it to the Grand Magician. Chevery riffled through the pages until he reached the most recent entry. There he found the spell, just as Calvyn had said. Chevery's frown deepened as he contemplated the evidence.

'I don't know many air spells, Sir. Are there any more that I can study?' Calvyn asked innocently.

This time Calvyn was completely unprepared for Chevery's response. Calvyn had meant the comment to be an acknowledgement of his own lack of knowledge in that particular area of magic. It was an attempt to mollify the Grand Magician by bowing to the man's superior learning and experience.

'What do you know of the elements, Acolyte?' Chevery snapped. 'Has Perdimonn divulged secrets to you that he should not?'

'I ... I don't know what you mean,' Calvyn spluttered, completely aghast at Master Chevery's suggestion. 'Perdimonn taught me a few basic spells and then gave me this grimoire. If that is "divulging secrets", then perhaps he has. As for the elements, I know only what Therone Jexis states in broad terms in his book on basic magical theory – that all spells draw energy from four basic elements: earth, air, water and fire. I have deduced a little more from applying that principle to the spells that I have already learned. They are only my theories though, and I have not categorically proved them yet.'

Grand Magician Chevery's expression appeared to waver between anger and suspicion.

'And what might your theories be, young man?' he asked, his voice losing its really vicious edge and returning to a more typical acidic tone.

'Well, Master Chevery, in equally broad terms, I believe that each of the runes belongs to an element group. Some are obvious, others are more subtle. Looking at the spells that Perdimonn taught me, the vast majority are made up from runes that I would group under the earth element. He did teach me a few very basic spells that were tied with the other elements, but it was almost as if he had specialised in a particular type of spell and advanced only in that one field.'

'Yes, well I don't want you to start filling the heads of the other Acolytes with such nonsense,' Chevery stated, his expression set in a particularly disapproving frown. 'If I hear any of the other Acolytes spouting your fanciful ideas, I shall expel you from the Academy personally. Is that quite clear?'

'Yes, Master Chevery,' Calvyn replied meekly.

'Very well. I shall be speaking with the other Masters about your exploits today, of that you can be sure.'

Calvyn took that as a dismissal and he gathered up his books, including his grimoire, and let himself out of the classroom. Inside, his stomach seethed with anger at the reaction of the Grand Magician to his hard work and obvious ability. What was wrong with the man? Did he not want his students to excel? He was not like any instructor or teacher that Calvyn had ever come across before. Fair enough, when Calvyn had broken the taboo on using sorcery in the Magicians' Academy, he had given the Master a right to be angry. The perfect execution of a homework exercise and the obvious extra research and practice that Calvyn had shown today had not.

Grinding his teeth as he walked, Calvyn promised himself that he would not give the Grand Magician an excuse to expel him. He would just have to continue to prove himself so far ahead of the rest of his class that Chevery would have no choice but to let him study with the senior Acolytes.

* * * * *

The loud 'thump, thump, thump' on the door startled Jenna from her daydream. The guest room that Lomand had arranged for her to stay in was very comfortable, but Jenna had nothing to do. Boredom and daydreaming had filled her with a desire to be on the move again. It was time to return to Thrandor and face Baron Keevan to explain her actions, but more than anything Jenna wanted to find Calvyn and tell him how she really felt about him. If justice had anything to do with it, the Baron would reward her for bravery and service above and beyond the call of duty. In reality, though, Jenna knew it was more likely that she would be disciplined and possibly thrown out of his army. Life could be cruel sometimes, but if facing the Baron gave her the chance to find Calvyn again, then any punishment that Keevan dealt her would be worth suffering.

Jenna opened the door and Lomand was standing outside, almost totally blocking the doorway with his vast bulk. He smiled at her warmly.

'Master Akhdar will see you now, Jenna. Please, come this way.'

Lomand turned and started off down the corridor without waiting to see if she followed.

'About time too,' Jenna muttered under her breath. They had kept her waiting around for more than a day, and whilst it had been nice to be able to eat regularly without worrying about how she was going to pay, the subtle draw of the path home was gradually increasing its tension. Jenna's resolve to return to Thrandor had strengthened with every passing hour, such that now she just wanted to walk out of the door and begin the journey.

The maze of corridors quickly worked their subtle magic on Jenna. After three or four turns she had no idea of where she was relative to her room anymore. Every passageway appeared the same – a threadbare central lane of dark red carpet on a wooden planked flooring, oddly placed and composed pictures dotted along the walls and lots of identical-looking plain wooden doors at irregular intervals on either side.

Lomand stopped without warning in front of a door that appeared identical to all of the others. He knocked with the same heavy thump, thump, thump, that he had used on her door a few minutes before. From inside a faint 'Come in' prompted Lomand to open the door and usher her inside.

Grand Magician Akhdar, sitting at his desk, looked up and smiled warmly at her as she entered. Pushing himself up out of his seat, Akhdar offered a hand for Jenna to shake in greeting. His long-fingered hand was warm as Jenna shook it and his kindly old face, snowy white hair and sparklingly piercing blue eyes, made her feel more welcome in an instant than she had ever felt before.

'Good afternoon, Jenna, it's a pleasure to meet you. I apologise that you have had such a long wait, but there has been a lot going on that has demanded my attention. Please, take a seat. You came here on something of a quest I understand?'

'That's right, Master Akhdar. I came in search of a recent travelling companion of mine. His name is Perdimonn. Can you tell me where I might find him, for I got the impression from his call that he was in need of help.'

Akhdar raised one eyebrow inquisitively.

'His call? What call was this?' the Grand Magician asked.

'A mental call. A magical call. Like a dream, but real. He contacted me in the same way to solicit my help a while ago. Of course I didn't know who he was then and I thought at first that I might be going a little loopy.'

'Wait a moment! Did you say that Perdimonn called you mentally at a distance and he had never met you before?' Akhdar asked incredulously. 'You are absolutely sure that you had never met before, even in passing?'

'Positive,' Jenna affirmed.

'And he called you personally, by name?'

'Yes.'

'Remarkable!' exclaimed Akhdar happily. 'I would never have thought it possible, but then I suppose that I should never be surprised at what Perdimonn has achieved. He has a remarkable knack for developing new and often unexpected spells. So what did he say to you in this call that brought you here looking for him?'

'Nothing really, Master Akhdar. I heard his call and then there was a vague impression that he had been startled by something, then nothing. I've had no sense of him calling me since. When we parted he was heading here to bring you warning of Selkor and Darkweaver's

Amulet. This was the logical place for me to come looking for him.'

Akhdar nodded, looking thoughtful for a moment and then smiled at her with the same almost grandfatherly smile that he had given her when she had first walked into his study.

'You have done well to find us here, Jenna. Many have come looking, but few find this place. I think that I must ask you to stay for a while. Perdimonn may yet call you again and the Council craves news of him. If it will calm your fears for him, we have had news of his whereabouts since he left us having delivered the news that you spoke of. The last we heard he was in Kaldea and was safe, though his news was equally as dire as the tidings of Darkweaver's Amulet. Events are overtaking us and I cannot allow a potential source of information out of my reach at such a crucial time. You do understand, don't you?'

The final question was put in tones that spoke volumes of necessity and paternal concern such that Jenna found herself telling the old Magician that of course she would stay while he had need of her. Even as she was saying the words her heart cried out against the restriction. Perdimonn was not here and therefore Jenna had no further call to stay. So why was she agreeing with this sweet old fellow with his twinkling eyes and his white hair? He had to be using magic of some form to persuade her, yet she felt no compulsion placed on her heart to actually stay.

As Lomand led Jenna out of Akhdar's study and back through the corridors to her room, confusion tangled her thoughts. Staying made no real sense. Perdimonn had called her, she no longer doubted that much, but weeks had passed since in which she had heard nothing more. Why should the vague possibility of Perdimonn calling her again at some indeterminate time in the future tie her to remaining here in Terilla? Certainly it might be true that the Council of Magicians required news of the old man and his quest, whatever it might be. If what Perdimonn had told her of the importance of his mission to Terilla in the first place was true, then what he was doing was of vital importance to the future of Thrandor as well as to the Council of Magicians. Did she have the right to just opt out and leave them to it when she might be able to offer a vital link?

Lomand said nothing all the way back to Jenna's room, but he had obviously sensed something of her disquiet.

'I know that you would rather be on your way, Jenna,' he said kindly. 'Please, don't go just yet. Akhdar was telling the truth. We need lines of communication and you have the potential to offer another line. If it would help to make your stay with us more comfortable I could introduce you to a fellow Thrandorian who has recently joined the Academy as an Acolyte. Would that help at all?'

'Another Thrandorian? Come to study magic? Do many come here from Thrandor?' she asked, curious that someone should ignore the prohibition and travel all this way.

'No indeed! We have not had a Thrandorian Acolyte for many years now. This young fellow is proving to be something of a revelation though. He is probably the youngest Knight that I have ever met and he is certainly causing a stir among the other students with his talents.

'Knight? A Knight of the Realm of Thrandor is here to study magic? Well that's certainly a strange turn of events for a country that has prohibited magic for so long. If the King found out... well he wouldn't be happy I'm sure.'

'Things have been changing rapidly in Thrandor after recent events I believe,' rumbled Lomand thoughtfully. 'You may be right of course, but this young fellow claims to be the new King's Adviser on matters magical. I'll introduce you at dinner tonight if you wish.'

Jenna was tempted. The thought of catching up on news from home was certainly attractive. But what if Baron Keevan had circulated a description of her as a deserter? A Knight of the Realm was an enforcer of the King's law. If he recognised her as a deserter, he would be forced to do something about it. Still, they were a long way from home. What could he do here, so far from the Thrandorian border? Jenna did not know, but she thought better of finding out the hard way.

'No,' she sighed. 'Thank you, but no. I will bide my time for news as I have a few things to think about. I can stay a short while, but I do have things that need addressing back in Thrandor. If you don't mind, I'd rather not rub shoulders with the aristocracy. Would it be all right for me to eat here in my room this evening?'

'Certainly,' Lomand shrugged, 'if that's what you want. The young fellow really isn't that aristocratic though. I'm sure that he would prove pleasant enough company even if you're not from the same part of Thrandor.'

'I'm sure that he would be charming company, Lomand. I, on the other hand, would probably be too distracted by problems at home to be able to return the compliment. Another time maybe.'

'Very well, Jenna. I will have your meal sent here later.'

'Thanks, Lomand.'

Lomand closed the door behind him as he left and Jenna found herself wondering even more about what was happening back in Thrandor. The King employing an adviser on matters magical – surely King Malo would have been better to get someone like Calvyn to fill a post like that, rather than some young Knight of the Realm. At least Calvyn knew something of magic. But then who could say where Calvyn was? Maybe the King would have given him the post if he had not gone missing. Then there was Perdimonn off doing something terribly important in Kaldea, wherever that was. Whatever it was that he was doing certainly had the Council of Magicians in a flap, as they were very keen to keep track of him. What would take him so far, so fast, that was so vitally important? Whatever it was, Jenna would have wagered that Selkor was involved.

Strangely, even as she was thinking about Perdimonn and Calvyn, Jenna began to imagine that she could hear them talking to one another. With a quiet chuckle, she threw herself onto her bed.

'I've been sitting alone in this room too much,' she muttered aloud. 'Maybe I should have dinner with this Thrandorian Knight after all.'

Jenna had expected that speaking aloud would banish the familiar voices from her mind, but they had continued their imaginary conversation despite her verbal interruption. It was then that it sank in. The conversation was not imaginary at all. Perdimonn was using his magic to speak with Calvyn and she was somehow mentally eavesdropping. Holding her breath to prevent the noise of her breathing from interfering with her ability to hear the two minds conversing, Jenna's eyes widened in shock as she suddenly grasped the gist of what they were saying.

CHAPTER 15

'How's the Thrandorian doing?' Chorain asked, eyeing Hammar with a seemingly casual interest from the other side of the table.

Hammar was not fooled by the dissembling for an instant. Chorain was nervous. Hammar could almost feel the tension in the Commander.

'Better than I expected,' Hammar admitted with a shrug. 'But I'm not stupid enough to bet on him defeating Serrius just yet.'

Chorain had arranged this meeting to find out how his 'investment' was shaping up. Hammar had already deduced that Chorain's arrangement with him was somehow to patch up a previous plan that had not gone as the Commander had expected. It seemed that Commander Chorain was still trying to convince himself that his plans were all still under firm control. If that was the case, and Bek beating Serrius was a part of his plans, then the man was delusional. Nothing in the arena was ever sure. Any one of a multitude of unpredictable factors could turn a fight from what seemed like a foregone conclusion into an upset. The only apparent constant in the arena was Serrius and it was that constant that Chorain was trying to destroy. Only a fool would bet on someone beating him, even if the someone they were betting on was Bek.

Bek had been a good fighter when Hammar had first seen him in the arena. After his recent spell of intensive training, Hammar was willing to raise that appraisal to excellent. However, excellence had never defeated Serrius in the past and there were certainly no guarantees that it would in Bek's case. There was a certain indefinable quality in Bek that Hammar could not quite place his finger on which *might* make a difference. It was not a feeling that Hammar would be willing to lay gold on though, and certainly not the amount of gold that Chorain would be paying Hammar if Bek did somehow defeat the top ranked fighter.

'Will he fight tomorrow?' Chorain asked.

Hammar nodded.

'Twice if all goes as planned in the first bout.'

'Good. The sooner this is resolved, the better. I need the Thrandorian and I need him soon,' Chorain stated boldly. 'See that I get him in one piece, Hammar.'

'I'll continue to do my best, Commander. The pot of gold at the end of the rainbow should give you confidence of that much. I can't make you any promises though. You're a seasoned soldier. You should understand why not.'

Chorain smiled tolerantly at Hammar.

'Every enemy has a weakness, Hammar. That is what my military training tells me. You just have to identify and exploit it correctly and even the mightiest of foes will fall.

'Excellent,' Hammar responded, his voice laced with sarcasm. 'Point out to me the weak link in Serrius' armour and I'll stick the knife in myself and save Bek the trouble. The rules have never seemed to apply to that man, but I'll be more than happy to be proved wrong. Do you know of such a weakness?'

Chorain's face hardened with anger. He was not used to people who did not bow and scrape at his every word, particularly people to whom he was paying a vast amount of money for a service. Hammar was hardly a typical employee though, and his lack of military training was more than evident by his attitude.

'No I don't. That is what I'm paying you for. Don't get clever with me, Hammar. Just keep the Thrandorian alive long enough for me to use him. Is that clear?'

'Perfectly, Commander. As I said, if I fail it will not be through a lack of effort.'

'Good.'

With that, Chorain pushed himself to his feet abruptly and stalked from the room. Anger pulsed from him with every pace, but Hammar did not care. The Weapons Master had made dangerous enemies throughout his life. It would have been difficult not to within his chosen career path. This Commander was dangerous in many ways, Hammar decided, but providing that he kept paying gold in such large quantities the Weapons Master was willing to face the risks involved in dealing with him. There was one thing that Hammar would most certainly *not* do for Chorain though, and that was to compromise his position in the arena by using foul means to gain the Commander's gold. If Bek beat Serrius then it would be done fair and square.

Chorain strode down the steps to exit the arena and barged past the guard without a glimmer of remorse for his rudeness. He had hardly walked a hundred paces from the gate when a beggar woman in a tattered black shawl intercepted him on the street.

'Please, Sir? Me children are starvin' an' me husban' ain't sent nothin' fer months. Could yer spare a copper 'r two fer a bite fer me children, Sir? Please?'

The young woman was filthy, but while she was skinny, Chorain would hardly have said she was undernourished. He did not even bother to reply. Given his mood and the fact that he was not the most generous-looking character to begin with, the Commander was amazed that the woman had had the gall to approach him in the first place. Without a second thought he moved to sidestep her, but the woman chose to step the same way and they collided. Something sharp jabbed into Chorain's side and he snarled at the sudden prick of pain.

'Sorry, S...'

The woman did not get a chance to complete her apology. Chorain's knuckles caught her hard on the cheek as he back-handed her aside.

'Get away from me, you clumsy cow!' he spat angrily.

Leaving the woman sprawled on the ground, clutching at her cheek and weeping loudly, Chorain stamped away with his mood darkened even more by the incident. If he had been Emperor, Chorain would have made begging illegal. Deportation to some remote land would rid Shandar of the dross that marred city streets across the land. It just took someone with the political will to make it happen.

By the time he reached the turning towards his lodgings Commander Chorain found himself strangely out of breath. His side throbbed where he had been jabbed by the beggar woman and he began to feel a little dizzy. What was wrong with him? He did not normally suffer breathlessness like this. Staggering slightly, as his head started to spin with disorientation, Chorain walked to the corner of the nearest building and propped himself against the wall for stability.

With a curse, he looked back up the street to where he had left the woman lying in the road. There was no sign of her.

'This is no time to fall sick,' he growled aloud.

His body did not agree.

After a few seconds, Chorain pushed himself away from the wall and tried to continue on to his accommodation. He would rest there, he decided. The proprietor could send a maid up with some weak dahl and a cold compress for his rapidly developing headache. He would feel fine after a good night's rest and a decent meal.

It took a few seconds to realise that he was no longer on his feet, but sprawled on the cold stone paving. Another few seconds and it sank in that he had retched. His body was quivering and jerking madly out of control. Muscles were no longer his to control and his vision was blurred and already darkening. He could not even call out for help though his mind urged his lungs to try. All that escaped was a low groan that ended in a long sigh as his body gave a final lurch and stilled in death.

Femke carefully dropped the poisoned iron pin down an open drain hole. It had done its job most effectively and the Emperor's top spy and sometime assassin promised to herself that she would use the supplier of that particularly evil brew again.

The Commander had not really connected hard with his backhanded blow, for Femke had long since learned how to roll with a punch. Despite her skill though, the blow had stung and would probably bruise. It was annoying, but a small price to pay, Femke decided as she wrapped her tatty black shawl around her shoulders and carefully slipped away unnoticed into the city streets.

* * * * *

The crowd in the arena seemed bigger today, a seething mass of humanity even more vocal than usual in supporting their favourite fighters. It might have been his imagination but Bek could have sworn that the loudest cheers of the day had been for his victory over Mandarbe this morning. The word was certainly out that there was a new fighter climbing the ranks. According to Hammar, Bek was the sole reason that the crowd was so large today. Not surprisingly, Garvin was delighted at the sudden surge of interest. The disturbing part of the news was that the Arena Master was reportedly considering changing the challenge rules to slow down Bek's advance towards what was already being mooted as an inevitable clash with Serrius.

This morning's clash with Mandarbe had gone precisely to plan with one exception. Mandarbe was dead. Bek had not intended to kill the man but the move that Hammar had taught him to use against the tall, dark-haired fighter had resulted in a momentary chance for a swift finish. Bek had taken that chance. He could not afford long, drawn out fights and if it meant killing his opponents, then that was what he would do.

Hammar had been pragmatic about the death of Mandarbe.

'It happens,' he had stated without emotion. 'You didn't set out to kill him, but the arena is a dangerous place. Forget it and move on. Don't dwell on past fights. Keep focused on the opponent at hand.'

If the crowd had been disappointed at the fact that Bek's fight had finished so quickly this morning, then they had shown no sign of it. The cheering and applause afterwards had been deafening and had seemed to last an age. For the most part Bek was oblivious to the crowd, but even in his determined and single-minded state he had not been able to totally ignore the barrage of noise that it generated.

He braced himself to face the roar of the crowd again. Zeffanes would be waiting for him this time. If he won this fight only one further bout would separate him from the chance to face Serrius.

'One at a time,' Bek muttered under his breath. 'Just take them one at a time.'

The words were Hammar's, drummed into him all week during session after session of training. Bek was fitter and faster than he had ever been in his life before. There was no doubt in his mind that if he ever did get back to Baron Keevan's army there would be none there to touch him in one-on-one swordplay anymore. True, the only person who had ever defeated him in friendly competition there had been Derra and that had been while he was in his first week as a recruit. However, the war against the Terachite Nomads had erupted before the annual challenge competitions had come around, so he had never had the chance to test himself against some of the better veterans. If there had been better swordsmen then Bek knew that he would never know. There would be none back home to beat him now. Unfortunately, that was not necessarily the case here.

The gate opened and Bek marched forward and out into the blazing heat of the arena. A glance to his left confirmed that Zeffanes was matching him stride for stride from a gate some twenty yards away. This would be a testing bout and Bek was under no illusions that it would go as easily as the one with Mandarbe earlier.

Zeffanes was of a similar height and build to Bek. He moved lightly on the balls of his feet and was renowned for his grace and poise. That he was only ranked tenth in the arena meant little, for Hammar had made it quite clear that if Zeffanes wanted to make the top five he could do so. Like several others though, he did not want to force a fight with Serrius, so he deliberately avoided moving up the ranks. Bek had never seen Zeffanes fight in the arena, but had watched him in training. All of the top fighters were fast, but Zeffanes moved with the grace of a dancer. He was cat-like in his ability to stay on his feet and his blade moved with the speed of a striking snake. In training Bek had never seen the man lose his balance or focus. If Bek was going to win, he would have to change that statistic.

In previous fights Bek had merely carried a single short sword, but at Hammar's insistence he changed the pattern this time.

'Don't give Serrius any more information than you have to,' the Weapons Master had advised. 'Use different tactics for each fight and he will not know what you are going to do against him.'

The resulting decision was that Bek would use a hand shield in conjunction with his sword this time. Bek had been trained to use a shield as a soldier in Baron Keevan's army. This small hand version, which was not much bigger than a dinner plate, required different techniques to be used effectively, but Bek had practised with it and had adapted quickly to the changes. He had also modified it slightly in a gamble to try to throw Zeffanes off balance. The shields were generally made of a hard wood, metal rimmed and reinforced. Bek had carefully removed about a fifth of the metal rim around his shield and had repainted it to make the change all but unnoticeable.

Bek reached the centre of the arena and saluted the Emperor's balcony. Turning to face Zeffanes, Bek eyed his opponent with the icy gaze for which he was fast becoming known: no emotion, just a cold, dispassionate appraisal. Zeffanes returned the look with a slight smile. His brown eyes held a warmth that was deceptive, for there was no doubt in Bek's mind that the man would gut him in an instant if given the chance. What was more, he would probably continue to smile as he did it.

The stalking began, a slow quartering step that gave nothing away. Both men stalked a careful prowling circle as they watched and prepared for the first blows. The crowd took up the beat of their steps with a slow clap, but neither man noticed. Like lovers in a crowded room, they were intent only on one another. Eyes narrowed and unblinking, the two fighters seemed almost to be battling silently with their minds before their blades even touched.

Bek recognised the slight bunching of Zeffanes' muscles and sprang forward to meet his attack. Blades clashed in a furiously fast exchange and the fighters seemed almost to spin past each other, returning to the stalking. Again Bek saw the faintest of hints – again he met the attack squarely. This time the exchange was a little longer, a clashing cacophony of steel on steel.

Zeffanes withdrew and the circling began once more. Bek kept his gaze as cold as death, though he began to imagine that he could see a small glimmer of respect in his opponent's eyes. Zeffanes was certainly fast and he used his hand shield very cleverly to develop openings for his blade. Bek was thankful for all of his recent coaching with Hammar. Within seconds Bek realised that had it not been for all of those extra training sessions learning the subtleties of arena fighting and the tricks that the fighters employed, he would have already lost this fight and possibly his life with it.

Bek had no intention of dragging this fight out and so he darted back at Zeffanes, taking the fight to him. As Bek expected, the Shandese fighter read his movement well and met his attack with perfect poise. A vicious exchange followed. Bek took a cut to the forearm of his sword arm, though he opened a similar cut just below

Zeffanes' shoulder. Both fighters felt the bite of steel and ignored it with equal indifference. Blades flashed and clashed with no reduction in speed until Bek played his trump card.

A wickedly fast, cutting stroke from Zeffanes was just what Bek had been waiting for. It came at such an angle that Bek could twist his hand shield so that the edge of his opponent's blade, instead of glancing off the shield, bit into the section of the hard wood rim where Bek had removed the metal. For an instant the blade jammed in the wood and Bek yanked his shield back as hard as he could. The move took Zeffanes totally by surprise and pulled him forward, completely off balance. Bek struck like lightning, his sword lashing twice at Zeffanes in the blink of an eye. Amazingly, somehow the Shandese fighter managed to twist and partially deflect both blows with his own hand shield. The first blow scraped harmlessly against Zeffanes' breastplate armour and the second opened a shallow cut across his forehead. Then his blade wrenched free of Bek's shield and he was instantly on the counter attack.

Bek was taken aback that his plan had failed to produce the quick result that he had wanted but he pressed Zeffanes hard in the following exchange, refusing to let up the pace. Once again the damage was not all one-sided. Both men were now bleeding in several places, though none of the wounds was serious enough to qualify either man the winner.

Time and again they clashed in a blaze of furiously flashing blades. The pace was breathtaking and the subtleties in the swordplay were enough to satisfy even the most critical of audiences. For Bek, every minute felt like an age. The last thing that he had wanted was a protracted bout and this looked as though it could last forever. Zeffanes and he appeared evenly matched, neither being able to land a deciding blow.

The fight ended strangely, or at least, strangely as far as Bek was concerned. Zeffanes was by no means beaten, nor was he badly injured, but with an abruptness almost as fast as his attacks, Zeffanes suddenly stepped back and laid aside his sword in the sign of surrender.

Bek did not know whether to feel satisfied, frustrated, relieved or just happy that he had emerged from the bout as the winner. The fact that he had progressed once more towards his goal was pleasing, but the manner of his progression made him feel somehow cheated of true victory.

Bek saluted the Emperor's balcony and as he had found in the past, the sound of the crowd became apparent again. They, at least, had enjoyed the fight it appeared. Zeffanes recovered his sword and gave his salute as well. Then the two men crossed the sand together towards the opening gate.

'Why did you surrender the fight?' Bek asked Zeffanes as they approached the gate. 'You could have won. The fight was in the balance.'

'True, I could possibly have won. There again, if I had not surrendered we would probably be still out there cutting each other to shreds, and for what? You want to fight Serrius: you are welcome to. You are at least as good as I am. Maybe you are slightly better, who can say? I decided to take the guesswork out of it and prevent either of us from giving the medics any more sewing practice! I have no desire to meet Serrius in the arena, so best of luck to you. If you beat him, then I'll come looking for a rematch and we'll fight until we drop if you like.'

Bek grinned at him.

'Thanks. I appreciate the sentiment!' Bek said dryly.

Zeffanes nodded and returned Bek's grin. Then they were inside and both were led away by medics to different rooms.

As Bek made the slow walk through the corridors to the medic's rooms the adrenaline that had been coursing through his veins drained away. The pain of his various wounds started to pulse and throb like the angry buzzing of a swarm of bees. A wave of tiredness swept over him and he staggered slightly, surprised to find that the energy and vitality that had filled him only moments before had all disappeared.

'Do you need help? Or can you make it to my workroom?' asked Bek's designated medic with concern.

'I'll be all right,' Bek answered stubbornly. 'Lead on. Just don't go too fast.'

Fortunately they did not have much further to go, for by the time that they had walked the last few yards to the medic's room, Bek was fit to drop. In a flash of insight, Bek suddenly appreciated what it was for some men to actually enjoy the dangers of the arena. Although he had not been fearful of death today, he had faced the possibility of it twice. Mentally and physically he had experienced a high of awareness and mobility superior to anything that he had known before. True, he had fought with swords since he was a boy. His father, being a Captain in Lord Valdeer's army, had encouraged him and coached him until he was more than just competent, but these arena fights were different. Competitions that he had participated in before had always been to first blood and the battles that he had fought in had been largely about survival and holding battle lines. The arena forced the fighters to live and perform at their peak, in the full knowledge that the opponent they faced would not stop at first blood. Somehow, facing that situation with the atmosphere of thousands of people watching and cheering had made Bek feel incredibly alive. He could appreciate that it was an experience that would be addictive for some – for some maybe, but not for Bek. For Bek the arena was merely a means to an end, a means to exact revenge and justice.

The medic opened the door to his workroom. Bek stumbled through the door, pushing past the medic, and all but collapsed onto the raised bench-like bed. The medic sighed and muttered something derogatory about 'damned fool fighters'.

Bek lay on the couch with his head swimming in a sea of pain and fatigue. He was vaguely aware of the medic cleaning up various cuts and removing his protective gear to get at others. A couple of times he flinched at shafts of particularly acute pain as the medic stitched his wounds, but for the most part he lay still, mentally swamped in weariness and pain. Bek was certainly not aware that Hammar had entered the room until the Weapons Master spoke directly to him.

'Well, Thrandorian, it seems that you have reached your goal,' Hammar said with a hint of sadness in his voice. 'You fought well today. I will be honest, I did not expect you to beat Zeffanes.'

'I didn't beat him. He gave up,' Bek mumbled.

Hammar smiled.

'You did not let him beat you. That is victory enough against such an accomplished arena fighter. I will say it again – you fought well today.'

Bek's mind suddenly grasped Hammar's first statement and he pushed himself up off the bed into a half-sitting position, resting on his elbows.

'What do you mean I've reached my goal?' he asked. 'What about Voldor? He's ranked five isn't he? I have only reached ten. Have the rules changed? Can I now challenge Serrius?'

'The rules have become irrelevant: Serrius has publicly announced his intention to challenge *you* in next week's games.'

'That's good, isn't it? It means one less fight at least,' Bek said positively.

'It might be good, then again it might not,' Hammar answered cagily. 'It might be that he wants to fight you before you gain any more experience of fighting top fighters.'

'You don't sound very convinced of that,' Bek observed wryly.

'No, because I think it unlikely,' Hammar admitted. 'It is much more likely that he feels he has identified a weakness that he can exploit. It appears that he has challenged you because he is sure that he can kill you.'

* * * * *

'Why are we still here, Derra?' Fesha whispered in her ear, though with the noise the arena crowd was making he could have shouted his question without fear of arousing interest.

Derra turned and gave Fesha one of her hardest stares. Most men who knew Derra would tremble in fear at the gaze she levelled at him, but Fesha refused to be intimidated by it. He met her look with an uncompromising stare of his own. After all, what they were doing was madness.

Half of Shandrim was looking for Derra at the moment. Her victory in the arena the previous week had won her instant fame throughout the city. When she escaped from the arena, rumour of the breakout had flashed through Shandrim like a forest fire. People who had seen her fight and win wanted her caught so they could see her fight again. People who had missed her fight wanted her captured so that they could see her in action. In short, everyone wanted Derra captured and returned to fight in the arena, yet here she was, along with her two rescuers, in the arena crowd. Madness.

'I came here to get Bek and Jez. Jez is beyond my reach but I will not go back empty handed when there's a chance of taking Bek,' Derra stated coldly.

'He doesn't *want* to come,' Fesha hissed.

'I don't care!' Derra said flatly. 'I came to get him. That's what I intend to do.'

Fesha shook his head and turned towards Eloise. The raven-haired beauty eyed him with an equally uncompromising expression.

'Women!' Fesha muttered under his breath, shaking his head in disgust.

* * * * *

'Ah, yes! Femke, of course. Come in,' the Emperor enthused. 'What news do you have for me?'

Femke was on edge instantly. Something was not quite right here. The Emperor looked all right, and sounded all right, but something had set the hairs on the back of her neck tingling from the instant that Femke entered the room. One did not survive to be the best spy in the business without developing certain instincts, and alarm bells were ringing within Femke's head as she gave her brief statement.

'The developing situation that I briefed you on last time continues to grow, your Imperial Majesty. Rumours abound on the streets now and it will not be long I fear before signs of unrest among the populace become more widespread.'

The Emperor looked thoughtful for a moment.

'It is to be expected I suppose,' he said with a sigh. 'Very well, do you have anything new to add?'

Femke shook her head slightly.

'Not on that matter, your Majesty. If you require the location of the Thrandorian woman and the couple who aided her escape, then I know where they're hiding out.'

'Excellent! Where are they?'

'They're staying in a small guesthouse in one of the back streets not far from the arena. They've made no moves to leave Shandrim, which suggests that they still intend to try to free the last Thrandorian. Would you like me to arrange for them to be arrested?'

Vallaine thought for a moment. He had heard something about a woman fighter from Thrandor today at the arena, but having only replaced the real Emperor after the last games, he did not really know the background to her being there or her breakout. In truth, he had little interest in the arena and its fighters other than the Thrandorian that he had seen fight today. That young man might prove very useful to Vallaine's plans. Still, it would not be proper to just let these people get away with whatever it was that they had done and he certainly did not want them to take the young Thrandorian fighter out of his reach.

Then, he had another idea.

'No,' he said thoughtfully. 'Instruct a select few of your colleagues to monitor them, but don't have them arrested just yet. I will consider what to do about them later.'

'Certainly, your Majesty. Also, the other matter that you asked me to deal with need trouble you no more.'

'Really?' the Emperor asked casually, pouring a little red wine into a glass and taking a tiny sip. 'How did you do it?'

'Are you sure that you want to know details, your Majesty? I would rather not say things about such matters openly where other ears might overhear. Suffice it to say that the deed is done.'

'Of course, Femke, of course,' the Emperor said, his tone placating. 'It is a weight off my mind to know that I can leave such matters in your capable hands. Now, I appreciate that you are probably tired after all your recent activities but I have a new mission for you. It's vitally important to the future of Shandar that a certain person be brought here to me. I cannot trust anyone else enough to do the job swiftly and discreetly. It will mean a bit of a journey, I'm afraid.'

'Of course, your Majesty. That shouldn't be a problem,' Femke answered, thoroughly intrigued. The Emperor had never sent her out of Shandrim before. Femke had spent so long buried in the shadier sides of the Capital that she had given up on ever getting involved in anything further afield. 'Who is it that I'm to find and what information do I have to work with?'

The Emperor looked intently at Femke over the top of his wine glass as he took another small sip. The hairs raised even higher on the back of Femke's neck. What was it that was bothering her? Something was terribly wrong but she could not put her finger on it at all.

He lowered his glass.

'Barrathos is his name. He is a very large man who, shall we just say, possesses a certain ability that I would like to make use of. It is because of his talent that I would rather keep his coming to the palace as low key as possible.'

'I understand, your Majesty,' Femke affirmed confidently. In fact she did not understand and did not really care to understand. The feeling of wrongness in the Emperor's chamber had got her so on edge that she was ready to say anything in order to be able to get out in a hurry.

'Good. I had a feeling you would,' the Emperor said, his voice pleased.

'There,' thought Femke suddenly, 'there was something in the Emperor's voice that just did not sound right.'

'You'll find Barrathos somewhere in the region of Shellia,' the Emperor continued. 'The last time I heard, he was trying to drown himself in ale. He may be a little nervous about coming to the palace, so just tell him to remember that his recent disaster brought ruin to many. It is time for him to come and repair the damage. Just say that. It should be enough to bring him running along.'

'Yes, your Majesty. Was there anything else, your Majesty?'

Femke could not wait to leave. The uneasy feeling that the Emperor's spy had experienced from the moment she had entered his study just would not go away. It was screeching on her nerves like fingernails scraping over a slate board.

'No, Femke. Swift journey.'

Femke bowed smoothly and withdrew gratefully from the room. Almost immediately the feeling of wrongness started to subside. Shuddering slightly at the memory, Femke walked quickly away through the palace and out to the stables to acquire a horse. Whatever it was that had caused the feeling required thought to sort out. Fortunately, she had been given time and space to give it the thought that it required. It would take her several days to get to Shellia and back. That was ample time to solve the mystery, she thought.

Vallaine dropped his disguise once Femke had left. The woman suspected something, he was sure of it. Nevertheless, she was a useful asset. The Emperor's top people were all talented and from what little Vallaine had learned of Femke, she was an excellent spy. Vallaine needed talents like that. He could not afford to squander such skills unnecessarily. If he just kept her at arms' length long enough to perfect his disguise properly, then there was no reason why she should not continue to work for him unknowingly for many years to come.

Knocking back the last of the wine in his glass Vallaine idly wondered what the last part of Femke's report had actually been about. The first part had most likely been to do with the rumours of the defeat in Thrandor. It made sense and the Emperor had certainly been monitoring the public mood. The second part had been self explanatory, but what the last part of her report had been about, he had no idea. Maybe Commander Chorain would know, he mused. Vallaine had discovered only a few hours before that Chorain had returned from Thrandor, and the Sorcerer Lord was eager to pump him for information about Shanier. It had been one of the servants that had mentioned the Commander and Femke in the same breath. Unfortunately, the unwitting fool had known nothing more of Chorain than his name, so Vallaine would have to send out his own operatives to try to track him down. It was a minor inconvenience, but an annoying one.

Information was what Vallaine needed more than anything else at the moment. He had neatly disposed of the Emperor and with him the threat of any more top assassins being paid by the Imperial purse. However, by taking the Emperor's place he had inherited a new set of problems that would not go away without some considerable effort.

If only he did not have to go through the motions of being someone that he was not, he might have more time to devote to the problems facing Shandar. Unfortunately, if he was to maintain the pretence of being the Emperor, he had to do the things that the man he had replaced used to do. Among other things, that involved attending the incredibly tedious arena fights all the time. What the man had seen to enjoy in men hacking at one another in an interminable bloodbath, Vallaine did not know. One interesting character had emerged though, the Thrandorian fighter named Bek. He was certainly skilled, and a bit of judicious digging had turned up the fact that he had been sent to the arena as a prisoner by none other than Shanier. There was mileage in that, Vallaine was certain of it. Keeping the young man's friends under surveillance whilst maintaining them out of harm's way would give him a second lever. If they made a nuisance of themselves he would have them arrested, but providing they stayed out of the way and continued to plot, Vallaine would be content to just keep an eye on them and be poised to spring his invisible trap in his own time.

'I'll call him up for a little Imperial chat after his next fight,' Vallaine promised himself, pouring a little more wine into his empty glass. 'With any luck he will know even more than Chorain. One way or another, Shanier will pay for deceiving me.'

CHAPTER 16

'...tell the Council that Selkor has managed to stay one step ahead of me all of the way. He now has three of the four Keys of Power and I have little doubt that he'll come looking for me next. Morrel has joined with us and we're riding hard for Mantor. I'll explain what happened when I see you. It's essential now that the Council put their doubts and fears aside and ride out to meet us. Only together and prepared will we stand a chance of preventing Selkor from gaining knowledge of the final Key. I'd like you to come with them, Calvyn. Also, bring Lomand if you can. I'm sorry that I can't tell you more, but I need to ride in haste and this spell takes a lot of energy. Just bring them all to Mantor.'

'Very well, Perdimonn, I'll do my best,' Calvyn replied dubiously. 'I don't know how they'll take such a demand coming from me, but I will try to shove them into action.'

'Good. Oh, and one last thing...' Perdimonn added, trying to sound casual about it. 'Bring your sword along with you. You do still have it, don't you?'

'Yes, I've still got it,' Calvyn answered, recognising instantly that Perdimonn was concealing something behind his casual request. Burning with curiosity, but very aware that Perdimonn probably did not have the luxury to explain, he decided not to pursue it. 'I'll be sure to bring it with me. Is there anything else?'

'No,' Perdimonn answered, a slight hint of relief in his voice. 'Just get to Mantor with the others as quickly as you can. I'll see you there.'

Perdimonn's presence in Calvyn's mind faded away. Rubbing his temples gently to ease the stress and the beginnings of a headache, Calvyn pushed his chair back from his bedroom desk. The pain had nothing to do with the mental link with Perdimonn and everything to do with having worked past midnight virtually every night since he had arrived at the Academy. Although the hour could just barely be classed as late afternoon, a wave of fatigue was rolling over him that clearly indicated his body was in need of rest. Just the thought of rest set Calvyn to yawning uncontrollably.

'It's no good,' he muttered after a jaw cracking yawn, 'I don't care if the world is going to end, I am going to bed early tonight regardless.'

Even as he moved towards the door of his room in order to take Perdimonn's message to Grand Magician Akhdar, Calvyn heard the commotion outside in the corridor. Someone was running along the corridor yelling at the top of their voice. Maybe it was because he was tired, but it took a moment for him to register that the voice was both familiar and calling *his* name. Eyes widening in shock as it dawned on him who was making the racket, Calvyn wrenched his door open and ran out into the corridor.

'Jenna!' he cried in amazement. 'Jenna? Is that really you?'

The slim figure had passed his room, but slid to a halt a short distance down the corridor, took one look at him and then hurled herself into his arms. Before Calvyn could begin to get over his astonishment Jenna was hugging him tightly, her head buried against his shoulder. Instinctively, Calvyn loosely wrapped his arms around her and made soothing sounds down into her hair as he could feel her weeping uncontrollably against him.

All along the corridor heads peered around doors and people stepped out of their rooms to see what all the noise was about. Observing the couple locked in an embrace was generally enough to sate everyone's curiosity. One by one they melted away until a few moments later the two were alone in the corridor. Standing still and holding Jenna for what seemed like an age, Calvyn struggled with the welter of emotions and thoughts that flooded his body. Finally he managed to link his mind to his vocal chords and he spoke gently.

'Come on Jenna. Let's get out of the corridor and sit down, shall we?'

Calvyn felt her nod against his shoulder so, not wanting to break the physical contact, he kept one arm around Jenna's shoulders as he led her into his room and over to his bed. They sat close, each with an arm about the other, not really knowing where to start until Calvyn reached over with his spare hand and offered his pillow to Jenna as a sort of outsized handkerchief. Jenna laughed suddenly and dried her eyes on the corner of the pillowcase.

'How in Tarmin's name did you find me here?' Calvyn asked eventually.

'I didn't really find you, because I wasn't actually looking for you,' she answered, still dabbing at her eyes. 'Oh, Calvyn, I'm *so* sorry that I was horrid to you back at the dormitory.'

'What? The dormitory? What are you talking about, Jenna?'

'The day before you were captured by the raiding party – I was horrid to you in the dormitory. It's been playing on my mind ever since. I only did it because I was jealous. I saw you with Eloise and I thought that you were falling for her when all along I had been hoping that you might... fall for me,' she said, cocking her head slightly to one side and looking up at him with her big brown eyes. 'I love you, Calvyn.'

'You do?' Calvyn exclaimed in surprise.

Jenna had said the words softly but their effect had struck him like a cascading avalanche.

'That was not what you were supposed to say,' Jenna said reproachfully. 'You were supposed to sweep me up in your arms, profess your undying love in return and then kiss me.'

'I was?' Calvyn replied in bewilderment.

'Oh, you're hopeless!' she declared and then pulled his head forcefully down to hers and kissed him deeply and firmly on the lips.

When they finally parted, Calvyn's expression was one of such dumbfounded shock that Jenna laughed.

'What's the matter, farm boy? Never been kissed before?'

'Not like that,' Calvyn admitted with a grin. 'It was very nice.'

Jenna looked at him, her manner coy and her eyes sparkling with pleasure and amusement.

'So, do you?' she asked with a cute, kittenish expression.

'Do I what?' Calvyn asked stupidly.

'Love me, you lummox!'

'Well, er, I... I suppose I do,' he said, finally recognising the reason for having missed her so acutely over the last few months.

'Suppose! Sup...' Jenna exclaimed, her voice rising in mock outrage. But before she could say anything further, Calvyn forestalled her by planting his lips firmly over hers and kissing away her protests. Jenna did not resist, but relaxed into Calvyn's embrace and was smiling happily when they eventually parted.

'Sorry to change such a very pleasurable topic of conversation,' Calvyn apologised softly. 'But what are you doing here if you weren't looking for me?'

'I came here in search of Perdimonn,' Jenna answered. 'I thought I heard him calling me a few weeks ago and...'

'Perdimonn!' Calvyn exclaimed suddenly, leaping to his feet. 'I have to get to Akhdar and the rest of the Council. I have to convince them to come to Thrandor and help Perdimonn and the other Warders.'

'I know. I heard,' Jenna said, grinning at his stunned look.

'What... how...?'

'It doesn't matter for now,' she answered. 'Let's go and

rouse these Magicians into action.'

'That might not be quite as easy as it sounds,' Calvyn muttered aloud, his eyes momentarily distant. 'Still,' he added, his voice firming as his resolve hardened, 'we must try. Let's go, Jenna. We can catch up on news later. I have so many questions, but we can discuss everything on the way to Mantor. There should be long enough on that road to fill in the details of the last few months.'

Calvyn caught Jenna by the hand and led her out into the corridor. They strode rapidly through the maze of corridors at an urgent pace, Calvyn turning with confidence at each junction and doorway. Within a minute or so of leaving Calvyn's room Jenna had no idea of where they were, but she no longer cared. It was true to say that Jenna was as happy as she had ever been in her life.

They stopped abruptly next to a door that looked no different from any of the others. Calvyn knocked and hardly waited for a reply before entering. Grand Magician Akhdar was still in the process of calling out his permission to enter as Calvyn led Jenna into the old man's study. Jenna recognised the room the instant that the door opened, and was torn between wariness and amusement at Akhdar's outraged expression with their cannon-ball style entrance.

'I hope that this intrusion is important, young Calvyn,' Akhdar began, his voice tinged with more anger than Calvyn had yet heard in the generally mild old Magician. Then his eyes took in Jenna as well and Calvyn could almost see the pieces falling into place behind the Grand Magician's eyes.

'Perdimonn needs help, Master,' Calvyn stated, his voice firm and uncompromising. 'He has called for the Council to meet him in Mantor as soon as possible.'

Akhdar's eyes narrowed slightly as his penetrating gaze assessed the situation. Firstly he took in Calvyn's determined stance, the set of his jaw and the defiance in his eyes. Next he looked at Jenna, who blushed slightly under the intensity of his stare but did not look away. Finally, he looked at the link between them – the joined hands – and a slow smile spread across his face. Jenna blushed more deeply and would have relinquished Calvyn's hand had he not squeezed hers with a reassuring pressure.

'So, that was Perdimonn's message, was it? An order for the Council to come to Mantor – I find it unlikely that even in extremis, Perdimonn would be so blunt.'

'No, Master, but that was the bottom line. The message was one of dire tidings, though I don't profess to understand their full import,' Calvyn replied without so much as a hint of apology.

'I'll be the judge of that, Calvyn. Now out with the message – all of it please.'

'Master, the message was for the Council, not for you specifically,' Calvyn answered determinedly. 'Also, Lomand should be here, for the contents involve him as well. I have told you what I will without the other Council members present.'

'How *dare* you withhold information from me, Acolyte! Have you learned nothing of respect for the Brotherhood in your short time here? We share with you the secrets of magic and you will not even entrust news, vital to the survival of our Order, to one of the most senior Grand Magicians! I suggest that you re-examine your priorities and loyalties, young man. Now tell me the message.'

'Master, with all due respect, the Magicians do not even share their secrets with one another here, let alone with mere Acolytes. This so-called Academy is ridiculously inefficient in its transfer of knowledge, and from what I've been able to determine, actually restricts the pursuit of true advances in magic. Your teachers drum into Acolytes the nonsensical idea that the development of new spells is somehow terribly dangerous and wrong. They don't encourage delving into the truths of how spells are constructed and how runes from the different elemental groups interact to produce various basic spell characteristics. All in all, it appears that your Academy is nothing more than a sham to prevent anyone outside of your little Council-clique from learning to wield any true power. Now, *Master* Akhdar, I don't deny that your knowledge is far greater than mine in the field of magic, but I object to having my priorities and loyalty brought into question when I've clearly been brought up to understand the true meaning of the concepts. Call your Council, or I will go to Lomand, who I suspect will have a more open mind to my request.'

Jenna was shocked to hear Calvyn speak to a venerable and wise-looking Magician in such a fashion and, judging by the old man's scandalised expression, so was Akhdar. The Grand Magician was clearly speechless at Calvyn's multitude of accusations, though it was interesting that he did not strike back instantly with countering answers.

'Master,' Calvyn said in a much friendlier tone, 'I respect the fact that you've shared at least something outside of the knowledge fed to other Acolytes. I have a suspicion that *The Oracles of Drehboor* may have some bearing on current events, but I can't make any sense of them at all. Please, Master Akhdar, just convene the Council. Maybe, if we can all just share a little more of what we know, then the whole situation might begin to make a little more sense.'

Akhdar looked at Calvyn sharply. The Magician was clearly not soothed one iota by Calvyn's platitude, but he did point at a bell hanging in a high recessed corner of his study and, muttering a short spell, he started it ringing.

'There are reasons other than selfish secrecy for what we do here at the Academy, Calvyn. Now is not the time for discussing them, but be assured that we will speak on this issue again,' Akhdar said shortly, his voice cold and hard where normally it was warm and friendly. 'I trust that you've not been discussing your ideas and beliefs with the other Acolytes.'

'No, Master, my ideas and deductions are my own. I have more sense than to spread dissent and disorder unnecessarily through the Academy. Some of the

Acolytes might figure it out on their own in time, though, particularly after my homework presentation in Master Chevery's class the other day.'

'Yes, I heard about that. I suppose I should have spoken to you immediately afterwards. Still, it's irrelevant now.'

Lomand arrived, his bulk looming in the open doorway.

'Is there anything I can be of assistance with, Master Akhdar?' he boomed, his deep voice rolling into the study like a peal of thunder.

'Come in, Lomand. The Council is convening and your attendance has been requested.'

'My attendance?'

'Yes, Lomand. Leave the door open, would you? The others should be arriving shortly.'

Sure enough, Master Jabal arrived only moments later, followed shortly by Master Chevery. When the final two Council members arrived, Akhdar introduced them to Jenna as Masters Ivalo and Kalmar. Calvyn had seen them both once before when they had come to Master Jabal's classroom in reaction to the alarm set off by the discovery of his sword. The encounter had only been brief though, for Akhdar had swept Calvyn off to his study before the other Masters had had much chance to talk with him. Not surprisingly, Ivalo and Kalmar gave Calvyn suspicious looks as they entered. Master Chevery wore a look that bordered on outright hostility, whilst Jabal merely looked curious. This would be an interesting meeting, Calvyn decided, pursing his lips into a hard line as he mentally braced himself for the inevitable arguments.

'Brothers, I have convened the Council on the behest of Acolyte Calvyn and a visiting guest from Thrandor. It appears that they have been contacted by Brother Perdimonn with a message that is of such urgency that we must all be present to hear it.' Akhdar did not attempt to hide the edge of irritation in his voice at the final clause, leaving all present in no doubt that he had no prior knowledge of the nature of the message. 'The floor is yours, Acolyte. What are Perdimonn's tidings?'

Calvyn took a deep breath and looked around at the gathering of Magicians. Not one of them looked really open to what he had to say, except maybe Lomand, but he was as difficult to read as a closed book. Nothing about this situation was easy.

'Masters, Perdimonn contacted me a short while ago and gave me instructions and information to pass on to you. He specifically said to "tell the Council", so I asked Master Akhdar to summon you before sharing the information.' Calvyn paused and let that sink in for a second or two before continuing. 'Perdimonn wanted me to tell you that Selkor has managed to stay one step ahead of him wherever he has gone. Selkor apparently now has three of the four Keys of Power and Perdimonn believes that Selkor will now turn and pursue him.'

The room erupted in a babble of confused and conflicting questions, as all five Grand Magicians at once tried to ask Calvyn different clarifying points. Surprisingly, it was Lomand who settled them.

'Quiet! All of you! Let the young man at least complete his message before you dissect it,' Lomand boomed, his voice bringing silence out of chaos.

'Thank you, Lomand,' Calvyn acknowledged, giving the huge man a quick smile of gratitude. 'Perdimonn said that it is time to put all doubts and fears behind you. He asks that you all ride in haste to meet him and the other Warders at Mantor. His words were, "Only together and prepared will we stand a chance of preventing Selkor from gaining knowledge of the final Key." Then he asked that Lomand and I accompany you to Mantor. He gave no reasons for that, but he was riding in haste. I suggest that we do the same.'

'Your suggestion is noted,' Akhdar said acidly, 'but it is the Council which makes the decisions here. Not Perdimonn, not Selkor and most certainly not you.'

'*Three Keys!*' exclaimed Chevery, obviously still in a state of some shock at that fact. 'Do you think Selkor really *is* "The Chosen One"?'

'That remains to be seen,' Jabal answered, his tone contemptuous of Chevery's obvious fear. 'He has not yet gained the final Key, but that is of little importance. If Selkor is "The Chosen One", then nothing that we could possibly do would prevent him from gaining it.'

'Surely just possessing knowledge of the four Keys does not automatically make Selkor "The Chosen One"?' Kalmar interjected. 'He would still have to fit the rest of the prophecies, wouldn't he?'

'Why should he?' Ivalo argued. 'Prophecies are hardly renowned for their accuracy. If the future is already set then what is the point in making any decisions. Surely if the future is already mapped out and set in stone, then whether we ride to Perdimonn's aid or not, we cannot affect the outcome of events.'

'That's nonsense, Ivalo, and you know it,' Kalmar said derisively. 'We cannot shirk our responsibilities by hiding behind such specious arguments. If we do nothing, then history will have every right to accuse us of our part in what could potentially be a calamitous disaster.'

'You are right, Kalmar,' Jabal said, nodding his agreement. 'We may not be able to prevent a thing, but that does not absolve us of our responsibility to try.'

'Excuse me,' Calvyn interrupted, fascinated by the arguments but unable to restrain himself any longer from asking the question that was burning his lips. 'Who, or what, exactly is this "Chosen One" that everyone keeps speaking of?'

Silence reigned and the Council members all looked at one another to see if any of the others would answer the question. For a moment, Calvyn thought that none would. Then Jabal started to speak.

'It is said that "The Chosen..."'

'Jabal!' Akhdar interrupted, shocked that the Grand Magician was actually going to explain it to Calvyn.

'He needs to know, Akhdar. He is involved too deeply in this affair not to know what we are dealing with here. It is interesting, and a measure of Perdimonn's integrity, that the lad knows nothing of it already,' Jabal retorted, and then he turned back to Calvyn. 'It is said that "The Chosen One" will wield all four Keys of Power. The Keys are special magical runes that can literally unlock the power of the elements. They are master runes if you like. These runes, even individually, if used for evil purposes would bring destruction on a worldwide scale. It was therefore decided long ago that the knowledge of these master runes should be safeguarded from misuse. As written knowledge could be stolen and the Magicians' Council proved corruptible, it was decided that Warders would be appointed as guardians: pacifist Warders who undertook solemn oaths that bound them to maintain the secrecy of their charge and never use it in anger or violence of any form. Each Warder was given knowledge of one of the master runes and part of the vow was to never attempt to gain knowledge of any of the other runes. Perdimonn is a Warder of one of those Keys...'

'The Earth Key! Of course!' Calvyn exclaimed aloud.

Jabal looked at him sharply, as did all of the other Magicians, but Calvyn did not notice. Suddenly everything was finally falling into place.

'Indeed, but which Key hardly matters now that Selkor has knowledge of the other three. Selkor is but one step away from becoming "The Chosen One", but what that means is difficult to say. There are many prophecies involving "The Chosen One", though they appear to be conflicting in what they say. Some name him the harbinger of eternal damnation, some the bringer of an age of peace. Still others speak of a path in the balance between the two. Who is to say what the reality will be?'

'Far be it from me to interrupt you gentlemen,' Jenna said, her voice so unexpected that it drew immediate attention from all present. 'It's simply that immediately before parting ways with Perdimonn, he explained to me that he felt Selkor still had some element of good still within him. Perdimonn was intent on coming here to enlist your help in order to prevent Selkor from being – I think his phrase was – "swept into the abyss". I take it from the fact you are still here and that Selkor is brewing even bigger trouble, you denied Perdimonn the support that he sought. Now he's crying out to you for aid again from a situation so dire that you are talking of worldwide destruction and eternal damnation. Don't you think that the time of talking and debate is past? You've heard Perdimonn's request that you ride to Mantor. What are you waiting for? The time of action is here. For good or ill we should ride to his aid and at least try to ensure that evil doesn't triumph.'

Jenna did not add that Perdimonn had also described the Council members as 'sour old men who steep themselves in memories of better days, so busy looking inwards that they have forgotten how to act'. The last thing that Jenna wanted was to alienate these old men, for Perdimonn had also pointed out that when they did act in unison, the Council still wielded considerable power.

The pause that followed Jenna's speech was an awkward silence. No one wanted to endorse her words for fear of being ridiculed by the others. After a few difficult moments, Akhdar spoke again.

'Much as it grieves me to say it, Brothers, Jenna is right. We can't just ignore events any longer. Selkor is out of control. Like it or not he is a Brother and, as such, falls under our responsibility. I say that we should ride to Mantor and meet with Perdimonn and... did he say if the other Warders were with him?'

'He didn't mention it, Master,' Calvyn answered.

'No matter. I think that we can reasonably assume that Perdimonn is gathering whatever defences he can muster to face Selkor. We should be a part of that defence.'

'I disagree, Akhdar,' Chevery said, shaking his head. 'If Perdimonn wants protection, then he should come here and stay with us. Why should we go chasing half way across the world to protect him?'

'We should go because it's our responsibility not only to bring Selkor under control, but also to ensure that the magical items that Selkor stole from us are returned,' countered Jabal. 'If Perdimonn is drawing Selkor to Mantor, then we should go and face Selkor where we know he will be. It's time that we owned up to the charges placed in our care when we accepted our places on this Council. Let's go to Mantor.'

'I agree,' said Kalmar.

Ivalo looked dubious, but nodded when Akhdar looked at him for confirmation. Chevery still looked set against going, but with the full weight of the gazes of the other four Council members looking at him, he shrugged in a grudging acceptance.

'It's decided then. We ride without delay. Lomand, take Calvyn and Jenna and prepare horses and provisions for the journey. The Council has matters to discuss and many things to organise in the short time before we depart,' Akhdar announced.

Lomand bowed to the Council and Calvyn followed suit. Jenna simply nodded and left with them as they marched out of Akhdar's study and back into the maze of corridors.

'You were just great in there, Jenna,' Calvyn said, placing his arm across her shoulders and giving her a friendly squeeze of congratulation.

'Hmm, I see that you have made your acquaintance with our young Thrandorian Acolyte then, Jenna,' Lomand rumbled, his tone amused by their familiarity.

'Thrandorian Acolyte? But I thought you said that the Acolyte was a Knight, Lomand?'

Calvyn cleared his throat with an awkward cough and Jenna shook herself from the arm around her shoulders, stopping dead in her tracks and looking at him disbelievingly. He shrugged almost apologetically.

'There are one or two items of news that we might need to catch up on along the way,' Calvyn said, looking distinctly ill at ease.

'A Knight! You're a Knight of the Realm?' Jenna's voice went from incredulous to hopelessly despondent in one simple phrase. 'But that makes it...'

'No!' Calvyn interrupted firmly. 'Don't ever so much as

think that, Jenna. It would have been difficult if I'd remained a Corporal and you a Private. Mixed rank relationships are generally frowned upon, but as a Knight I'm a free agent. I can court any lady I choose, and if that lady happens to be a Private in the army then who is to gainsay the choice of a Knight of the Realm?'

Lomand had paused to wait for them, but did not allow a full-blown discussion to develop.

'Come along now. I see that you two have a lot of talking to do, but we don't have time for that now. You'll have lots of time on the journey. Even pressing hard on horseback it will take several weeks to reach Mantor. You can court and talk to your hearts' content when we're underway,' he said with an amused smile.

Jenna looked as if she was not going to move for a moment. Calvyn felt that, even without the aid of magic or sorcery, he could almost see the jumble of thoughts cascading through her head. Reluctantly, Jenna nodded and Calvyn held out a hand towards her. With a shy smile, she placed her hand in his and they set off down the corridor at a brisk pace to go and prepare for the long road ahead.

* * * * *

'Dead! What do you mean, he's dead?' Vallaine stormed at the luckless servant.

'Just what I say, your Majesty. Commander Chorain was found dead on the street. Apparently there was no obvious cause of death. It seems likely that his heart failed, your Majesty. The medics claim that this is not that uncommon an occurrence, even amongst the fittest of men.'

'Not that uncommon! Heart failure! Do you think that I'm a fool?' Vallaine raged, punching his right fist into the palm of his left hand with a resounding smack. 'Did they check to see if he had been poisoned?'

'I... I don't know, your Majesty. I am merely a servant bearing bad news. I don't know the methods and skills of the medics. I will gladly go and ask them if you wish, your Majesty.'

'Yes! Yes! Go!' Vallaine snapped.

The servant could not leave quickly enough. He virtually ran from the chamber and the door banged shut, with very little decorum, behind him.

The High Lord of the Inner Eye did not notice.

Lost in angry thoughts, Vallaine paced back and forth across the large, beautifully woven carpet. Things were not fitting together at all as he had anticipated. True, none yet suspected that he was an impostor, except maybe Femke, but that was little consolation to salve the huge problems facing him. Vallaine had known that soothing the populace after the disaster in Thrandor would not be easy. What he had not counted on was his inability to make full use of the Emperor's spy network because there were so many questions that he could not ask for fear of giving himself away. Now the potential to use one of the Commanders who had been firmly in Vallaine's pocket had been taken away as well. With the information-gathering network effectively unavailable to him and few loyal allies in the locality to help, Vallaine realised that his position as Emperor of Shandar was perilously fragile. Of course, Vallaine did still have one potential ally – the Thrandorian fighter. If the Thrandorian was pliable to Vallaine's will, then the largest of the Sorcerer's problems could be resolved swiftly and with the minimum of fuss.

'I'll have a little talk with him after the next games,' Vallaine muttered to himself, still pacing furiously across the room. Suddenly, he stopped as a thought struck him. Slowly he lifted his left hand up in front of him to gaze at the line of rings on his fingers. Most of them had belonged to the recently departed Emperor – most, but not all. One had been in his possession for a very long time. This particular ring was not overly ornate or precious, though it was made of gold. It was just a plain gold band with a flattened oval area, engraved with a simply etched picture of a closed eye.

Vallaine sighed and scratched absently at the back of his neck as he contemplated the ring. It would be a huge gamble to give the ring to the Thrandorian, for it would leave Vallaine more vulnerable than ever and that thought caused him to shudder. The ring had saved Vallaine's life more times than he cared to think about, for many Sorcerers had coveted his position as High Lord of the Inner Eye and had tried to depose him by sorcerous means. Every attempt had failed and, with each failure, Vallaine's reputation as one that was unassailable by force of mind grew ever stronger. The truth of the matter was that the ring prevented attack by sorcery. How it had been made and by whom, were secrets lost in the mists of time, but Vallaine had learned of its power when he had still been a young man. Once he knew the ring's secret, it had only been a matter of time before Vallaine had found the ideal opportunity to perform a suitable act of treachery. After all, there is more than one way to grab power.

All of these years the ring had proved an invaluable defence against the other Sorcerer Lords, many of whom were more than inclined towards treachery of their own. Surprise attacks on Vallaine had merely left the attackers open to an instant reprisal. Some, Vallaine had killed as an example to the others. The rest, Vallaine had given a severe mental beating and had left in no doubt that had he wanted to kill them, he could have done so.

'A difficult dilemma,' Vallaine mused to himself. 'To send the Thrandorian against Shanier without the ring would be like sending a lamb to the slaughter, but send him with the ring and Shanier might well die before he even realised that sorcery was useless. Then again, if I give the Thrandorian the ring, then I make myself vulnerable to attack by sorcery. What to do?'

The more Vallaine thought about it, the more convinced he became that giving the ring to the fighter would be the best course of action. After all, Vallaine was no longer surrounded by Sorcerer Lords all seeking to take his place – he was in the Imperial Palace. It was true that being here brought many dangers, but the threat of attack from one of his fellow Sorcerers was relatively remote. On balance, the risk was worth the potential reward. With Shanier's head on a pole, it would be much easier to demonstrate to the Shandese people that the Emperor was still in control of events. Vallaine had also sent out orders for the Legions to gather at Shandrim over the next few weeks. The populace would soon see that the Emperor meant business. As Emperor, Vallaine knew that he could not ignore the disastrous loss of the Legions in Thrandor, so he had decided to bring together a huge show of force in order to convince the people that he was going to exact revenge.

The unrest amongst the people should be quietened by these displays of Imperial force. If they did not work then Vallaine had one final weapon that might just prove pivotal in controlling the masses – conscription. If nothing else cooled the hot heads, then Vallaine reasoned that he would draft every able-bodied man into the Legions and send them off to fight someone other than their own Emperor. It was a drastic measure, but Vallaine had few doubts that it would prove effective enough should it be required.

Having resolved in his mind to give the ring to the Thrandorian, Vallaine chuckled. First he would place a compulsion in the fighter's mind to seek out and kill Shanier and then he would give him the ring. That way no one would be able to remove the compulsion, as it would be protected by the ring's power. The fighter would be like an arrow that homed in on its target with such force that it would slice through shield and armour alike to strike the heart of the enemy. All Vallaine had to do was to call him up to the Emperor's balcony after his next fight.

Rumours had abounded at the last games that a fighter called Serrius had challenged the Thrandorian to fight at the next games. Vallaine knew virtually nothing of arena fighting. He certainly did not know the fighters' names, but he had watched what seemed to be an inordinate number of fights in the short time since taking the Emperor's place. The Thrandorian had looked faster and fitter than anyone else he had seen. Having seen him fight a couple of times it was difficult to imagine that he might lose. He could not picture a fight more furious than the last one that the Thrandorian had won, so Vallaine did not worry about it. Besides, the Thrandorian was but one spoke in the wheel of his plan.

The last of Vallaine's anger subsided away. Chorain's death was a nuisance but, irritating though it was, his demise would not overly hamper Vallaine's plans after all. Shanier would die, Thrandor would fall and Vallaine would be more powerful than ever.

CHAPTER 17

'Have the Thrandorian brought up here to the balcony after his fight today, would you?' Vallaine asked Garvin, who was hovering around the Imperial Balcony like a humming bird, dashing from person to person looking for the sweet nectar of praise. If Garvin had, in truth, been responsible for the recent increase in interest in the games then praise would certainly have been his due reward, but the reality was that fate had dealt him some very good fortune. First came a brilliant young fighter, both foreign and a prisoner, that everybody in the city seemed to be talking about, next a woman fighter who had won a bout in the arena before mysteriously escaping, and now Serrius had issued a public challenge to the young Thrandorian. It was hardly surprising that the arena was packed with the biggest crowd it had ever held. There was not a space anywhere to be seen in any of the stands.

Garvin stared at the Emperor, dumbstruck by the request.

'Did you hear me, Garvin? I said to bring the Thrandorian up here to the balcony after his fight today,' Vallaine repeated slowly.

'Yes, your Imperial Majesty, I heard you. I was just a little surprised. You want me to bring his body up here after the fight? Well that can be arranged, I suppose, though it's very unusual.'

'His body? What makes you think that he's going to die?' Vallaine asked, his face implacable.

'What makes me... ho, ho, ho! Very good, your Majesty. You really had me going for a moment there. I honestly began to believe that you favoured the Thrandorian over Serrius. Ha, ha, ha! That's good. That's really good.'

Vallaine gave Garvin a quick smile to solidify the Arena Master's belief that the Emperor was joking with him. Inside, though, his heart sank. It appeared that the Thrandorian was considered the underdog here and was more than likely to be killed. Vallaine mentally kicked himself for not studying the background of this arena fighting and its main characters before taking on the persona of someone who was clearly regarded as an authority on the subject. Serrius must be a Master Swordsman indeed, Vallaine decided, to be considered such a strong favourite against a fighter as good as this young Thrandorian. Now that he was alert to the fact, Vallaine listened in on conversations around him and all were about the same impending fight – Serrius and Bek. Amazingly, from what Vallaine could gather, very few people were betting on who would win the fight, but there were incredible amounts of money being placed on how long Bek would last before Serrius killed him.

Vallaine could already hear Garvin telling people of the Emperor's 'joke' and that tale would certainly grow in the telling. The Arena Master was an irritating little fellow who, judging by his stunted and twisted appearance, should have been put down at birth. The Emperor had obviously had some respect for the strange little fellow though and, despite the Emperor's miscalculation that had resulted in Vallaine killing him, the High Lord of the Inner Eye had learned a lot of respect for the Emperor's shrewd mind. The Emperor had loved the arena and would not have suffered a fool to run it. On that basis alone, there had to be more to Garvin than met the eye.

Vallaine ground his teeth silently in frustration. Garvin and his merits were really of little consequence. What mattered was the fight due to take place between the Thrandorian and this Serrius fellow. Vallaine was very wary of using blatant sorcery to swing the outcome of the fight in the Thrandorian's favour. Somewhere amongst this enormous crowd of people there would almost inevitably be one or two who would detect that sort of interference. Even a fairly subtle enchantment might compromise him, so sorcery was out of the question. Short of an Imperial Order to prevent the fight, there appeared little that Vallaine could do but hope that the Thrandorian would defy the odds and survive.

* * * * *

Derra squeezed along the row to where Eloise was waiting.

'Is everything set?' Eloise asked anxiously.

'Apparently,' Derra replied calmly. 'As far as I can tell, Fesha is in position. You should go and wait where we agreed. I will meet you tonight for our little get together regardless of the outcome and then we'll all go home.'

'I do hope... our friend is able to join us,' Eloise said carefully.

'So do I,' Derra agreed softly. 'Go on now. Off you go,' she said more loudly. 'Thank you for keeping my place. I'll tell you all about the outcome this evening.'

In keeping with their latest disguise, Eloise bowed her head in the local sign of respect from employee to employer and then began squeezing her way out along the route that Derra had just come in. Derra watched her for a few moments and was amused to note that few men seemed to mind Eloise brushing past them. The ladies, on the other hand, were not so enamoured. Beauty, it seemed, was a double-edged sword.

Derra moved her attention back to the arena where two fighters had been slugging away at one another for some time with great broadswords. The fight had been brutal but slow and the crowd was clearly not taking much notice of it. Everyone was waiting for the same thing – to see Serrius fight Bek. Not surprisingly, as the day had worn on and the fight that the crowd was waiting for had still not happened, people began to get impatient and restless. Garvin had worked the schedule to milk every last drop of money that he could from the crowd, and who could blame him? The Arena Master was unlikely to see another crowd like this again for some time.

Derra clapped absently as one of the two fighters finally bludgeoned his opponent into submission. The mission that she had embarked on with Calvyn and the other two might have had a good chance of success had Calvyn not been sidetracked to Terilla. Fesha, Eloise and she had done their best without Calvyn and his powers of magic and sorcery, but they had been too late to save Jez and this last attempt to free Bek relied totally on him surviving his fight today. It was pointless to try to free Bek before the fight, because he had already made it quite clear that he would not come with them. Revenge for Jez's death was Bek's controlling motivation at the moment and while Derra disapproved and disagreed with Bek's course of action, she was powerless to prevent it. In her mind, Derra had already promised herself that if the young Corporal did survive to ever make it back to Baron Keevan's castle, she would give him a very one-sided interview on his arrival.

'It's all down to you now, Bek,' Derra growled under her breath. 'Don't go proving all our efforts worthless by getting yourself killed.'

* * * * *

'Remember, Bek, don't be tempted into drawing your second blade too early in the fight. If you do, then you will certainly die. Serrius won't draw his second blade unless you do. That's his nature. He'll be surprised enough to see you carrying it at all. Use that as a lever. Play on what uncertainties you can raise in his mind.'

'Don't fret, Hammar, I intend to see that Commander pay you in full. We've been through the game plan a hundred times. I'm as ready as I can be,' Bek replied with a grim and determined smile.

'Forget the gold, Bek. The Commander died shortly

after your fight last week. I'll be getting no more money from him. Rumour has it he was assassinated. I guess he pulled one string too many.'

Bek's eyes widened in surprise.

'But if he's dead, then why...?'

'Why did I continue to train you?' Hammar finished with a tight grin. 'Because I wanted to. You're a good fighter, Bek. You deserve your chance. I honestly believe that you have it in you to beat Serrius today. I still don't know why that is, but it is the truth. Serrius is the better fighter, so don't go arrogant on me, but you have just got... oh, I don't know. It's more of a gut feeling on my part rather than anything I can lay my finger on. Let's just say that it is a strong enough feeling for me to have placed a little bet of my own.'

'You have?'

'Yes, but don't noise it around. I rarely place wagers and I try to keep it very low key when I do.'

Hammar gave Bek a comradely slap on the shoulder and then inspected his straps and plates again. What Hammar was looking for Bek could not begin to imagine, for they had both checked everything several times. It was obviously Hammar's way of coping with his nervousness, Bek decided, even whilst unconsciously adjusting his sword belt for the twentieth time in as many minutes.

A loud knock sounded at the door, making them both start.

'It's time,' a gruff voice stated. To Hammar's amusement, despite the guard's obvious effort to sound as uncaring as normal, the man had been unable to totally conceal an undertone of excitement. Bek was oblivious to the subtleties in the guard's voice, as his pulse had started to race the moment that the guard had knocked on the door.

Bek and Hammar looked at one another.

'Good luck,' Hammar stated simply.

'Thanks,' Bek replied gratefully. 'Thanks for everything, Hammar.'

They left the room together and set off down the corridor behind the guard who was striding away ahead of them. Then, without saying another word, Hammar turned aside up a flight of stairs to go and find his vantage point from which to view the fight. Bek marched on behind the guard. A hand on each sword hilt prevented an embarrassing tangle of legs with blades and gave him something reassuring to grip as his heart pounded with anticipation.

The knowledge that the stands were full to bursting and the reality of the sight were two completely different entities. It was impossible to totally blank the crowd out as he walked out of the pits and onto the sand, though a quick glance across at Serrius revealed that he was experiencing a similar distraction. The arena was simply a heaving mass of yelling, cheering and waving humanity. Garvin had teased this crowd to a frenzy, Bek noted. Aside from scheduling this fight right at the end of the day's events, he had even made them wait while a group of men had come out and swept the sand in the central area of the arena perfectly flat, just to heighten the tension even further.

Even as the two contenders walked out into the very middle of the sand the crowd started to chant.

'SER-RI-US, SER-RI-US, SER-RI-US,' roared down from the tiers causing even the normally emotionless Serrius to allow himself a slight smile of satisfaction.

The smile was short-lived for, gradually becoming audible through the first chant, a counter-chant began.

'THRAN-DOR-I-AN, THRAN-DOR-I-AN.'

It was Bek's turn to smile quietly to himself as the chants boomed in competition with one another throughout the arena. If it was just down to supporters, then the fight would be a closer run contest than many here had thought, he mused.

Bek stopped in the middle of the arena and he sensed Serrius stopping to his left. Looking up at the balcony, Bek noted that even the Emperor was not sitting in his usual casual position. His Imperial Majesty sat on the edge of his seat, mirroring the few others around the arena who were not already standing.

Bek saluted at the same moment as Serrius, and up in the stands Derra sent up a quick prayer to the gods, while Hammar leaned forward against the wall at the very front tier and strained his eyes intently towards the two fighters, his heart hammering in his chest. Vallaine gave the Emperor's usual wave of acknowledgement and the two fighters turned to begin the fight.

To Bek's surprise, Serrius did not even pause before leaping forward like a cat springing on a mouse, and Bek was forced to retreat as he defended frantically against a barrage of lightning-fast sword strokes. Finding speed and reflexes that he did not realise he possessed, Bek met every cut and thrust whilst constantly backing away under the seemingly relentless onslaught from Serrius.

Bek had practised extensively over the past two weeks at fighting with a single sword while wearing a second on his right hip. Although he had managed to fight effectively enough against Hammar with the second sword constantly bumping and tapping at his thigh, it had always been a distracting irritation. Defending for all he was worth, as he was at this moment, the distraction was proving almost more than he could bear and the temptation to draw the second blade was immense. Hammar had been so insistent that he should not try to use two blades early in the fight that Bek resisted the urge to use it and concentrated instead on looking for opportunities to try a counter-attack.

In a whirling fever of blocks and parries, Bek finally managed to spin himself far enough away from Serrius to gain a brief respite. In the stands, Derra let out the breath that she had unconsciously been holding, and Hammar nodded to himself with satisfaction. Bek had survived the first test, but the pause in the action was short indeed as Serrius quickly resumed his attack.

The massive crowd's cheering was like the roar of a stormy sea on a rocky shore; a loud, constant stream of noise that rolled unnoticed over the two fighters. The

Shandese crowd had never seen Serrius like this before and had certainly never seen him face another fighter who could cope with such ferocious speed and power. Every now and then through the constant wall of white noise the chants of 'SER-RI-US, SER-RI-US,' or 'THRAN-DOR-I-AN, THRAN-DOR-I-AN,' would punch their way through, but the contestants remained oblivious.

Bek backed up again under the pounding hail of strokes that Serrius was hurling at him with blinding speed and precision. Then, for a second or two, Bek managed to hold his ground as he began to anticipate Serrius slightly. It was not until he felt the sting of steel twice in quick succession that he realised that Serrius had duped him into a trap. Bek had taken the bait, but Serrius had turned down his first chance to finish the fight because Bek had left no opening for a killing stroke. Leaping back out of range, Bek flexed the muscles in his arm where Serrius had struck. The cuts were clearly not deep and Bek looked the advancing Serrius in the eye for the first time.

'Why?' he asked simply.

Serrius ignored him, his eyes glittering cold as ice and hard as diamonds. The Master Swordsman attacked again and Bek responded as before with a brilliant sequence of blocks and parries, but could not seem to find the edge of pace that he needed to launch a real counter-attack. Once more, Bek sprang clear and addressed Serrius.

'Why does it always have to be the kill, Serrius?' he asked mockingly. 'Are you so frightened that someone may learn enough of your skill that they might just prove you beatable?'

No flicker of emotion or acknowledgement touched the face of Serrius. He merely attacked again with another storm of blows that battered against Bek's blade like an avalanche. Bek retreated smoothly, though again he felt the sting of another small cut opening on his sword arm.

'Not fast enough, Serrius,' Bek taunted. 'Come on, is that the best you can do?'

Again, the words seemed to have no effect. Serrius just kept pushing forward with the same cold, unswerving determination. Bek could see that the sheen of sweat on Serrius' skin was now dotted with beads as the heat of the sun and the effort of the fight sucked water from his body in an ever increasing flood. Bek's own body was already drenched and rivulets of sweat ran freely down his back and arms.

'Come on, you fatherless son of a worthless washerwoman, can't you do any better than that?'

Bek braced himself as Serrius' eyes widened slightly in shock and then narrowed with a deep-seated anger. Hammar had been right to say that Serrius would respond to that particular insult, though he had certainly not lost control of his anger. If anything, Serrius looked more deadly now than ever.

'You will not live to repeat that remark outside the arena,' Serrius growled dangerously. 'And when I've finished with you, I'll deal with Hammar as well. Oath-breakers do not deserve to live, retired or not.'

It was Bek's turn to display a little surprise. Hammar had told him to use the phrase but had not explained its significance. Apparently Serrius *was* the illegitimate son of a washerwoman and Hammar had somehow known about it. Now was not the time to try to explain that Hammar had broken no oath of secrecy, far from it. Bek only had to look at Serrius to see the fury in his eyes and knew only too well how that was going to manifest itself.

Sure enough, Serrius attacked with even more speed and power than before, and sparks flew in showers from their clashing blades. Bek had been hoping for mistakes in that offensive but found none to exploit. Instead, he found himself struggling to stave off the most deadly rain of blows yet. Ducking and whirling, blocking and deflecting, Bek wove a protective path of survival through the savage assault and was more than relieved to break clear from Serrius without further injury.

'You cannot run forever, Thrandorian,' Serrius said, his voice as cold and hard as a block of marble. 'Come. It's time to die.'

In the stands even Vallaine was on his feet, unable to remain in his seat through this fight. One-sided though it had been so far, the atmosphere was still electric and everyone around the arena was yelling and screaming their favourite on. Vallaine, from his prime vantage point, could see that the two fighters were conversing and he would have given a lot to know what they were saying, but he dared not use that sort of sorcery for fear of someone penetrating his disguise.

Hammar was standing at the front tier, his hands clenched so tightly into fists that his nails were cutting into his palms; and the normally impassive Derra was shouting so loudly that she already felt that she would have little voice left for days. Everyone around the arena could see that Serrius held the upper hand from the start, but that was expected. Bek's defending under extreme pressure had been little less than miraculous so far, but the vast majority of the crowd knew that it was only a matter of time before Serrius killed him.

The two fighters clashed again and once more it was Serrius who pushed forward, driving Bek back and back. This time, however, something snapped inside Bek and having suffered the niggling irritation of the blade hanging at his right hip through each of the previous clashes, he suddenly decided that he could stand it no more.

Just as Serrius had arced his blade into a descending slash, Bek whipped out his second blade to form a cross with the blades above his head and caught Serrius' blade in between them. With a heave, Bek pushed Serrius back and the Master Swordsman staggered slightly as for the first time since starting the fight, he was forced to take a back step.

Bek locked eyes with Serrius and was only mildly surprised to note a slight satisfied smile settle on his adversary's face. In a slow, deliberate movement Serrius drew his second blade. Unbeknown to Bek, Hammar briefly buried his face in his hands and shook his head in dismay.

'Too early, Bek – much too early,' Hammar muttered to himself. The Weapons' Master did not look away for long. Even in this dispirited moment he could not bring himself to miss even the slightest part of the fight. Bek had obviously been forced to abandon their carefully worked out strategy, but the fight was far from over in Hammar's eyes and the next few seconds would be vital.

Serrius leapt back in towards Bek, his blades flashing in a dazzling sequence of strokes. To everyone's surprise, including Serrius, the attack was met by a solid defence and it was he who leapt back having felt the sting of steel parting skin. Serrius glanced at the cut on his arm. He had not seen the stroke that opened it and that drove a spike of doubt into the pit of his stomach. Was this Thrandorian really better than he had been making out? Had he actually been dissembling until now? Was that possible? There was only one way to find out.

Serrius attacked again and met the same solid defence. This time one of Bek's blades scored the leather of Serrius' chest protector and instead of backing away Bek advanced, pushing Serrius back with a dazzling display of coordinated sword work.

The roars of approval around the arena were deafening. Seemingly from nowhere, the fight was suddenly in the balance with the scales tipping in Bek's favour. After Serrius' demonstration about two months before, when he had killed five trained fighters with his two-handed skills, everyone had assumed him to be unmatched in the simultaneous use of two blades. What nobody appreciated was that Serrius had no one to hone those skills against. He practised forms and sequences with two blades regularly and was devastatingly fast and accurate at the drills and variations that he knew. What no one, including Serrius, had realised was that Hammar had observed him practise on many occasions and knew all of his set pieces by heart. Hammar had quietly developed counter sequences and identified the exact weak spots in Serrius' patterns. Bek had then been the fortunate benefactor of Hammar's knowledge. It was probably true to say that Bek had experienced more one-on-one practice with two blades in the last two weeks than Serrius had ever known. Moreover, his practice had been with a highly skilled and adaptive opponent – something that Serrius had never really encountered.

Despite Bek's surprising degree of ability at fighting with two blades, Serrius was far from ready to lose this battle. The Master Swordsman had not gained his position of top ranked fighter in Shandrim by set piece blade work alone, and for the next few minutes the crowd were treated to a scintillating display of swordplay from both fighters. First Bek had the upper hand, forcing Serrius to retreat as he carved his way forward with some brilliant sequences of strokes. Then Serrius rallied hard and pushed Bek back again. Around and around they span, dancing a deadly tango in which a single wrong step could cost a life.

Bek rapidly learned to appreciate why Hammar had insisted that he should survive as long as he could with a single blade before switching to two. If he had managed to wear Serrius down more before surprising him with his unexpected skills, the surprise might have been enough for him to have beaten and maybe even killed Serrius in that moment of advantage. He knew now that he had wasted his trump card by playing it far too early, and unless he did something spectacular soon the fight would almost inevitably go Serrius' way.

There was one final tactic that Bek had worked out in his head. He had not even considered discussing it with Hammar, as he knew that the Weapons' Master would have dismissed it as madness. Here in the arena, gritting his teeth with effort as he twisted, blocked, slashed and cut his way out of another clashing exchange, the idea did not seem so crazy.

Steeling himself, Bek charged Serrius and deliberately made an error that he knew Serrius could not help but exploit, for he clearly left an opening for a killing thrust. Bek was gambling everything on Serrius going for that opening and, knowing that the thrust was coming, that his own reactions would be fast enough to prevent Serrius from succeeding.

Sure enough, Serrius thrust into the gap, in turn creating an opening for Bek. Twisting and just managing to partially deflect Serrius' blade, Bek felt the icy burn as the steel blade sliced through his body even as he felt the satisfying resistance of his own blade driving into Serrius.

The two men staggered apart and the crowd's frenzied cheering died to an almost eerie quiet as each man looked down at the blade embedded in his own body. Tear-blinded with pain, Bek dropped his second blade and carefully put both hands to feel where Serrius' blade entered the side of his stomach and exited his back. Even as he touched it with his hands he knew that he had been lucky. The blade had penetrated close enough to his side to avoid penetrating any vital organs. Providing the medics acted quickly, he should live to tell of this bout. Looking up again and focusing through his tear-filled eyes, he realised that Serrius might not be so fortunate.

Even as Bek watched, Serrius fell to his knees with his hands clutching at the blade protruding from his middle and then slowly toppled onto his side. If the winner was the last man standing, then Bek had won, but winning meant nothing to him.

'That one was for you, Jez,' Bek gasped. 'Rest easy, old friend. I'll find Calvyn in good time and then you'll be properly avenged.'

Gritting his teeth, Bek grasped the hilt of Serrius' sword in his right hand and pinched the flesh against either side of the blade with his left. Even as he pulled the blade from his body he could hear someone running towards him and yelling frantically.

'No! No! Leave it in! Leave it...'

It was too late. Bek pulled the blade free and sank to his knees as blood flushed over his left hand and a fresh wave of pain threatened to totally overwhelm him. He felt the medic press pads against the wounds, front and back, and heard him ordering others to help as he bound them in place with bandages. Hands supported Bek from all sides as the medic worked swiftly, and through the waves of pain he was pleased to recognise the medic's voice. It was obviously someone who had patched him up before and the tone of concern in the familiar voice brought comfort.

More people arrived and an argument broke out.

'The Emperor! Don't be foolish, man. Can't you see that the only place this man is going is to my medic's table? If I don't get him there quickly he may die,' the familiar sounding medic said angrily in a loud voice.

'That is not my concern, medic. I have been commanded by the Emperor to bring this man to his balcony for an audience with His Imperial Majesty and that is what I am going to do.'

There was a brief pause and Bek could almost feel the medic's eyes looking at him.

'Madness!' the medic muttered angrily. 'Very well, if it must be so, then let us do it swiftly before he has a chance to lose too much more blood.'

Bek was beyond wincing and was barely conscious as he felt strong hands lift him to his feet. He was all but carried across the arena and was vaguely aware of thunderous applause and cheering as they went. Then they were inside and bumping through doorways, along corridors and up flights of stairs. Bek began to think that it would never end and wanted to just be allowed to sit down, or even better to lie down and rest.

Suddenly they were back out in the daylight and people were clapping and cheering all around him. Bek tried to focus and could vaguely make out several very well-dressed figures ahead of him. He recognised the Imperial Box and realised that he must be in the presence of the Emperor, though at first Bek could not distinguish him from the others.

'Well done, Thrandorian. That was without doubt the most spectacular fight that I have ever seen. You have done what most thought impossible. You beat Serrius.'

Bek tried to respond but all that came from his mouth was a groaning sigh.

'He has been sorely wounded, your Imperial Majesty,' the medic at Bek's side said bravely. 'Please, I beg you. Keep this brief or I may not be able to heal him.'

'Yes, of course, good medic. I merely wanted to give the Thrandorian a gift in recognition of his great victory today. Here let me just place this ring upon his finger.'

Using the tightest tendril of mind power that he could form, Vallaine reached into Bek's mind with the intention of planting the compulsion to kill Shanier, only to find that it was unnecessary – Bek's thoughts already centred on exacting revenge for Jez's untimely demise. Satisfied that Bek was already primed as a weapon, Vallaine carefully withdrew his mental probe and removed his most precious of rings from his hand. He could not resist one final glance at it before he lifted Bek's right hand and placed it on his middle finger.

'There,' he whispered to Bek. 'This will help you when you go after Shanier.'

Bek started at that name.

'Must... kill... him,' Bek groaned softly.

'Yes, yes, all in good time,' Vallaine purred, suffused by a glow of satisfaction as he realised that the Thrandorian would need little encouragement to go and seek out the renegade Sorcerer Lord. 'Go and recover your strength now and we will talk again of Shanier another day.'

Vallaine stepped back and nodded to the medic.

'Thank you. Heal him well, medic. He has a glorious future ahead of him.'

'Yes, your Imperial Majesty.'

Bek felt himself turned around and led back down under the stands. Something jabbed him slightly in his wounded side and he groaned at the pain.

'Damn it, man!' the medic swore. 'He's going to die if I don't do something for him soon. Tell me, is there an exit from the arena around here? Doesn't the Emperor have his own special way in and out of the stands?'

'Well, yes there is, but...' the other man said, his voice

full of uncertainty.

'Take me to it then. There's no time to work our way right around the arena to my workroom. He'll die before we get there. My house is not far from this side of the arena. We'll have to take him there.'

Something jabbed Bek in his injured side again and he groaned again at the pain that blossomed at that touch. It felt like the medic was poking him deliberately to make him react.

'Come on, man, don't just stand there. The Thrandorian sounds like he could die at any second and you heard the Emperor – he ordered me to heal him well. Now I'm telling you that my best chance of doing that is to take him to my house,' the medic urged.

'The Emperor's gate has a constant guard...' the other man started.

'So? You're a guard too. Just tell them that we're taking the Thrandorian out on the Emperor's orders – that is what we're doing, after all.'

The guard grumbled, but they started moving again and a short while later they were ordered to stop by someone with a deep, gruff voice.

'Stand aside and open the door, Lawdrin,' the guard helping the medic ordered. 'The Emperor has commanded that the Thrandorian be taken to a nearby house of healing.'

'Very well,' the deep voice replied unquestioningly.

Light appeared ahead but all was still a foggy haze to Bek, whose pain-soaked senses had all but shut down to block out the agony. They moved forward again and out into the streets. Bek slipped into unconsciousness shortly thereafter and felt nothing as the two men carried him between them into the labyrinth of streets that surrounded the arena.

Bek roused slightly when he was laid down gently onto a narrow bed. The pressure against the wound in his back forced a brief and painful awakening. Everything was so confusing. The medic looking down at him did not look like any medic that Bek knew; yet his face was

315

familiar. The fight, the Emperor, the medic, the room –
all was a blur of senseless images that refused to make
any sense.

'Thanks for your help,' Bek heard the medic say to the
guard.

'No problem. I'll see that a couple of guards are sent
across to help you get him back to his quarters once
you've stitched him up,' the guard replied.

'Oh, I don't think that will be necessary,' the medic said
cheerily. There was a soft thud followed by a gurgling
sigh and the sound of a body collapsing onto the floor.

'Bek... Bek!' the medic said insistently, shaking Bek's
shoulder. 'Bek, it's me – Fesha. Well, you did it,
Corporal. You proved to everyone that even here in
Shandrim you're still 'First Sword'. It was an incredible
fight and I'm sure that I'll never forget seeing it. You
realise that you are probably being written into Shandese
history right now as the man who beat Serrius? Now it's
time to get you back to Thrandor where you and I belong.'

Bek felt Fesha's hands gently checking the bandages
that covered his wounds and groaned gently at the pain
that even that light touch triggered.

'Sorry, Bek. Listen, things didn't quite go as planned in
the arena and I had to improvise a bit. The others have
no idea where we are and I'm going to need their help to
get you fixed up and away from Shandrim. The pads and
bandages seem to be holding the bleeding under control
for the moment. I'll be back as soon as I can with Eloise
and Derra. Just hang in there, Corporal. Don't go dying
on me while I'm gone now, will you? Derra won't be
happy with me if you die and you know how she gets
when she's narked off with someone. I know that you
wouldn't wish that on anyone, so I'm going to trust you to
concentrate on staying alive for a little while, all right?'

With that, Fesha's face withdrew and Bek could hear
the wiry little Private changing clothes in a hurry. Fesha,
Eloise and Derra were still in Shandrim and, despite Bek
having told them to leave him and return home, they
were still determined to rescue him. It hardly seemed

possible but even as consciousness slipped away from him once again, Bek's face twisted into a contented smile. 'Perfect,' he thought. 'With Serrius out of the way, I was ready to go and hunt down Calvyn anyway. There's still a score to be settled and Calvyn, or Shanier, or whatever he's calling himself now, will pay the rest of the blood price for Jez's death.'

Here ends Book 3 of The Darkweaver Legacy. Book 4 – *The Chosen One* will bring the series to its spectacular climax, as Selkor's hidden agenda behind the gathering of magical power is revealed and Calvyn discovers the horrifying meaning of the strange Oracles of Drehboor.